666 CHARING CROSS ROAD

By Paul Magrs and available from Headline Review

Never the Bride
Something Borrowed
Conjugal Rites
Hell's Belles
The Bride That Time Forgot
666 Charing Cross Road

666 CHARING CROSS ROAD

PAUL MAGRS

headline
review

First published in 2011 by
HEADLINE REVIEW
An imprint of HEADLINE PUBLISHING GROUP

1

Cataloguing in Publication Data is available from the British Library

ISBN 978 0 7553 5947 9 (Hardback)
ISBN 978 0 7553 5948 6 (Trade paperback)

Typeset in Garamond by Avon DataSet Ltd,
Bidford-on-Avon, Warwickshire

Printed and bound in Great Britain by
Clays Ltd, St Ives plc

HEADLINE PUBLISHING GROUP
An Hachette UK Company
338 Euston Road
London NW1 3BH

www.headline.co.uk
www.hachette.co.uk

Prologue

Where was Shelley?

Somehow Daniel had forgotten her. She hadn't come home that night, which was just as well, of course. He'd other things to concentrate on. Other fish to fry.

The apartment was in a godawful state. Candles had dripped on to the carpets. There was blood on the shagpile and sofa. There was the acrid reek of smoke damage. There'd been a little fire some hours before: he'd doused it with tonic water. He'd been drinking all night, and now – in the early hours – he couldn't quite be sure what was real and what wasn't.

Ricardo? Had Ricardo been round? That sexy Latino? Daniel shook his head confusedly. Surely not. He wouldn't have been so stupid as to invite him. He couldn't have smuggled him in. But how did . . .

He sat up gradually. It was still dark outside. The clock said five o'clock. An evil hour on a December morning.

Something was very, very wrong. No Shelley. Shelley was gone. She hadn't even been home. And he felt so strange. Like he'd been on a long run. He was exhausted. He looked down at himself. He was naked and covered in blood, and for a few minutes he was terrified. What had he done to himself?

And then the memories started leaking back.

He moved to the blinds and peered out at the night. Snow was falling. Gently, remorselessly, unexpectedly. He looked down into the street and saw that it was settling. Everything down there looked so smooth already.

He found the grimoire on the sofa. It lay unassumingly on the black leather. Battered and a bit bloody, just like Daniel himself. It was open, quite casually, at a frankly terrifying etching of a demon from hell.

Oh no.

Something stirred. Something murmured and shifted in its sleep inside Daniel's mind. Like a cat dreaming of shredding its prey, the thing in Daniel's head flexed its claws. It snickered at Daniel as he became aware of its presence.

What have I let in? he thought. Madly, furiously. He hardly knew what he was thinking.

Then: the ritual. I did the ritual. I tried it out. I invited him . . . I . . .

And then he started choking and coughing. Great wheezing gasps doubled him over. It was like he had something caught. Something stuck in his throat. He cried out, retching. His throat was parched. He was thirsty. Yes, thirsty, of course. He'd never been so thirsty in all his life. He had never known anything like this.

In the kitchen alcove, he ransacked the cupboards and fridge. He drank milk straight from the carton. Then tonic that had lost its fizz. There was some soda Shelley had left, and he gagged on its saccharine taste. No. This wasn't what he needed.

The creature in his head was stirring awake. It was languid and amused. It knew where it was. It stretched and gloried in its liberation. It spoke to Daniel. It told him why he was thirsty. It explained everything. In a voice that was little more than a purr, a voluptuous murmur, it laid down the law to Daniel. It told him how things were going to be.

Daniel bowed his head and listened.

For a few moments he baulked at the things the creature was saying. His human self rebelled against the chocolatey voice in his head. Those deep, gorgeous tones telling him what he must do to survive . . . he could ignore them, couldn't he? He could pretend they weren't there. He was strong-willed. He didn't mind being thirsty. It surely didn't have to be that way.

Oh, but it did. The voice gave an oily chuckle.

Daniel had opened the book. He had read aloud the correct words. He had understood the invocation. He had known what it was meant to accomplish. And this was a fate he had brought upon himself.

He should be pleased. He should be astonished. This was promotion, wasn't it? He was going to be king of the city. He'd be the first of his kind. Prince of New York.

And tonight was when it would all begin.

Come along, Daniel, the voice commanded. It curled around his limbs. It tingled through his nerves. It played about his every fibre so suggestively. So in control of his every move. Come along, Daniel. Let us go together, you and I. While the snow falls and pacifies the city that never sleeps.

Let us glide across the fresh formed drifts. Our feet need hardly touch the ground. You have powers now, Daniel. Powers you don't yet even know about or understand. But I can show you. I can be your mentor. I can tell you everything you need to know. But first . . . first we must slake this thirst. We share this intense hunger tonight, and it must be appeased. You are newly formed and you must be blooded. I am very old and I have not feasted for more than a hundred years. Can you imagine what that must feel like?

So tonight . . . right now . . . We have hours before the weak December sun comes up over Manhattan island . . .

All right . . . all right, thought Daniel, addressing the creature inside his mind. We can go. We can go outside. Just . . . tell me what to do . . . Direct me . . .

I know there is no escape from you.

Good, very good, said the being. You're correct. You invited me in. There's no going back now. Now that I'm free. And at last I can see this fabled city. Somewhere that, in life, I often dreamed about visiting . . . a city of the future, and a great concentration of throbbing life . . . Tell me, is it really the twenty-first century?

Oh yes, said Daniel. How long have you slept?

Since 1896, said the creature. So you can imagine my plight. My thirst. My desperation. Thank you, my dear, for hosting me. So very kind.

Daniel gasped as he felt the creature writhe with pleasure inside him. He shuddered and gave himself no time to think. He suppressed his thoughts. The creature would hear him. He had, instead, to throw on some warm clothes. He had to brave the early hours outside. Eighth Avenue, Hell's Kitchen, the meatpacking district. They would find what they were looking for. They were bound to.

Time to go hunting, Daniel, said his mentor. Time for us wolves to go running in the snow.

Chapter One

Just over a month ago . . .

He stared up at her handiwork and shuddered. It wasn't the reaction that Shelley had been hoping for.

'My God. What a horrible old thing. Where did you dig *that* up?'

Despite herself, Shelley grew flustered in the face of his cool disapproval. 'Apparently it's been in storage for years. Down in the basement.'

Her boss sniffed. The sharp noise echoed in the gloomy exhibition hall. 'Best place for it. Hideous thing. What's it doing out now?'

Shelley coughed. It had been her idea. It had seemed such a great one at the time. Putting this larger-then-life effigy at the centre of her exhibit.

'I thought it would work brilliantly, as part of the "Women and Madness" show . . .' Her voice trailed off as she watched Daniel peer even more closely at the tall, witchlike figure. What was it made out of? Shelley didn't even know. Bones and leather, wool and papier mâché. The stringy hair was like dried grasses. The ancient garments were grimy tatters. All Shelley knew was that when she had found the thing, hidden away in a trunk deep beneath the New York Museum of Outsider Art, she had to rescue it. She had to put it on display.

Not *it*.

Her.

The feeling had been very strong. It was starting to wither slightly now, as Daniel pulled faces. 'It smells awful as well,' he said. 'What is it? Mould? Formaldehyde?'

Shelley found that she was in awe of this effigy, this gigantic doll, no matter what Daniel said. From the very first, she had had a keen sensation that this was an extremely old creation. It had travelled a long way, and the fact that it was still intact was a miracle. To Shelley's way of thinking, this object needed to be shown prominently in the museum where she worked. 'Women and Madness' month seemed to be the perfect slot.

Shelley hadn't worked for very long here, at the Museum of Outsider Art, tucked away between offices on Lincoln Square. She had been dating her boss, Daniel, for an even shorter time. Well, only a few dates yet. Early days. Technically he was her line manager, which made Shelley feel strangely awkward. Especially at moments like this.

'I wonder where the dreadful artefact came from in the first place,' he mused. 'Was there any paperwork with it?'

'Scotland, according to the records. One of the islands. She's some kind of effigy. Probably built to be sacrificed, like a—'

'Guy Fawkes dummy?'

Daniel was English. Shelley loved his accent. She loved his whole manner, apart from when he was being stiff and slightly pompous, like right now.

8

'I think it's more . . . pagan than that,' she whispered.

'God help us,' he sighed.

To Shelley, there was something very human about the effigy. The more she studied it, the more anguished its expression seemed. That tattered, faded dress, could it even be a wedding dress? Something about the giant doll made her conjure up terrible images. Burning and sacrifice. When was it from? When *had* the remote tribes given up their strange festivals and rites?

The yellowed teeth were too real-looking, set inside that twisted mouth, giving the withered turnip skull a slightly mocking, dangerous look.

'Well, I'd never have dragged it out of cold storage,' Daniel said. 'But I guess it'll make a striking centrepiece for your . . . um, "Crazy Ladies" display.'

He turned neatly on his heel and clipped away down the corridor, leaving a faint scent of lemon and tea tree aftershave. Funny how offhand he was with her at work, when he could be quite different in their time off. It was as if he was trying especially hard to maintain a professional distance. She'd not figured him out totally yet. He had a certain mystique. But maybe that was just his being English.

Just then, Shelley was joined by Ruthie from the gift shop. Ruthie was covered in junk jewellery, so you could hear her coming from a mile away. She wasn't the usual kind of person you might see working in a midtown gallery, but the Museum of Outsider Art was a curious sort of place. It was dedicated to the preservation of work by untrained and unheard-of artists from all over the world. Ruthie was similarly inclusive in outlook: warm and loud. She made people feel welcome. She boasted that she had worked in gift shops of every possible kind, the length and breadth of Manhattan Island. This job was her favourite so far, she claimed, because it was the quietest. She thought some of the academic-looking men about the place – especially Daniel – were *hot*.

Now she was staring at the Scottish Bride, as Shelley was starting to think of the effigy. 'Jeez. Would you look at her! Are you sure about this, Shelley?'

Earlier this morning it had been quite exciting. When they'd brought the packing crate into the exhibition space it had been unnerving, but tinged with pleasurable anticipation. With Ruthie helping her, Shelley had felt a bit like Howard Carter at the opening of the tomb of King Tut. She saw at once as they hoisted and lifted that her instincts during stocktaking last week had been right. She knew in her gut that this monstrous woman would be a fine centrepiece for the display.

My first exhibit, she reminded herself. With her straw-like hair standing up every which way and her gown hanging in faded tatters over her twiggy limbs. She was holding out a cobwebby bouquet of some kind.

'No one's gonna forget seeing her,' Ruthie said. She was more used to the tamer exhibitions of dumb paintings, needlepoint and weird pottery they showed here. Usually she was politely mystified by the stuff they put so reverentially on the walls. Shelley's mystery lady was different. It spoke to her somehow . . .

'That poor dame,' she said now. 'She looks like she's been through a tough life.'

Later on, that lunch break, Shelley found herself thinking about what Ruthie had said. She'd picked up some soup and a sandwich from a crowded deli and wandered into the park, finding a favourite spot on a bench by the pond. It was chillier, certainly. She was glad she'd brought sweet and sour soup, which she blew on and sipped carefully, watching the ducks. Daniel had been so dismissive of her female effigy. Almost disparaging. Could she really see a man romantically who was inclined to put her work down like that?

Her phone went and she had to juggle her lunch bags as she reached into her jacket pocket. 'Aunt Liza?'

She wondered if her aunt was in the park this lunchtime. But she tended to walk Rufus later in the afternoon, when the crowds were thinner.

'I'm downtown, shopping,' said her aunt. That deep, scratchy voice of hers burst loudly into Shelley's ear. 'I'll pick up anything I think you might like. How's work?'

Shelley put on a tight, bright voice. 'The exhibition's almost done. I can't wait for you to see it.'

'Yeah, yeah, sure,' said her aunt. 'I'm looking forward to it, honey. Listen, I just wanted to check that you and your new friend are okay for tomorrow night, and my little gathering . . .'

Shelley cursed herself. She hadn't reminded Daniel. Somehow she just knew he wasn't going to be pleased if she badgered him about this. But she wanted him to meet her aunt, and one of these gatherings at Liza's tiny apartment was the best possible way. There he would see her at her best and most relaxed. Shelley wanted more than anything for him to like her aunt. That was the ultimate test of a boyfriend, she thought. If they didn't get on with Aunt Liza, then they could forget it. Nine times out of ten. Her aunt's approval was important to her.

However, she was just a bit worried about what kind of surprise Liza might have laid on for her guests. Daniel was pretty strait-laced. Sometimes Liza's entertainments could be a little risqué.

'Sure, we'll be there,' she assured her.

'We can't miss a Hallowe'en together,' fretted Aunt Liza. 'We never have and we never will, right?'

Shelley allayed the old woman's fears, talking and sipping spicy soup at the same time.

'Okay, listen, I'm meeting a young man for lunch. My friend from the bookshop, Jack. I gotta go.'

Shelley put her phone away, shaking her head ruefully. Here she was, about to go back to work for the long slog of the afternoon, her desk aswarm with paperwork – to counteract the fun of unpacking the Scottish effigy. And there was her aunt, skipping about merrily in Greenwich Village and having lunch with young men. Shelley sighed.

At least she had Daniel.

The first time Jack had met Liza, he'd thought she looked like someone from a different era. She was old, but had kept herself glamorous. She was in a perfect costume, something preserved from the 1950s.

He had met her at the bookshop where he worked, Fangtasm. He understood she had patronised the place for years, even before it became the specialist mystery / horror / fantasy bookstore that it was today. Way back when, Fangtasm used to be antiquarian, but there was no money in that nowadays. Not according to the owner. Jack wasn't paid to have an opinion. Secretly he was glad not to be handling old and dirty volumes. He liked the smooth shininess of the new books they stocked. They were colourful and cheery, these gothic romances and cosy mysteries with their embossed spatters of blood and shiny titles.

From the first, Liza had engaged him in conversation. She spoke to him like someone she'd known for years, and at first he wondered if he'd been mistaken for someone else, or if she was crazy.

When he asked her about this later, she told him, 'You just have one of those faces. Reassuring, you know? Like someone I must've thought I'd met before.'

He was a bit affronted by this. One of those faces? Reassuring? He'd rather be bleakly beautiful; strange and savage looking . . . or even austere, like some of those boys you saw about the Village. Unapproachable and impossibly attractive. This had been very disappointing news from Liza. Still, he guessed there were worse things to be than friendly.

So they talked every time she came by the bookstore. Then she took him to her favourite place for coffee, and told him the story of her life. It was so long and involved it took a whole week of lunch hours, and still Jack didn't think he was getting the full picture.

Liza had sat bundled up in her ratty fur coat and talked about bringing up her children in the fifties. Living in NYC as a single mom and having small children. Making a living by writing copy. Churning out words and words and pages by the yard: words about anything the customer wanted. Working late into every night. 'But also, you know, the city was wonderful then. It still is, but it was especially wonderful then. It was like a playground for the kids. All the museums, galleries . . . I let them go where they wanted. Every day there was something new to see, to find . . .'

Listening to her, Jack started to see it through her eyes. He realised how jaded he'd become. He was seeing nothing new for himself. He'd lived here most of his adult life. Even on Christopher Street there was nothing he hadn't seen a thousand times before. This tiny old woman was telling him to get some of that sense of wonder back.

'Sense of wonder?' she'd laughed. 'Nah. Just stop looking so intense, that'll do. Get out and get laid or something.'

They were on Christopher Street again this lunchtime, at one of the few places open at this hour. After trying out a number of coffee houses, they had settled on a favourite. This one was a bit wholefoody and earnest, but they liked the seclusion of its rooms, populated by many rubber plants and the strange antiques arranged as *objets d'art*. They liked it best because there was a conservatory out back and they could sit as long as they cared to.

As they sat with huge bowls of cooling milky coffee, Liza was bitching about her workload.

'My tiny apartment is overrun. I can hardly even get in the door. Galley pages and printers' proofs and bound proofs everywhere. They're stacked twenty deep in the hallway. And there's me throwing a party tomorrow night. What are my guests gonna think? They'll think I've gone feral. I'm like one of those old dames who can't throw anything out . . .'

She always complained about her job as a publisher's reader. To Jack, it sounded wonderful. Certainly better than working a till and stacking shelves and fending off weirdo customers for minimum wage. Liza got to read all day, every day. She could take her work wherever she wanted. She could sit in MoMA or the restaurant at Macy's or up Dog Hill with Rufus. Jack pictured her there, perched on the edge of a bench with a thick manuscript on her knees, making notes. She was so short her legs would be dangling in free air, and her beagle would be tearing about, delirious with freedom.

She was famous for her caustic reports, typed up fiercely and swiftly and emailed back to publishers at record speed. She was the best reader there was – Jack knew it from bits of insider gossip he had picked up at work subsequent to meeting her and figuring out who she was. When it came to genre stuff – romance, mystery, paranormal – Liza's taste was queen. All the publishing people worked nearby, on Hudson Street or further uptown – but they'd all visit Fangtasm, and it was from them he learned about the old woman's reputation. Her instinct for genre. Jack knew that, to the insiders, Liza's approbation was valued.

Right now she was running through the colourful catalogues for the spring releases and pulling faces. 'Crap, crap, crap. All terrible. Awful. But you'll have to stock 'em anyway. This is good. She's good. Not her best. This is great, too. And this.'

Not that Jack was in any position to act on her advice. He didn't get to do any stocking or ordering. That was all down to the owner, Mr Grenoble, but Jack liked to think he was in on the skinny from this dumpy old lady. And besides, he took her recommendations for his own reading, which was – if not as vast as Liza's – still pretty voracious.

Suddenly she stopped flicking through brochures and sighed. 'Sometimes I get sick of brand-new stuff.'

'Really? I love it. The thought that these are books only one or two people have read so far . . . it's all straight out of someone's imagination . . .'

'Hmmm,' she said darkly. 'I prefer things that have stood the test of time, I guess. Let some dust gather. I wish . . . I wish your shop still sold old stuff . . .'

'There are plenty of antiquarian bookshops.' Though Jack knew full well that many in Manhattan had closed in recent years, probably due to online selling and sites like eBay.

'I don't mean the usual old stuff. I mean weird old stuff. Books no one's ever heard of. Mystery and ghost stories. Black magic. Fairy tales. I dunno. I miss the smell of mildew . . .'

Jack found himself turning up his nose a bit. Personally, he loved the smell of binder's glue and the soft new pulpiness of fresh pages.

'Never mind me,' Liza said. 'Season of mists and yellow forgetfulness. The autumn's in full swing and I'm apt to get nostalgic. I'm a foolish old woman. C'mon. I guess we'd better get up and go. The afternoon's waiting. I gotta do some shopping for my shindig tomorrow night. You *are* coming, aren't you?'

Jack paused. He'd never been to her apartment before. He was picturing a roomful of elderly people, and the look on his face gave him away.

'Hey, I'll understand if you say no. It'll just be a bunch of writers and publishing people. And witches.' Liza shrugged and grinned at him, shouldering her tapestried velveteen bag, which looked far too full and much too heavy for her.

Jack's eyes lit up at the mention of writers. 'And witches? Real ones?'

She tutted. 'Would I waste my time entertaining fake ones?'

She tossed her head (her perfectly set perm hardly moved) and gave him her card. He glanced at an address on Second Avenue. Somewhere in the Eighties. He guessed it was undesirable: it wasn't somewhere he had been before. 'Bring your partner or whatever if you want,' she added.

Jack shrugged. 'It'll just be me, I guess.' Then he was conscious of sounding a bit doleful about that. He brightened up determinedly. 'Okay,' he promised. 'I'll come by.'

It was a long time since he'd been the youngest guest at a house party. Ever since he'd left the family home in Carlisle, Pennsylvania. There, he'd always been the baby.

Here, at thirty-one years of age and living in Greenwich Village, Jack felt destined to sit longer on the shelf than any of the paperbacks he went on to spend the afternoon unpacking.

Chapter Two

Daniel was complaining about being rushed. He had been home to his apartment and changed, and now he was out meeting Shelley again. When she saw him loitering about on the corner of 57th and 8th, she knew he was in one of his moods when he was keen to wrangle. He looked gorgeous, though, in a blue Paul Smith suit. Was it weird of her to feel turned on by those greyish streaks in his hair? What was that about?

Shelley had had to get out of town and back again. Back to her rotten one-roomed place at the other end of the tunnel. At home, she had tried on every stitch of clothing she had bought in the last six months, and all of it was wrong. Everything looked awful on her. She took a long hard squint at herself in the blotchy full-length mirror: at the gangly, gawkish body she always thought looked too much like a boy's. She felt knobbly and awkward in whatever she wore. Her aunt was usually great for raising her spirits, though. 'Are you kiddin'? Back in the sixties we'd have killed for those long legs, that gamine look of yours. And those huge eyes you got!'

When Shelley looked at herself in the mirror, she always looked a bit too startled, as if she'd had a fright. And her nose was bent – inherited from her dad, as her aunt had pointed out, not her mom. Her straight blond hair fell just anywhere in no kind of style, and she never found the time to sort it out. But it would have to do for tonight. There just wasn't the time for beautifying herself as well as getting in and out of the city four times a day. Her hair and make-up would have to do, and so would the same pale pink cocktail dress she'd worn for her aunt's last party. She realised this embarrassing factoid a bit too late, on the subway rattling back into Manhattan. Hopefully no one would notice. She tended to blend into the background at these things anyway.

'I don't see why it has to be so early,' Daniel grumped.

'Some of my aunt's friends are elderly people. They don't like being out late.'

They hurried down the grimy sidewalk just as it was hardening and crisping with frost, and stopped by a deli on 7th to pick up some wine. Daniel spent ages choosing which kind, glaring at labels and aggravating the queue. Shelley hung back, enjoying the wonderful mixed aromas of the Chinese food sizzling on hot plates. As she eyeballed glistening peppers, baby corn, shredded spicy beef, the tangles of squid and octopus legs, her stomach growled at her. If she lived midtown, she'd be in these places all the time. She'd never cook a thing for herself. She'd be bringing back cartons of Chinese food and anything else she could think of. My God, I'd be the size of a house. If I lived somewhere great, I'd end up huge. But she didn't live anywhere near here, thankfully. So that was some consolation, anyway, for living in a dump. A faraway dump.

'I had tickets tonight,' Daniel said, as they hit the cold street again. There was scaffolding up, forcing the busy sidewalk narrower and pushing Shelley and Daniel closer. Great gouts of steam from the subway came billowing out, buffeting the pair of them along. The wind was sharp, catching their breath as they marched against it.

'You never told me that.'

'I didn't want to spoil the evening. You were so set on going to your aunt's.'

Yeah, but you could still tell me about it, she thought, uncharitably. They were crossing in front of Carnegie Hall. Daniel had an idiotic habit of jumping in front of traffic, leaving Shelley with no choice but to follow after him, yelling apologies at cab drivers and everyone else.

'We were meant to be going *here*,' he said. He was nodding at the posters outside Carnegie Hall. Shelley peered at them. Some kind of fancy recital. A woman with satiny hair and a pained expression was draped all over a cello. Old classical kind of stuff. Nothing Shelley knew about. She looked at Daniel. He was wearing a stoic expression. 'And you're sacrificing your pleasure for the sake of my aunt?' she said. 'Well, that's great. She'll appreciate that.' Shelley decided she had to show him: she was no pushover. She stalked off ahead, shoes pinching worse than ever, proud that she hadn't given in to him. It was one of her worst traits. Giving in. Making peace. Anything for an easy life. Her natural impulse was to look at his fake crestfallen expression and tell him: 'Let's go to your concert instead. My aunt won't mind. Let's go listen to your cello lady.' But this time she kept her mouth shut. She was determined not to seem as desperate as she most often felt around him.

They crossed the corner of the park, skirting the pond, which was a mistake, since it turned out ice was sheeting on the tarmac. She had to grip his steady arm. 'My aunt's really important to me,' she sighed. 'She's all I've got in the world, relative-wise.'

'I know that.' He patted her bare arm. Why the hell hadn't she brought a coat? She had rough gooseflesh all over her. The word for that, Aunt Liza – the wordsmith – had once told her, was horribilation. Great. Daniel was stroking her arm as they walked in Central Park and she was horribilating all over. Some romance.

Daniel was going on. He made it seem as if he was wrestling with what he wanted to say. 'The thing is, Shelley love, you can't let your aunt go bullying you. You really can't. I've known you for how long now?'

'Four months,' she said. She didn't add how many days and hours on top of that. He'd think that was weird.

'Well, in that time – and I'm a pretty good judge of character – I'd say you were quite a passive personality, Shelley. A walkover for some people, including your aunt. She just has to crook her little finger and you come running. It's true, isn't it? And I think she enjoys this power she has over you.'

'You've never even met her!'

'I pick up on the signs,' he said. 'I'm very sensitive. And I know the signs because – believe it or not – I used to get manipulated like that too. Until I learned to assert myself and my needs above those of other people.'

They fell silent then, walking alongside the darkened zoo. Shelley was vaguely listening for the muffled cries and mutters of the animals beyond the foliage. Settling down for the night in their cages.

'Who are all these people anyway? That she's inviting?'

'Publishing people, mostly,' Shelley said.

'Oh, I forgot. She's some kind of bigwig, isn't she? Very influential.'

'Hardly.' Shelley smiled fondly. 'She was in advertising once, before I was born. She hated it. For as long as I can remember, all my aunt has ever done is *read*. That's her job. Reading novels and telling people what she thinks of them.'

'Nice work.'

'You enjoy your work, don't you?'

He shrugged. 'I want more, Shelley. I'm quite ambitious, you know.'

'Are you?'

'Of course! One has to be! Otherwise . . . what's the point? All appetite and longing. Just grubbing about, feeling unfulfilled. We're simply animals then, aren't we? Life's a very superficial thing without ambition, Shelley. You must feel that.'

'I . . . guess I do.'

But she didn't.

They exited the park near the Met. It was still a long walk across several blocks to Aunt Liza's. Daniel lost his patience with all this traipsing around. The streets this side of town looked rather rough and seamy to him, so he flagged down a cab and wasn't happy until he was seated in the warmth.

The cabbie tried to talk to them: what a cold night it had turned out to be. Must be the first real night of winter. Happy Hallowe'en, guys.

Daniel ignored him, scowling.

Shelley mulled over what he'd said about ambition. He was showing a whole other side of his personality to her. A harder edge. Even a ruthless edge. But maybe that was good? Maybe that revelation counted as Daniel opening out to her a bit more.

'You're late!' Aunt Liza cried, letting them in. Her hallway was cram-packed with boxes of proofs and stacked novels. Liza hugged her, and barely had time to introduce Daniel before her aunt started rattling on again. 'I thought you were blowing me out. Everyone's already in the party mood. You two are gonna have to warm up and get into the swing of things pretty snappy . . .' She snatched Daniel's coat off him and was appalled that her niece wasn't wearing one.

Shelley loudly admired her aunt's filmy frock, all swirling Bridget Riley patterns. Daniel politely followed suit, though he thought the small old woman looked peculiar.

'You know where the drinks are, Shelley. You help yourselves. Don't mind them, apple-bobbing. I've made my famous black toffee? Can you smell it? Yeah, it burned a bit. Look, here's Rufus to welcome you . . .'

Her beagle came romping through the press of bodies in the L-shaped living space and stopped still to growl at Shelley's guest.

'Daniel, huh?' Liza smiled. 'Rufus isn't so sure about you. He isn't sure about this one, Shelley. Look at his expression!'

'It's me,' said Daniel, rather embarrassed. 'I've never been very fond of mutts. They don't like me for some reason.'

'Don't call Rufus a mutt!' Shelley nudged him. 'You're making it worse.'

Liza smiled. 'How strange. Well, never mind. Is this for me? Very kind! Is it fancy?' She examined the bottle Daniel had handed her. She yanked off the tissue paper, squinting at the label. 'I can't drink fancy-schmancy wine, Shelley will tell you. Gimme something cheap I can hold down . . . Oh, look! Here's another young person . . .'

Daniel had been staring about the place – frankly appalled at being surrounded by ancient old hags, most of them quite eccentrically dressed. Freakishly, even. He reminded himself it was Hallowe'en. Presumably they didn't always look like this.

One whole wall of books in the L-shaped room snagged his attention. They seemed to be well cared for and dusted. They were probably valuable. He could see rare editions of some folklore classics that he was instantly coveting. Some rather arcane texts up there, not a million miles from his own anthropological areas of interest. He wouldn't have minded a closer look, but the crowd was packed too tightly to squeeze through. His curiosity would have to wait. And then the music went up a notch. Something ghastly from about a century ago . . . some late-seventies disco thing.

Aunt Liza was steering them towards a bewildered-looking young man. Plumpish and obviously gay, to Daniel's eyes. Wearing a Baby Dee T-shirt and looking quite out of place. Gulping a Bloody Mary.

'My other young person,' Liza was saying. 'My latest find, Shelley. You'll like him. Jack is the bookseller I told you about.'

Jack winced. 'I work the till at a bookstore downtown. I'm hardly a—'

Liza waved his objections away. 'He shares my passions, Shelley.

24

He and I met a little while ago and got talking about our favourite books and authors and we just clicked. Like that. You know that instant kind of chemistry? Between folk who chime in at the deepest possible level?'

There was a pause then, as Liza looked Shelley and Daniel up and down. 'Well, perhaps not. Now, I've got some little pastry things under the whatchacallit, the broiler, and I'd better attend to them. Can I leave you youngsters to look after yourselves and each other?'

She was off. Daniel rolled his eyes. 'I wish she wouldn't call us *youngsters*.'

'We are, to her,' Shelley said. 'Even you, Daniel, with your sexy silver streaks.'

Daniel flushed with irritation.

'You're Shelley,' said the young man called Jack. 'Your aunt has told me quite a lot about you.'

'And you. You're her new best friend, huh?' Shelley caught herself sounding just a teensy bit sarcastic. But she had known these faddy friendships of her aunt's before. When so-and-so who worked at FAO Schwarz or who clipped tickets at the local cinema was all of a sudden the most amazing and fascinating person in all the world. Her aunt called herself a *people* person – a phrase that never failed to make Shelley wince.

'Why is there a pole in the middle of your aunt's living room?' asked Daniel abruptly.

He was right. There was a shiny metal pole in the middle of the room, connecting floor to ceiling. As they looked, a small space was clearing all around it. The elderly guests were drawing back excitedly.

Shelley looked as puzzled as her boyfriend, until Jack explained: 'They were erecting it as I arrived. It takes some doing, to get it jammed solid between floor and ceiling.'

'But what's it for?' asked Shelley, fearing the worst.

It turned out that her aunt had found an extra-special novelty for her Hallowe'en party. She had hired a pole dancer, who, it turned out, actually *was* Polish. Aunt Liza announced this loudly to the assembled company, as if it was the wittiest thing she had ever heard.

Then the woman in question came hurrying out of the bathroom, where she had been changing into a flimsy Arabian Nights-type outfit.

Shelley could feel the mortification spreading over her boyfriend as he stood beside her, watching. She could see that Jack was wanting to burst out laughing at it all, but couldn't because of the reverent silence that had fallen over the rest of the room. The music changed to some eerie Eastern-style tune. Next thing, the woman was upside down, undulating round the pole, just like the snake out of *The Jungle Book*.

'Rita is a sibyl,' Liza explained. 'Not only does she perform amazing erotic dances, but she tells the future as well.'

Everyone applauded.

They watched Rita writhe about for a while. Daniel was acutely uncomfortable. The woman was too stockily built to be doing stuff like this, especially upside down. Jack was turning purple with suppressed merriment. Shelley didn't know where to look.

Then the sibyl spoke. Her accent was pure New Jersey.

'I am the voice of the future and . . .' She stopped abruptly. 'I can see! I can see what will transpire! Here! In this very apartment! To some of the guests gathered here!'

She had large blue eyes painted over her eyelids, and when she closed her real eyes it was quite effective. But this wasn't just theatrical fakery, the way she was talking right now. There was a strange, tense atmosphere. Liza was suddenly leaning closer, gripping hold of her niece's forearm. She was genuinely alarmed, Shelley could tell.

Rita the sibyl spoke again: 'There is . . . a very great evil heading this way. Evil like I have never known. An ancient evil. And it will come here. It will grace this very apartment with its presence. You must be so careful! All of you . . . you must be very, very careful, for it will destroy you if it can . . .'

With that, the enchantment seemed to leave her and she slithered heavily off the pole and on to the carpet. One of the old men hurried to examine her – he was a medic got up as Boris Karloff for the night. 'She's okay. Nothing broken.'

'Thank God for that,' Liza snorted. 'Fancy letting go of the pole like that. That's the last thing I need in my living room – a New Jersey sibyl with a broken neck.' She hurried to the old-fashioned music centre and put her party record back on, urging her guests to make light of the pole dancer's pronouncements. It was just a bit of fun, wasn't it? Rita always went a bit melodramatic. What she said oughtn't bring the party down!

Then Liza took Shelley aside. 'I've never seen Rita like that. She's a great prognosticator. I think maybe she really has seen something dire in the near future.'

Shelley shook her head and tried to laugh it off. She went to see that Daniel was okay. He was sitting on a chairful of coats, still looking mortified. On her way over, Jack smiled and delayed her.

'This is great,' he said. 'I've met two of my favourite writers and heard horrible predictions about the future. Are your aunt's parties always like this?'

Shelley nodded. 'Always. Who here are your favourite writers?'

He nodded to a lanky, sour-faced woman in a tinsel boa by the venetian blinds. 'Erica Stott, author of the acclaimed *New York Times* bestseller *Werewolf Hooker* series. And Jessica Collings, who did an amazing trilogy set in a parallel universe. But she's in the bathroom. Throwing up, I'd guess, from the state she was in.'

'Wow, you really do like the same stuff my aunt likes, don't you?'

'I love my spooky mystery series, yeah,' he nodded. 'And my paranormal romance. And even some SF and F, so long as there's lots of hot sex in them.'

They were interrupted then by a loud cry from Daniel. He was yelping furiously. Shelley jumped. She was attuned to his mood so strongly that she dashed over immediately to see what the matter was. He was sucking his fingers and aiming a swift kick at Liza's Rufus, who went bounding away through the forest of legs.

'Bit me! Her dog bit me!' Then he was standing up. 'C'mon. We're going to the emergency room. I need a tetanus booster. I'm taking no chances.'

'But the party's just starting really . . .'

Daniel gave Shelley a very level look. He was livid, she could tell. He really was bleeding. She found a handkerchief for him in her bag. It wasn't very clean. This wasn't like Rufus, she tried to protest. She hoped he hadn't hurt the beagle.

'I'll do more than *kick* the mutt if we stay a moment longer.'

They left without saying goodbye to Aunt Liza, or anyone.

Chapter Three

A couple of days after the Hallowe'en party, Liza was still very much on Jack's mind.

The whole evening had proven far more entertaining than expected. Following the departure of Daniel with Liza's niece Shelley, things had stepped up a notch. More people had arrived and it all became a lot more raucous. Jack was surprised to see how determined these old folk were to have a good time. He thought it was a shame Shelley had had to leave so early. Later, Liza confided tipsily that she thought her niece was wasting herself on that uptight Englishman.

Now, on Wednesday, Jack was back hard at work, as Mr Grenoble instructed all his staff to make Fangtasm ready for their most important evening event of the year.

There was going to be a book launch for the lauded and prestigious Moira Sable, author of the exceedingly erotic vampire series, *Dark Juices*. The renowned Ms Sable had chosen Fangtasm as her ideal venue. Mr Grenoble was very flattered and pleased by this. Now he was determined to make everything perfect, and he was prepared to crack the whip to get all hands on deck.

All the shop's casual staff were drafted in for overtime. Jack found himself doing everything from setting out chairs to folding slivers of smoked salmon on to buckwheat blinis – much too early in the afternoon, he felt. He grumbled about this to Lame Wendy, who was his closest friend on the staff. She was what his mother would call 'homely' in looks. She had a squint and a limp and a home-cut hairdo, but she was kind-hearted, loyal, and often agreed with Jack. She too thought that the buckwheat blinis would be all soggy with the crème fraiche and the dill by the time the party began. But Mr Grenoble was flustered and would brook no arguments. He was intent on doing things his way. He had visions of his shop becoming the single most important independent venue for this type of launch.

Jack managed to snatch a break before the author and her entourage arrived. He went to the fancy chocolatier round the corner and ordered himself a minty mocha.

The boy at the counter was the most perfect being Jack had ever seen.

'Hey,' he said, and Jack croaked something back at him. When he was younger, Jack seemed to have moments like this on a daily basis. At least now his infatuations were more widely spaced through his week. But this was a biggie.

Ricardo, his name tag said. No mistaking that look he was giving, and yet Jack indeed mistook it at first. He thought Ricardo had noticed something funny about him – a smut on his nose or something weird. And that was why he was giving him a second look. But it wasn't. Ricardo was giving him a second look because he wanted to. Realising this at last, Jack almost hyperventilated. He took his paper cup to a window seat and concentrated on pretending to watch the crowds swanking by.

He jabbed at his iPhone with trembling fingers. I'm being watched by him, he thought, as his phone connected. By *Ricardo*. The boy was suddenly nearby, wiping round the surfaces where customers brought their drinks. Jack had to move aside the copy of *Title Tattle*, the publishing industry insider mag he had just opened up. I'm being cruised! he thought excitedly. By the boy who's made me the most perfect frothy mocha.

'Yeah?' Liza picked up her phone, sounding gruff. Could she still have a hangover, two days after her party? He remembered her doing tequila shots at the breakfast bar in her apartment as he was putting on his coat to leave that night. 'Whatizzit?'

'Are you coming to our launch party?' he asked hurriedly. 'Remember? Moira Sable? We're doing her a lavish evening at the shop to celebrate the publication of *Bloody Anguish*, the next in her vampire series . . .'

'Yeah, I know. I've read it. Ghastly. What time is this do?'

'Seven thirty. You've got enough time . . .'

'Yeah, enough time to throw on some old rags and schlep all the way downtown.'

'You might meet some interesting people . . .' Just as he said this, Jack inadvertently caught the chocolate boy's eye again. He winced with shame. Being pretty obvious there. Maybe the boy's eyebrows were too primped. Maybe he looked a bit queeny. Hell, I'm nitpicking. He's wonderful. 'Liza? C'mon, it might be fun. We've got blinis. And loads of that pink Frizzante stuff Mr Grenoble's so fond of.'

'Blinis, huh?' He could hear her thinking. 'Well, I've eaten nothin' for days. I've been working like a dog. Maybe I should

32

come out. Hmm. I don't like that Moira Sable, though. She's a stuck-up bitch.'

'It doesn't matter. 'Cause listen, there's something else I wanna tell you. I found an advert in the trade paper . . .'

She chuckled. 'Oh yeah? What's this, the lonely hearts column?' She knew that his single status irked him, and had decided to keep on making jokes about it. She saw no harm. 'Aw, come off it, Jack. Don't take offence. You're so young! An amoeba! What do you gotta panic about being alone for? The right boy will come along some day. You don't gotta to resort to the classifieds . . .'

He frowned. 'No, it's not lonely hearts!' he burst out. Ricardo looked across the chocolate shop at him, and he could have kicked himself. 'Listen up. It's a bookshop. That's what I found in the classifieds section.'

'Uh-huh?' She sounded nonplussed. He had the idea that she was still reading something as she spoke to him.

'It's just the kind of bookshop you want, Liza. What you were talking about the other day . . . old stuff, creepy stuff . . .'

'Oh yeah?'

He read her the advert from the back pages of *Title Tattle*, lowering his voice now, conscious that, even as he served other customers, Ricardo was listening in with keen interest.

'*Vintage and antique books bought and sold. Ghost stories, spook stories, vampire tales. Good prices. Clean copies. Excellent service. Postage to anywhere in the world. Rare and unheard-of tomes. Long-buried horrors and mysteries unearthed especially for you . . .*'

He heard Liza gasp, and was pleased that he'd caught her attention. 'Where is this place?' she asked.

'It's in England.'

She sighed. 'I knew it was too good to be true.'

'But they post to anywhere in the world!'

'Is there a website?'

'No! Not even an email address or a phone number! Isn't that amazing?'

'Very quaint,' said Liza drily.

'But don't you think it sounds wonderful? Can't you just imagine the stuff they must have there? Books that no one else even knows about . . .'

'Uh-huh.'

He knew she was imagining the aroma of mould and mildew. Paperbacks so old and neglected they'd have to be opened with great care. Calfskin-bound private editions of weirdo texts by depraved aristos . . . lurid pulp fiction from a more innocent era . . .

'There must be an address, at least,' she said.

He read it out proudly: '666 Charing Cross Road, WC2H, London. The United Kingdom. What about that, huh? Classy or what?'

'We need to find out more,' she mused.

'I thought you'd like the sound of it. So anyway, are you coming to this party tonight?'

She thought for a couple of seconds. 'Go on then. On one condition.'

'Which is?'

'You gotta ask the boy you've been watching all the way through this conversation. You've gotta ask him along too.'

Jack lowered his phone and stared at it. How the hell did she know?

'I just know. I'm a witch, remember? Second sight and all that. Seriously.'

His eyes widened. When had she told him she was a witch? Maybe when they were completely zonked on punch the other night at hers. He knew she was deep and mysterious under all that brashness. But could she really have powers? He looked across at Ricardo and found him looking straight back. Damn.

'Okay,' he told Liza, finishing the call, and taking his life into his hands. He went straight to the counter and asked Ricardo what time he got off work. Something he'd never, ever do, usually. Liza was taking him out of his comfort zone. If Ricardo laughed at him, he could say – there's a witch on Second Avenue making me do this stuff. It isn't really *me* to be forward like this.

But Ricardo smiled – brilliantly – and told him he was just about finished right now, and what did Jack have in mind?

'Shelley, that effigy of yours is attracting attention from some very strange people.'

This was Daniel on Thursday morning. He was stropping up and down the polished floors of the museum looking peeved. And looking for someone to take it out on. Already he had moved along several viewers of what was fast becoming the most popular exhibit of 'Women and Madness' month; indeed in the museum as a whole. He didn't approve of loiterers. The people he was having to deal with today weren't ones that Daniel liked the look of at all.

'That's what she's there for, Daniel. She's very striking. People are struck by her.'

'Weirdos.'

'Oh come on. We're in a Museum of Outsider Art. It's all *about* weirdos! We *love* weirdos and mavericks, remember?'

'I don't,' he said coldly.

They took this out at lunchtime and carried on the conversation in a French-styled coffee bar at the southern entrance to the park. She watched him nibble his way around a macrobiotic starter and fiddle with his elderberry tea bag. He told her how much he'd rather be working right now in a legitimate gallery. One with real art and proper artists. Not somewhere filled with the loony daubs and outpourings of the mentally ill and – worse, the untrained.

'I hate outsider art, I really do.'

She – who loved it – was shocked. 'But what are you doing working there? How did you get the job?'

He shrugged easily. 'I faked it. It was just an interview. You don't really have to believe in anything you say in those circumstances, do you?'

Shelley went a bit numb at this. She heaped brown sugar into her strong coffee and went to order a muffin. I'm so naïve, she thought miserably. Of course Daniel's just looking for the next step up on his career ladder. The museum and outsider art mean nothing to him. He's just a curator with no love for this particular art form. It's all too messy to him. Too real. Too painful. Of course he wouldn't like it. Yet as she mulled this over, she also knew that there was more to him that that, whatever he said. He had a passion for strange things, ancient things. He really loved old folklore and mystical, totemic objects. He had amassed quite a collection of curious artefacts and hefty, expensive books on the subject, and she had examined them in his apartment. She knew he wasn't as superficially cynical as he pretended to be. Deep down, he really cared about something, no matter what he said.

She came back to sit down and looked at him. He was so sharp, so neat. It was so unlikely he should be with her. She still didn't understand how it had happened. He was even tidy and exact when he was having sex with her. She found herself blushing at the thought, and then she felt ungrateful for feeling that making love with Daniel was just a bit too controlled and pernickety. She felt like one of the machines at his gym . . .

'What are you thinking?' He reached for her hand.

She glanced down quickly. 'About making love with you,' she said.

He frowned. 'Hardly appropriate, Shelley, when we've got to return to work any minute. We've been chatting here for ages. We're almost late. We're out of control.'

She chanced her arm suddenly. 'Oh, let's go back to yours, Daniel. Let's go mad.'

'What?' He looked at her, shocked. 'Go home? In the middle of the day?'

'We can call in sick. We can say I tripped on the street and banged my head and had concussion. And you can take me home and have your wicked way with me . . .'

'Certainly not!' he gasped. Then he went on to list all the vastly important tasks he had to complete that afternoon. Was she insane? He couldn't afford to let anything drift – not one single thing. And, frankly, he was appalled that she thought she could. All for the sake of a tawdry afternoon encounter.

'Tawdry!' she burst out. 'I thought it would be romantic.'

His tossed his head. 'I don't believe in romance.' Then he led the way out of the café and back on to noisy, pushy Broadway and up to Lincoln Square. Back to the Museum of Outsider Art, where he was glad not to fit in.

Shelley ambled miserably around her feminist exhibit. She was cheered slightly by the larger than usual crowd assembled, peering at the artefacts and the paintings. Most of them were congregating around her Scottish woman, of course. They were women of various ages, some of them academic-looking, some of them younger, freaky, alternative sorts. Others were more ordinary. One woman was a vagrant and pretty stinky. Daniel wouldn't be pleased at all by the heterogeneous mix. The women were talking animatedly amongst themselves. Speculating about the tall effigy with her rictus grin and her twiggy fingers and the dark, soulful eyes under that thatch of unruly hair. Who was she? Why was she here? How had she found her way into the New World?

The vagrant woman – swaddled in masses of filthy old clothes, she looked as dreadful as the Scottish Bride herself – had caught hold of Ruthie, Shelley noticed. Ruthie was listening kindly, as she would to anyone, hardly noticing that the filthy old woman was grabbing her arm too hard, making her bracelets jangle. She talked fiercely for a while, punctuating her words with a stabbing finger, and then she was off. It was as if she left a miasma of street dust and bad karma behind her.

Shelley hurried over to her bemused colleague. 'Hey, what was that about? Who was she?'

'Beats me.' Ruthie shrugged. 'Your Scotch lady is getting some pretty strong reactions. They mostly love her, though. There's no denying it. She's become, like, the most popular thing in the place, almost immediately.'

Shelley felt a little glow of pleasure at that. It had been she who had found her, lying neglected all this time. No one could deny her that small piece of success.

'We could have merchandising for my shop,' Ruthie said, her eye – as ever – on the business and touristy end of things. 'T-shirts and mugs. Posters.'

'Really?'

'Honey, I know what tourists will buy. They'll all love her. Listen up, she needs a name.'

'You're right. What about . . .'

'Crazy lady told me what her name is. Just then, by the door.'

'She did, huh?'

'She said – get this – she said that the Scotch woman whispered it to her. Crazy lady leaned forward and touched her cheek and the effigy told her her name.'

Shelley shook her head. Daniel was right. They were attracting the wrong sort. And at the mention of patrons physically touching artefacts, she felt her own prissiness rising up. 'Go on then. Hit me with it.'

'Crazy lady says that our new guest of honour's name is . . . *Bessie.*'

Chapter Four

Dear sir or madam,

Your advertisement in the back pages of *Title Tattle* was pointed out to me quite recently by a young friend in the book trade. I was delighted to see it.

My tastes tend to the esoteric and the somewhat slightly weird and macabre end of things. I desperately want to get my clutches on a number of elderly – mostly English – ghost stories and novels dealing with supernatural themes. All of them are out of print and mostly unheard of by the general reading public. None of them are available here in the Big Apple. Don't ask me why. You'd think there'd be some kind of specialist bookstore somewhere on the whole of Manhattan island that could slake my fervid desire, wouldn't you?

Fervid desire – you like that? Pretty Gothic, huh? Well, the thing is, every bookstore I have patronised for decades has turned its attention to the all-new and the all-shiny. Even the establishments that used to keep a dimly lit and select corner for used-and-second-hand have cleaned up their acts and made way for the new. As a lady of a certain age I could take it as a personal insult – this decluttering and despoliation of the detritus. It sends shivers through my very soul, this lack of respect for the redundant and the old.

I'm just so pleased to see that – judging by your lack of a website or even a phone – you have steadfastly refused to enter what is laughingly known as the twenty-first century. Seriously, guys, how do you manage that? How do you keep afloat in the modern world, doing enough business to survive, if you ignore the usual means of communication? Don't get me wrong – I am agog with admiration at your bloody-mindedness. Blessings on your anachronistic behaviour, 666 Charing Cross Road!

Your address is so evocative to me. I've never been to London, though I would dearly love to visit. It is the home of so many of my favourite purveyors of spook stories. I fondly imagine the gloomy streets that Sir Oswald Arthur tripped up and down as he thought out his spectacular plots. Wandering about in a thick peasouper. Wearing an Ulster and a deerstalker, probably. And Lady Lucretia Noggins, that well-bred floozy. Her tales of torture and depravity are among my earliest loves in the genre. Fox Soames, of course, too, that great debunker of black magicians – his books, also, are unavailable here in NYC. Is this some great conspiracy, do you think? Is this the concerted efforts of the puritanical New World – keeping out the feverish and magical nightmares of the Old? I could heartily believe it.

So – I enclose a handful of American dollars. Go to it! Those three names I mention above – these are where I wish to start on my dark odyssey back into the creepy and not-so-remote literary past. I would be grateful if you could furnish me with volumes by these three luminaries – not expensive editions. (My tastes are cheap. I want reading copies. Paperbacks with the tackiest covers you can find. Pan paperbacks from the 1950s would suit me down to the ground.)

My eternal thanks, sir or madam! I am risking my dollars to the vagaries of our postal systems and flinging them upon your mercy. You might simply ignore this letter of mine and pocket the cash. I fervently hope you will comply with my request and hunt out the volumes I dreadfully desire. I lie here panting and delirious on this frosty November afternoon high above 84th and 2nd – dreaming of ghostly English writers. Don't let me down, you guys!

Yours very sincerely,
Elizabeth Bathory

Liza wrote her letter the morning after the bookshop party. She had what she would have called a towering inferno of a hangover, and vague recollections of having been in some sort of terrible argument the previous evening. She took an Alka-Seltzer and tried to ignore the stirrings of her conscience. She used an old-fashioned nibbed pen and purple Indian ink to compose her letter to London.

When she finished, she read it back with great satisfaction, imagining the delights to come by return of international post. She made fiendishly strong coffee and wolfed a banana, which always helped her with hangovers. Then Jack rang from his bookshop.

'I meant to call, to thank you for inviting me last night,' she said. Though she couldn't remember great swathes of the evening, she *did* recall Jack bundling her roughly into a cab at some point. Had there been a falling-out between them somehow?

Right now he sounded a bit off with her. 'I wanted to make sure you hadn't died in your sleep. Maybe swallowing your own forked tongue or something.'

'What?' she gasped. 'Whaddya mean?'

'I mean, my job's in jeopardy here because of you. Everyone knows that you were here on my invite last night. Mr Grenoble says he's very tempted to fire me on the spot.'

'Fire you? But the place was packed for Moira whatsit's party. It was a huge success, wasn't it? With her launching her *Anguished Juices*, or whatever it was called.'

'Oh, sure,' hissed Jack. 'It was going great. Until you decided to pick a fight with the celebrated author.'

Liza gulped. 'I did?'

'You don't remember, do you?'

'Erm . . .' Actually, it was starting to come back now. She remembered coming face to face with the primped and painted clown, that dreadful Moira Sable person. She remembered feeling her blood begin to boil. She had groaned aloud all the way through Moira's reading from her vampire novel, drawing strained looks from fellow partygoers. And then she had marched up to Moira and told her she was a phoney.

Moira Sable was a faded glamourpuss. Liza decided that she had put her bosoms on show in a misplaced attempt to distract her audience from her godawful prose – and told her so. 'The thing is, I can tell,' she had said. 'I can sniff out phoneys and fakes. And you, my dear, have faked it. You've never had any true, first-hand experience of magic or mystery in your entire life, have you?'

The novelist stared at her. 'What? Why should I? I . . . I use my imagination . . .'

'And a pretty poor one it is too!' Liza barked. 'Well, I have lots of experience of real magic and mystery, as it happens, and I'm here to tell you, lady, that the stuff you put about is all lies. It's dangerous lies. What you're doing is glamorising the undead and those awful necrophiliacs who mess about with them. They're filthy cadavers! Monsters! Trust me, I know all about this stuff! And you're playing a despicable game, making them seem desirable . . .'

Moira Sable was starting to look alarmed by now. Of course it had fallen to Jack to sort out the situation. He prised Liza none too gently away from the famous novelist and guided her to the door. What was she yelling about? Real vampires and monsters? Where was she getting this stuff from?

Mr Grenoble had announced that he was banning Liza from his store for a month.

'A month!' gasped Liza, hearing this awful news now. 'What am I gonna do?'

Jack gave an audible shrug down the line. 'You should be glad it's not even longer. Mr Grenoble is still furious this morning. Moira Sable says she'll never darken our door again.'

'Pah.' Liza reflected that it was a good thing she'd put her order in with the shop at 666 Charing Cross Road. If she kept on getting banned from places, she would need all the new outlets she could find.

And what had she been thinking of? Blurting out to all and sundry about her actual experiences with the world of monsters, demons and dark forces? She'd have them all laughing at her. They'd think she was a mental case, some mad old coot.

She had vowed never to let any of that stuff slip past her lips. Not in public. Not to anyone.

Liza had seen too much. Too many spooky things.

And she had to keep quiet about them. She certainly wasn't meant to rant about them drunkenly in the middle of Greenwich Village cocktail parties. Those days were far behind her now.

'And you never said what you thought of Ricardo,' said Jack, bringing her out of her reverie.

'Who?'

'My date. At the book party last night. He was enthralled by the whole thing. He thought you were fabulous, by the way, for starting a fight like that.'

'Oh!' Liza tried to picture him. Jack had a date? Jack had introduced him to her? She couldn't remember at all, so she pretended. 'He seemed very nice.'

'You told me last night that he didn't look very much like a reader to you.'

'Did I? I'm such an awful snob.'

'But he is! He's a big Moira Sable fan. In fact, it was Ricardo's strategic grovelling that calmed Moira down, after you attacked her for being such a phoney.'

'Don't remind me! I'm so ashamed!'

But something in Liza's tone alerted Jack to the fact that

she wasn't ashamed one bit. In one way, he looked forward to getting old, if it meant behaving appallingly and getting away with it.

'Did you really mean it?' he asked. 'That the only supernatural stories worth anything are the ones with some basis in reality?'

'Of course!' she said. 'Don't you think so too?'

'But . . . but *none* of it's real, is it? Isn't it *all* made up? All the spooky stuff?'

'Oh dear, Jack,' she chuckled. 'Do you really think that?'

'Well . . . yes, I guess I do.'

'Ah. Hmm. Well you've got an awful lot to learn, sweetheart.' There was something very dark in her voice. There was so much lurking beneath the surface of everything she said, he realised. Yeah, I've got a lot to learn, he thought.

And this was the season that Jack's education really began.

Chapter Five

November was well and truly with them now, making early mornings harsh and difficult. Especially for Shelley, she felt.

She and Jack met up a couple of times – having found out that they got on. Liza had brought them together as friends. They found they had things to discuss. Jack had a brand-new boyfriend, and there was lots to talk about there. Shelley's relationship was a little older and she was thinking about taking it to what she called 'the next level'.

They took a walk in the park to chew it over. The trees were putting on one last burst of glorious colour. The two new friends ate spicy nuts from a twisted paper bag, sitting on the grey granite rocks, watching the city at play.

'It's too cold to sit for long,' Jack said.

Shelley smiled at him for being an old woman. They had a loose sort of arrangement, about heading to Dog Hill later in the afternoon and meeting Liza. For now they were content to wander and gossip about their boyfriends. Actually, Shelley had heard enough about the marvellous Ricardo by now. She hadn't met him yet, but she felt like she knew way too much about him. Like many gay men, Jack could dish far too much information about some things.

It was as they were walking down one of the broader boulevards, luxuriating under the stirring shadows of the dying leaves, that she came out with her news.

'You can't!' Jack gasped.

'Why not? I'm sick of going back and forth on public transport. And it was Daniel's idea, anyway. It's not like I'll be imposing . . . or moving too quickly . . .'

'But moving *in* with the guy.' Jack whistled. 'And giving up your own place.'

'My place is crappy. You've never seen it. It's a single room and it's damp and cold. It's like sitting in a drowned woman's handbag.'

He stared at her. 'That line's one of your Aunt Liza's, right?'

'Yeah, it's what she said the one time she came to visit. About a year ago. The depths of winter is when my place is at its best. When the mould on the four walls is glistening and black.'

'It sounds charming.' Jack was thinking of his own place on Thompson Street, and how proud he was of it. How long it took him to get it. And how he wouldn't let it go, no matter what.

'So it's pretty spiffy, I'm guessing, Daniel's place?'

'Five-storey brownstone in the West Nineties. He's got two floors. He must have some serious money behind him. Family money.'

They meandered on a bit, stopping to stare at red squirrels as they dive-bombed and caromed about on the grass. Shelley was mentally kicking herself for sounding like some money-grabbing whore and wondering how to make herself appear better to her new friend.

'I'm glad to hear it's love as well,' Jack said at last. 'Not just, like, shallow greed.'

They both laughed.

'Love him?' She thought about this. 'I suppose I must do. To want to take it to the next level like this.' But really, she thought, I'm thinking less about love than I am the shortened commute to work. Or his beautiful polished wooden floors. She didn't think much of the creepy paintings he had on the walls, or his rather masculine furniture . . .

'Don't do it, Shelley,' Jack suddenly burst out. 'It's a huge mistake.'

'What?'

'I mean it. Your aunt would say the same, I bet. You try her out. She'd be appalled at you giving up your independence, just for an easy life.'

'How do you know? You hardly know her . . .'

'Just look at her! Your Aunt Liza has been independent all her life. She's lived alone in her own place for over forty years. She'll be horrified at you meekly moving in with your snobby boyfriend.'

'Snobby!' she gasped. 'Meekly! Who says I'm moving in meekly?'

A family were passing them. Father with a toddler sitting on his shoulders, the older kid on a little bike. The mother raised both eyebrows. Shelley was sounding just about hysterical, Jack thought, as she defended herself.

He shrugged at her. 'It's up to you. But I wouldn't trust him. I'm sorry. I've held off saying so, but I don't think he's right for you.'

'What?'

'I know I haven't known you for long . . .'

'You're right there, buster. What gives you the right . . . ?'

'But I just have this feeling. And so does your Aunt Liza!' He looked triumphant for a second. Then he saw Shelley's face fall and felt instantly ashamed.

'What? She doesn't like Daniel either? She said that?'

Now he tried to wriggle out of it. 'I'm sorry, I shouldn't have said anything. It's up to her to tell you what she thinks.' He started walking on ahead, hoping the crunch of dead leaves on gravel would drown out his guilty qualms.

'But she's confided in you? About Daniel? And me?'

He stopped. 'Yeah. She did. I'm sorry, Shelley.'

'Oh!' Shelley looked as if she'd been slapped. Her long hair blew about around her face, some of it sticking to her mouth. She had a kind of careless, guileless look that made his heart go out to her. 'How come you were talking about me like that?'

'Because . . .' He sighed. 'Because we were both talking about Daniel and how we . . .'

'How you what?'

'Don't like him much, I guess,' he mumbled. 'I guess that was the tenor of the conversation, yeah.'

They carried on walking in silence for a while. Their Sunday peacefulness was ruined, even though the sky was a bright, impeccable blue as they strolled purposefully, deeper into the park. Soon they would catch up with Liza, who'd be out with Rufus now, letting him off the lead in their special place, even though she wasn't really supposed to, according to park rules. When they caught up with her, Shelley thought, her aunt would have some tricky questions to answer.

*

Dear madam,

We are very glad to have received your letter and your order. We hope that the books that we have chosen for you go some way to rewarding your faith in our ability to fulfil your needs. Please find enclosed four books. Three are by the authors you mentioned in your letter. We have chosen the three rarest of their works, all in pleasingly gaudy paperback editions.

We have taken the liberty, also, of including something we thought you might enjoy. A bumper volume of macabre stories edited by Fox Soames, *The Best of the Books of Mayhem*. Altogether the price of these first purchases from our humble shop comes to the equivalent of seven dollars ninety-six. This leaves you with a surplus of thirty-two dollars and four cents. Should we hang on to this and consider it credit for your next order? Please advise.

We, the staff at 66b Charing Cross Road, hope you will be pleased with this first foray into our endless stock. We hope you will remain a good customer of ours. We find that we have very loyal customers, with whom we have long-term and interesting relationships. Do note, however, madam, that our address is 66*b* Charing Cross Road. You appear to have misread it in our advertisement as *666*. The satanic implications are amusing but not, I'm afraid, hugely practical. Our postal service has gone very downhill in recent years and any little mistake on the front of your envelope might result in it going astray for ever. So please *do* watch out. Some of the staff here did have a little chuckle with me, however, when I showed them your tiny slip. As it turns out, no one has ever made that connection before, between our address and the infamous number of the beast.

I must draw to a close here, and hope once more that these enclosures will delight you and that we will hear from you again, before long.

With very best wishes,
Mr K. N. Wright

He called me madam! Liza laughed.

She read the letter through again and smiled to herself. She'd never been addressed so formally or politely in all her long life. It seemed ludicrous somehow, almost parodic. But on reading the letter through once more, she detected no hint of sarcasm or mockery. This must be what was known as olde-worlde charm. And she loved it! Immediately she could picture this Mr K. N. Wright. He'd be tall and dapper. Silver-haired and oh-so-careful in his approach to everything. Like a Jeeves-type character, all-knowing and prepared for anything. She loved the idea of him typing this letter (on an actual typewriter! The letters were slightly misaligned and uneven) and thinking very carefully about how he should approach such a valued new customer.

And the books . . . !

The parcel was lying open on her Formica breakfast bar. She hardly dared touch them, they were so perfect and . . . old. And yet they were beautifully preserved, as if everyone who had read them over the years had been extra-careful not to crack their spines or bend their colourful covers. They were indeed, as Mr Wright had said, rare specimens. She had never even heard of *The Books of Mayhem* before, let alone *The Best of*. She flipped it open reverentially, to scan down a list of contributors' names that was half familiar, half unknown. Here lay a cornucopia of new writers to explore. A whole world of the supernatural was about to open up to her. Long-forgotten English ghost-story writers. Just holding up that thick tome and riffling through the yellow pages made her breathing and her heartbeat go that bit faster.

She wanted to fling herself into her chair straight away and make a start. Forget everything else she was reading. All that current stuff. All that slight and superficial stuff. The things she read for work and the slim pickings she worked her way through on her own account. Always it felt like she was on the trail of something elusive and alluring . . . and yet she was always let down in the end. The books were too unsubtle. Too bloody, or not bloody enough. Not at all creepy, or too downright schlocky. There was a sensibility she hankered for . . . a certain restraint and a particular kind of gallows humour . . . Somehow she just knew she had it here, with this package. This was the mother lode. Mr Wright had stuffed her first parcel with books that were bound to become her favourites, she could just feel it. He was like some kind of darkly benign Santa Claus.

But she couldn't sit in her reading chair just now. It was nearly eleven o'clock. All she had accomplished this morning was a trip to the market for dog food and celery and hummus. This blessedly marvellous parcel had taken up all of her attention. But now she remembered she had appointments to keep. She was due at a meeting or two this afternoon. She had to pick up some new galleys. Her opinion was required.

Liza stared with longing at her chair by the window, where she loved to read, watched over by the tall windows and pointed gables across the street. But she knew she couldn't stay here this afternoon. She had to be out and doing stuff. She set the new books down on her console table by the chair, and folded the letter from Mr Wright into her purse. She'd be seeing Jack for coffee later on, when she was done with her last appointment on Hudson Street. She imagined showing him the letter and giving him full credit for inspiring this wonderful connection. He'd be so pleased, she thought.

That is, if he'd shut up for just one second about that new boyfriend of his.

Before leaving her apartment, she folded away the brown paper that Mr Wright had wrapped her books in. Who still did parcels that way? Brown paper and hairy string? It was like something out of the wartime years. Liza found herself studying the stamps with the Queen's head on. She realised she was longing to go to England. She always had.

But it was the England of ghosts and ghouls and yellow fogs that she wanted. She longed for the England of the classic supernatural tale, the bloody folk legends, the stories of demonic romance. Was it really there? Did it actually exist?

One thing was certain: 666 Charing Cross Road existed for sure. Even if the address *was* wrong. That establishment alone – harbouring its treasures right in the heart of the modern metropolis – seemed magical enough to Liza.

Chapter Six

They ventured over to Daniel's apartment. It was Shelley's idea and her invitation. Thanksgiving at her new place.

Liza wasn't keen. Thanksgiving wasn't something she paid much attention to these days. She hadn't really since the kids were little. Her Jennifer and Bryan. Back when she was a young mother, she'd make the special effort for their sake. But now, with them grown and gone so far away – one to Texas, the other to Los Angeles – there hardly seemed any point. Jen and Bryan had their own homes and kids and family traditions. And they were all a lot more traditional than the eccentric way in which they always accused Liza of bringing them up. Now Liza was alone and liked being on her own, apart from Rufus, that was. She saw no reason for forced celebrations and togetherness: all that kind of thing embarrassed her. When other people were laughing and smiling she often found her thoughts miles away, and caught herself scowling, which was no good in polite, festive company.

Somehow, though, she couldn't refuse Shelley and Daniel's earnest invitation to give thanks with them this year. Besides, she wanted to see this fancy pad of Daniel's. Also, she'd have a young man accompanying her, which made it easier somehow. It was a long time since she'd enjoyed having an escort like this. She was glad Jack had been invited as well. It felt like moral support.

The two of them made their way across in the early afternoon.

'You've spruced yourself up,' she told him.

'Aren't I always spruce?' He looked at her outfit. More of a costume, with a tweedy green cape and a dinky hat. He didn't think he'd seen Liza in the same outfit twice.

As they strolled under the bare trees lining the broad streets, the addresses were getting fancier and the homes more and more luxurious looking. Liza was completely unfazed by it all. Jack had the idea that she could fit in just about anywhere.

Now she was telling him about the latest order she had placed with the bookshop he had found for her. She was breathless with excitement about it.

'So I'm working my way through this anthology they sent me, and I've asked for further books by some of these guys I've never heard of before.' Her eyes gleamed. 'I thought I was some kind of expert in this stuff. Now I find I know hardly anything. There's a whole world of supernatural fiction out there, just waiting for me . . .'

'I'm pleased I discovered the advert,' Jack said, reminding her where credit was due.

The streets were strangely quiet. Everyone was indoors already, enjoying the closeness of their families and celebrating in private. A sudden gloom stole over Jack, as he remembered how he'd told his mom and the rest of his family that he wouldn't be home for Thanksgiving this year: he was staying in the city. They had been very disappointed in him. What could he say, though? That this year he had new friends, and a new boyfriend, with whom he wanted to spend the day? He hadn't known any of these new people in his life for very long, though.

Just as they thought they were getting close to Daniel and Shelley's address, they became aware of someone running up to them from behind. Jack felt Liza tense immediately, ready to spring to their defence, as if she thought it might be a mugger. But it was Ricardo. Looking immaculate in a red cashmere sweater and a scarf slung casually over one shoulder.

'You remember each other, don't you?' Jack said. 'From that launch at Fangtasm?'

Ricardo grinned. Beautiful teeth, Liza thought. She could recall that much through the haze of her memories of that night. 'Of course. He mollified that Moira Whatsit after I riled her up for being such a phoney. So! How's it going, you two, huh? Must be getting serious, if you're spending Thanksgiving together . . .'

Jack blushed furiously, but Ricardo was made of sterner stuff. He simply smiled, hefted up the sack of provisions he had with him and said to Liza, 'My mother is having a shit fit. I'm all she has in the world and I have told her I'll be out all day.' He shrugged. 'I tried to tell her, what does Thanksgiving mean to us anyway? Zilch. And she hates eating food in front of other people. Other people make her choke, she says.'

Liza smiled, ambling along and counting down the addresses. 'You should have brought her along. I'm sure Daniel wouldn't have minded. And my niece is very laid-back . . .'

Except today Shelley wasn't in the least bit laid-back.

When they found the right building, and had themselves buzzed up to the fourth floor, they toiled up the wide staircases, and found Shelley looking sweaty and furious on her doorstep. Everything was going wrong. She had messed up every single stage of dinner and was probably about to inflict food poisoning on them with her dodgily defrosted turkey.

'Happy Thanksgiving,' said Liza ruefully, and effected the necessary introductions.

'Omigod, sorry,' Shelley burst out. 'Hello, Ricardo. Come on in, everyone. Make yourselves at home . . .'

In the vast space of the stylish living room (Shelley had been quite correct about the very masculine furniture), Daniel coolly held court by the cocktail cabinet. He mixed them mercifully strong martinis and welcomed them to his home. If he felt even the slightest bit irked at sharing his holiday with this odd mixture of guests – all of them Shelley's – he didn't show it.

He was the perfect host, even Liza had to admit. Perhaps a bit too smooth. That always gave her the creeps. Shelley had said he came from some rich, posh English family. That's where he got all that polish from, then. So you'd never be able to tell what he was thinking or feeling. How would Shelley ever put up with that? He kind of belonged in one of those ghost stories from the Olde Worlde that Liza was enjoying so much – all frosty and haunted, stiff and repressed. Great to read about, sure, but who wanted to be shacked up with a guy like that?

'Dinner smells wonderful,' Jack told Shelley. 'I don't know what you're fretting about.'

'I've overcooked all the vegetables. I got nervous and put them on too soon. We're having soggy sweet potatoes.'

'Who cares?' said Ricardo suddenly. 'What matters, surely, is the spirit of the thing, huh? We're all in the same place, celebrating together and enjoying each other's company.' He urged them to stand up for a toast, and Jack grinned at his self-possession. Liza had just gotten comfortable on the black settee and resented having to stand again. Daniel looked as if he was thinking, 'Who is this guy, proposing toasts in my apartment?'

Then Daniel put on his *Chill Out with the Classics* CD and stalked off to the kitchenette to supervise Shelley's progress.

She looked like she was about to cry. The oven door was open and she was prodding at the huge bird, as if that would do any good. Daniel sighed and thought longingly about last year, when he had still been seeing a former colleague called Amanda. They'd taken a cabin in the woods for the holidays. She had been a luscious deaf mute, and it was the relative quiet and calm that appealed most right now.

'Just calm down,' he grunted at Shelley. 'You don't have to impress anyone. They don't want anything fancy.'

She looked at him and seemed a bit wild. 'I want everything to be nice for them.' It was more than that, though. She wanted it to be perfect for her aunt's sake. She wanted Liza to see that moving in here was the right thing for her. And that Daniel was the right guy for her, too.

'I'm sure it's nice enough for them,' he said, and shrugged as he sipped his drink. It was silvery and perfect. 'So who said Jack could bring along a friend? What is this, a soup kitchen?'

Shelley was shocked. 'Ricardo's his boyfriend.'

'Oh, of course. Indeed. Long-term thing, yeah? They look to me like they've only just met. He probably picked him up last night. Somewhere insalubrious, no doubt.' Daniel was scowling. 'Keep an eye on him. Make sure he doesn't steal anything.'

'Daniel! You can't—'

'I don't like the look of him. Of either of them, actually.'

Frazzled, Shelley turned her attention back to her hopeless-looking vegetables, which were still stewing on the hob. 'What's not to like about them?'

'I don't like faggots.' He shrugged. 'The way they look you up and down. Wondering. Speculating about you. Me. I mean, one. And the way they talk. And walk. I can't bear them. I hate being around fellows like that. I wish you'd never invited them.'

Then he was gone, returning to the living room to be the charming host. Shelley stared at the space he'd left behind, shocked. She stayed like that until Jack popped his head in. 'We're all starving. Can I help you carry things into the dining room?'

Oh God, the table wasn't even laid properly. She'd started but then she had been distracted. Daniel would be bound to have something to say about that.

'Is everything okay through there?' she asked Jack.

'Everything's fine.' He smiled. 'Don't worry so much, Shelley. Everyone's having a lovely time. Liza's telling us all about her correspondence with Mr Wright at the bookshop on Charing Cross Road in London.'

Shelley tutted. 'Can you believe that? She's got a crush already on this bookseller she's never even met. She says he comes across very nicely in his letters. He could be saying anything to her and she wouldn't mind, so long as it was in a polite English voice. Huh!' She wiped her damp face with the tea cloth. 'Is Daniel being okay with everyone?'

'He's being charm itself,' Jack said. 'I'm sorry that I was so candid about my feelings before. When I said he was horrible. I

60

rushed in too quickly to judge him. He seems much nicer, now that I'm getting to know him. I'm glad things are working out for you, Shelley. You seem so at home here.'

'Yeah,' she said, wanting to cry. 'I really am.'

A couple of days later, Jack was spending his afternoon off with Ricardo. Ricardo had been pretty quiet since the Thanksgiving dinner at Shelley and Daniel's. Jack was hoping that the awkwardness and ultimate failure of that day wouldn't spill over . . .

'No, no, I've just been busy, you know. My mother's very demanding. She's in this situation with her landlord. All the people in her building are in dispute with him . . .'

Ricardo seemed *muy* devoted to his mother. This made Jack feel vaguely guilty about the way in which he neglected all the members of his own family.

'This is the first day I've been able to get away to see you,' Ricardo told him. 'Honestly.' He grinned at Jack as they walked along, and then, to Jack's amazement, took hold of his hand. Jack blushed as they walked along like this through the early afternoon crowds on Eighth Avenue.

They were going to Shelley's work, to see her much-vaunted exhibit. She had tried to explain it to them over dinner the other day, but the alcohol had gotten to them and discussion of the 'Women and Madness' show had dissolved into helpless giggles.

Since then, there had been a review in a local free paper, and a mention in the *Times*. Shelley had almost fainted to see something from the Outsider Art gallery – let alone something of hers – mentioned in the press. She had been positively glowing with pride for two whole days. Now the museum was even fuller, with a broad mix of visitors flocking to see the eclectic range of works every day. They were all mostly there for the Scottish Bride, however. Bessie was the true draw in the show.

Even Daniel had to hand Shelley the credit – albeit surlily – for Bessie's success.

'I still don't understand what it is we're going to see,' Ricardo said.

Jack tried to explain. It was thought to be some kind of sacrificial object, perhaps as much as two hundred years old. Something that the Scots might have intended to burn on a ritualistic pyre as a kind of, like, propitiation thing. Or she might have been intended for death by drowning. Perhaps she was a gigantic fetish doll or represented some sort of witchy creature who had to be cast out of the community. No one knew for certain. The only knowable fact was that the giant effigy had turned up in a crate at the museum, quite forgotten in the cellar, and Shelley had unearthed her. And now she was causing a sensation, under the name bestowed upon her by a drunken vagrant. A number of starkly horrible pictures had been taken, and these had found their way into the press. Bessie was enjoying the limelight like a grisly and ancient Broadway starlet in the throes of an unexpected late blooming.

They had to queue for some moments to get into the unassuming museum. Once inside, they bought tickets and milled around in the foyer with a crowd of people, all a little unsure where to go. A boisterous woman was doing a roaring trade in the gift shop, selling visitors outsize T-shirts with the Scottish Bride's image printed on.

'Oh, I'll have to have one of those for my mother,' Ricardo said. 'Aren't they great?'

Shelley had appeared magically at their sides. She hugged them both briskly. She was slightly different in her manner here at work, noted Jack approvingly. Less jittery somehow. More in command. She unhooked a braid barrier to let them through. 'There's a queue, but my friends can come straight in,' she said.

'Er, has your aunt been yet?' Jack said. 'Surely she must be fascinated by all of this?'

Shelley admitted that Liza hadn't visited yet. 'But she loves the collections we get here. She's promised to come before the week's out. She's been very busy, as you know . . .'

Jack nodded ruefully. 'Yeah, she's spending all her spare time with these books she's getting from London.'

Shelley led them through the miniature maze of exhibits until they stood before the Bride herself. They stared up at her podium with something approaching awe.

'She's much bigger than she seems in the pictures,' said Jack at last. The thing stood about a foot taller than he did, up on its plinth. She was grinning down at him with broken teeth. And there was a nasty, sweetish smell, like something gone off. He had expected to be visiting something quaint and unusual. He had expected to be politely diverted by this visit. But Bessie was making his flesh creep. He had to look away.

'I can see why you call her a bride,' said Ricardo. 'She's like a dead bride. Drowned. In the tatters of her wedding dress. And that bouquet, the poor thing . . .' His words faded away and the others looked at him in surprise. Ricardo seemed very affected by the sight of the figure.

'We've had to fix her in place a bit more firmly,' Shelley told them. 'She's nailed to a post now. That's why she's standing a bit hunched like that. She looks more . . . menacing than she did. But we had to do it. Daniel's orders. Someone pulled at her the other day and she toppled forward into the crowd. Luckily she had a soft landing and nothing was damaged. And no one was injured, thank God.'

A shiver passed through Jack as he imagined this hideous creation teetering forward and falling on to him. He'd have a screaming fit, he knew.

Shelley glanced at her watch and made her excuses. 'I have to get back to my desk. But I'll see you both soon, won't I?' They all hugged and the boys watched her clip-clop away on expensive heels. Jack remarked that he had never seen her looking so smart and professional.

'If I had a proper job I would love to be like that,' Ricardo sighed. 'All efficient and tidy. Marching about the place and knowing what to tell people to do.'

Jack smiled. He couldn't imagine Ricardo being anything like that. His attitude at his fancy chocolate shop was pretty slapdash, on the whole. He had also alluded to doing some porno for pin money, though those days were over now, since at twenty-two he was obviously getting too old. Jack had been shocked to find himself turned on by this glimpse of Ricardo's resumé.

'I like Shelley a lot,' Ricardo confided, as they took a last look at the effigy and then a walk around the remainder of the exhibition. 'It's good, being with you. I've met interesting new people. Liza's great, of course, too.' But then he scowled suddenly. 'I don't like Daniel, though. I could do without being around him. Shelley's too good for the likes of him.'

Jack shrugged. He was amused by Ricardo's fast-changing emotions and the way he tended to act them all out very deliberately. 'Oh, I know, but what can you say? They're together. There must be another side to him besides all that snobbiness and stiffness . . .'

'Huh,' snorted Ricardo. 'There is another side to him all right.' Now they were in the gift shop, which was less crowded. They could examine the new Bessie T-shirts in peace. 'That was something I discovered at that Thanksgiving travesty . . .'

Jack watched him unfolding a tiny shirt and holding it against his narrow chest. 'What do you mean? What are you getting at?'

'I'll have to tell you. I can't *not* tell you.'

'Tell me what?' Jack gasped. Sometimes Ricardo was a bit overdramatic, frankly.

'When I went to load the dishwasher. You know, helping out, doing my bit. Because Shelley looked fit to drop by then. And everyone else was completely messed up on martinis.'

'Yeah?'

'Well, I was cramming all the crockery into their dishwasher and Daniel followed me into the kitchenette, right? And at first he's, like, telling me I'm doing it all wrong and how I'll smash the glasses and anyway they don't belong in there . . .'

Jack held his breath, all of a sudden knowing what was coming next.

Ricardo nodded, bunching the T-shirt in his hands. 'Yeah. Next thing I know, he's right over by me. All over me. He's got his face pressed right into mine, trying to get his fat tongue in my mouth. And his hands are all over, grabbing after my dick. The

65

man's a classic closet case, Jack. He's a fricking menace. How're we gonna break it to Shelley?'

Jack just gawped at him.

Ruthie shouted over from the till, 'You guys buying that shirt or what?'

It was like a limp twisted rag in Ricardo's hands: he would have to buy it now.

Chapter Seven

Rufus was acting out of character this afternoon.

On those days when it was warm enough still for Liza to sit reading outside, there was nothing he liked more than going with her. Sometimes she would take him to the particular spot in the park he loved the most, and she'd let him off the leash. He knew that mostly he would have to stay close to her, though, but that was okay. Rufus liked Liza. They had been together years. He knew that theirs was one of the longest and most satisfying relationships she had ever been in.

Only thing was, she was terrible at taking any kind of advice. And, him being a dog, she found it pretty easy to disregard the stuff he was saying to her. She would pretend she couldn't understand his warnings. Like now.

'What is it with you today, Rufus?' He was pulling away from her. He was refusing to settle. He wasn't even enjoying the things she knew he normally liked. There was no sniffing around trees and glaring at squirrels. He wasn't even diverted by the figures gliding around the rink. It was as if he had gone into some terrible mood and nothing would distract him.

Well, Liza didn't have time for temperamental mutts. Rufus would just have to shake himself out of it.

Still, it was strange. He was usually the most easy-going of companions, but today, he had even growled at her. She shook her head, thinking about it. She, who had taken him in when he'd had nowhere else to go. He was a rescue puppy. A scraggy one no one had wanted. When Liza first clapped eyes on him, her heart had bled. She'd taken one look at that ripped ear, that endearing slobber he produced in his excitement as she lingered outside his pen. An indissoluble relationship had been formed that day.

But the woman was pig-headed, Rufus thought. He had learned that much over the years. She had her flaws, just like anyone else. Although, obviously, she was still the most wonderful person in the world to him, and they had never been parted.

Yeah, he had growled at her. He felt a bit ashamed of it now, and he knew she was thinking about that moment too, as they ambled through the frosty park. Maybe he had gone too far with the growl.

All he knew was that there had been a funny smell in the apartment all morning. More than a smell. A heaviness in the air. A low vibration. Outside the bandwidth of human ears, obviously. And the smell was oily and corrupt.

It had arrived with the morning's mail. His hackles had gone up when Liza came bustling back in with an armful of letters and a parcel. Another parcel bundled in brown paper. Smelling of coldness and the hold of an airplane and a different country. Many hands had touched this parcel, masking the whiff of what lay inside until Liza had excitedly cut the string and unpeeled the paper, revealing the pile of books within.

68

And that was when Rufus had smelled the horrible smell.

Liza was quite unaffected. She gasped with pleasure and excitement. Rufus knew that these book things were important to her. She seemed to get a lot out of them. She spent all her time around them and her livelihood was intimately bound up in somehow working with them. He had never quite figured out what it was she did, exactly, to make a living. He just knew that books were important. And she was especially fond of old, stinky ones, which tended to play havoc with her pooch's heightened senses.

The three paperbacks were old and innocuous. He wasn't bothered about those. But there was a fourth book. A hardback bound in black leather. It was only the size of Liza's hands and he watched her pore over it, turning the pages with such care and attention. She was holding her breath. Her heart was beating like mad. It was obviously something that had come as a very great surprise.

'What's Mr Wright sent us this time, hey, Roof? Another freebie! Look at this thing, would ya? Must be worth a fortune.' She held it close to her face and inhaled its rich scent, then paused and lingered over the strange book. She wasn't sure she liked that smell, actually.

Rufus found himself dancing on the spot nervously, claws clicking on the kitchen lino. Ridiculous! Dancing like a puppy! Whimpering!

'Roof?' She turned to him and blinked. 'What's a matter?' Then she opened up her purse and slipped the new, ancient volume inside.

That was when Rufus had growled at her.

Yeah, he was ashamed of himself now. Baring his teeth at her. Giving her his most fierce warning. Right there, in the kitchen where she had nursed him through sickness and tended to him and fed him his every dinner. He was ashamed, but he knew he was right.

She shouldn't carry that thing about with her. That dead thing. That dead, wicked thing that somehow . . . somehow was speaking. Shrieking. Quivering with vileness inside her purse.

Liza was disturbed by her dog's behaviour. Never had he carried on like this. Maybe he was sickening for something? Whatever the case, he distracted her and she forgot about the sickly smelling volume that had been sent her.

Really, it had made her feel as jittery and odd as Rufus had seemed. There was something very wrong about that book. Something that nagged and pulled at her. It roused her instincts and her memories of a time in her life she thought she had laid aside for ever . . .

But now her attention was on her nervy, sulky dog and the necessity of getting him some exercise. Maybe he could walk off this rather sour mood.

Soon they were trotting about in the park, puffing out lungfuls of clean white air. Rufus could almost forget about their unfortunate start to the day as they breezed past joggers and skateboarders and tried to keep pace with the horses and carriages and yellow cabs.

As they wandered briskly through the zoo, however, he was reminded of his fear. Wherever they went, they were observed by alert, intelligent eyes. Usually the animals were pretty blasé. They'd seen it all before in there. They regarded their visitors with easy tolerance. But today Liza and Rufus were made to feel distinctly . . . unwelcome. The penguins turned tail pretty sharpish. They scuttled away as Liza paused to watch them. The snow monkeys halted in what they were doing. One of them stared hard at Liza and gave in to a sudden, wild panic. That set the others off and they started gibbering madly, tearing at their long hair.

Every caged beast that Liza and Rufus passed that afternoon had the same reaction. By the time she decided they should leave the zoo – she was causing too much fuss – Liza was beginning to feel paranoid. It was like being a famous person in the animal kingdom. Wherever she went, she set off this bizarre behaviour. She was growled at everywhere she turned. Even someone's kid in a stroller gave her a weird look as she hurried on by, under the clock and out of there.

'So it's not just you, hey, Roof. I'm *persona non grata* today. Maybe I should change my scent, huh? Shelley bought me this one last birthday. I never really liked it . . .' She was babbling as they walked along. She was disturbed, though. Nothing like this had ever happened before.

What was different about today? What was different about her?

Rufus tried to explain again.

'Stop whining,' she snapped at him. She sat on a bench, far from everyone. She took out a bag of scraps and crumbs and looked for squirrels to feed. Not a one. They'd all scrammed. She sighed and took out the book she had brought with her.

Rufus whined again and she frowned at him darkly. She'd had just about enough already today.

Time to examine this latest free gift from London more closely.

It was an ancient kind of anthology of texts and spells. The word *Grimoire* was stamped in gold lettering on its spine. The pages were messy with different languages and handwritten notes. There were some peculiar woodcuts in smudgy black ink.

That feeling was back. Deep in her stomach, like she'd eaten bad takeout. And that nagging in her memories. Warning her. Telling her to stop this before she went any further . . .

Liza hated listening to her subconscious, especially when it was issuing warnings.

Some of the pages in the middle were stuck together. A whole handful were clumped and hardened with a black, crusty substance. Some of it powdered on to her fingers. It smelled horrible, like something that was rotting.

Rufus set about whining again, and pawing at the mulchy leaves on the gravel. 'Put a sock in it, boy, wouldja?'

Well, Mr Wright, she thought. What's this you've sent me? I can't read a word of this tiny script. It's all pretty mysterious. And smelly, and just a bit disturbing. A shiver went through her just then, as an icy breeze came scudding through the air. The atmosphere of the park changed all of a sudden. One moment it was a bright, perfect day. The tall buildings stood as mute silver sentinels at the corner of her vision. Here in the park, she was used to feeling that she could relax and spread out complacently, but all the while know that she was in the heart of the city. The buildings were always in sight. She always knew exactly where she was and where civilisation lay.

But the breeze toyed with her and played around her. The dead leaves lifted and danced around her and her dog. She shuddered and snapped shut the questionable volume.

The frigid wind died down. Oh wow. This wasn't normal. This wasn't right.

Liza knew at once that something creepy and bizarre was happening to her and her dog. And the dog had seen it coming before she did.

She was a foolish old woman for ignoring the signs. She should listen to her stomach, her subconscious, and most of all, her dog.

She apologised to Rufus, stowed the book in her bag, and set off for home.

'Now, now, children. I'll have no squabbling round here . . .'

Liza tried to smooth things over as best she could. Her niece was flushed and she looked hectic somehow. Daniel seemed to be badgering her about something.

'It's okay,' Shelley said. 'We're just having a small difference of opinion . . .'

Liza studied her two dinner guests and judged that they had probably been bickering for hours. Daniel was simmering with rage, but was otherwise impeccable in his dark suit. His hair was slicked back just so. Shelley, on the other hand was utterly frazzled. There was no other word for it.

'I've made my world-famous paella,' Liza said. 'And I've made much too much, so I hope you guys are hungry.'

Daniel had been wrinkling his nose ever since he'd stepped into the apartment. There was an acrid burning smell, but that was simply how Liza liked her paella. He'd have to learn. He coughed and passed her a chilly bottle of extremely dry white wine.

'Er, where's Rufus?' asked Shelley nervously. Part of their row coming over here tonight had been about Aunt Liza's dog, and the bite wound that had only just healed up on Daniel's hand.

'Don't worry. I've shut him in the bedroom,' Liza sighed.

'Just on our account!' gasped Shelley. 'The poor thing. You don't need to lock him away . . .'

Liza shrugged. She bustled around the tiny dining table she'd folded out by the window and was laying out lace place mats. 'He's been in a very strange mood these past couple days. Sort of snappy and not himself. I dunno what's wrong with him.'

There was something peculiar about her aunt's manner too, Shelley thought. Something had happened. Something that was disturbing the old woman as she fussed around with crockery and cutlery in the fug of singed paella. She was lying, Shelley realised. Her aunt *did* know what had disturbed the dog, but wasn't saying.

Daniel simply looked pleased that the mutt was nowhere in sight. 'Shall I open and pour?'

'So,' said Liza, once they were seated in the living room with glasses, 'what were you bickering about? Sign of a healthy relationship, I always think. A good bicker now and then, especially in front of other people.'

Shelley couldn't tell whether her aunt was being sardonic or not.

Daniel sniffed again. Surely the old dear couldn't intend to let her paella smoulder away like that, quite so much? He said, 'Shelley has several unfortunate habits to do with tidiness. Or rather, untidiness. It turns out that she prefers rather a lot of clutter about the place.'

Liza nodded approvingly at her niece.

'Well, you've seen the size of my apartment . . .' Daniel went on.

'Yes! It's colossal!' said Liza. 'You could do with a bit more stuff in it! Make it a bit less . . . austere.'

Daniel's eyebrows went up. 'I happen to like austere.'

Shelley was rolling her eyes, and he caught her. 'Perhaps I was rash to let my own place go,' she mused. 'I'm missing my independence . . . my tiny space . . .'

'You let your own place go?' said Liza, scandalised. 'You never said that! How could you give it up? A woman needs her own place in the world . . .'

'Exactly what I've been saying all along,' sighed Daniel.

'You need your refuge . . . your own things about you . . .'

'But no,' Daniel grumbled. 'She kept saying she was in love with me. That we were both so head over heels, how could we bear to be apart? So she was in like a shot.'

'Oh, Shelley!' said her clearly disappointed aunt.

Shelley scowled at them both. 'My place was a fleapit. It was expensive too. I'm glad to see the back of it.'

Daniel shrugged. 'Now all her stuff is in boxes in my hall. She hasn't even unpacked it. And she keeps bringing home all this rubbish from work.'

'She's a pack rat.' Liza laughed. 'So was her mother. So am I. It's in the family. You gotta live with that, Daniel. Now, if you lovebirds will excuse me . . .' Off she went to scrape the blackened paella off the bottom of her pan.

Minutes later her guests were struggling with the burned masses on their plates. Daniel toyed with a singed prawn, gazing appreciatively once more at the books on Liza's shelves. 'It's true that your place is full of stuff, Liza. But you really have some wonderful things. You have marvellous taste.'

She was wolfing her paella and grinned at him through a mouthful. She knew he was just buttering her up. 'Yes, well, it's true. I've seen you appreciating my bookshelves.'

'A rare collection. I must introduce you to mine some day.'

'Daniel's big on folklore,' Shelley said. 'He's got some really fine volumes . . .'

He shot her a glance, Liza noticed. A quivering tension strung out between them once again. He's really trying to control her, Liza mused crossly. We'll just have to see about that. She wasn't happy at all, but this wasn't the place to sort it out. Instead she decided to engage his attention. 'I must show you this,' she said, putting her fork down with a clatter. She went to a drawer in the cabinet by the bookshelves and produced something wrapped in a piece of white muslin.

Daniel dabbed his fingers with a napkin and took the object out of her hands. He unwrapped it to find the strange volume that Liza had received from 666 Charing Cross Road. Their special-offer volume that had been slipped without fanfare or fuss into her second parcel. It was heavy in Daniel's hands and it had a queer aroma, he noticed at once. Something heavy and dark that he could smell even through the reek of burned rice and fish.

'Oh my,' he said quietly, as he turned over the cover and flipped the first few pages.

'Interesting?' Liza asked. She watched him carefully. His eyes were those of an expert, she thought. He was used to handling artefacts such as this. He knew what to look for. She had a feeling he might.

'Very interesting,' he said.

'What is it?' Shelley put in. 'One of your old books of ghost stories, Aunt Liza?'

'Not quite,' she said. 'Daniel?'

He was staring at the curious woodcuts. Peering at the impenetrable text. And yet it all seemed to mean something to him. Liza could see that at once. His expertise, she suspected, was about to come in rather useful. He came to the pages that were clumped together with that dark, powdery substance. 'Goodness,' he murmured.

'What is it?' Shelley asked again, leaning over to see.

Daniel looked up at his hostess. He looked as lively as she had ever seen him. Usually he was so urbane and dry. So controlled. Now there was an electricity about him. His eyes were lit up. His mouth quivered momentarily as he tried to frame his thoughts.

'It's a grimoire.'

'A what?' said Shelley.

'A book of ancient magic,' he elaborated. 'Of spells.'

'Hmm,' said Liza. 'I thought as much.' She frowned at him. 'A thing of power, is it? Valuable? Rare?'

'Oh yes, yes,' he said. 'Well, I imagine so. I know a little . . . just a little bit about things of this sort. I did a paper once . . .'

'Dangerous, is it?' Aunt Liza asked, with the air of a woman who already thought she knew the answer.

'What?'

'Those pages are stuck together with *blood*, Daniel,' Liza said. 'Surely you can't have failed to notice that?'

Shelley gasped. 'Blood? They sent you a book, all the way from London, and it's covered with blood? Isn't that insanitary? And illegal?'

'Just about fifty pages or so,' Liza said. 'They're impossible to prise apart. But I bet I couldn't read what was on those pages anyway, even if I could open them. The whole book's impossible to decipher. At least, it is to me.'

Shelley had never heard her aunt sound so mystified. Especially by a book. Liza lived in a world of books. Nothing was closed to her. If she couldn't understand something, then she would learn about it. She would find out. She would demystify it. She always used to tell Shelley that all human knowledge and experience and accomplishment was there before her, arrayed in books. In the public library. She only had to put the work in to find it all out. Those words had always stayed with her.

But here was her aunt, admitting defeat before this odd little tome.

More than that. She sounded . . . disturbed by it.

'Can I take this away?' Daniel asked suddenly. 'I would like to give it all my attention. I'd like to study it properly.'

'No!' Liza cried out. 'No way! It stays here! Do you hear me? It stays right here!'

They both stared at her.

'I'm sorry,' she said, trying to laugh off her outburst. 'I want to look at it longer myself. Gimme it back. I'll put it away. Rufus hates it, by the way. That's why he's locked up tonight. Maybe it's the smell of blood, but he keeps trying to get it in his jaws to rip it apart. I kind of wish Mr Wright had never sent it . . .'

As she burbled on in this way, she was slipping the wrapped book back into the cabinet drawer.

Shelley glanced at her boyfriend and saw how hungry he looked. And it wasn't just because the paella was inedible.

Chapter Eight

On her way across town to Shelley's museum, Liza posted another order to England:

Dear Mr Wright,

What the hell kind of thing was that you sent? My so-called free gift? Young acquaintance of mine tells me it's what's known in the black magic world as a grimoire. Well, I sort of knew that from my not inconsiderable reading around the subject area. But come on! Really? This is fer real?

White magic I believe in, of course. But – maybe naïvely – I never really thought that there were ever such things as black magicians, plying their trade and publishing cookery books.

So what the hell are you doing sending me their books of spells? And what is that gunky stuff all over the middle fifty pages, huh? Is it really someone's blood? I really, really wish you hadn't sent me this thing. I thought about returning it to you under this cover, but couldn't find an envelope big enough. No, I'll hang on to it. But whatever possessed you to think it was something I might like? What the hell do you think I am?

Anyway. I enclose with this letter a list of titles culled from the biographies page of *The Best of the Books of Mayhem*. Some of these are for me, but a bunch of them are for Christmas presents. I really hope that you can supply my wants in time, before the festive season hits us full pelt. I've been bragging about your swift and amazing service and your stock in arcane fiction to my friends over here – so don't you go letting me down!!

With all best wishes for the season – and no more creepy old non-fictional tomes, please! Just the made-up stuff will do me fine!

Regards,
Liza Bathory

She was still carrying the offending book in her purse. She didn't want to leave it in the apartment with Rufus. However well she stowed it away, she had a feeling her old mutt would sniff it out and rip it to shreds. He had taken to growling at her purse recently, rightly assuming that was where she was keeping the strange old book.

Somehow her new acquisition weighed more heavily on her thoughts with every day that passed. It felt like a bit of an albatross around her neck.

How she wished she could really be the woman she'd pretended to be in her affronted letter to Mr K. N. Wright. She longed to be someone who didn't know all that much about the true black arts.

She wanted to be naïve and only slightly irked by the presence of this grimoire.

But of course she was better informed than that. She had learned, during the course of her long life, so very much about that twilight world of necromancers and ne'er-do-wells. She knew more about magic – real magic – than she'd ever care to own up to. And so she wasn't just irked by the grimoire that had fallen into her possession. She was scared of it.

Somehow, though, she couldn't just wrap it up again and parcel it off back to where it came from. The idea occurred to her a couple of times, and she brushed it away. Her curiosity was piqued. No, it was more than that. She knew that this was something important. Dangerous, perhaps, even deadly. But it was important, and it had been entrusted to her for a reason.

Liza arrived at the Museum of Outsider Art and tried to put these disturbing thoughts out of her mind. There was a queue trailing out of the main door, which surprised her. She had visited the place only a handful of times before, but Shelley had talked repeatedly about numbers being down, and how hard it was to get people through the doors, when most mainstream galleries and museums put on such glitzy, crowd-pleasing exhibitions.

There were posters outside and in the foyer, showing the Scottish Bride in silhouette: a hulking, misshapen form. A tremor of excitement passed through Liza as she queued. She wasn't sure why. She had a sudden sense of foreboding.

She clutched her bag to her chest as she shuffled into the dowdy hallway. Was that her phone ringing, set to vibrate? Apparently not. Something was tingling, though.

'Aunt Liza!'

Shelley was delighted to see her, and Liza hugged her niece, amazed all over again at this smart and professional-looking young person in her workplace. So unlike the rather haphazard Shelley she knew in everyday life.

'C'mon, we can jump the queue. It's one of the perks.' Shelley grasped Liza's arm and ducked her under the barrier.

'Are you sure?' Liza was conscious of raised eyebrows from those patiently standing in line.

'Hey, it's my show.' Shelley laughed. 'I found her, right? There'd be no one here if I hadn't unearthed Bessie.'

That was right – the effigy had a name now. Liza remembered reading something in the *New York Times*. The story was picking up momentum, and several journals and papers had run with it. Hence the queues and the buzz about the place. As Liza let herself be led into the heart of the museum, she felt a terrific sense of pride in her niece.

'And here she is,' Shelley grinned, leading her smartly up to the exhibit.

She sealed off the room for a few moments, so her aunt could study the effigy in peace. Liza was embarrassed by the special attention, but her reservations soon dropped away.

She stood and gazed up into the face of the Scottish Bride.

'Pretty impressive, huh?'

The mothbally and musty scent was almost overpowering at first. And there was something denser and nastier in the atmosphere around the so-called Bessie that made her visitor want to back away at once. But Liza stayed there, ineluctably drawn to staring straight back into those dark, shrouded eyes.

The lopsided grin was the most awful thing. It didn't mean to be horrifying. She could see that the Scottish woman was trying to smile, but her jaw and teeth were all wrong and so there was something almost malevolent in that expression. Her stringy limbs were slightly raised, as if to place themselves around you. There was something frightening in that, too, as if she wanted to hug you and then strangle you, and throw your limp body into a ditch.

'I can see why people are flocking here,' Liza said, very quietly. 'There's something compelling about her.'

'More and more so,' said Shelley. 'I think she's blossoming with all the attention. When I first found her, she was like a heap of old rags. But – and this sounds crazy, I know – with all these people looking at her and studying her, it's as if she's becoming more . . . human with every day.'

'Hmmm.' Liza peered even closer. She sniffed hard. 'Shelley . . .' she murmured. 'Erm, you *did* check out what this effigy is made from, didn't you? I mean, you had her examined properly, didn't you?'

'What?' Shelley frowned. 'She's just natural materials, isn't she? Wood and twigs . . . and old material. Hessian rags. Woollens. And woad, I guess. All organic stuff.' She was perturbed by this line of questioning. Was her aunt trying to say that the Scottish Bride was some kind of fake? That she'd been thrown together much more recently than Shelley had thought?

'Oh, I can see that she's . . . organic,' said Liza. 'I can smell that fact. It's just that . . . Had you considered . . .' Her voice trailed off. She was momentarily distracted by something in her purse. Shelley watched as her aunt slapped irritably at her handbag.

'Aunt Liza?' What was the matter with the old woman? She was behaving pretty strangely.

'It's okay,' Liza said. 'Look, will you tell Daniel that I don't mind at all if he borrows my book.'

'Your book?'

'The grimoire. The one he seemed so interested in the other night. I'd be glad if he wanted to study it. In fact, I'd be glad to have the awful thing out of my hands.'

'Oh, sure,' Shelley said. Daniel would be pleased, she knew. More than pleased. After leaving her aunt's place the other night, he had rambled on about that strange book for ages. Shelley had gotten sick of him going on, as a matter of fact.

Now Liza was fumbling in her purse, fetching out the book.

'So what were you going to say?' Shelley asked her.

'Hm?'

'Just then? You seemed to have a thought about Bessie here. Something important. When you asked if I'd had her properly examined . . .'

'Oh! Yes!' Liza shoved the black leather volume into Shelley's hands. Almost immediately she felt better. The headache she'd been nursing all morning started to fade. 'See that you give it straight to Daniel, won't you? He seems to know more about this kind of thing.'

'Sure.' Shelley nodded. 'But what about Bessie, Aunt Liza? What were you going to say?'

'Ah.' Liza squinched her mouth up and frowned heavily. 'It's just that you've been assuming she's made out of stuff. Like a scarecrow. You've been assuming she's someone's effigy, right?'

'Yeah, I have . . .'

'But what if she's more than that? That doesn't look like wood to me. Or leather. That face looks like dried skin. Human skin and bone and real teeth.'

'What!'

Aunt Liza breathed in deeply and looked at her niece worriedly. 'What if Bessie's not someone's effigy at all? What if she's actually someone's *mummy*?'

'This isn't the time or the place,' Jack told Ricardo.

'But it is! It *is* the time and the place. I have to have it out with you.'

'Look, Mr Grenoble's watching. He hates us having personal friends coming in. He hates us having lives outside the shop, period.'

'I am a customer! I have money! I could be asking you about something I want to buy. My mother reads mysteries. She reads four mysteries every single week . . .'

Jack knew that much was true. She had been living in his tiny apartment for a week now, and he had become more familiar with her habits – not just her reading ones – than he ever wanted to be.

How had it happened? How had this boy and his mother suddenly taken up so much of his life like this?

Consuela had come round one evening, bringing with her bags and bags of supplies for fixing them dinner. She was a diminutive woman, swaying unsteadily with her groceries and goodies up the clanging fire-escape stairs to Jack's front door. He had dashed down to help her. She had gazed about approvingly at his tiny space, with the kitchen alcove and the bookshelves everywhere, and had launched into a voluble appreciation of her favourite mystery novels as she took over his kitchen.

Hefting down his heaviest pans and tutting over the state of his ovenwear, this tiny woman was a dynamo, talking in a loud voice as she scrubbed and peeled and chopped and sautéed.

She had been in his kitchen for a week now. He had to shimmy and limbo around and about her, and so did Ricardo – who seemed very pleased that his mother was there so often. Who are these people? Jack had to keep asking himself. And he kept pinching himself: it was like a dream – ghastly and blissful in equal measures. For although he could have done without the hugely noisy Consuela on his dilapidated couch – an afghan pulled about her shoulders, reading murder books through the night – he was having a lovely time with her son. Most of his time was spent listening to Ricardo. He wasn't allowed to get much of a word in. Ricardo never stopped. Even during sex he could spin a pretty coherent anecdote. He staggered Jack.

Ricardo recounted tales. That was what he loved to do. How much was true and how much did he make up on the spot? Maybe his story about Shelley's boyfriend Daniel making a clumsy pass at him during Thanksgiving was just a fabrication too?

'No!' said Ricardo, scandalised. 'I would never lie about a thing like that!'

Now here he was at Fangtasm. Already it seemed like ages since breakfast this morning, which had been some kind of folded omelette rich with paprika and tiny mushrooms, served up triumphantly by Consuela, who had the big black rings of the habitual insomniac around her eyes. Jack was terrified in case she ever heard him fooling around with her son in the other room: his apartment was so small. Obviously she was okay with it, but it was embarrassing nevertheless.

This morning his two new house guests were so voluble and irritating, Jack had ended up yelling at the two of them. They yammered away in Spanish like two transvestite hookers in an Almodavar movie, and Jack just snapped.

That was why Ricardo was at Fangtasm now, during a break at the chocolate shop. He was pretending to be a customer, and Jack was leading him irritably around the shelves.

'It's a classy shop this, with the antiques and the . . . what are they?'

'Aspidistras,' sighed Jack.

Ricardo sat down heavily in a cosy armchair and let Jack bring a pile of paperbacks to him. 'No, she won't read anything with brutal death in it.'

'They're murders. They're all brutal.'

'You know what I mean. She wants cosies. She just likes cosies. My mamma has seen too much violence in her life. My father was very bad to her. She just needs books about revenge and bad men being killed, but not on the page. Not so she sees it. Offstage is where she wants it. And she likes strong female characters. And cats, cats too. She likes it when the cat helps to solve the mystery.'

Jack went to find him some cat mysteries. He had already heard the saga of Consuela's cat. One of the many reasons why she couldn't face returning to her own apartment was that her cat Cleo had been killed on the street outside it. 'I am in mourning. And also, my apartment is shitty. It's a shitty place to live.'

'Don't be hard on her,' Ricardo said. 'Will it kill you to let her stay for a little while?'

'Well, no . . . I . . .'

'And she loves you. You're the first boyfriend I've had that she loves. All the others she has wanted to kill on sight. She hates the thought of her little boy going with these terrible men. But you, you she loves.'

'She does?'

'Of course. What's not to love?'

Jack glowed at this, and went off to fetch more books, deciding he could use his staff discount. He knew he was being flattered into agreeing to house Ricardo's mother a little longer. He had a vaguely defeated feeling just under the surface of his flattered ego . . . but so what? He'd take what he could get.

'Anyway,' Ricardo said, when Jack returned and Ricardo was flipping through the lurid paperbacks. 'I'm not here to talk about my mother. She's okay. I knew you two would get along fine. No, I'm here because of Paolo.'

'Who's Paolo?'

'My cousin. My mother's sister's boy. We email now and then. We were the only close ones in our family. The other cousins hated me, but Paolo was always friendly. And now he's in London, with a wife and a baby.' Ricardo sighed. 'We have never seen them. The baby can walk and my mother has never even seen her. They live somewhere horrible in London. It sounds like a slum and it weighs very heavily on my mother's heart. Her sister is dead, you know, and—'

Jack – who realised that his boss Mr Grenoble was eyeballing him across the plush room – broke in. 'Look, what's this about? Tell me!'

'He has gone missing,' Ricardo said simply. 'His wife replied to my latest email. This morning. She sounds in a panic about it. It isn't like Paolo. He went out yesterday afternoon into the middle of London and he hasn't come back.'

Jack frowned. He was sorry to hear about it, but he didn't see what it had to do with him, really. Or what he could do about it.

'Ah, but he was on an errand,' Ricardo said. 'He was doing it for *us*.'

'He was?'

'I sent him. Out of interest. Well, he's already in London, isn't he? It should be no effort for him, really. And I was intrigued. Why, the way that the old woman was talking on Thanksgiving. Remember? The way she's been talking to you, too. About the bookshop.'

'On Charing Cross Road?' Jack asked. 'The bookshop I found for Liza?'

'Yes! Exactly! And I found it all so intriguing. It was like a romance, a mystery, almost. These strange parcels she gets. I wanted to know what the shop itself was like. I wanted to find out for her – for Liza – and for you. And then I remembered – my cousin! Paolo! It would be no effort for him to go into the city and to find the shop on Charing Cross Road . . .'

Jack's heart was beating wildly. Strange that he had become so invested in this story, and in the idea of this shop, just as Liza had. He felt responsible for the whole thing, because he had pointed out the advert. But his heart was thumping too, because he had a feeling that Ricardo was telling him something important and horrible.

'He went yesterday. He was pleased to do something for us. After my mother and I sent all those romper suits and knitted things for the baby. So he went yesterday on the . . . what do they call it? The Tube? And he never came back. His cell phone is dead. His wife Vicki is in pieces. Something has happened to him, is what she thinks. And so do I, Jack.'

Jack stared at him. Dumbfounded.

'Jack, I mean it. I think we have sent him into somewhere very bad. Six six six, Jack. The bad number. The beastly number. And we sent him there. Him with a new baby and his whole life ahead of him. We have sent him into an evil bookstore!'

At this point Mr Grenoble marched over and demanded to know what was going on. He wasn't having melodramatically raised voices in his shop, thank you very much. Ricardo glared at him, chose six novels seemingly at random and sashayed straight to the checkout desk, with Jack scuttling after him.

Chapter Nine

Daniel was really, really good-looking.

Shelley lay awake that morning and stared at his profile. It was haughty and arrogant, silhouetted against the flowing softness of the muslin curtains. Even when he slept, his expression didn't soften; he would twitch and frown in his sleep. As if he was wrangling with people, even in his dreams. He always had to be right about things, Shelley knew that much by now. She guessed that he argued the people in his dreams to a standstill, just as he did with those in everyday life.

The covers had fallen back off him. He didn't seem to mind the chill coming in from the open windows. He tended to keep his apartment rather cold, and that was something else Shelley found it hard to adjust to. She schlepped about the place in a woollen dressing gown and bunny slippers, shivering the whole time. Daniel didn't even notice the cold. Right now, his beautiful pale limbs were bare and he was almost like a classical statue. Like some marvellous piece of sculpture out of the ancient world, like all those things he had made her look at on trips to the Met. He was enthralled by those naked people from days of old in weird positions. She knew he would kill for a chance to be working in a legitimate museum full of that kind of stuff. She knew he felt thwarted where he was. That was a very Daniel word. She'd never heard anyone use that word in real life, until she'd met Daniel.

She tried to cover him with the quilt, but in his sleep he brushed her away irritably. He twisted round and she stared at the fine structure of him. Those corded lines of muscle down his body. She loved the sparse dark hair on his chest and stomach, though when she said anything about it, or praised him in any way, he looked politely mystified. Now that she thought about it, he never reciprocated by praising *her* in any way. It was as if he lived in some other realm of the senses. He wasn't much of a physical being at all. He was all intellect and spirit. The gross and fleshy world meant little to him.

Which irked her quite a bit. Especially when she'd woken early and felt a little bit sexy, like this.

'Daniel?' She woke him by stroking his muscular shoulder. 'Sweetie?' She knew that sweetie was quite the wrong endearment for him, but it was a placeholder till she found the right one. He groaned and started to surface out of his dreams.

Shelley squooshed up in the bed next to him, as if huddling for warmth. It was her imagination surely, but the apartment seemed even more frigid this morning. It was as if the temperature had dropped sharply overnight, far more than the forecast had predicted.

'What is it? It's early, Shelley.' He frowned, and narrowed his eyes at the alarm clock.

'I thought you might be, you know. In the mood.'

'What for?'

She sighed. 'Never mind.'

'Intercourse?' He laughed. 'You've got to be kidding, Shelley.'

'Why?' She sounded brattish, she knew.

'I've got to conserve my energy. I've some important meetings today.'

'Oh. Okay.' She lay still for a moment, staring at the ceiling fan. She heard his light, fluting snores starting up again. She was envious of the way he could just fall asleep, easy as anything, like changing channels on the TV. She grew irked at him. Conserving energy indeed.

Oops. She'd better pull herself out of this mood. This was no good. She'd get in a bad frustrated funk and be a bitch all day at work if she didn't watch out. She got out of bed, hopped lightly across the polished boards and dragged on her heavy dressing gown, wincing at the frosty air. But it was hard not to feel rejected. Daniel had made it sound like an early romp with her was some onerous thing. Some kind of workout routine he'd be happier skipping.

Shelley stomped off to the kitchen. She needed coffee. Maybe she'd make him a pot of his herbal elderflower nonsense as well. And spit in it.

As the kettle boiled on the gas hob she remembered something. In her purse on the dining table. Something her aunt had given her yesterday, and which had completely slipped her mind. The book. The – what was it – the grimoire? She had been saving it for a special moment. She had intended to give it to Daniel with a flourish: Ta-dah! Look what I've got for you! Aren't I great?

Suddenly she was aware that he was in the room with her. He was stealthy. Light on his feet. He'd emerged from the bedroom and crept up behind her without Shelley realising it until the very last minute. Now he was standing right behind her. She froze as his strong arms went around her waist and he held her tightly from behind.

This was more like it. He nuzzled her neck and murmured apologies. The kettle boiled, puffing out clouds of steam, and Shelley flushed with pleasure and relief.

'I'm a useless boyfriend,' he was saying. 'I'm so selfish. And you're so lovely. I could just eat you up.'

He was pressing himself against her. She felt his hardness even through the thickness of her robe. He turned her around gently. Then grasped her a little less gently and tugged at the knotted cord of her gown.

She had never seen him like this before. 'We can't do it on the kitchen surfaces,' she said.

'We can do it where we want,' he said.

'No, I mean, there's not enough room, there's . . .'

He sighed and his hands dropped to his sides. 'Where do you want to do it, then?'

She blushed now, and moved to the kettle. She felt a bit awkward. She tried not to look at him, naked in the kitchen with that raging hard-on. The moment had passed for her, definitely, and he was starting to look ridiculous. 'D-do you want your herbal tea?'

He tutted and turned back to the bedroom to get his own robe.

Shelley watched him go. The sex wasn't working. She knew that now. They just couldn't get it together, and when they did, there was something about it that didn't quite gel. That was the wrong word. It was as if they didn't click . . . She had been pretending to be more into it than she actually was, and that was just to flatter him, to make him feel okay about it. And now she felt guilty for that, like she had been leading him along . . .

She went to her purse and took out the grimoire, wrapped in its square of white cloth. It tingled under her fingertips, she could have sworn. Maybe it was just the cold, playing havoc with her nerve endings. Maybe it was just a frazzle of thwarted desire (now she was using that terrible word!). She sniffed. The book still smelled weird.

'What's that?' Suddenly Daniel was beside her again. He was in his robe and he was frowning. Then he gasped and his voice went higher. 'It's the grimoire, isn't it? You got it off her, didn't you? Off the old woman?'

She hated him calling her beloved aunt the old woman. She barely had a moment to explain before he snatched the thing out of her grasp.

'Oh, you clever girl. You beautiful girl. I could kiss you!'

But in his haste to take possession of the book, he didn't. Shelley was left standing there by the table, like a proud mom on Christmas morning, watching her precocious child pore over his first set of encyclopedias.

There was something almost feverish about Daniel as he leafed through the book once more. 'I can't believe you talked her into letting me have it! Oh, this is brilliant, Shelley. This is great. I can learn so much from this . . . given time.'

'I didn't have to persuade her. Aunt Liza brought it to me yesterday. She brought it to the museum when she came to see the Scottish Bride. She said she thought you'd probably get more out of it than she would. But it's just a loan, of course. She's not giving it to you . . .'

'Yes, yes, of course,' he said dismissively. He took his nasty pale tea and moved out of the kitchen, to examine the volume in the bright searing light of the living room. 'Look, if this is what I really think it is . . . we've got something very important on our hands. I spent some time in the City Library yesterday. I may have a lead on who the compiler of this book was. And the bloodstain . . . that's very important, too.'

Shelley listened to him rambling on. 'I'm taking my coffee to the bathroom,' she said. 'I'm getting a shower.' She was chilled right through. Weirdly, her fingertips were almost numbed with cold, as if contact with the leather tome had drained them of their living warmth. 'Daniel? I'm off to get ready for work.'

'Sure,' he said, hunched forward on the sofa, studying the book's frontispiece. 'Uh, listen. When you go in, tell them I'm sick, will you? Get my secretary to cancel my meetings.'

'But you said they were important . . .'

'I'm staying home,' he said sharply. 'I've got to work on this. Can't you see? Don't you know how important this is, Shelley?' He stared at her, and there was something almost like scorn on his face. His lovely face. Twisting it out of shape. Sending her out of the room and into the bathroom.

She turned on the shower and let its gradual warmth bring her to life. Its noise drummed at her soothingly. She prepared herself to face the day almost mechanically. She didn't let herself think too much about Daniel. About her and Daniel.

This isn't working, she thought minutes later, as she squinted in the mirror to put on her make-up. It was a tiny thought – the only one that escaped through her barrier of dull routine that morning. But it was enough. This isn't working. She had made a ghastly mistake.

That morning – as things later showed – she made a much bigger one.

Midweek drinking. It wasn't something Shelley had intended to do. But when, just before work finished, Jack phoned out of the blue and asked her out, she found herself agreeing readily.

'You need to get out and enjoy yourself,' Ruthie from the gift shop told her. 'You're looking a bit down, girl.'

Truth was, she didn't relish the idea of getting back to that apartment and fixing another dinner that Daniel would hardly touch. He was so preoccupied by Aunt Liza's mysterious book these days, he was barely eating a thing. He simply sat hunched, gazing at endless pages. He had sheets of scrawled notes all around him. He'd printed off hundreds of documents from the internet. He was getting into some pretty weird stuff these days, she thought. And he sat there with fingers dirty from that old book. The dark red ancient blood that it had been saturated with.

So it was a relief to get out and to go downtown for the evening.

She met the boys in a bar in SoHo, a place that seemed a bit fancy for her mood. They chose fiddly little dishes of ravioli and salad from the oversized menu and settled in for a long night of chatting.

'And ever since she said that, I can't look at Bessie in the same way,' Shelley found herself telling them. The boys were agog.

'So what are you saying? That the effigy's . . . changed in some way?'

'No, no, of course not. Well, I dunno. It's just that, since Aunt Liza came to look at it – on the day she gave me the grimoire – I'm not sure . . . I feel a bit differently about the thing. I keep thinking – my God, what if it really *is* a mummified corpse? And I've just put her on display there. I thought she was all stitched together rags and stuff but . . . now that you look at the face . . . it's kind of leathery . . . like old skin. Like Egyptian mummies look . . .'

Ricardo was staring at her, both primped eyebrows raised. 'That is horrible. You should know for sure whether this is a corpse or not. You could bring down a curse on your head. There could be a bad spirit, wandering about the place . . .'

Shelley laughed uneasily, but Jack elbowed him sharply. 'Stop it. Don't make it any worse.'

'I don't know if I believe in stuff like that or not,' said Shelley, sipping her lurid cocktail thoughtfully.

'I do,' said Ricardo. 'Bad spirits. Evil intentions. You have to be very, very careful about this stuff. Didn't your aunt warn you? She's a witch, isn't she?'

Shelley rolled her eyes. 'She likes to think she is.'

'But she is,' Ricardo said. 'A powerful one. I can sense it. My . . . goosebumps go up when she's near. Not in a bad way, but she has certain powers. I know.' He clicked his fingers. 'My mother. She knows about all of this business. She has seen some funny things in her time. She should come and see your Scottish Bride. She will tell you if you've anything to worry about.'

Jack shuddered and tried to attract the waiter's attention. 'I can't stand all this weirdo voodoo stuff. Can we change the subject?'

98

Shelley was pleased to. She had a pressing practical concern to deal with. 'Look, I need to get out from under Daniel's feet for a few days.'

'Why? What's he doing?'

'We're just getting on each other's nerves at the moment. We need a bit of a break. Maybe a few nights. He's working late on a . . . research project, and he gets very involved.'

'Ah,' said Jack. 'He's quite intense, isn't he?' He caught Ricardo's eye, and just then the waiter bobbed up, and they ordered some more deliciously sweet, sickly drinks.

'I am not surprised you need to be away from him, Shelley,' Ricardo said. 'I know why. I know what it's all about.' He glared at Jack, who had started kicking him under the table. 'Ow. What is it? I am just saying what I think.'

'Well Shelley doesn't need to hear what you think about her boyfriend. She just needs our support.'

Shelley smiled at him gratefully. 'Would you mind . . . I mean, I feel silly, really. Having let my apartment go. My aunt said it was a mistake, and she's right. And now I'm in this position, like, straight away. Would you mind, Jack?'

'Mind what?' But he kind of knew what was coming.

'If I borrowed your couch for a few nights? Just to get out of Daniel's hair for a while? Maybe give him a shock, make him see what he's missing? You wouldn't mind, would you?'

'Ah,' said Ricardo.

'Hm,' said Jack. 'I'm really sorry, Shelley. But the couch is taken, for the duration, it seems.'

'By my mother,' said Ricardo. 'She doesn't sleep much. She's an insomniac. But she takes up a lot of room.'

'Oh,' said Shelley. 'You never said you were putting her up, Jack. I shouldn't have asked.'

'No, it's okay,' Jack said. 'I'd love to help out, Shelley. I just don't know how long Consuela is . . . um, planning on sticking around.'

Ricardo said darkly, 'She's very unpredictable.'

'And volatile,' added Jack.

They greeted their new drinks, glad of the interruption. Then the evening went in to fast forward for a bit. They finished up in the restaurant and went to a little bar Ricardo knew, which was somewhere in the East Village and, as far as Shelley could tell, not very nice. It was painted in black and scarlet and had a half-finished look about it. There were no ladies' toilets and there was a go-go boy on the bar giving a desultory shimmy now and then to a remix of an old Talking Heads song.

Ricardo surprised her by being quite drunk. Because the place was crowded, they were squashed into a corner, and she found him telling her some long, rambling story about his cousin in England. She didn't quite get the gist of the tale and realised that Jack was trying to break in and distract his inebriated boyfriend. He was embarrassed! Jack was actually embarrassed by Ricardo's hopelessness, leaning against a plaster pillar, just about drooling.

A week or two ago Jack had been like someone who could hardly believe his luck. Having Ricardo near him was like he had won some fabulous prize. How quickly things change about, Shelley thought woozily. Now she was feeling the worse for wear herself. Her head was knocking with alcohol fumes. What was this beer she was drinking?

Suddenly Ricardo was saying to her: 'It is better that you move away from him. You are right to leave him. That apartment isn't you. That lifestyle isn't you. He isn't you.'

'What are you talking about?' She was getting irritated now. There was something insinuating about his manner. Jack had popped into the bathroom and there was no getting away from Ricardo's mumbling.

'Daniel. I'm talking about Daniel. He isn't right for you, Shelley. You are doing the right thing.'

'How would you know?' She let her anger flash out at him, and enjoyed it.

Ricardo shrugged and smiled. 'Because of Thanksgiving. What happened on Thanksgiving. I never told you, did I? I promised Jack I wouldn't tell you. But when we were at Daniel's apartment. When you were doing all the work that day on feeding us, he was looking at me.'

'Looking at you?' Yes, she thought. And she knew why. Daniel hadn't wanted Ricardo or Jack to be there. He had said as much. So he had made them uncomfortable, deliberately. Now Ricardo was telling her how terrible it had made him feel.

'He came into the kitchen. When I was doing the dishwasher and stuff. He came after me, Shelley. You have to believe me.'

'What?'

'He was all over me. Grabbing my cock. Trying to kiss me. Getting his hands all over my ass.'

Shelley stared at him.

Ricardo stopped talking. He saw that the message had got through. There was nothing more to say except, 'So it is good you're moving away from him. He's a bad bad closet case. He's lying to you, and to himself.'

Shelley's breath was caught in her throat. She had to get out of there. She was flushed, too hot. She was going to be sick. She was half aware of Jack returning to their small group just then. He was plucking his warm beer bottle out of his lover's grasp and stepping aside to allow Shelley to stumble backwards.

'Hey, what's up? What's the matter?'

She didn't say anything. She couldn't. She found herself staggering across the packed room, squeezing through pressed bodies and coming out the other side slick with sweat, her shoes sticky with spilled booze.

Outside, the air was freezing, and she sucked in huge lungfuls. She stared up and down the street as the confusing noises came rushing at her. Honking taxis. She needed a cab. She needed one fast. The smokers outside the windowless club stared at her as she teetered on the spot. I look out of control, she thought. That's bad. I'd be easy prey for a mugger. For anyone. She rallied herself to the spot and clutched her purse. She swore furiously inside her head. Men. Men. Fricking men.

Then she thought: Aunt Liza. Aunt Liza makes wonderful black syrupy coffee. She's got that old angular coffee pot thing she brews up on her gas ring. That's what I need now, if I'm ever gonna sober up.

By the time she'd flagged down a cab and was hunting in her purse, checking she had enough cash to take her to Second Avenue, she had decided that she would fling herself on her aunt's mercy. Hot black coffee first, with loads of sugar. And then begging her for a place to stay. It was something she had been loath to do. Her aunt would be furious all over again that she had let her own place go. She'd lecture her about keeping her independence and the importance of self-reliance. It was a lecture Shelley knew she had coming to her.

She didn't care.

The cab veered and jolted, sallying forth up gaudy canyons. The driver looked piqued that he'd picked up a woman as drunk as she was. He said something stern about vomiting. She tried to allay his fears.

'My aunt will sort it out,' she said. 'It'll be okay. She'll fix it all up.'

When she got to her aunt's apartment block, Liza was holding a late-night soirée for some authors and publishing friends. This time it was a pre-Christmas event, and the theme was elves. When Shelley appeared in her doorway looking dishevelled and helpless, Liza could see that something awful had happened. She knew at once that her niece needed her.

She cleared her apartment in five minutes flat. Turning off the Christmas tunes, snatching cups of punch out of elves' hands and making polite but firm apologies to her assembled guests.

When they were all gone, Shelley fell into the sturdy arms of her diminutive aunt and burst into loud and messy tears.

Chapter Ten

Ricardo woke suddenly in the middle of the night. His head was pounding and his throat was dry. The tiny room he shared with Jack was suddenly much too hot, and too small. There wasn't even a window in here. When the door was closed, it was absolute darkness. He could hear Jack stirring and felt the bed creaking as his boyfriend moved about. Jack was a much heavier sleeper than Ricardo. This made Ricardo vaguely envious, usually. Tonight he was glad of it as he stumbled clumsily out of bed and slipped out of the door.

Then he was in the windowless bathroom, and as he stared woozily into his own puzzled face, the voice came into his mind again:

'Are you listening, Ricardo? Can you hear me?'

Exactly as it had been in his dream. He turned on the taps and splashed water all over his face. He was sticky, delirious, still drunk. All of those things. He was having hallucinations. Maybe someone in the bar had spiked his drink.

'It's me, Ricardo. I'm calling out to you. Across the city. We have a connection, you and I . . .'

He gripped the sides of the washbasin and fought back a wave of nausea. He almost threw up. He knew that voice had followed him from his dreams.

'Ricardo? Are you there?' Now the tone was mocking him. Cajoling him. It wanted him to do its bidding.

He slipped out of the bathroom. In the kitchen alcove he moved around as quietly as he could. By the glow of the fairy lights looped round the shelves that held Jack's cooking supplies, he set about making a pot of coffee. It would keep him awake the rest of the night, sure, but a bit of lucid, wide-awake calm would do him good. He spooned out coffee and prayed that his mother wouldn't wake. Peering over the breakfast bar, he could see the mounded shape of her under an afghan on the couch. On the floor beside her were the murder books he had bought her, two of them splayed open.

'Ricardo? No one else can hear us . . .'

'Go away,' he said firmly, inside his head. He looked at himself in the reflection in the dark window above the sink. The apartment faced on to a blank brick wall and was a perfect mirror. He watched his lips move silently, addressing the stranger in his head. Or rather, the near-stranger in his head.

'Get away from me, Daniel. Leave me alone.'

Was he going crazy? How could he even believe that Shelley's boyfriend could reach out to him like this across the city rooftops? His telepathic voice bouncing from roof to roof, swinging round the skyscrapers and finding its way to its target here in SoHo?

'It really is you, isn't it, Daniel?'

'Hello, Ricardo. I told you we had a strong connection.'

Ricardo was superstitious. His mother believed in all kinds of things. Folklore, mysteries of the unknown, spirits, ETs, every-thing. Ricardo had grown up accepting her somewhat off-kilter view of the world. In recent years he had come to question some of her more outrageous beliefs, but it was hard to shake off completely her faith in the unreal.

Now, in the dark window, he could see a swirl of mist. It was looping and coiling before his eyes. In the mist he could see a figure.

'What are you showing me?'

'Watch . . .'

The coffee things lay abandoned on the bench beside him. The kettle wasn't even switched on. Ricardo was devoting all of his attention to the weird scene materialising before him. He swayed on the spot, feeling his stomach roiling inside him again. But this wasn't being drunk and overtired. This wasn't just some hallucination. He knew absolutely that what he was watching was magic, and it was real.

The window was showing an image of Daniel, in his own apartment, on the Upper West Side. The mist drew back and Ricardo recognised some of the details of the apartment where he had spent Thanksgiving: the tall windows, the immaculate fireplace and the framed Paul Klee poster. And there was Daniel now, naked in the moonlight in his living room. He was staring straight out at Ricardo.

'Can you see me?' he said tauntingly.

Ricardo nodded dumbly, and unconsciously licked his lips. Daniel had a fantastic body. Long-limbed, lithe, toned. Ricardo hadn't suspected for a second that he'd look like this without his clothes. He watched with fascination as Daniel knelt on the sheepskin rug and started fiddling with an assortment of strange objects arranged about him. It looked like he was engaged in some sort of ritual. Ricardo gulped. Maybe if he'd known Daniel was so hot, he'd have reacted differently in the kitchen on Thanksgiving.

Now he could see less of the handsome museum curator, but his attention was still held as he watched the spectre lighting candles, taking up a small knife and making a cut in one palm. Now he was letting the blood drip into a saucer.

Ricardo frowned. He had seen things like this before. He remembered Mrs Beatty, his mother's one-time neighbour in an apartment block when he was a kid. In Brooklyn, this was. For five dollars a pop, Mrs Beatty would put hexes on people. After the first few worked out, Consuela had gone back almost weekly, and Ricardo had gone along to watch. He remembered the stench of cooking spices and cat piss in Mrs Beatty's rooms.

Now he was watching another such ritual. But a far more exciting one. His heart caught as he watched Daniel rise to his feet. He stared at the semi-erect cock – he couldn't help it – slapping about the place as Daniel smeared his own blood over his face and his chest. This was getting pretty weird.

Now Daniel was chanting something out of the small book he held. He was fondling himself, and Ricardo felt like he was watching some kind of sexy webcam footage of a suitor across town – but this time involving black magic.

The smoke started swirling again, obscuring the image here and there. This was frustrating, as Ricardo found that he was wanting to watch Daniel as he proceeded to bring himself to a noisy climax.

Jesus. No wonder Shelley wanted a few nights away from this guy. She never said he was doing stuff like this . . .

And at precisely that moment, just as Ricardo felt his own cock stirring in mute response to what he was witnessing, something hideous happened in Daniel's room.

His ritual worked.

Something emerged from the tiny book. It was like more smoke, at first, a dark reddish-brown cloud of mist, and as Ricardo stared in horror, it assumed for a moment a man-shaped aspect. He could almost make out terrible twisted features in its skull-like head.

He heard Daniel cry out as he came and suddenly realised what he had summoned into being.

The spirit had been *inside* of the book, Ricardo found himself thinking.

'Yes, yes,' Daniel said. 'You're right. He was . . . he is here now . . .'

His voice was shaking. He had shocked himself by what he had done.

The picture in the window frame was starting to break up. The connection was fragmenting like a bad digital channel. Or the buffering on a dodgy MPEG clip, Ricardo thought wildly. The image froze and shattered. In those last few seconds he saw a glimpse of the book's evil spirit bearing down on Daniel. Daniel was offering himself up bravely. He was terrified, but he knew there was no escape. He was spent and frightened, kneeling on the rug amongst the ritual's bric-a-brac . . . and the spirit came for him.

It entered through Daniel's eyes and his open mouth as he screamed . . .

Ricardo blinked.

The illusion was gone.

He turned and clicked the kettle on.

No. It had been real. Every second of it. He had seen something that was actually happening, at that very moment, across town. But why? Why would Daniel call out to *him*? What did he want, help? Or was it something else? Did he want Ricardo to join him in this bizarre—

'You're making coffee at four in the morning?' His mother's voice shook him fully awake. She was in her dressing gown, with some terrible hairnet on. She was holding open the bead curtain and he realised he hadn't even heard her approach. How long had she been standing watching him?

'Uh, want some?'

'I won't sleep again now.' She scowled. 'All that crashing about. What are you playing at?'

'I . . . I don't know.'

Her eyes narrowed at him. She stared at him with a mixture of fondness and head-shaking despair. Ricardo stood a full foot taller than his mother, and he smiled uneasily down at her. If he told her now what he had witnessed, what would she say? She'd believe him, because . . . well, he was her son and why would he lie? And also, she believed unequivocally that practising evil magic in the dead of night and summoning spirits was just something that people *did*. Of course they did. Especially rich people.

She might think him dirty, though, if he told her about the nudity and the masturbation part. There was no way he'd mention that. And thank Jesus he'd not started jerking off in the kitchen as he'd watched, as he'd felt compelled to. He couldn't imagine anything more more mortifying.

'Are you all right, Ricardo?'

'I'm just tired. I drank too much tonight . . .'

She shrugged. She wasn't about to tell him how to behave. He was her baby, but he was a man now. He could do what he wanted. 'Were you celebrating?'

He shook his head. 'Not especially.'

'Something has happened to you,' she said shrewdly. 'I know you. I know you better than you know. I know that something has happened to you tonight.' She sniffed sharply, and it was as if she could detect the eldritch ceremony in the air.

'Bad dreams,' he said. 'Tequila always gives me bad dreams.'

He wished that was all it was, though. He wished he could dismiss what he had seen as a dream. But he couldn't. He knew it was true. Daniel had called out for him to be a witness.

Only he in the whole of NYC knew what had happened to Daniel tonight: the terrible thing that had somehow taken him over.

But what was Ricardo supposed to do with knowledge like that?

When she was a child, Shelley would come to the city to visit her aunt. Her mom would look vaguely terrified about putting her on the train, and she would be issued with instructions and notes and everything but lucky charms to keep her safe on the journey. In truth, she had never been in the slightest bit nervous about boarding that huge brown and silver train and sitting in one of the wide seats with her weekend bag beside her, watching the landscape sliding by. First the soft rolling green of the countryside, farms and shingled houses, then the industrial swamps and wastelands of New Jersey.

Every minute of it she had enjoyed, reading her book and knowing that at the end of her odyssey her beloved aunt would be waiting for her at Penn Station, ready to sweep her up in her arms. Aunt Liza made Shelley feel brave. She made her feel that the whole of the Big Apple was her backyard, which really, in a sense, it was. From the age of ten Shelley had tried to emulate her aunt's easy relationship with the place, ambling about the deep canyons of the streets as if she owned the whole shebang.

Shelley had slept on the fold-down settee in her aunt's apartment. The worn velvet drapes had been drawn to shut out the pulsing lights of the city, but still the street noise came filtering up to her. She had loved those nights, feeling safe as houses in the apartment. Reading *Charlotte's Web* by the light of her digital watch.

Tonight – so many years later – she was back in the same place. At the age of nearly thirty, she was under the heaped comforters and cushions of her aunt's elderly settee, and she was very glad of it.

Aunt Liza had of course shown her mercy, and here she was, making like she was ten again. The comforting was doing her a lot of good. It had been such an awful night. She felt sickly and drunk, and dreaded having to throw up in her aunt's tiny bathroom, knowing the sounds would wake her aunt and possibly make her cross or ashamed. Shelley didn't want to be a bother; she already felt a fool. I'm homeless and drunk and my boyfriend doesn't give a shit about me. She kept checking her phone, but no, he hadn't texted her or tried to get in touch. She even looked at his Facebook page to see if he'd said anything in his status updates. She let the phone drop out of her hands.

It was almost four o'clock. A dreadful time of night. She felt that she was at her lowest ever ebb: as if her heart could slow to a standstill and she would just die, here and now. And no one would even care or notice. In fact, she herself probably wouldn't even notice, because she was just so negligible. Who cared about *her* feelings?

Certainly not that Ricardo. She'd decided that she hated him. He was a liar. He was jealous. What did he stand to gain by making up horrible lies about her Daniel? He just had a nasty mouth. What did Jack see in him? Jack wasn't superficial. He wasn't just swayed by the boy's obvious – if *too* obvious – beauty?

Anyway. Didn't matter. Who cared? She wished she'd never gone out with them tonight.

Shelley was just thinking about going to the bookshelves to see if she could find her aunt's first edition of *Charlotte's Web* – it was just the right time for a reread – when she dozed off. Sleep suddenly found her out and put a bag over her head, like a benign kidnapper.

When she woke, it was sometime before five a.m. and there were some very strange noises in her aunt's flat.

She definitely heard footsteps. Heavy, uncertain.

Her heart froze somewhere up in her throat. Her scalp tingled.

There came another footstep. Something scratched. Scritch-scritch-scritch. Was it a cat? Clawing at something, trying to get out, wanting to be fed? Her aunt didn't have a cat. Not any more.

112

Could it be her aunt? Awake in the night? Had she had a stroke and was dragging herself about the place, unable to speak? Pleading for help?

Thud. Thud. That was a dining-room chair knocking against the table. Someone had been into the kitchen. They had passed through the living room. They were just yards away from the couch. Shelley raised herself minutely on her elbow and squinted into the darkness. But she could see nothing at all. The drapes were too thick. Not a speck of illumination penetrated the gloom. She stopped breathing, and listened with every iota of her frightened being.

Was it Daniel? The crazy thought shot through her head. He had realised where she must be. She was his beloved. He had come for her forgiveness. He had somehow let himself into her aunt's apartment. He had smashed the lock. He had kicked in the door. He had let nothing stand in the way of this early morning reunion. He loved her . . . he worshipped her . . .

There was a funny kind of smell in the room. It wasn't the heady, fresh scent of the lemon and tea tree cologne Daniel had imported for himself. It was a much more pungent aroma. A not unfamiliar one. Like old leather and mothballs, maybe. Or chemicals in a lab experiment. Formaldehyde . . .

Shelley let out a strangled gasp and almost died on the spot.

She knew that smell. She knew what it was.

But it was impossible. It was completely impossible.

Very gently she reached behind her and gathered curtain fabric in her hand. She tweaked back the drapes only slightly, allowing a spill of street light to filter into the gloom.

There was a rustle. A creak. A thump.

There was a figure in the room with her. A tall, spindly figure, swaddled in ragged clothes.

It was positioned awkwardly, frozen in one position. On the alert because of the light and knowing that it had been seen.

Creaking noises accompanied its every tiny move. It clicked and scratched and rustled like old leaves.

Shelley took in a slow, deep breath and let it out in the most bloodcurdling scream she could manage, hating herself the whole time for being the kind of woman who would scream.

Her aunt came running, quicker than she would have thought possible. She was dragging on her robe and shouting, 'Whuh? Whazzit? Whatizzit?' Her eyes were still gummed up with sleep, but as soon as they could open and focus, she saw what Shelley could see.

Standing there, quite impossibly, on the rug in the bend of the L-shaped living room.

Aunt Liza flicked on the lights and hefted the baseball bat she kept under her bed. Then she let out a squawk of pure astonishment.

The Scottish Bride turned her raddled head to look at her new hostess.

She was tall and ghastly. She looked like a corpse dragged from the Hudson River. She looked like Miss Havisham turned gangrenous and rabid.

'You musst help mee,' said the effigy, in slow, halting speech. The voice scraped across the tautened nerves of both women. 'Yoou gave me life . . . and now yoou musst help mee . . . pleease . . .'

The Bride held out those wretched twiggy fingers in supplication.

And then she collapsed in a faint, like a dead weight.

Chapter Eleven

Where was Shelley?

Somehow Daniel had forgotten her. She hadn't come home that night, which was just as well, of course. He'd other things to concentrate on. Other fish to fry.

The apartment was in a godawful state. Candles had dripped on to the carpets. There was blood on the shagpile and sofa. There was the acrid reek of smoke damage. There'd been a little fire some hours before: he'd doused it with tonic water. He'd been drinking all night, and now – in the early hours – he couldn't quite be sure what was real and what wasn't.

Ricardo? Had that Ricardo been round? That sexy Latino? Daniel shook his head confusedly. Surely not. He wouldn't have been so stupid as to invite him. He couldn't have smuggled him in. But how did . . .

He sat up gradually. It was still dark outside. The clock said five o'clock. An evil hour on a December morning.

Something was very, very wrong. No Shelley. Shelley was gone. She hadn't even been home. And he felt so strange. Like he'd been on a long run. He was exhausted. He looked down at himself. He was naked and covered in blood, and for a few minutes he was terrified. What had he done to himself?

And then the memories started leaking back.

He moved to the blinds and peered out at the night. Snow was falling. Gently, remorselessly, unexpectedly. He looked down into the street and saw that it was settling. Everything down there looked so smooth already.

He found the grimoire on the sofa. It lay unassumingly on the black leather. Battered and a bit bloody, just like Daniel himself. It was open, quite casually, at a frankly terrifying etching of a demon from hell.

Oh no.

Something stirred. Something murmured and shifted in its sleep inside Daniel's mind. Like a cat dreaming of shredding its prey, the thing in Daniel's head flexed its claws. It snickered at Daniel as he became aware of its presence.

What have I let in? he thought. Madly, furiously. He hardly knew what he was thinking.

Then: the ritual. I did the ritual. I tried it out. I invited him . . . I . . .

And then he started choking and coughing. Great wheezing gasps doubled him over. It was like he had something caught. Something stuck in his throat. He cried out, retching. His throat was parched. He was thirsty. Yes, thirsty, of course. He'd never been so thirsty in all his life. He never known anything like this.

In the kitchen alcove, he ransacked the cupboards and fridge. He drank milk straight from the carton. Then tonic that had lost its fizz. There was some soda Shelley had left, and he gagged on its saccharine taste. No. This wasn't what he needed.

The creature in his head was stirring awake. It was languid and amused. It knew where it was. It stretched and gloried in its liberation. It spoke to Daniel. It told him why he was thirsty. It explained everything. In a voice that was little more than a purr, a voluptuous murmur, it laid down the law to Daniel. It told him how things were going to be.

Daniel bowed his head and listened.

For a few moments he baulked at the things the creature was saying. His human self rebelled against the chocolatey voice in his head. Those deep, gorgeous tones telling him what he must do to survive . . . he could ignore them, couldn't he? He could pretend they weren't there. He was strong-willed. He didn't mind being thirsty. It surely didn't have to be that way.

Oh, but it did. The voice gave an oily chuckle.

Daniel had opened the book. He had read aloud the correct words. He had understood the invocation. He had known what it was meant to accomplish. And this was a fate he had brought upon himself.

He should be pleased. He should be astonished. This was promotion, wasn't it? He was going to be king of the city. He'd be the first of his kind. Prince of New York.

And tonight was when it would all begin.

Come along, Daniel, the voice commanded. It curled around his limbs. It tingled through his nerves. It played about his every fibre so suggestively. So in control of his every move. Come along, Daniel. Let us go together, you and I. While the snow falls and pacifies the city that never sleeps.

Let us glide across the freshly formed drifts. Our feet need hardly touch the ground. You have powers now, Daniel. Powers you don't yet even know about or understand. But I can show you. I can be your mentor. I can tell you everything you need to know. But first . . . first we must slake this thirst. We share this intense hunger tonight, and it must be appeased. You are newly formed and you must be blooded. I am very old and I have not feasted for more than a hundred years. Can you imagine what that must feel like?

So tonight . . . right now . . . We have hours before the weak December sun comes up over Manhattan island . . .

All right . . . all right, thought Daniel, addressing the creature inside his mind. We can go. We can go outside. Just . . . tell me what to do . . . Direct me . . .

I know there is no escape from you.

Good, very good, said the being. You're correct. You invited me in. There's no going back now. Now that I'm free. And at last I can see this fabled city. Somewhere that, in life, I often dreamed about visiting . . . a city of the future, and a great concentration of throbbing life . . . Tell me, is it really the twenty-first century?

Oh yes, said Daniel. How long have you slept?

Since eighteen ninety-six, said the creature. So you can imagine my plight. My thirst. My desperation. Thank you, my dear, for hosting me. So very kind.

Daniel gasped as he felt the creature writhe with pleasure inside him. He shuddered and gave himself no time to think. He suppressed his thoughts. The creature would hear him. He had, instead, to throw on some warm clothes. He had to brave the early hours outside. Eighth Avenue, Hell's Kitchen, the meatpacking district. They would find what they were looking for. They were bound to.

Time to go hunting, Daniel, said his mentor. Time for us wolves to go running in the snow.

Chapter Twelve

The next morning was pretty horrible for Shelley. It was just one thing after another.

Normally she would have loved waking to find the city blanketed in snow. Today she hardly noticed it, except as one more thing to be overcome. Her new winter boots were slipping all over the place as she hastened across the park.

At first light she had phoned Daniel. Whatever had happened between them, she needed his help. The events of the previous night were just too weird. Besides, she had to get into the apartment to pick up her things for work. She still had to earn a living, didn't she?

No answer from Daniel. She had an obscure feeling that he was punishing her. He could hear her leaving increasingly frantic messages on his machine, and on his mobile, and he was simply ignoring her. He was rolling over in their bed and snoozing away the wintry morning. Finding it so easy to block her out of his mind.

So she set off determinedly in her new, slippery boots, trudging through the snow.

She felt a bit guilty leaving her aunt with . . . with *the thing*. The creature called Bessie. But Bessie hadn't moved or spoken again, or done anything untoward, since she had collapsed full length on the carpet in the L-shaped room. She had simply lain there, impossibly. Shelley and her aunt hadn't discussed it properly yet. They didn't dare. In the pale light of the early morning they had stared at each other, and their expressions were reflected in the other's face: are we losing our minds?

But Bessie was real. She was lying there, all too evident to their senses. When Aunt Liza examined her apartment door, the evidence there was pretty plain, too. Somehow the strange intruder had picked the several locks with her twiggy fingers.

'There's bad magic tied up in this,' Liza said darkly, curling her hands round a hot mug of coffee. Shelley merely gawped at her aunt. Bad magic? Since when did her aunt start talking like a character in those books she read? 'How did she find us here?' Liza was musing. 'It's a relatively long way from your museum.'

Shelley couldn't believe how rational and calm her aunt was being about it all. She was mulling over these practical considerations as if the Scottish Bride's sudden appearance in her apartment was an everyday kind of occurrence.

Liza had taken note of Shelley's incredulous stare. 'Someone has to be pragmatic about this, sweetheart. It's no good having conniptions.'

Heading back to what was supposed to be her own home these days, Shelley was very close to having conniptions again.

Once inside Daniel's building, she raced up the several flights of stairs. She was wondering how she was going to explain any of this to him. She just knew he'd be looking immaculate and businesslike and ready for work at this time in the morning. He'd be so calm and reasonable. He'd think she was crazy, hurtling in wearing yesterday's clothes, reeking of stale booze and probably formaldehyde too.

But what she found in their apartment shocked her.

The place was unlocked. But the door hadn't been forced. It was as if Daniel had flown out, and in his rush had neglected to secure it. Perhaps, she thought – with daring hopefulness – he had dashed out to go looking for her. Perhaps he couldn't stand even a single night alone without his Shelley.

What she found inside the apartment perplexed and worried her even more. She found the burn marks and bloodstains on the living-room furniture and the rugs. She shivered uncontrollably at the frigid breeze coming in with the billowing muslin curtains. And there was that book. That wicked-looking book. It was closed and lying on the settee, apparently so innocent.

'Daniel?' The place had an air of disaster about it. Even with the windows open wide, there was a strange scent in the air. One that made her hackles rise.

She checked the time. Whatever weird stuff was happening, time was moving on. She had to be at work. Holding it together. She remembered her aunt's practical tone. Shelley could only pray that the snow would delay the whole world this morning. She could do with some more time. Just a little more time, so she could start to figure things out . . .

The apartment was so silent. She moved from room to room, looking at their empty, rumpled bed. It seemed like years already since they had lain there together. She found spatters of dark blood in the bathroom, and her heart leapt in fear. Where was he? What had he done?

Shelley thought about practical matters. She would be like her aunt. She would tackle things head on. She couldn't do that in worn clothes and with dirty hair.

But the blood . . . ! What had he done to himself? Shelley wiped it up quickly and neatly. Shaving. He must have nicked himself shaving.

After a shower and a change, she felt better about coping. She made more coffee and let the noise of the kettle absorb the frightening silence in the air. It was the kind of silence that fell after a terrible argument. It was as if the air was still ringing with raised voices and the threat of violence. Should she phone 911? That blood . . . there was no sign of Daniel . . . and the open door. Had someone been in? Had they attacked him? But there had been no burglary. Daniel's laptop and his wallet – she noticed with a sinking heart – were both splayed open on the small table by the bookshelves. Where would he have gone without his wallet?

She phoned Ruthie at the museum. She was always one of the first in the building.

'Hey, doll,' said her friend. 'You better get ready for this. You'll never believe it.'

Shelley winced. She braced herself for Ruthie's news. 'Tell me.'

'We had a break-in. The alarms failed. No one saw a thing.'

'Oh God.' But she knew this already. She knew what Ruthie had to tell her next. The whole thing had a sick inevitability about it.

'And you'll never believe what else.' Ruthie sighed heavily.

'They never took money. Nothing valuable. But the sick bastards took something else.'

'Y-yes?' She had never heard Ruthie swear so bitterly before.

'I'm sorry to hafta tell you this, Shelley. But they took our Bessie. They took her away last night. What do you suppose the shmucks want with her? What sick kinda thing they gonna do to her?' Ruthie sounded close to tears, Shelley thought. She could understand the feeling, though in her case it was stress-induced. 'This is what we get for garnering publicity like we did. There are some nasty weirdos out there. And now we've lost Bessie for ever.'

Oh my God, Shelley thought suddenly. They're going to think Aunt Liza and I stole the damn thing! Her instinct was to soothe Ruthie; to allay her fears and to break the news to her. She felt like she ought to say, 'It's okay! It's all right! I know exactly where Bessie is!'

But how could she? Without looking like a thief and a freak?

And besides, there were very much bigger considerations to take into account. Not just that the Scottish Bride had been carried out of the museum. Not just that she was ostensibly missing. More disturbing yet was the fact that Bessie had walked out of the Museum of Outsider Art by herself and made her own merry way in the middle of the night to the Upper East Side. That was the most pressing matter here, really.

'Look, I've got to go,' Shelley told Ruthie. 'I'll be in soon. If this snow doesn't hold me up.'

'Right. The cops are here. I guess they'll want a statement from you, and everything.'

'Okay.' Shelley's heart was pounding. How was she ever going to seem natural and normal about this? 'Is Daniel there yet?'

'Uh, no. Isn't he home?'

'No, er . . . he left pretty early this morning.'

'Okay, hon.' The line clicked off, but Shelley's thoughts were elsewhere. Daniel was gone.

It was him. He was behind this. It had to be. He had somehow . . . made all of this happen. He had done something . . . something bizarre with the Bride. Only he could get into the museum after dark. Only he could go to these lengths to . . . to accomplish *what* exactly?

She phoned her aunt. Her fingers trembled as she stabbed the digits.

She said, 'Aunt Liza, I think Daniel is behind this.'

Her aunt said simply, 'She's awake again.'

Consuela wouldn't be put off.

'You care about him, don't you? You're his boyfriend?'

'Well of course,' said Jack, a little sharper than he meant to. He lowered his voice, as a knot of tourists passed them on Christopher Street. 'Of course. You know I care about him. But I don't know what you're talking about. You're being very vague.'

She scowled at him. Jack paused outside a pet shop window. About a dozen Pomeranians were sprawling and tumbling over each other in a basket on display. Despite himself, his heart melted at the sight of the puppies. He wished he lived in a place that allowed dogs. What did he have instead? A Latino ex-porn star and his quarrelsome mother.

'I told you, I found him in the night. He looked so strange.'

'He's often restless,' Jack said.

'But he was like that as a child. I have seen him disturbed like this before. He was a sensitive boy.'

Jack tutted. 'Weren't we all?'

'I mean, sensitive like he saw things. Spirits. He saw things no one else could see.'

'Really?' Jack was intrigued. Ricardo had never mentioned anything like this before. He'd said his mother was a supernatural nut, but not that he thought he was in any way susceptible himself.

'Surely you must have seen how strangely he has been behaving these past few days?'

Jack pursed his lips as they carried on down the long street. It was lunchtime and he was heading back to work. He'd been hoping to spend the hour with Liza in a posh coffee shop, but Liza wasn't answering her phone for some reason. Instead he had been stuck with this crazy woman, who was intent on acting like a soothsayer and tagging around after him.

'Surely you must think so too,' she urged him. 'You haven't known him long, I know. But there is something different about my son.'

He agreed with her, but he didn't want to say so. Ever since Thanksgiving, in fact, and their visit to Shelley and Daniel. Something had got to Ricardo and altered his mood, though Jack couldn't exactly say how. It was something to do with Daniel, obviously, and this pass he had apparently made.

Consuela was hugging herself as they crossed a busy road. She was wearing only a shawl over her flimsy tasselled dress. Suddenly Jack felt touched by the sight of her. He thought about her devotion to her son. The way that she had come dashing out to consult Jack on his lunch hour, full of concern about Ricardo. Jack found it hard to imagine his own mother acting quite so obsessively. She was keener to let him confront his own problems and what she described as 'lifestyle choices'. She was more concerned with the affairs of the various charitable and cultural committees she sat on.

'There is a chill wind,' Consuela was saying now, in a lower voice, so that Jack had to walk slower and bend towards her. 'Can't you feel the cold? It's coming from the east. From the old world. Something *bad* is blowing in . . . *something* has come to the island . . .'

Jack found himself actually shivering. Real foreboding suddenly hit him in the chest, and his heart started beating faster.

'There is something bad here, Jack.' She looked up into his face, and he thought suddenly that she looked like a little doll. That perfectly painted face, with its eyebrows arched like Marlene Dietrich's in *The Devil Is a Woman*. Her shiny boot-black hair was scraped back into a tidy bun. He felt a quickening of compassion for this tiny, ardent woman and the way she kept herself looking so perfect, even when camping out on his sofa and living out of laundry bags.

She saw that her message had got through to him, and so, after patting his hands firmly, she let him return to work at Fangtasm.

All that afternoon, Jack got on with his usual tasks by rote. It was a quietish day, and he filled the time by dusting the glossy rosewood shelves. He spent some time shuffling some of the stock back into order. His gaze fell on the paranormal romances and the vampire books. Could it be that Consuela simply read too many of these things? Was she blurring reality with the myriad crazy fantasies in her head?

Jack really didn't know. All he knew was that Ricardo's mood had shifted. He was surly, incommunicative. He had become brusque and demanding in bed.

Well, maybe that feature of the mood shift wasn't *that* bad.

But also, he looked at Jack sometimes as if he hardly knew who he was. Jack sighed. That had an element of truth to it, though, didn't it? They had hardly known each other for any time at all. They had moved much too fast in their urge to be together.

He talked with customers and his boss, and with Lame Wendy, who came to relieve him for the evening shift. He even felt his cares and worries drift away a little as the street lamps came on outside and he realised suddenly it was time to go home. Now the snow was ankle deep, and it startled him to see it coming down so thick and fast. It looked wonderfully seasonal out there, and it was almost a shame to leave the cosy, antiquey ambience of Fangtasm for the short trip home. It was only a few blocks to Thompson Street, hardly a major schlep. He borrowed some of the trade mags to show Consuela which books were being published in the next six months. She'd be pleased, he reckoned, to get some insider gossip about them. And maybe he'd think about inviting her to the Christmas soirée at Fangtasm, the evening after next. She'd be bound to love it.

He trudged home through the snow, secretly delighting in it, even as it buffeted him along the streets. The smells of hot food from street vendors still braving the weather reached him as he hurried along. Hot dogs, boiled onions, sweet crisp waffles . . .

they were making his stomach ache with hunger, but he kept on, hoping that Consuela would be cooking up one of her feasts again.

When he made it up the fire escape, he found that neither Consuela nor Ricardo were home. A sudden cold pang went through him. She's out there somewhere. Without much of a clue where to start, Consuela was hunting for her son. Determined to bring him safely home.

Chapter Thirteen

Liza didn't know what to do that day. In her life she was used to being the practical person; the one that everyone else turned to. Any quandary, any bizarre situation. Nothing could faze her. She had seen it all in her very long and interesting life.

However, she had to admit that this new situation – this *visitation* – was reasonably unusual. Even for her life.

All that day she was forced to stay indoors. There was no way she was leaving that . . . that person alone in her apartment. Poor Rufus whined and scratched at the door to be out. He was desperate for his trot around the park and the streets. The dog could smell snow on the air, she was sure, and he was keen to go racing about in it. But she wouldn't let him. Not yet.

She wasn't sure what to do.

Maybe when Shelley came back from work that evening, maybe then Liza could slip out with Rufus. And Shelley could watch over . . . the woman. The thing. The Scottish Bride, as Shelley called her. Bessie.

'How are things going?'

'Oh, fine,' growled Liza. It was after lunchtime, and Shelley sounded far too breezy at the other end of the phone. Her aunt knew she was faking that casual tone. 'Has, er, has . . . anything happened?'

'No,' snapped Liza. 'She's sitting on the sofa and staring straight ahead. She's hardly said a word.'

'Right . . .' Shelley's voice trailed off.

Liza was trying to make a sandwich, one-handed, with the phone clamped to her ear. She was starving, but she wasn't keen, for some reason, on eating in front of her intruder. I'm like a hostage in my own apartment, she thought wildly. When she had asked the . . . woman if she wanted something, the interloper hadn't said a word. She appeared to be back in a deep sleep.

'I've talked to the police. I've given a statement to the press. It's been chaos here.'

'And Daniel?'

'We don't know where he is. He never turned up for work.'

'You still think it was him, huh?' Liza said, crunching down on a pickle.

'Don't you?'

'Fact is,' said Liza, 'the thing's . . . the effigy is still . . . doing stuff it shouldn't be. Like walking and talking, y'know. I don't see how Daniel can be responsible for that.'

'Me either,' sighed Shelley. 'But from the museum's point of view, it looks pretty suspicious for Daniel. He vanishes, and so does our prize exhibit. He's dropped himself right in it.'

'Huh,' said her aunt, thinking that Shelley sounded much too pleased about that fact. 'In the meantime, I've got another new lodger.'

'Look,' said Shelley hurriedly, 'I gotta go. I'll be home around seven.'

Home, thought her aunt, clicking off the phone. Shelley thinks she's moved in with me permanent. Great.

Suddenly Liza had a feeling she was waving her old, comfortable, mainly solitary life goodbye.

She stared at the woman-shaped creature on the sofa. In the harsh winter light of day from her tall windows, the face on the effigy looked a bit more human. She was pinched and pale in complexion, but she didn't look quite so monstrous, perhaps. Her hair hung in tatters, as did the rags she was wearing. Now that Liza took a good long look at her (she felt braver now, in the more prosaic and bright afternoon), Bessie looked rather less like a desiccated mummy than she did some poor soul who'd spent years living rough.

She was rocking, very gently, on the sofa. Back and forth. Slowly, almost imperceptibly. Liza drew closer and saw that the woman's eyes were slightly open. They were shrewdly taking in her surroundings. The dark pupils darted back and forth, fixing at last on her hostess.

'You're awake,' Liza said. 'Are you hungry? *Do* you eat?'

The woman made a strange noise, deep inside her sunken chest. It sounded rather like the rumbling strings within an old piano. 'I haven't eeaten in soo long,' she said at last. The voice was just as weird as it had been last night, in the terrifying dark. That unplaceable accent. Was it really Scotch? Liza couldn't tell. She put it out of her mind, the fact that she was talking to something made out of old bones and skin and patchwork.

Suddenly, irrevocably, this was a real woman. For Liza, this was the moment that Bessie became, once and for all, an actual person. With rights and a history and everything else a person could want.

'You're starving, huh?'

'I've beeen asleeeep soo long,' said Bessie. 'And I'm still soo coold.'

Liza swung into practical mode. 'All right then, let's get movin'. I got some sweetcorn chowder in the refrigerator. Can you handle that?'

'Soouup?' asked Bessie, looking up so hopefully that Liza's heart went out to her. The woman's face was withered and grey with neglect. She was filthy, Liza realised. She was encrusted with the dirt and dust of ages. But could she withstand a bath or a shower? She looked like she might dissolve at the first touch of hot frothy water. 'I'd like soouup, yesss . . .'

Minutes later, Liza had seated her visitor at the small kitchen table, and was studying her as she taught herself to eat again.

'Who are you?' she asked Bessie. 'Where do you come from?'

Bessie looked up at her and blinked. She licked her dry lips with a dark tongue. She gulped and winced as the soup scalded her throat. 'I doon't know,' she said, at last. 'I doon't knoow anny moore.' Her eyes stared straight at Liza then. Liza jumped a bit, because the eyes were suddenly a marvellous green. A glittering jade. Alive with a strange intelligence and an intensity she had never seen before. She was sure those eyes hadn't been like that earlier.

It was as if the woman was returning to warm and vital life, step by step, right before her own astonished eyes.

'When they found you and put you in the . . . in the museum,' said Liza, 'they decided to call you Bessie.'

The stranger's face twisted into what Liza realised was supposed to be a smile. The spoon was halfway up to her mouth as she tested the name out. 'Besssieee. I like thaaat. It'ss a goood naaame.'

'Bessie it is, then,' said Liza. Then she burst out with, 'You're magic, aren't you? I mean, you're not natural. You're real, but you're not in any way natural at all. You shouldn't really exist, should you?'

Bessie stared at her. There was some glimmering of understanding in those jewel-like eyes. 'Yees. I reememberr thaat. I amm not a natuural wooman. I am not like otherr woommen aarre . . .'

Liza felt an overwhelming urge to pat Bessie's hand. It was a like a bundle of twigs under her palm. 'Never mind, honey. You're in New York City now. You can be any kind of woman you damn well want.'

It had been the toughest day Shelley had ever spent at her museum. Not only had she had to field questions from the police and the press, she'd had Ruthie's barbed comments about Daniel all day too.

'What's he want with an effigy anyway? Kinda creepy, huh? Guess he's English, I suppose. They can be weird, with their private schools and all.'

Shelley refused to be drawn. She'd had enough to contend with, dealing with disappointed visitors who'd come to see Bessie. For the moment they were content to stare at the empty plinth where the Scottish Bride had stood, but she knew that novelty wouldn't last long.

She was glad when it was time to go home. But then she thought about what she was heading home to face, and how it wasn't really her home anyway. She'd be sharing Aunt Liza's settee with the woman this whole fuss was about in the first place. A woman who didn't even really exist.

As she shrugged on her coat and prepared to brave the wintry streets, a queer thought struck her.

This had all begun with that book.

Now, Shelley trusted her intuition. It was wild and impulsive, but it had got her out of more scrapes than it had put her into. She remembered Aunt Liza standing here with that weird book she'd got in the post. She was talking about how she'd give it to Daniel to study.

That book of magic spells . . .

She shook her head. This was crazy. Black magic stuff. But it was nonsense, wasn't it?

And yet, last night, she had seen the Bride, Bessie, alive. If that wasn't supernatural, what was?

She said good night to Ruthie, who was wearing a Bessie T-shirt and a mournful expression, and counting up the day's takings. 'Do you think there'll be a ransom note?' Ruthie asked.

Shelley blinked. 'For Bessie? You're kidding, right?'

'She was getting famous around town. She'd been in the newspapers. People get greedy and they look for opportunities.'

Shelley shook her head. 'Maybe you're right. G'night, Ruthie.'

As she made her way through the quickly trudging crowds, the traffic, the litter, the endless noise and city smells, Shelley wondered about the feasibility of perhaps making an all-new Bride out of odds and ends. Maybe they could put one together and fake her for the sake of the viewing public? Just a few old rags . . . a papier mâché head . . .

She steeled herself to march across town to Daniel's place. She'd need a few of her own things if she was going to be camping out. She'd call a cab from his building to get all her bags to her aunt's. She felt desolate as she strode and slithered through snow that had turned to demerara sugar on the pavements. This was the end of her thing with Daniel. Almost even before it had begun.

She walked the streets feeling like she was about to start living on them. She'd hardly had time to get used to her fancy address, her fancy living. Now she'd be living under that heap of boxes, or in the alcove behind those filthy bins. That was the life she'd blundered into, and all because she'd staked too much, too soon, on a bad relationship.

All her relationships had been rotten, hadn't they? Every single one. This was failure. It was worse than failure, actually, because something messed up and spooky was happening at the same time, as well.

She hauled herself up the stone stairs in Daniel's building and knew, before she even got to the top, that he was home again. There was just something in the air. Some kind of tingle. Some indistinct signs of life that she could sense, even before she heard the music coming from behind the apartment's front door.

It was Bauhaus, the old British Gothic band. God, Daniel was dragging out his vinyl records. He had come home and was clearly having some kind of nervous breakdown, revisiting the music of his teenage years. Once he had confided to Shelley how he'd been a punk, a Goth, a crusty, a raver . . . anything and everything that would have shocked his rather conservative parents. She remembered the tale of how his father had once angrily taken a heap of his punk records and burned them on a bonfire in their huge back garden. Daniel had tried to stop him, begging and weeping, and been beaten for his insubordination. This scene had haunted Daniel. He'd cried when he'd told Shelley the story, which had touched her. She'd tried to comfort him, but he'd pulled away, covering up his upset with a harsh laugh.

She knew that this music, blasting out like this, had a secret significance. For some reason it scared her, as if something beaten down in Daniel was choosing to reassert itself. Something inside him that had turned bitter and hard over the years.

Shelley let herself into the apartment, wincing at the noise. And then she blinked with surprise. There was a party going on in here. This was something Daniel had once said would happen in his immaculate place only over his dead body.

About a dozen young people were hanging about in the living room and the kitchen. They were slouched and sprawled decoratively on every surface. They were all elegance, model-slim, perfect, pale, epicene creatures. Androgynous men and women of every race and description. Shelley gazed around in astonishment at what looked like an R-rated fragrance ad.

They were rather strange, all of them. They moved very slowly, as if drugged, as if they were breathing a more languid atmosphere than Shelley. They were necking and fondling each other, but in a measured and elegant fashion. It was as if a very gradual orgy was taking place, and Shelley had come crashing slap-bang into the middle of it.

'Daniel!' she yelled. A few of the beautiful young people turned to look at her, smirking. 'Daniel, are you here?' My God, she thought. Maybe they're all squatters. Weird, sexy squatters.

She found Daniel in their bedroom. He was with a young

woman and a young man, both lying on the bed. Shelley almost fell through the floor in shock. Luckily, they were all dressed. Well, apart from the young man, who was shirtless. Daniel was sitting cross-legged on his wickerwork chair, and straight away Shelley knew something was wrong with him.

He looked ghoulish and pale. His eyes were black as caviar. When he grinned at Shelley, he looked maliciously pleased at how upset she was.

'Daniel! What are you doing? Who are all these . . . people?'

He shrugged. 'New friends. Do you realise, I've not gone out and made new friends in years?'

'What?'

'I've been working so hard. So focused on my career. On boring stuff. Getting stuck here with you. Playing happy couples. That wasn't really me, Shelley.'

She gasped, still fighting to be heard over the music as she threw back: 'And is this you, Daniel? Asking strangers back to our place and letting them run amok? Playing Bauhaus records?'

He shrugged. He really didn't care what she thought or said. She realised that he really didn't care at all.

She went on, 'And what are you doing here, in our bedroom? With these people . . . in our *bed*?'

He snickered. 'Uh . . . guess?'

Shelley blanched.

'You're welcome to join us,' he said. 'Why not? You can join my little gang.'

'I'm your girlfriend! What are you talking about? Get them out of here! And what do you think I've been doing all day? I've been covering your ass at work . . .'

'Oh, work,' he sighed. 'I've had enough of that ghastly place. I won't be going back until I feel like it.'

'Oh yeah?' Shelley found herself growing wild. She started dragging her suitcase down from the top of the wardrobe. 'And what are you going to do instead, huh?'

'Well . . .' said Daniel, pretending to give it some thought. 'I can do anything I want.'

'You can?'

'Of course. Of course I can, Shelley. I am a very talented man.'

She shook her head at him. 'You're not the Daniel I met.'

'That's very, very true.'

At that moment, the toilet in the en suite flushed and out came another figure. Another young man. He was wearing a red silk kimono that Shelley had been saving for a hoped-for luxury holiday. Or even honeymoon. She saw the dressing gown first and cried out in furious recognition. And then she did so again when she saw that it was being worn by Ricardo.

'Oh!' said Ricardo, when he saw her.

'You might well say oh,' Shelley shouted. 'So I guess you told the story the wrong way around, huh? It was actually you that made a pass at Daniel. That makes sense now. What the hell are you doing here?'

'You're so hidebound in your thinking,' Daniel told her. 'You astonish me. What's wrong, really, with giving ourselves up to the joys of the flesh?'

'What?' She almost laughed at him. 'You're sounding like some low-rent *Rocky Horror Picture Show*! What the hell are you doing, Daniel? Tell me it's not crystal meth . . .' Then she rounded on Ricardo. He had the same dreadful pallor. Like someone who hadn't been outside for days. This was what clubbing all night did to you. Ecstasy. Ketamine. Whatever else these idiots were on. 'What am I going to tell Jack, huh?'

Ricardo braved her belligerence. 'Tell him he'll see me when I decide I want to come home. Tell him I've joined the gang.'

'The gang?'

'My gang,' said Daniel. 'I've always wanted a gang. Now I've got one. And I feel happy. Happier than I ever was with you, you shrill harpy. Now, if you're not staying to join in the fun, then I think you should bugger off back to your hideous old auntie. Okay, love?'

Shelley gasped, but didn't give him the satisfaction of responding in words. She emptied a couple of drawersful of smalls into her case, under the laconic eyes of her bedroom's invaders. Then she bolted out of the apartment.

And I'm never coming back, she thought. That's it. He's gone mental. He's completely lost it.

Then she was out on the dark street, clutching her case, sobbing and trying to flag down a cab. She'd packed away presents for Daniel, ready for Christmas, in the back of the wardrobe. She hadn't even wrapped them yet. It was going to be their first Christmas, together in a place of their own. But he'd blown it for ever.

Chapter Fourteen

'You look completely wrecked and frazzled.'

'Thanks for that, Aunt Liza.'

'Tough day at work, huh?'

Shelley just scowled and flopped down on the sofa. She caught a whiff of mustiness and chemical preservatives. 'Where is she?'

Her aunt was bustling around the kitchen alcove. She was fiddling with the coffee maker in a slightly evasive kind of way. 'She? Oh, you mean Bessie.'

'Of course I mean Bessie! Who else? I've spent the whole day thinking and talking about her. Trying to deal with the fact that she's vanished off the face of the earth. All the while knowing she's round here, at yours! What have you done with her?'

'She was worn out, poor thing,' said Liza. 'We had a little lunch and we talked for while. And since then, she's been having a lie-down.'

'You talked for a while?'

'Oh, yes. Well, she's very interesting, you know. Once she gets going.'

Shelley shook her head, marvelling at her aunt's ability to get on with things so blithely. Nothing was extraordinary to her: she took it all in her stride. Now here came Rufus, padding about on the carpet. He was sniffing the air and looking twitchy because his territory had been invaded twice over.

'So where is she lying down?'

'In the hall closet. And she's standing up. She prefers it for sleeping she says. She spent years lying down in that box in the museum's basement.'

'She's asleep in your closet.' Shelley could suddenly hear the hysteria in her own voice. 'What are we going to do about her? What can we do about this whole thing?'

As the coffee pot started to bubble, Liza was studying her niece. She could see that there was more going on. 'What's up?'

'I went to Daniel's apartment. I needed to pick up some clothes and stuff . . .'

'Was he there? Have you seen him?'

Shelley nodded. Then she described what had happened.

'Ricardo? He was there?'

'Oh, it was horrible. It was like . . . I don't know. I don't know what he was doing.' Shelley stopped herself. She had been about to say something about that black book. The grimoire that Liza herself had placed in Daniel's care. But that was irrational, wasn't it? She couldn't just start blaming her aunt for Daniel's freakazoid behaviour. That would hardly be fair. 'I really can pick 'em, can't I?'

Her aunt brought her coffee and then set about making them both something to eat. The cupboards were running low. Everything – all her routines – had got out of kilter because of recent events. It was no good, thought Liza determinedly: she'd have to get a grip and keep life on an even keel. Whatever happened, there had to be regular meals and groceries. Otherwise there was anarchy.

She set about preparing one of her casseroles, which involved tossing into the mix all the leftovers in the refrigerator. Shelley's heart glowed when she saw this. It was her favourite dinner, going back to childhood visits here.

Shelley went to the tiny bathroom, splashing cold water on her face. She realised that she was numbed through with cold and shock. Oh, Daniel, she thought. What have you done? I thought we were going to be so happy this Christmas. I really thought we could be.

On her way back to the living room, she paused outside the door of the hall closet.

Bessie was inside there. Standing up like a scarecrow, eyes closed, conserving her infernal strength. Now that Shelley listened hard, she heard fluting, whistling breath from behind the door. Was it her imagination, or could she really hear the rustling of twiggy old limbs? Skin as dry as autumn leaves, crackling inside the dark confines? She could smell the old Scottish Bride much more strongly now. It wasn't, in the end, such an unpleasant smell. The mothbally reek of old stuff kept at the back of the closet. The mulchy fug of the countryside in October. Just a hint of mushroomy basements.

Bessie. Who was she?

Over dinner and some eggnog that Liza unearthed from her cocktail cabinet, aunt and niece attempted to cheer each other up. Liza even put on the Ronettes' Christmas album, which felt just right, rather than silly, as they toasted each other.

'Daniel calls this a snowball,' Shelley sniffed, holding her glass aloft. 'Eggnog with soda. It's like an English thing.'

'Forget him for now,' said Liza. She was furious with that young man. How dare he mess her niece around? Liza didn't understand any of this. What was he playing at? With those people in his apartment? Was it really drugs? Or something worse? Liza's intuition had always screamed at her about Daniel. She had taken against him at first sight – as had Rufus, she remembered. But she hadn't wanted to weigh in too heavily to warn Shelley. Not when Shelley was looking so pleased with herself for hooking this man. Silly girl. Liza shook her head fondly.

And then she remembered the black book. She swore to herself. It was with Daniel. She had let him study it, hadn't she? She knew it was important. Valuable, even. Now, if there was a big breach between these young people, perhaps she'd never get it back again?

And somehow she knew that was bad news.

Because, really, she had given Daniel the book because she herself hadn't liked being in possession of it.

That was true, wasn't it? That little book had disturbed her, for a reason she couldn't easily give a name to, though she had a few dark suspicions. She had been relieved when Shelley had taken it to give to her man. But it had been weak of Liza, very weak, not to take responsibility and do something about it herself.

She was digging around in her everything-outta-the-refrigerator stew and she suddenly froze. *It's all down to me.*

I tried to offload the wicked book on to Daniel. Somehow the book is doing this. All of this. It's the book behind everything weird. And it's all *my* frickin' fault.

A lump of sausage stuck in her throat and she choked. Her eyes watered and Shelley dashed for a glass of water. Oh, Mr Wright! What have you sent us? What kind of curse is this?

Shelley was patting her on the back. Too hard.

'It's okay, I'm all right,' Liza gasped. 'I just had a nasty thought. A very nasty thought.'

'What?' said Shelley, looking alarmed.

She's not equipped for this, thought her aunt. Shelley likes a nice easy life. Everything running smoothly. She can't deal with . . . anything spooky. Anything macabre. It's just not her thing. She gave Shelley a watery smile.

And then: thump thump thump.

They both jumped at the hollow sounds in the hall.

Bessie was awake again. She had smelled dinner and she wanted out of her closet.

'Oh my God,' Shelley whispered, as she heard footsteps and the living-room door opening. Her aunt put on a bright smile and started fixing up a third place setting.

'Bessie dear, come and sit with us. Good evening, my dear.'

Jack was delighted when Ricardo actually turned up at the Fangtasm Christmas party. Things were in full swing, and some impromptu dancing – to the swinging sounds of Les Baxter and his orchestra – had broken out amongst some of the older set. Mr Grenoble looked floridly pleased with himself as he went round greeting his most valued customers, colleagues and staff. He was in the process of flattering and flirting with the dolled-up Consuela when Jack noticed that his boyfriend had arrived.

Not that there should have been anything very surprising about that. Ricardo had promised several days ago to be here. But the fact was, he had been missing for nearly as long as that. Even though his mother and boyfriend had spent some hours patrolling the streets and bars and clubs, there had been no sign of him. The only thing that had prevented them from calling the cops was the word of his boss at the chocolate shop, who said that Ricardo had called in to explain his absence. He was sick. Which was news to his worried loved ones.

Now here he came, swaggering through the crowded store, easing his way past the literati. Or at least as close to the literati as Fangtasm ever came. The bookish revellers were excitedly sipping sherry and discussing vampire mysteries and romances, and so enthralled were they with each other's company, they barely took any notice of the singularly pale young Latino steadily making his way towards Jack.

Jack saw at once that something was changed and strange about his lover.

They kissed and Ricardo smiled blandly. He wouldn't answer any of Jack's questions about where he had been, or what had been happening.

He looked good. He looked a bit weird, but good. There was a curiously self-possessed air to him. A calm confidence that Jack had never noticed before. And his clothes . . . these weren't Ricardo's taste, were they? That was an expensive leather jacket. He had on a heavy charcoal-grey silk shirt. Ricardo's usual things were gaudy, flashy. Jack felt disloyal even calling them that inside his head. But he was trying to give a name to the changes in Ricardo. It was as if the boy had aged overnight. And had become more sophisticated or something.

147

'What is it?' Ricardo asked him. 'You're staring at me so hard. People are looking.'

'Screw people,' Jack burst out. 'I'm worried about you. So's your mother.'

Ricardo pulled a face. 'Shit, is she here?' He tensed.

'Just what is it with you?'

'I don't feel like explaining anything right now. I just came to see you. I knew you'd be here. I wanted to make sure you weren't worrying about me.'

'Well I was. I am.'

'You needn't.'

'You've met someone else, haven't you?' As soon as he said it, Jack knew that it just had to be true. The new attitude, the costly threads. Ricardo had gone off and found himself some sugar daddy. A rich older guy was exactly what he needed. Jack couldn't hope to fulfil his true needs.

'Yeah, I've met some people.' Ricardo shrugged. 'But, you know. Nothing that should alarm you, Jack. Nothing that should hurt your feelings.' Now he looked Jack straight in the eye. Jack flinched a bit, dazzled by his emerald gaze. 'I still want you, honey.'

Jack's stomach flipped and he shivered. He was furious at his own excitement. He wanted to be aloof, to punish Ricardo. But he felt like a puppy dog, instead, prepared to roll over and beg at this least sign of encouragement.

'Ricardo!' came a huge and shrill cry from across the room. There was some flurrying and bustling then as Consuela came hurrying through the crowd. Her son hugged her to him and kept hold of her. Her shouts and sobs were muffled through his new clothes. She seemed to be berating him and weeping joyously in equal measure.

'I've only been gone a couple of days . . .'

'We have never been separated,' she gasped. 'In all your life.' She aimed kisses at him and he submitted laughingly to her attentions, oblivious to the amused smiles and stares of the partygoers. Jack smiled to see Consuela so happy. Even his newly cool boyfriend had cracked a smile by now, which was a relief.

All of a sudden, Consuela drew back. 'But . . . are we okay?' She frowned at him. A dark expression. Her mouth was agape. Her perfect hair was awry. 'You are well, aren't you?'

'I'm fine, Mamma. I have never been better . . .'

Her frown deepened. 'Are you sure?' There was a flicker of . . . was it distaste on her face? Jack moved closer. 'You are so cold, my son . . .'

Ricardo tried to laugh away her concern. 'It's ten below out there! I've walked downtown in a blizzard. Have you even looked out there since the party started?'

Jack gazed past mother and son, and the others, and saw through the tall front windows of the bookshop that a wonderful snowstorm was in progress. There were some bright flakes in Ricardo's hair. They still hadn't melted. That was why he was so pale and chilled, of course. And his lips were so scarlet and his eyes so bright.

His mother put a small, clawlike hand to his cheek. 'This is no good. Why are you running about in the cold? In such a flimsy shirt? And where did this jacket come from? You didn't steal it, did you?'

'Mamma, you're embarrassing me . . .'

149

'We're going home right now,' she told him. 'Jack as well. I have some soup. I need to feed you.'

To Jack's surprise, Ricardo consented to being led along by his mother. He looked like a small boy being dragged home from school. Following them, Jack made his apologies to Mr Grenoble and others for leaving the annual gathering early. Family crisis, he mouthed – and the words felt good. Ricardo and his mother were really starting to feel like his family by now.

He wrapped himself up warm to brave the icy winds. It wasn't far to Thompson Street. Just a few icy corners and howling boulevards to negotiate. And, once home, once they'd eaten and were out of Consuela's fussy way . . . he'd have Ricardo all to himself. He thought about those lips . . . that perfectly pale complexion . . .

Chapter Fifteen

After a day in the woman's company, Liza had decided that, though Bessie's speech was rudimentary, her feelings were complicated.

There was a great deal going on under the surface as the person they had once thought an effigy struggled to come to terms with her new life and her new surroundings.

Actually, her speech wasn't as bad as it had been. She was slurring less and speeding up slightly. It was as if she had been petrified or sealed in ice or something. Now she was warmed through with the central heating in Liza's flat. She sat on the sofa like any other visitor, looking less like a hunk of wood and straw. Even Rufus had come out of the bedroom and wasn't quite so aggressive towards her. As he sniffed around her, Liza told him again and again that Bessie was a friend. He wasn't to attack her or any of his other tricks. Bessie herself gazed down at the dog with those vast, luminous eyes and looked very sad, as if she was remembering a dog of her own, lost to the distant past.

Yes, there was a great weight of sadness that the Scottish Bride carried around with her. But she wasn't a miserable person. Actually, she was quite good company, once you got to know her.

Yesterday evening she had watched TV with Liza and Shelley and had sat there enthralled through the most awful shows. Reality TV, cop dramas, MTV videos. Her ragged mouth had hung open in sheer astonishment as the rude noise ripped through the apartment.

'What are we going to do with her?' Shelley had hissed, as her aunt made yet another pot of coffee. It turned out Bessie had an insatiable thirst for java. The first sip she had taken had just about blown her tattered socks off.

'Do with her?' Liza frowned. 'She's all right here. She takes up hardly any space. She says she's happy in my hall closet.'

Shelley wanted to broach the subject of returning Bessie to the museum, but she could see that would be difficult. Her aunt clearly regarded her new friend as an actual person now, and not something to be put on display. Maybe it was best this way. The museum thought Bessie was lost for ever. Stolen as part of a prank. The police had been to see Daniel at the apartment, but he had managed to deter them, by all accounts, by being his usual suave and persuasive self, and claiming he had had a bout of flu. He had acted amazed that the effigy was missing.

'I wish I could persuade her to put on some decent clothes, though,' said Liza sadly. 'Those old rags of hers are falling apart. I offered her one of my jogging outfits so we could go out shopping for something more suitable . . .'

'You're gonna take a . . . mummified corpse shopping? You're taking her to Macy's?'

Liza nudged her. 'Don't call her that! She's not mummified.'

'She's not natural.' Shelley frowned. 'She was dead and she came back to life. What do you want me to call her? A zombie?'

Her aunt looked furious. 'You can go back to your precious boyfriend if you're going to start that nasty kind of talk.'

Shelley had looked sullen at this. There was no way for her to go back to Daniel. No way that she could see.

That evening, to get out of Shelley's hair, and to give both Rufus and Bessie some much-needed fresh air, Liza decided that they were going to walk in the park. Actually, she didn't know whether Bessie needed exercise or air at all, but she guessed she did, smelling of formaldehyde and all musty like she did. She produced a huge quilted black coat she had bought for herself in the sales last year. It had been much too big for her, but it was perfect on Bessie. Now she just looked like a gawky and very tall woman, but not particularly noticeable or unusual.

Bessie shivered inside the new garment. 'Thisss is wondeeerful,' she said, in a low voice. 'This isss something newww and waaarm.'

Liza fetched Rufus's leash from the hall and the dog went wild, dashing circles round her. 'Glad you like it. I thought I'd wasted my money on it. C'mon.'

Shelley waved them off and lay full length on the sofa. She wanted to stew over her various problems in silence for a while.

Bessie was a bit apprehensive as the two women ventured down the snowy street outside in the direction of the park. The city noise made her jump and twitch every few yards. Each yellow cab or dark-windowed car that swished by in the slushy snow caught her attention, and she marvelled at the Christmas lights in all the buildings.

'This is aaa miracuulous place, Lizaa,' she said. 'I have seen nooowhere like it. When I awooke . . . I didn't know if I wass in heaven or hellll. It is so different to the plaace . . . the place I was uuused to.'

'And where was that?'

'I doon't knoow!' She flapped her twiggy hands sadly. 'I can't reeemember anymooore!'

Rufus was pulling crossly on the leash. They weren't moving fast enough for him. He could smell the snow and longed to be dashing about in the drifts somewhere on Dog Hill. It was dark now, and the low clouds were dense with more snow, lit with a wash of pale orange light.

'Perhaps your memories will return gradually,' said Liza. 'Piece by piece. You can't rush these things. You've had a great shock, waking up all of a sudden like this.'

They walked in companionable silence until they entered the park. Once underneath the dark, spreading trees and on the meandering paths, Bessie became much more relaxed. There were fewer people and the light was gentler. More mysterious. Almost like being in a fairy tale. They stuck resolutely to the paths as they wound through the woods. Liza was very aware of her new friend, stalking along beside her, her face squinched up with effort.

Together they clambered up the hill where Liza liked to let Rufus off his leash. They watched him hare about and roll in the snow. At one point Bessie even laughed at his antics. It was a guttural laugh. It sounded unused. The moon was up and looming large over the tall hotels at the edge of the park.

'I wonder why you were woken up,' said Liza airily. She darted a look at her new friend. 'Hm? Whaddya think?' She was tired of puzzling over how this queer miracle had taken place. Now she wanted to know why. 'Because I guess there has to be a reason, doesn't there?'

'I don't knooow,' Bessie said, lapsing into her slow, dragging speech again. It was the cold, seeping back into her joints. 'Peerhaapss.' Then she jerked suddenly, like a marionette. Something had pulled her strings. 'Yess! A purpose!' She turned to Liza with a grin. It was a ghastly grin in many ways, like something carved into a pumpkin head, but the sight of it warmed Liza's heart. Bessie hadn't smiled very much yet at all. 'Yess! I am brought back to life because I aaam needed! That is alllwaaayss the waaay!'

'It is?'

'It haass happennned before that waaay. Yess. I musst bee needed here, in thisss time and plaacce. No?'

'I guess,' said Liza doubtfully.

'I have a purposse heeere. My spirit iss summoned . . . when my powers are requirrred.'

'Your powers?'

'Yess, yes . . . my powerrs . . .'

Then she seemed to clam up, thoughtfully. Her thoughts turned inward. She was rummaging with the tail ends of memories, Liza could tell. They finished up their walk in the park and called Rufus back. They were getting too cold. Even Rufus knew it was time to head home.

'Oh no!' Liza burst out. 'I'm missing the Christmas bash at Fangtasm! I knew there was something happening tonight.'

'Fangtaaassm?'

'It's a bookstore. I promised Jack as well. Damn.' She glanced at her watch. Nah. It was too late now. She'd phone him. Suggest lunch or something. She hadn't seen him in days – and there was a lot to catch up on.

'Bookstooore,' Bessie was intoning. 'Boooookkksssss . . .'

Liza smiled at her. 'Hey, Bessie. Whaddya say we swing by the Chinese market on Eighty-first? Take some noodles and gunk home for Shelley?'

'Nooodless and gunk?'

'It's what she used to call sweet and sour noodles when she was a kid. It was a special treat for her.'

'She neeedss a treat.' Bessie nodded seriously as they rejoined the main path, stamping the snow off their boots. Liza realised she should have found Bessie some new and stouter footware. 'That girrrl. Without herrr I wouldn't be back aliiive, would I?'

Liza had to agree that Bessie was quite right there. Shelley was the one she had to thank for her new life. Noodles and gunk was the very least they could fetch to say thanks.

Chapter Sixteen

Jack and Liza spent the day together Christmas shopping midtown, and though they did a lot of talking, they weren't completely honest with each other. For some reason they were concerned to keep the other from seeing how anxious they were.

They had brunch in a deli on 57th and 7th. Jack watched Liza demolish a plate of corned beef hash, while he sipped his coffee and nibbled at a roll. He knew she was burning with some new kind of knowledge. What it was he had no idea. Something to do with Shelley moving out of Daniel's place, he was sure.

'Actually, I'm glad she's out of there,' Jack said. 'And you never did like him, did you?'

Liza shrugged. 'Whether I liked him or not was kinda immaterial. My concern was whether Shelley was happy, and at first, she was okay with the guy. She threw in everything to move in with the shmuck . . .'

'Bad mistake.'

'Uh-huh.'

'So what made her move out? What was it he did?' Jack felt a bit uncomfortable, playing dumb, remembering how Ricardo had made Shelley flee the bar the other night, telling her how her boyfriend had come on to him.

Liza was squirming a bit too. No way did she want to tell Jack what Shelley had told her: that Ricardo had been among the strange young people round Daniel's pad. She shook her head, muttering darkly. Kids these days couldn't make up their minds about anything. It seemed to her like they had too many distractions, and too many opportunities to indulge and enjoy themselves.

'Anyway,' Jack said, 'you've got her staying with you now, where you can keep a eye on her.'

'It's getting kind of crowded in my apartment,' said Liza ruefully.

'Poor Shelley's not having much luck at work, either, is she?' he continued. 'I read about the effigy disappearing. That's a bit weird. Though we went to see it, and it gave me the shivers. There was a strange atmosphere around that thing all right. Did you go and see it before it vanished?'

'Oh yes.' Liza nodded. She thought back to seeing Bessie for the very first time. On the day she had given Shelley the grimoire. Perhaps the beginning of all their misfortunes.

Since then, Bessie had described that day as the one on which consciousness started to return to her. She had suddenly become aware that she was perched immobile upon a podium in a strange and cavernous room. She grew to realise that people were looking up at her. Feeling was returning to her desiccated limbs. She longed to move, to come to life once more . . .

'Hope you don't think this rude,' said Jack, 'but you seem really preoccupied.'

'Oh, it's nothing . . .' Damn, the boy could see through her.

She should have known. She'd chosen him for a friend. Any friend of hers was gonna be extra perceptive and smart, right?

'I wish you'd come to Mr Grenoble's Christmas party the other night,' he said. 'Everyone was asking after you.'

'I wish I could've as well. But I was looking after someone . . .'

'Shelley, huh?'

'No, I've another guest staying with me. That's why we're so crowded. It's uh . . . a childhood friend. From Brooklyn. A distant cousin, I think, but we grew up together. She's got some domestic problems and I'm . . . uh, helping her.'

'Your place is turning into a women's refuge!' Jack laughed. He was disturbed, though. Liza was acting so strange. Why was she being so evasive about this old friend from Brooklyn? It was like she was a secret, or shameful, or . . . Maybe she was Liza's *lover*? Maybe Liza was a lesbian? But why would she be covert about that?

They paid their bill and wandered towards Broadway, struggling with their heavy bags. It was the wrong way to wander. They were forced to go single file through the crowds and almost lost each other in the confusion of sightseers, serious shoppers and nuts ringing handbells and shouting about Jesus. Jack remembered that they were supposed to be heading towards the Rockefeller Center to watch the skating. No way would either of them be having a go. But Liza had expressed an interest in the sport of watching other people falling over.

They ambled on to a slightly quieter cross street. Liza found she was wondering what to buy Bessie for Christmas, which seemed like a queer thing to be thinking. What would Bessie care or even know about Christmas? But she'd have to get her something, wouldn't she? And what would happen when Jack wanted to come over to her place for the season – as he undoubtedly would – bringing his unfaithful boyfriend with him? They'd recognise Bessie straight away. They wouldn't be fooled by this cousin-from-Brooklyn shtick.

She deliberately changed the subject as the snow started falling again around them. 'Hey, your place is like a refuge too, huh? You still got your boyfriend's mother taking up your couch?'

'Yeah,' he sighed, pretending to look rueful. Secretly he was glad of Consuela's presence. He didn't know what he would do without her. He would think he was going crazy, wouldn't he? He would be left alone with Ricardo . . . and Ricardo had changed so much. So quickly. He was aloof and distant most of the time. So different from his usual warm, spontaneous, almost childlike self. He could be demanding and even rude with his mother and lover. They both found themselves ducking and dodging around these new moods of his, for some reason eager to please him. It puzzled both of them, why neither gave him a slap and simply told him to get a grip. But they didn't. Ricardo was taking over their minds and their wills with his bad behaviour.

He slept through the daytime like an adolescent. But even as a teenager he had never been like this, Consuela confided in Jack. He had never been rude or nasty, especially with his mamma. And there had been none of this sneaking about at night. Without telling his loved ones where he'd be going, he would slip out. They'd hear the door bang and know he was gone. He'd be back before dawn. Jack shook his head sorrowfully just thinking about it. And then blushed, thinking of how, in the dawn, Ricardo would shake him awake, demanding sex. Rough sex. Sex like Jack wasn't used to, with Ricardo or anyone. This was something he hadn't told Consuela about, naturally, and nor was he tempted to confide in Liza this afternoon. But the whole situation was disturbing to him. Recent experiences with Ricardo had shaken him very deeply.

But did the great sex stuff make up for all the weirdness?

Jack was ashamed to admit – even to himself – that it kind of *did*. Sometimes he could be shamed and relieved and pleased all at the same time to find himself so shallow, like any other man. But the sex was great. What was he going to do? Say no?

The afternoon passed by pleasantly, with no more confidences being shared by the friends. They jostled along, book-shopping in a big chain store (Jack feeling disloyal to Mr Grenoble), cruising round the Rockefeller rink, and examining the lavish window displays on Fifth and Sixth Avenues. As time wore on they were both bursting to tell each other more about their strange situations, but in the end, neither did. The daylight failed, the crowds doubled in strength, and it was time for the two to split up: for Jack to head back to Greenwich Village and Liza to return uptown to her house guests. She was fixing them a big dinner. Again, she mock-complained. Shelley and Bessie had huge appetites.

'Bessie?'

'That's my friend's name. My friend from Brooklyn.'

'Oh, of course.' Jack nodded and smiled, as they headed down into the subway. Liza's lesbian lover was called Bessie, huh.

Once under the sidewalk, they were about to go their separate ways when something remarkable happened. It was hard to make out what was going on at first, in the tireless jostle of the commuter crush. A small gap opened up in the crowd. Shouts rang out in the confined tiled space. There were echoes of gasps and screams. Surely it was just a mugging? A pickpocket disturbed in the act? So then why all the noise? It was an everyday occurrence, right?

'Someone's been attacked, I think,' said Jack. He was taller than Liza, of course, craning his neck over the press of bodies. 'I think they've been stabbed.'

'Christ,' muttered Liza, though she was thinking more about the delay. At least they hadn't actually witnessed anything. They wouldn't have to hang around giving statements.

Jack went on, 'There's someone down on the ground, hurt. They're gathering round him . . .'

'Where's the attacker?' Liza's eyes flew about. The stabber must still be in the crowd. She imagined him amongst them, a dripping flick knife held aloft, prepared to slash and stab his way out into the open . . .

There was a great cry then from the subway crowd. A piercing scream blotted out all other sound for a few moments. Then Liza and Jack and a few others who were standing on the edges saw the perpetrator of the attack come bursting through the crowd.

Jack grabbed hold of his friend and drew her back. Others did likewise, giving the young punk room. He looked crazed and ashen, as if shocked at what he had done. Right there, in front of everyone. This pale-faced young man. He had attacked someone. Left them lying there on the tiled floor. In the split second for which he paused, before darting off into another tunnel, Liza and Jack got a good look at him.

Just a young punk in a hooded top. A young punk who looked feral, somehow, insane, like a wild animal that had been cooped up too long. His mouth was set in a rictus grin. He was slavering frothing crimson blood. Somebody else's blood was bright and wet down his neck and his white T-shirt.

Liza and Jack stared at him before he whirled around and fled back into the darkness.

Nobody followed him.

Jack looked at Liza. She looked very grim, staring after the young man.

She said simply: 'Vampire.'

Chapter Seventeen

That particular dark afternoon, Shelley was spending some time at her aunt's apartment, alone. She had heard from Ruthie that Daniel had deigned to return to the office today, and so she had decided to work from home. Easier to install herself on Liza's bed settee with her laptop and sheaves of reports.

Outside, the snow continued to fall, remorselessly. It looked like hazy interference on a broken TV. Shelley felt herself drawn to watching through the blinds and lapsing into a daydream. Every now and then she'd wake with guilty thoughts of work she had to get through. It was her responsibility to file the paperwork pertaining to the loss of the effigy known as Bessie.

It seemed a bit ridiculous, given that Bessie was propped up dozing in the hall closet not five yards from where Shelley was currently sitting. The very thought made her shudder. She wasn't comfortable thinking about Bessie. She wasn't as blasé as her aunt about the whole business of Bessie's presumed humanity. She thought this was probably because she had been the one to disinter the body from its coffin-like crate in the museum in the first place. She knew that Bessie had lain there, uncomplaining, for several decades . . .

What time was it? Maybe she should think about fixing some dinner. Her aunt would be home soon, frozen and exhausted and laden down with Christmas packages and bags. It was only fair that Shelley prepared their food tonight. She wanted to do her bit around the place and earn her keep. Outside, it was completely dark by now.

Just as she was closing the laptop and scooping away heaps of disorganised paperwork (she hadn't made much headway, truth be told), there came a short, sharp knock at the apartment door. Rufus started barking immediately. It couldn't be Liza, lost her key. Rufus would never bark like that at his mistress. He'd be yelping and jumping up, delighted that she was back.

The knock came again. Rufus growled, low in his throat. 'Heeyy, Roof,' Shelley calmed him, but he was rigid with tension, leaning forward. He whimpered when she brushed past him, on her way to answer the summons.

Shelley squinted through the fish-eye lens of the peephole. The brightness of the corridor outside made her blink. Then she saw him.

Daniel. In his Paul Smith suit. Tugging his tie straight. Clutching a bunch of dark crimson roses. Even distorted in the peephole he looked extraordinary. He looked wonderful.

Shelley couldn't stop herself. She unlatched and unbolted the heavy door. She left the chain on for a moment as she eased open a gap.

'Daniel? What do you want?'

'Let me in.' He grinned at her. Wolfishly. Little pig, little pig. I'll huff and I'll puff. 'I brought you roses, look.'

She could already smell them. It was a dense, overwhelming

scent. Fecund. Almost rotting. She looked at their unfurled heads and saw that they were overripe. Crisping at the edges. But Daniel, though . . . Daniel looked marvellous. She had never seen him looking so . . . bright and glowing with vitality. His eyes sparkled as if at some delicious shared joke. Snow had settled in his dark hair like jewels. Suddenly she wanted him. She didn't know how he had done this to her. He had never had quite so dramatic an effect before. But right now she wanted him. Her mouth went dry.

'Come on, Shelley love. Let me in. What am I going to do? We need to talk.'

Rufus wouldn't be mollified. He knew it was a terrible idea for Shelley to take off the safety chain and open the door fully. He went crazy as Daniel stepped over the threshold at Shelley's invitation. This time, though, the small dog didn't race at Daniel's ankles. He didn't dart at him and try to bite him, as he had done before. This time he whimpered and made only a show of protest. As Daniel swept into the living room, Rufus scampered away, fearfully, to hide under Liza's bed.

'Some guard dog he is,' sighed Shelley. 'What's the matter with him?'

Daniel was gazing round at the apartment. He had a half-amused, half-disdainful look on his beautiful face. Yes, beautiful. Shelley had known he was attractive. But she had never thought of her boyfriend as beautiful. Not really. She shook her head to clear it. 'What is it you want, Daniel?' She felt he was taunting her by his very presence.

'This place is in a horrible state,' he observed.

Shelley blushed. Yeah, the apartment was pretty messy. She

had meant to have a clean round while her aunt was out Christmas shopping. It was hard, though, three women – one of them seemingly undead – and a small dog sharing such a tiny space.

Daniel glanced at the paperwork mixed up in the comforter and blankets. 'You're working and sleeping on the same bed settee?' He shook his head, tutting. 'How can you go from the comfort of our luxurious apartment to this, Shelley? Do you really hate me that much?'

'I d-don't hate you,' she said.

'But you must. To run right across town like this. To choose to live . . . in such squalor.'

Her heart flared up in protest. She forgot to be entranced by him. 'This isn't squalor! It's just a bit untidy! How dare you say that about my aunt's place?'

He shrugged, as if her aunt meant nothing to him.

This reminded her of something. 'Oh. She wants the book back. The grim-whatsit.'

'The grimoire,' he said, almost purring the word.

'Yeah, it's valuable, she says. She should never really have let it out of her sight.'

'I still have it,' he said, steel entering his voice. 'I am still *using* it.'

She frowned. Not 'reading' it. *Using* it. 'Are you doing spells, Daniel? Are you messing with . . . black magic?' It sounded so stupid, the way she said it. She felt foolish. But then she saw that Daniel was listening. He was taking her question quite seriously.

'Am I?' He grinned. It was a wonderful grin. It was salacious and sexy and filled with hot promises. He tossed the bouquet he was still holding on to the mussed sheets and blankets and museum paperwork. 'I could show you something magical, Shelley,' he said. 'Right here and now.'

She groaned. Half persuaded, but also at the obviousness. Exquisite he might be, but it was all pretty cheesy. Suddenly Rufus was barking out a warning in the next room, as if he had been listening to every word *and* its subtext.

'Uh,' she said. 'No thanks.'

'I want you to come home with me, Shelley,' Daniel said suddenly. His tone was still commanding, but there was a tinge of . . . was it desperation? She hoped so.

'I'm not going anywhere.' But she was uneasy. He was holding out his arms to her. He seemed suddenly vulnerable. He looked lost without her. How did he do that? He was twisting her around his little finger. She knew he was. She knew what stunt he was pulling. But she loved it. She loved the tugging sensation in her bones as she gravitated towards him. He was making her dance . . . almost floating through the overwarm air of the apartment towards him. He is seducing me all over again, she thought . . . And this time it's so easy.

'It will be better this time, Shelley,' he was promising her. 'We had difficulties before. But they were petty things. Silly things. Mundane human concerns. We are above such things. Our love is above such things, surely.'

'Yes, yes,' she said, inching towards him. He was right, and she felt ashamed for the things they had argued about. Sharing space. Belongings. Clutter and mess. Possessiveness. How silly it all seemed now. Compared with this deep-rooted need . . . this hunger . . .

He reached and reached with those long fingers . . . and she felt him touch her hair. He took up handfuls of it and tangled it round his fingers, playing with her . . .

'There are good times coming, Shelley. Good times for the likes of you and me. We will enjoy the coming months and years together, as we ought to. As it was written. Our union is predicted. It is meant. There is a golden dawn coming, Shelley, and we shall greet it as king and queen . . .'

His words were swimming about her in gorgeous eddies and ripples of sound. But then something suddenly snagged her attention. What was it? Oh, yes. He was talking bullshit.

'I mean it, Shelley. We can be king and queen. Of this city. Of this whole country. It will be so easy. The power is at hand. Will you share in it? The power grows day by day, hour by hour. I can feel it coursing within me. Every day more followers flock to my cause . . . we bring them into the fold . . . more and more people are with me . . .'

'Uh, Daniel,' she said, breaking into his flow. She tried to pull back from his cloying fingers. They tangled in her hair, making her cry out. 'Leave go of me!' she yelled.

'Shelley, I . . .' He stared at her. His eyes were blazing.

Okay. That was weird. That wasn't natural at all.

'What are you talking about?' she gasped. 'You're talking about crazy stuff. I thought you were here to win me back! I thought you were talking about *us*!'

'I was! I am! You have to rejoin me, Shelley. I have my pick. I could have any one of my converts and followers. But I choose you, Shelley. You are marked out. You are mine . . .'

She had had quite enough of this. This was drugs talking. This was something outside of himself, taking control of him.

He'd flipped out completely, and she was listening to no more.

'I want you to go now, Daniel.'

But he wouldn't. He stood his ground and carried on for some moments with his bizarre imprecations.

'What are you?' she gasped. 'Are you in some kind of cult?' That was exactly what it sounded like to her. He had that *zeal* about him.

'I *am* the cult.' He sniggered suddenly. '*I* am the one they are following. I am Daniel.'

'I *know* you're Daniel! Just get a grip. And I want you to get out of my aunt's apartment – right now!'

He could see that his blandishments had failed. His expression changed alarmingly. It became twisted, feral. He lunged at Shelley with both hands. She saw the move coming and darted away. She shrieked as he came after her.

'Daniel!' she yelled. The walls here were paper thin. Would any of her aunt's neighbours hear? Rufus was barking fit to burst, but he didn't come running to help. Daniel was chuckling. Toying with her like a great sleek cat would its prey. Shelley backed away and stumbled on the coffee table. She fell backwards through the air, scattering papers and unwashed crockery, landing awkwardly on the makeshift bed.

'I have you now.' Daniel grinned at her, licking his lips.

For God's sake, Shelley thought! The creep is actually licking his lips. She stared at him as he advanced. She knew now that she was at his mercy. Maybe she could reach a glass . . . she could smash it and . . . and what? Would she really slash him with broken glass?

'Don't come any closer,' she warned.

170

'What are you going to do?' he jeered. 'You're mine. I can do what I want with you.'

'Daniel . . .' she said, and started to scream.

He laughed at her. He was laughing so hard that at first he didn't hear the scuffling noise in the hallway.

Shelley did. Was Rufus coming to help at last? Or had her aunt returned? She didn't even care about the shame. She wanted her aunt there. Shrieking and calling the police. Thump *thump*. Heavy footsteps. The crash of a door. Wood splintering.

This wasn't Aunt Liza.

Even Daniel – in the throes of his weird excitement – heard these sounds.

The heavy approach as she came up behind him.

'What . . . ?' he said.

And then Bessie walloped him.

That was the only word for it, afterwards, when Shelley tried to explain the scene to people, primarily Aunt Liza.

'She simply took him in both hands and I thought she was going to tear him into pieces. He didn't know what had hit him at first. Even when he did, when he got a good look at her, he clearly didn't believe what was happening. She bounced him around the room. She . . . walloped him. She kicked his ass. When he came to his right senses, that was when he fled. With his tail tucked between his legs.

'She was a monster, Aunt Liza. Like a thing possessed. I really thought she was going to kill him . . .'

'I hate to be . . . to beee liiike that . . .' Bessie moaned. 'I hate tooo hurt people . . .'

The woman had her head in her hands. She was moaning and shaking, perched heavily on the bed settee. While Shelley brewed up a strong pot of coffee to bring her out of her shock, Aunt Liza stood patting her on the back. 'I'm sure you did just what you had to do.'

'I try not to hurt people,' Bessie said. 'I aamm not dangerous, Liza. Not anny mooore. Youu must believe me. Youuu aaare my frieeend, aren't youu? Booth of youu? You and Shellley?'

'We are, we are,' said Liza. Though truth be known, she was a bit disturbed, coming home with her Christmas shopping at the end of the day – having already witnessed one strange scene of violence – to discover her apartment in utter disarray. And Bessie sobbing over the way she had beaten up Daniel.

'I try not tooo let my aaangerr get the betterrr of meee.' Bessie shivered, gratefully accepting the mug of coffee that Shelley brought her. She breathed in its fragrant steam and seemed to calm somewhat. 'In the past I . . . I did some terrrrible thiiingss, when I wasssn't in my riiight mind . . . When I was beeeing used and taken possession of . . .'

Liza and Shelley exchanged a swift glance. Who exactly *was* Bessie? What on earth were they sheltering here in the apartment?

'I'm sure that Daniel deserved the walloping you gave him,' Liza said decisively. 'As far as I'm concerned, that young man's been cruisin' for a bruisin' for weeks now.'

'I could heeear, in my closet,' said Bessie. 'Heee was going to huuurt Shelley. The things he was saying . . .'

'What was he saying?' Liza asked her niece sharply.

'Crazy stuff!' said Shelley. 'I was scared, actually. For his sanity as much as my safety, as it happens.'

Liza gazed ruefully at the ruined dining-room chair and the scattered books. A lamp she'd had for forty years was smashed and in pieces on the carpet. She sighed deeply. What was happening to her life? What had happened to her quiet evenings spent reading? Her days so mundane they merged blissfully into one?

Even Rufus the beagle was worried. He stood nearby, whimpering and looking out of his depth.

'I could have killed himmm,' said Bessie. 'He made me angry again. I do not want to beee angry again. Thiss is my neew life. I do not have to beee the monsterrr I wass . . .'

Aunt and niece nodded at her consolingly – though they had no idea what their guest was talking about.

Shelley told her, 'Your kicking his ass was most appreciated, Bessie. You have to believe that. And I'm sorry if the fight has disturbed you.'

'I have made a mess of my neeew friend Liza's home. I have broken thinngsss . . .'

'Don't you worry about that, sweetheart,' Liza said. 'Just a lamp. A chair. I've had worse brawls than that, I can tell you!' It was quite true, actually. She flashed back suddenly to a fracas between two novelist pals of hers, New Year's Eve before last. They were the worst, of course, novelists.

Bessie sipped her cooling coffee and regathered her thoughts. As she did so, Shelley was marvelling at her greater articulacy. Her lifelikeness. It was hard for her to credit that this was the same entity as the patchwork doll that she and Ruthie had set up as the centrepiece of their 'Women and Madness' exhibit, what felt like fifty years ago. Bessie still looked weathered and scrawny, but tonight there was a florid tinge to her cheeks. Her emerald eyes were sparkling with a fresh vitality. Whupping Daniel's skinny butt had clearly done her a lot of good.

Liza was trying to make light of the situation now. She was chuckling to herself and wondering aloud about what a fool Daniel must feel. He had fled into the Christmassy night, all battered and bleeding. Shamefaced – and so he should be. Heading back home feeling – undoubtedly – mighty sorry for himself. She said to Shelley, 'I reckon that'll be the last you see of him.'

Bessie looked up and made a strange noise in her throat. It was almost a growl. 'Oooh no. Yooou'll see him again. We will all see him again. Oooh . . . yesss. Thisss will not beee the end of it. Not by a looong chalk.'

'What do you mean, Bessie?' Shelley was disturbed by her tone.

'Heee and his kind dooo not give up so eeeasily.'

'His kind?' frowned Liza. 'You mean the English?'

Bessie shook her head, and her straw-like hair rustled. 'Surely yoou knoow. Heee is vampyr.'

Silence. Shelley and her aunt baulked and glared at the woman on the sofa.

'What!'

'Suuurely you kneew? He isss not a natural man? I thought youuu reaaaalised?'

They shook their heads, dumbfounded. Shelley was the more shocked. Aunt Liza felt something like sick dread seeping up through her very frame, soaking into her like cold wet slush through her winter boots. She had known this was coming. Known in her gut. None of this was natural. There had to be something behind it all. Daniel was a vampire. Of course he fricking was. Liza had seen all this before. She had been through these adventures and these dangers a long time ago. She sat down heavily in her reading chair and cursed aloud.

'I have seeen thisss many times, in many places,' said Bessie. 'I have fought them before. This scourge. Even here, in the future . . . your moderrrn wooorld . . . *they are here* . . . the agents of daaarkness . . .'

Shelley blinked and shook her head. 'Hang on. Let me get this straight. You're saying that Daniel, my Daniel . . . the reason he's been acting like he has . . . the reason for everything is that he's a vampire?'

Bessie looked up at her steadily. Those green eyes! Shelley found she had to look away.

'Of course. I amm sorrrry, Shelley. I could smell it on him. He reeeeks of it. Of ooold black blood. Coagulating inside of him. He isss undead. Did you not smell himm when he was here with youuu?'

Shelley pulled a face. She hardly liked to point out that Daniel smelled of nothing but citrus cologne compared with the Scottish Bride's brackish scent.

'He isss a powerful one,' said Bessie. 'I know that much. Heee is their prince.'

Shelley gasped. 'That's what he was saying! He was coming out with all this garbage about us being king and queen of New York City! He was talking about his followers . . .'

Bessie nodded. 'Heee will be making a nessst. He will have a hive. A swarm of converts.'

'Omigod,' said Shelley. She was thinking about the way her erstwhile shared apartment had been overrun by all those young people the other day. 'He's already started. He's building a gang!'

'What must we do, Bessie?' asked Liza, pragmatic as ever.

Bessie met her determined eye. 'There is an outbreak heeere in your New York City. An outbreak of ancient eeevil. And weee are all going to have to dooo something about it. That is why we are here, together. When there is eeevil like this, there are alwaaaays those best placed to fight it. And this is us.'

'Us?' said Shelley. 'What can we do?'

Bessie stood up stiffly and turned to gaze out at the snowy city. 'I was wooonderiiiing . . . And now I know. I have returned juuust in time. I am here to dooo battle with theeese forces of darkness and deeestruction. Again. Once again. And you both most help meee. We must work together and put a stop to theeese creatures of the endlessss night.

'Thiiss is why I was brought baaack to life. Thisss is my reeeason for being heeere.'

Chapter Eighteen

As Christmas approached, it seemed to Jack that the whole world had gone vampire-crazy.

Or is it just me? he wondered.

At work, there was a big push on vampire-related titles and series. Following the celebrations of various lurid and bloodily best-selling paranormal romances that season, Mr Grenoble had Jack rearranging the window displays. Fangtasm's festive windows were covered in fake snow and splattered blood. Daubing it on in full public view, Jack felt a little queasy.

But it wasn't just the world of literature and pulp fiction that was getting to him. It seemed that wherever he went, people were talking about vampires. He sat in coffee bars downtown on his hours away from work and picked up snippets of alarming gossip. People had disappeared. Others had been attacked and barely escaped with their lives. Some people had been bitten by strangers and were terrified, waiting to see what would happen.

There was something in the air. Something frightening and exciting all at the same time. As Jack listened to the whispers and the gossip, and kept his eyes on the local downtown papers and the news reports and the buzz on internet forums, he realised that it wasn't just straightforward fear that the denizens of his town were exhibiting. They were excited as well. There was a frisson of delicious, exotic terror about all of this. Real vampires . . . real danger . . .

Jack couldn't share in any of that excitement. He enjoyed them in fiction. He got off on the whole paranormal thing and loved the books they sold at Fangtasm. And it was a cool look, too, the vampire thing. But when any of that shit came close to real life – nuh-huh. He wanted nothing to do with it.

He thought about that early evening panic and crush in the subway station the other day, Liza grasping his arm as they were swallowed by the crowd. For a second, as screams had rung out, it had felt like there would be a stampede. He could see again that boy with the blood on his T-shirt and round his mouth. That foul slobber. Jack felt his throat tighten and his gorge rise at the very thought of someone else's blood. The very idea of drinking it, of feeling it warm and gushing in your mouth. Your teeth digging so sharply into another's skin that they pierced through, deep enough to puncture blood vessels. It made him shudder. It made him feel ill.

He didn't want to hear any more about it.

But at work, Mr Grenoble and Lame Wendy wouldn't stop going on about this outbreak of vampire gossip.

Tuesday evening and the boss was at the cash desk, crowing over the increase in sales. 'I tell you, it's very good for business.'

'It's a bit sick, though,' Jack said. 'Isn't it? When people are going missing and there's this sense of panic underneath everything . . .'

Lame Wendy shrugged and slurped out of a huge paper cup of

tea. 'I think it's all coming true. Everything outta the books that we sell. I knew it was all true. Creatures of the night. The undead. It all hadda be true, didn't it?'

Mr Grenoble smiled at her kindly. 'So long as profits are up and no one gets hurt, then who am I to complain?'

'But what if people *do* get hurt, Mr Grenoble?' said Jack.

The old man waved his hand disparagingly. 'It's a fad. A craze. It's just young people dressing up and enjoying themselves. Do you really think they're biting each other? Do you really believe in black magic, huh? All that jazz?'

'I do,' Lame Wendy said. 'Oh God, do I. I just wish one of them vampires would getta hold of me one of these days. I keep hearing the rumours, but I ain't seen nuthin' yet. Not a whiff of anything demonic.'

Jack stared at her. 'You'd better hope that it carries on like that. You don't really want to get into the supernatural, do you?'

Mr Grenoble chuckled and stepped down, wheezing arthritically, from the raised dais where the old desk stood. He looked at the two of them. 'You kids. What are you like? Getting so scared over silly things. The supernatural. Pah. You shouldda been around in my day. Then you would have had something to be frightened of. We had it hard in my day, oh yeah . . .' He went off mumbling, doing his last rounds of the shop before closing time.

'My girlfriends, they seen stuff,' Lame Wendy said to Jack, confidingly. 'Not when I was there. But they was out in the Village, and they got approached. By these pale boys. They said they was so pale and gorgeous. They was promising them the usual stuff, like dope and booze and a good time and stuff. But there was more to it.'

179

'What happened to them? They didn't go with them, surely?'

Lame Wendy laughed. 'Nah. They cried off, the babies. Wouldn't go off anywhere with them. Said they were creepy. Me? If I'd a been there, I'd a been gone in a flash with them guys. Pale boys. Whew. Yeah, I'd a been gone. But I guess they wouldna have wanted me, you think?'

Sometimes Jack felt sorry for Lame Wendy. She had a whining voice and sometimes went fishing for compliments or attention. Other times it was like life was passing her by even as she stood there. She was ready and up for anything, but life somehow went streaming by her day upon day and nothing new ever happened to her. Something about her hopefulness – and her hopelessness – touched a chord in Jack.

Today he just warned her, 'You be careful, Wendy. There are some strange guys out there.'

She smiled lopsidedly. 'Yeah, I'm in no danger, sweetie. Those creepy guys never come nowhere near me. More's the pity! They see me limpin' along and they run a freakin' mile!'

The lights shuddered and blinked. They were going out one by one, all around the shop. The effect was eerie, as Mr Grenoble turned off one source of antique lighting after another. Jack couldn't help shivering as the shop floor grew dimmer and shadows gathered round the book stacks.

'Good night, ladies and gentlemen! Good night!' Mr Grenoble was calling out as he did his rounds, as he had done almost every night of the forty years he had owned this shop, under its various names and specialisms. 'Good night all! We'll be open again tomorrow!'

It was more like a reading room in some ways, with all the cosy chairs and comfortable corners. Fangtasm's browers seemed to stay there longer than they did in any other bookstore Jack knew of. But did they buy enough? He knew that the boss was worried about how to keep open and going. It was difficult. That was why he welcomed this vampire fad as a bit of free publicity.

They closed the shop and said good night on the doorstep, watching Mr Grenoble locking up. The snow had settled thickly and was starting to fall again as Jack pulled up his collar and turned to go home.

He was met by Consuela. She was barrelling towards him, looking harried and unkempt. Jack was alarmed. He had never seen her in public looking less than immaculate.

'What is it?'

'It is Ricardo. He won't wake up. He has slept all afternoon. I thought he had a fever. I thought he needed his rest. But then when I went to wake him just now . . . he wouldn't respond. His breathing was shallow . . . I thought he was dead for a moment. His eyes are open, though. They're staring at the ceiling. But there is no life in him . . . Please, please, Jack. He will wake for you. I am sure he will. He loves you. I know. He loves his mamma too, but he will not stir. Please, come . . . come now, Jack . . .'

She wouldn't leave go of him as they stumbled along through the snowy streets. She hampered their progress with her clinging and her rambling words. Jack tried to be reassuring. He tried not to panic. He dragged them both back home to Thompson Street, where Ricardo was waiting, comatose on the sofa.

Oh God, Jack thought. Don't let it be true. Don't let it. *Please*.

Consuela stood there wringing her hands. 'Wake him. Wake him up. Bring him back to himself, Jack, can't you?'

Jack looked at his boyfriend and knew that he couldn't. He knew that something dreadful and profound had happened to Ricardo.

It seemed altogether more straightforward to Shelley simply to get on with things at work. Pretend like nothing had happened.

Oh yeah. That was easy.

Easy to turn up at the museum unflustered and immaculate. When her life was upside down and she was sleeping on her aunt's settee and there was an effigy called Bessie living in the hall closet. An effigy who had come to life and – oh yes – become her aunt's new best friend. And who had whupped her ex-boyfriend's ass. Oh yeah, easy.

And it was Christmas coming up. Everyone seemed so happy and pleased with themselves. Even those who looked harassed and stressed Shelley found herself envying this season. At least they had normal lives. At least they didn't have weird shit happening to them.

Oh God, Daniel.

What had happened to him?

The hardest thing was facing him at work the day after the famous ass-whupping episode.

What would he say? What could he possibly say?

Now he knew where Bessie had gone. Now he knew that she was alive. Somehow, mysteriously, impossibly, Bessie was alive. And dangerous. And round at Shelley's aunt's apartment.

Would Daniel land Shelley in trouble over this? Would he simply exact revenge for the ass-whupping by telling everyone where the Scottish Bride was to be found?

She went to work shaking that day. She felt sick to her stomach. She had to stop for a glass of warm milk in a coffee bar to settle her nerves.

But when she went into the museum at last, Daniel didn't say a word. He looked pale and angry when he spared her a glance, but he never alluded to the strange episode at Liza's place. Not in front of anyone else, and not when they were alone – brief though those moments turned out to be. He was clipping about on his exquisite hand-stitched shoes and ordering his staff around. Business was as usual.

Shelley took a deeply relieved breath. Maybe she'd get away with this.

Then she was fuming. *She* would get away with it? Wasn't it he who had attacked her? And all that strange talk he had come out with . . . all that garbage about the two of them becoming king and queen of the city . . . Why, it was he who should be worried, wasn't it? What if she started telling people about the weird stuff he was getting into?

Ah. That was it. He depended on her quiet, just as she did his. At least for now. Here at work they were suspended in a kind of complicity. She hated the feeling. She hated his smug, sly looks and his insinuating glances.

He knew the Bride was alive. He knew where she was holed up.

Shelley looked at the empty plinth in the main hall of the museum and she felt guilty. When she saw the posters and the T-shirts in Ruthie's gift shop, she felt guilty and alarmed all over again. Bessie had become a big deal for the museum. She might just have given them a bit more hope in these days of financial troubles. The queues had been good to see. The board and the trustees had been pleased by the surprise success of that twiggy, wretched-looking woman.

But Bessie wasn't content to be an exhibit all her life. She had changed too much for that. She was here in New York for a reason, just like she'd told them the other night – in her moment of lucidity and epiphany in Liza's flat. She was here to do battle with evil.

Oh, brother.

'Hey, doll,' said Ruthie. 'So what's up with you and lover boy?'

Shelley gave her a watery smile. Ruthie already knew the bare bones of the tale. She knew that Shelley had moved out of Daniel's place – scant days after moving in. Yeah, she'd moved in too quickly. She was foolish. Staking too much on him.

I hardly knew him, she thought. I know him even less now. He's completely crazy. But she couldn't say any of that to Ruthie. 'It's gonna be a great Christmas,' she sighed. 'It's all my own fault, though. I was so keen to have a boyfriend. To move in.' She winced. 'And dating the boss, too. That's a terrible thing to do.'

Ruthie grinned at her. 'He make any trouble for you here and I'll sort him out. You'll see.'

'Thanks, Ruthie.' Shelley smiled weakly, and went back to her tiny office upstairs. She knew that she was holding out on Ruthie. Ruthie knew there was more to this than met the eye and she had given her friend every chance to confide in her. But Shelley hadn't. There was no way she could even start to explain her various predicaments.

Ruthie watched her go, feeling sad for her, and also as though her friendly gesture had been spurned.

In her office, Shelley toyed again with the idea of building a new Scottish Bride. Maybe get just some chicken wire and plaster of Paris . . . Who did she know who was good at handicrafts? Who could be relied upon to keep their mouth shut?

Oh, it was hopeless. They would never make a perfect replica. No one would be fooled. As far as the museum was concerned, Bessie was gone for ever. It would just have to stay a mystery.

There was a knock at her door. Daniel.

'Y-yes?'

He grinned at her. 'I could make things so much easier for you.'

'What?'

'I can see you, holding back the panic. You're up to your neck in it, Shelley. You don't know what to do.'

'Shut up.'

'There's all this stuff happening around you, Shelley. Weird stuff. Dark stuff. Magical stuff. And you don't know what any of it means, do you? You don't know what's happening at all.'

She ground her teeth together and wished she could block out the sound of his voice. That seductive purr. 'I don't have to put up with this. You're my boss, but you don't own me.'

'We're still lovers, Shelley,' he said. 'We always will be. We are fated to be together.'

'Go away! I mean it, Daniel. I'll . . .'

'You'll what?' He laughed at her. 'I really could make all the panic stop, you know. Everything that seems terrifying right now, or confusing . . . I could clear it *all* up.' He clicked his fingers in her face. 'Like that. I could make everything quite straightforward.'

'H-how?'

'I could give you everything you ever wanted. Just like that.'

Now she was looking up into his face. In the pearly mid-afternoon light, she could see the mark that Bessie's hand had left on his cheek. His flesh had an unnatural, greyish tinge to it.

'You can't give me anything,' she burst out, breaking the momentary spell.

He withdrew, laughing. 'You'll see, Shelley. You'll come running, soon enough.' Then he turned and left her alone in her office.

Chapter Nineteen

It was true. Consuela had been quite right. Ricardo looked dead.

This wasn't natural sleep. It didn't look restful.

'I hate him like this,' his mother hissed to Jack. 'He is such a sweet boy. He was always a good boy. He would come to me and hug me when I was upset, when none of his brothers and sisters would. When they were too old or too busy with themselves to notice how their mother was going through hard times. Only Ricardo saw. He was always close to me . . . too close, perhaps. And now to see him like this . . .'

'I-I don't know what to do,' Jack whispered. He felt pathetic. Useless. Could they lug him downstairs, down the fire escape? Could they carry him, swaddled in bedclothes, to the emergency room? But what would they say when they got him there? How would they explain that they were worried about him, and what he had become?

He was sleeping very steadily and still, with his limbs too straight and tidy. He was grinning in his sleep as if he could see something hilarious in his dreams. There was something savage in that grin, as well. Something feral.

Consuela was looking at Jack in the dim light that came

through the bedroom blinds from the street outside. Because the snow was still falling, it gave the shadows a grainy, shifting appearance. Consuela was in black and white all of a sudden, and a guilty pang in Jack's chest had him wishing that he was watching this on a screen somewhere. That this was some cheesy old scary film and it wasn't happening in his bedroom at all.

'This is a demon's work, isn't it?' Consuela said. 'I know this now. I have been avoiding it. Thinking he is just ill. It is something that will pass. But this . . . the way he is today. This is some evil spirit that is in him. This is magic.'

Jack looked at her and couldn't say anything. He knew through Ricardo that she had history with magic and deep beliefs in the supernatural. In a way he was amazed she hadn't started going on about it sooner. Now he could see that she had dreaded giving a supernatural explanation to Ricardo's plight.

'I think . . . there is no cure for this,' she said. 'No way out. We simply have to look after him the best we can . . .'

At last Jack found his voice. 'But what is he? What has he turned into?'

They both knew the answer to that one. They looked at each other and neither said the word.

The two of them ate desultorily that night. Consuela put together two plates of leftovers from the fridge, and they sat before the evening news with the volume turned down. Jack sat on his couch, resting on the heap of neatly folded bedclothes and pillows where Consuela would later make up her bed. On the evening news there was talk of strange attacks, several maimings, worsening weather conditions – and further disappearances. Young people simply leaving their homes and vanishing. Leaving the outlying districts and suburbs and last seen heading for the city. For the middle of the island. Not enough to call it an epidemic or a crisis, but enough to make the evening news. They were being drawn to something. And they weren't going home again . . .

Consuela said, 'Whatever happens, we mustn't let him leave us. We can't. I can't lose him. I have lost my other babies. Only Ricardo stayed. I will not let him go. Whatever is going on here . . . they can't take him from me . . .'

Jack gave her a watery smile. Now he felt utterly trapped.

When it came time for him to go to bed, he felt weird climbing in with Ricardo. He thought about staying away. About maybe cowering in the living room with Consuela, sleeping in a chair. But he couldn't do it. Something drew him to Ricardo's side. Even though he was freaked out by the way Ricardo was, and the whole thing scared him, he knew he still had to lie in that bed beside him. *Just in case.*

He crawled in under the covers, wearing his boxers, and gave a little jump as Consuela's head peeped round the door. 'Good night, sweet dreams, my boys,' she hissed.

Jack wasn't at all happy about being looked at in bed like this, right next to his comatose boyfriend. But then what was he to do?

Soon it was quiet. As he lay in the dark, he could actually hear Ricardo's slow, easy breathing. It was reassuring. More like normal.

The stress had made Jack tired. No sooner had he stretched out and thought to himself that sleep would never come, he was under. It felt like a great weight simply rolled over him, squashing him into submission.

He dreamed that Ricardo woke. Easily, naturally, and with a huge, hungry yawn. It was early, bright morning and the snow had stopped. The sky was a wonderful cornflower blue, and Ricardo rolled over to take Jack in his arms. He hugged him so hard that all the breath was squashed out of him. Pleasurably, thrillingly. Jack felt himself waking up and coursing with life and energy. The whole length of their bodies was pressed hard one against the other, and as Ricardo pushed him over till he was in the uppermost position, Jack marvelled again at how they seemed to fit each other so perfectly. When they lay like this, they couldn't even have swiped a credit card anywhere between them. They would stay like this, pressed tight, until limbs went numb and buzzing and it became hard to tell which bit belonged to who.

Jack turned over in his sleep, grumbling with contentment. His dreams spooled on, becoming more involved. Dirtier.

His movements woke Ricardo for real.

Ricardo sat up abruptly. He basked in the warm darkness of the room, the stifled air. His grin never faded for a moment. He spared a quick glance at Jack, but that was all, before he slipped out of bed and picked up the first items of clothing he came across. Some dirty jeans, a vest top, a hoodie. He slipped them on with smooth, fluid movements.

In the living room, he didn't stop to do anything more than pick up his shoes.

He was on his way out. He scooped up his leather jacket. His key was in his hand as he headed for the door. There was no time to waste. His heart was thumping heavily in his chest. A bass line, a tempo, a greedy need to get out there.

Consuela was watching him through a crack in her heaped bedclothes. All night she had lain awake, waiting for this moment, which she knew must come. The digital clock on the wall said it was exactly two a.m.

With her eyelids barely open and her own heart beating fit to burst with fear, she watched her son glance around the room. She stayed as still as she could.

He was still grinning.

He unlocked the door, flung it open, letting in the howling sounds of the wind and the sirens out there in unsafe New York City. Then his heels were ringing out loudly on the iron steps of the fire escape. He let the door slam shut behind him and he was off.

But Consuela wasn't letting him get away with that.

Under her bedclothes she was still fully dressed. She had a heavy shawl wrapped around her daytime clothes, and her stoutest shoes were still on her feet.

Feeling woozy as the indoor air mixed with the freezing night wind, she crossed the room without a thought. She opened the door and propelled herself outside after her son. She didn't pause long enough to question herself or to let the fear take a hold of her.

She just had to follow him, as best she could.

She wouldn't let him out of her sight.

The small woman bustled along in the snow. She drew her outer clothes around her till she was looking out of a narrow slit, but still the cold air stung her face. She was dogged, however, keeping that boy of hers within her sights.

The streets were mostly empty. A few taxis whizzed back and forth in the slushy snow, but she saw very few people roaming about. Never had she seen the city so emptied out, and that only added to this horrible feeling of unreality. The whole place had become an inhospitable backdrop for this strange powerplay between mother and son.

Yes, powerplay – because there was a psychological dimension to this. He knew she was here, hard on his heels, pushing and panting along on the icy surface, trying to keep up with him. Buffeted and assailed on all sides by the knifing wind, Consuela kept tottering onwards. Ricardo was only about twenty metres ahead. He seemed to glide effortlessly. She even took a weird kind of pride in the way he sailed into the dark. And she knew he knew she was behind him. Several times he glanced backwards, and she got a glimpse of his pale skin, his flashing eyes.

He didn't increase his pace. He didn't dash away or try to give her the slip. He knew she was pursuing him through the city streets, and he let her continue. She didn't wonder why. She was just glad she was allowed to keep pushing forward like this, snow caked ever thicker on her stout shoes, her face numb with the oncoming blizzard.

The streets were busier north of 42nd Street. Even in the darkest hours, the skies were pink with light pollution, like a fake approaching dawn. There were more people about, and the day was on the brink of starting up. Eighth Avenue swirled with snowy vortices of litter and wind. It was almost as if things were normal. Consuela felt less peculiar; less locked into some nightmarish fairy tale.

Still her son ploughed on ahead, a slim, sure silhouette in his leather jacket. She felt pride and fear. Those were the ways sons always made you feel – but now the feelings were multiplied hundredfold.

Once or twice, when there were other people around, she found words bursting out of her: 'Ricardo, my son! Come back! Someone stop him!' But he didn't look backwards on those occasions, and no one else took any notice. A man carrying a whole split pig from a van into a building dodged around her, and she was flustered for a moment, thinking she had lost her son. But there he was, one block ahead and still heading north.

At last they came to Daniel's apartment, though Consuela had no knowledge of who it belonged to, or why Ricardo should be going there. She simply followed him to his destination, and here it was, in this smart part of town. She knew the apartments here were very expensive. She had cleaned here years ago, in these streets by the park.

Ricardo let himself in at the front door and left it obligingly open for her. He really wanted her to follow him.

She stepped with infinite caution into the clutch of shadows in the hallway beyond.

If I die, I die, she thought. Anyone could jump out and get me here. But if I die, at least I have tried, I have done my best for my son.

There was a strange tangy scent in the stone-floored hallway. It grew stronger as she went into the stairwell. Ricardo's hurried footsteps rang out around her. He was going to the very top, up flight after flight of granite steps. Her strength was almost gone.

The front door clanged shut behind her. The noise made her jump.

Up she toiled after him.

And in the apartment at the very top of the building, she found the nest.

'Hello?' she croaked, stepping through the open door. Here, that smell was dense and rank. She recognised it now. The same coppery tang as the slaughterhouse where she'd once worked. Another terrible job she had held down. There, you soon got used to the heavy scent of death. Here, in these luxurious surroundings – all this fine furniture and these smart pictures – it was incongruous. Obscene.

There were young people here. In the messy disarray of the apartment they lolled about the place, on sofas and rugs. For a moment she thought she had wandered into some strange party as it wound down, with everyone too exhausted to even move and go home. But she knew that wasn't it. These people were like animals . . . like a pride of lions, seeking solace and company together in the night. How many? Twenty, thirty of them, crammed into this space?

Heads went up, looking at her with sleepy insolence. They marked her shambling progress into the room. There was a low buzz of attention, somewhere a snicker of laughter.

Ricardo was there, in the kitchen. She called to him.

'Nightcap, Mamma?' he asked.

She saw the bleached corpse on the kitchen table. A young woman laid out with her veins gouged open. A variety of kitchen bowls catching the drips as if from a leaky faucet. They were siphoning her off and it was plain she had been dead for some time. Ricardo was holding out a bowl of her dark blood.

'Oh nooo,' Consuela moaned. She shrank away from him. Her

limbs turned to water. It was as if up till now she had been pretending things could be all right. It might all be some horrible mistake. She had followed her son in order to find out that she was quite wrong in her nasty suppositions. Now she saw that he had allowed her to follow because he wanted her to know the truth.

She watched him lap like a cat from the bowl that brimmed with the dead girl's blood.

Then she saw that her son's friends had crawled out of their corners of the room and come to see.

And then they grabbed her.

Chapter Twenty

It was the absence of noise that woke Jack.

He had grown so used to nights in his apartment with Consuela bustling about, making hot drinks, tuning in the TV to obscure channels to watch soap operas in the middle of the night . . . The complete absence of all nocturnal commotion woke him some time before dawn.

Also, Ricardo was gone. That was more normal these days. He came and went as he pleased, and Jack was hardly aware of his movements. There was nothing in between that coma with its rictus grin and his complete absence. Ricardo was out in the city somewhere, and Jack was preparing to face the day alone.

When he saw that Consuela was also missing, his heart started hammering. He knew at once that she had gone after Ricardo. She was caught up with him somewhere. And Jack had let them both down by sleeping through it all. Her blankets on the sofa were mussed and her reading glasses and her recent novels were scattered on the rug. She had lumbered out of bed in a hurry, knocking over a glass of something milky.

Jack stood still, unsure of what to do.

He filled the kettle, letting the drumming noise soothe his

nerves for a moment. He had to think clearly. He had to think straight. Ricardo would never hurt his own mother, he was sure of that. Whatever state he was in, whatever bad stuff he was into, he would never let Consuela come to any harm – would he?

Jack looked into the opaque blackness of the window above the sink. He searched for his own reflection, but couldn't find it. His heart leapt as an incandescent swirl of light took form in the glass. It was like cream being stirred into coffee . . . dissolving into cloud shapes . . . And he saw . . .

He saw Daniel's apartment, across town. It was as if his own window looked straight into Daniel's. But that was surely impossible. This was a kind of stress-induced hallucination . . . a waking nightmare . . .

But it was quite true. It was real. He recognised the print of the wallpaper, the large pictures on the walls. Some kind of party seemed to be in progress. Jack frowned and drew closer . . . and gasped at what he saw.

There were lots of strangers congregated in Daniel's living room. Young people – fit and lithe and wearing hardly a stitch. They were engaged in all sorts of depraved stuff, Jack suddenly realised. They were having sex in all kinds of combinations – rough, savage sex. And some were feeding on each other. There was blood running across limbs and chests, and rubbed in people's faces and hair. It was one great tangle of bloody flesh, laying waste to Daniel's living room.

And then Jack saw Consuela, caught up in the middle of this scene of Dionysian ritual. She was holding what looked like her worry beads up to her face, kissing them and staring at the floor.

Ricardo was holding her by the scruff of her neck. He had her arms locked behind her in his own strong grip, and Jack saw that he was laughing fit to burst. That same leering expression on his face.

Consuela was shouting out now, and screaming. Her mouth was a large black O with no sound coming out.

Daniel was there. Looking calm and in command. He walked towards the young man and his mother. He spread his arms to welcome the old lady, as if he expected her to run to him, for solace or succour. Ricardo pushed Consuela towards Daniel, roughly, flat-handed, and laughed as she staggered.

Daniel's hand shot out and grasped at the beads and the crucifix around the woman's neck. She shrieked and writhed, falling to her knees.

Jack watched as she was shaken and rattled like a bag of rubbish, or an unwanted present on Christmas Eve.

They were going to kill her. He knew it now. They were going to slash her and drain her of blood before his very eyes.

He fumbled for the phone. Gripping it with both hands, he still almost dropped it. He called the police and it wasn't until they connected him with someone calm, insistent and ready to take down details that he realised he was reporting an incident that he was seeing in some kind of mystical vision. How was he going to explain that to the forces of law and order?

As he gabbled into the receiver, describing what he was seeing, that very image was starting to fade. It swirled again, like the cream dissolving and fading into the dark coffee. The last lingering impression was of all those young people leaving their enjoyments and clustering around Consuela. They were hemming her in, and in her eyes it was obvious that she knew there was no mistake. She was like a mouse caught in a nest of vipers. Jack saw the hope burning fiercely in her eyes – and then it started to fade as the circle tightened and the vision all but vanished from the window pane.

'Sir? Sir?' That urgent voice on the phone brought him to his senses.

There was no use trying to explain all of this. They would never believe it. Keep it simple, he thought. Focus on what's important. He gave them Daniel's address. He told them to send someone round immediately. He gave a hint as to what he thought was going on. He found himself saying something about a 'blood sex black magic ritual', and realised what an idiot he sounded. He added that he believed that a senior citizen was in terrible danger.

That call finished quickly, with the switchboard lady promising prompt action (but did she mean it? Had he come across too much like just another freak? Just how believable had he sounded, giving details like that down the phone line?). Then he phoned Liza's number. Shelley needed to know what was going on in her apartment.

It was more than that, though. He needed their help. Those women on Second Avenue. They just had to help him with this.

The phone rang twice, and then there was a rustling sound as someone picked up the receiver.

'Yeessssss?' said a voice Jack didn't recognise at all. 'Thiissss iss Lizzza's home. Caan I heeelp?'

'Yes, yes please. Is Liza there? Or Shelley?'

'Yeess, they are both stilll sleeeeping . . .'

'Could you wake them, please? This is an emergency.'

'Could I aasssskk whooo is calllling?'

'This is Jack, Liza's friend. I'm a good friend. She knows me. She won't mind me phoning at this hour.'

'I have nevvvver answered the telephone beforrrrre,' said the strange woman's voice. 'Where arrreee youuu? Arrrre you faaar?'

Jack was impatient – and a bit disturbed by now at the peculiar voice. 'Look, who is this?'

'I ammm Bessssie. Wait a moment, Jaaaaack. Lizzzaaaa is heeeere . . .'

Thank Christ, Jack thought. Liza at least he could rely on. This night was getting more horrible by the minute.

It was light when they eventually let her go.

She knew that they had merely been playing with her. Had these young people wanted, they could have taken her life in a flash. She saw they had no qualms about death. The apartment was sticky with blood, and there were body parts in the kitchen, as if some messy cannibalistic chef had been given free rein.

They toyed with her, nipping at her playfully and pushing her about.

Consuela screeched and howled, but she never begged. Some deep-seated pride in her wouldn't be broken, even by a scene as terrible as this. Battered and bloody, she refused to give up. Only one thing brought her close, and that was the fact that her beloved son Ricardo was one of this pack of jackals. The way he grabbed her and shook her and pushed her into the foul embrace of these creatures . . . all of this quietly broke her heart, but she tried to keep that inside her. She couldn't give in to despair. Not yet.

And then they let her go. She bored them.

She hastened towards the stone staircase, the first moment she could make her way to the door. The young people were losing interest, turning to each other again and carrying on with their filthy activities. The wide room was filling with pale, snowy morning light, which made it seem even more hellish and foul. It walls and furnishings were streaked with darkening gore.

Consuela took her chance and fled. Her legs shook as she hurried down the stairwell. Her insides had liquefied. She attempted a quick inventory of herself as she bowled along, and realised she had incurred only flesh wounds. They had slashed and nipped at her. They need me alive, she thought. For something. They want to use me for something . . . but what?

It was like wading through molasses in a dream. She was shaking so much she couldn't move as quickly as she wanted.

Could she pound on any of the other apartment doors? Didn't the neighbours know what was going on in their very own building? True, it wasn't particularly noisy. In fact it had been eerily quiet, given the number of people involved in that macabre orgy.

Images were burned on to Consuela's retinas. Images from hell that she knew she would never forget. She had heard of these things from priests and read accounts in her studies of the Bible. Tonight, she thought, I have seen a true hell on earth, here in our city. And my son has found his place there.

But she wouldn't think of that now. She was out. She couldn't afford to cave in. She needed help. Who could help with a thing such as this? Who was qualified?

Since moving out of her last home, she had cut off contact with her own community and the protection of her small church and padre. There had been ructions, and there was bad blood there. He was too liberal, too modern. But I need his protection now, she thought.

From the top landing there was a rustling and a rushing noise.

Hurried footfalls on the stone. Giggling.

They are coming after me, Consuela thought wildly.

But aren't you creatures of the night? Shouldn't you lie down to sleep now that dawn is here?

The stairwell was drenched in a wonderful pearly glow from the skylight straight above. It felt like God's own holy gaze staring down at them. But it didn't deter the young people at all.

Consuela picked up her skirts, sobbing, and ran.

She reached the bottom of the stairs, flung open the door and staggered outside.

She left great blotches of dark blood on the thick snow as she loped down the street. But no one saw her. There was no one about yet, which felt terrible and wrong, as if her own nightmare had taken over the whole city. As if she had slipped sideways into a world that contained only her and the creatures who were using her as a plaything.

She glanced backwards and saw a gaggle of the young people coming after her. Not especially hurried. Not even trying. Just coming after her, assured of getting what they wanted out of her.

Consuela's lungs and heart were bursting in her chest. All of her organs were swelling up, it seemed, and crushing the life out of her from within.

She had a vague plan about getting to the park. Surely there would be more people there. Policemen on horses, traffic heading uptown and down. Early walkers and joggers. Yes, she could hear the noise. The welcome susurration of city sounds . . . She made towards it. Using every scrap of energy she had left, she staggered onwards on her aching feet.

She thought about Daniel. Their leader. Their prince, they called him. He referred to himself loftily, with no irony, as the King of New York. She had shrunk from his embrace. He had taken her in his arms and they'd all laughed as he'd kissed her, lingering over the crêpey flesh of her neck and her bosom. She was mortified, lying there in his strong arms, under their mocking, wicked eyes.

'Yes, we are a plague, Consuela,' he had laughed at her. 'An infection. A pestilence. Just as your good book always promised. We are what happens when mankind doesn't clean up its ways.'

She had bitten her tongue until it bled. She wouldn't speak with him. To engage in conversation with the devil was a way to let him in. He'd find the tiny hairline cracks in your resolve. He would work his way into your good heart. He would toy with your words and make you believe all kinds of terrible things. Consuela would not speak with Daniel if she could help it, because she firmly believed this was the devil before her, in the form of this handsome man. This kind of embrace she should feel safe inside. For years she had toiled alone and wondered one day about being held like this again by a man. She had secretly longed for it.

But now it came like this. Being taunted and rocked in the arms of Satan.

'We have our own book. Would you like to see? This grimoire. Our little black book. Our magic book. Isn't it beautiful, Consuela? Have you ever heard of such a thing? Blessings on Liza Bathory, who made all this possible. Who brought us the grimoire from England.'

The other young people took up these words as a chant. 'Blessings on Liza Bathory,' they intoned. They said the name again and again. Somehow it rang a tiny, furtive bell in Consuela's mind.

'This book tells of the past, but also tells what will happen here,' Daniel said. 'And you are mentioned, Conseula. You and your son are part of this splendid renaissance in modern New York. Imagine that, my dear! You are written about, in a book from many years ago. See? You are important, after all. You thought you were just nothing. A cleaner. A money-grubbing peasant. An elderly whore atoning for her many sins by shuffling along earning a pittance in the twilight of her years. Let down by life, battered and bruised. Relying on her faggot son and his nasty boyfriend for charity. With nothing and no one left to love. Tolerated. Homeless. You thought that was all you were, didn't you, Consuela?'

'No . . .' she moaned. Then jammed her mouth shut. Don't say a word. This is how Beelzebub taunts you. He forces you to speak. This mockery is to cajole a response from you.

Daniel laughed and stroked her wiry hair. Then he wrenched her tresses free of their habitual bun. 'But I know there is more to you than that. I have read the chapters in the unholy grimoire that deal with these days. And you are mentioned, Consuela. You are the mother of Ricardo, one of our most beloved sons. You have a wonderful and wicked role to play here.'

She wriggled and wrenched free of his grasp.

'And you will play that role, Consuela. You're the old bitch who suckled one of our most beloved princes. You fed him venom and bile with your mother's milk. You nursed this wickedness into

204

him. You are responsible, in part, for the beautiful horror that will take over this city . . .'

Daniel was overcome with mirth at this point. He threw her to the sticky carpet and she felt broken glass in her palms and knees. It was then, picking herself up, that she saw her moment for escape. No one was coming to save her. Like so often in her life, she would have to save herself. And so, seizing her moment, she fled.

Now she was coming up to the park, somewhere near the Natural History Museum. And yes, there was traffic noise and people. I look like a crazy lady. A woman living rough, she thought. Will anyone listen to me?

She stood in the street and shrieked like a siren. 'Don't let them get me! Please!'

People heard, and some came running to help. She realised how desperate she must look. She sagged into their arms and felt helpless and hopeless. They took her away to be looked after.

But she knew that those young people were still at her back. Watching from the street corner. Waiting.

Chapter Twenty-One

Jack took a deep breath and knocked hard on Liza's door. He was holding out a paper bag of pastries he had brought for breakfast, and it was sweating damply in his hand. He was nervous. He knew that it was time to tell his friends what had been happening with Ricardo. It was time to seek help, and it made him nervous. What if they thought he was crazy when he told his tale?

He needn't have worried.

Liza and her niece were dealing with even weirder stuff themselves on the other side of that reinforced apartment door, as Jack was just about to find out. His revelations would – if not pale into insignificance – soon seem a little less impossibly outrageous.

Liza opened the door and stared at him. She was blinking in the harsh light of the corridor, looking older than Jack had ever seen her. 'Ah,' she said, taking the chain off the door. 'Now, you're not a screamer, are you?'

As he shuffled past, Jack didn't know how to take that. He felt vaguely offended, and he caught his reflection in her hall mirror. He looked as rough and tired as his hostess did. She took the pastries from him and led him to her main living area, scooting past the tottering stacks of paperbacks and bundles of paper on the way.

'I mean, dear, you aren't going to overreact or anything, are you?' she said. 'We're trusting you.'

'Trusting me?' Jack thought he had come here to enlist help for dealing with his own living nightmare.

Apparently not.

Shelley was in the messy living room, looking like hell. She smiled an awkward hello. On the sofa sat a third woman. A tall, thin woman Jack didn't know. She looked the most unkempt of the three, with hair sticking out in all directions and a strange dress hanging in tatters from her bony frame.

Liza fussed with coffee mugs at the breakfast bar. 'Jack, I believe you talked already with Bessie, over the phone earlier?' For a moment she sounded absurdly like her cocktail party self, cheerily making introductions as she saw to refreshments.

'Er, yeah . . .' said Jack. He looked straight into the seated woman's weathered face and felt his pulse rate skyrocket. He stared into her fathomless eyes – which returned his stare full force and made his own eyes tear up immediately. 'Oh my God,' he said quietly.

'Bessie has moved in with Aunt Liza for a while,' explained Shelley wearily. 'She had nowhere else to go.'

'But . . .' Jack began. He looked rapidly from niece to aunt and back again. Liza scooted calmly out of the kitchen alcove with a tray of coffee things. 'But . . .'

'It isss a pleasssuuuure to meeeet youuu, Jaaack,' said the ancient woman on the sofa. She held out a twiggy hand for shaking. Jack took it and tried not to recoil from its brittleness and the creaking noise it made as he gingerly squeezed. 'I haaave heard sooo much about yoooou from myyy neeew frienddss.'

Now that Jack looked, it was obvious that the ruined dress she was wearing was a bridal gown. A yellowy-grey, sea-stained, rat-nibbled wedding dress God knew how many centuries old. This couldn't be. It couldn't be happening. But even as he struggled with his next sentence, with all three women looking at him so expectantly, he knew that it was.

'Hello,' he said to Bessie. He tried to sound as polite and normal as possible. 'We haven't met. But I have seen you before. In the museum.'

'Oohhh?' said Bessie calmly, reaching for her own coffee. She held the mug under her pointed nose, basking in the warm steam as if it could revitalise her terribly dry skin.

Jack felt a note of panic creep into his voice. 'Yes, sure. I saw you in the Museum of Outsider Art where you were on display as an exhibit! And you were just a dummy, and an effigy, and you weren't making social calls and answering the phone! Shelley . . .' He glared at her beseechingly. 'What's going on here?'

Bessie looked thoughtful, and just a touch melancholy. 'Aaah, you saaaw meee then, did yooou, Jack? Thaat waaasss before I came baaack to liiiife.'

'Right,' he said.

'Jack,' Liza broke in. 'It turns out that Bessie isn't just some effigy after all.'

'Okay,' he said. 'I can see that now.'

'Yes,' smiled Liza with enforced brightness. 'She's a delightful new companion.' Just then there came a muffled barking from Liza's bedroom. Rufus had evidently heard Jack's now familiar voice when he raised it, and despite the presence of the Scottish Bride, the dog wanted out.

'He can't come in here,' Liza explained, motioning Jack to sit. 'Every now and then he goes wild around Bessie. He tried to pull her arm off yesterday.'

'I haaave neeevver beeen good with animaaals,' said Bessie sadly.

Shelley looked at her, 'Never mind. Rufus will get used to you. Hey, your speech is getting better, you know. You're slurring a little less.'

'I ammm waaarming up,' Bessie agreed. 'The oooold sineeews and tisssssues are filling up with liiife. Soooon I will beeee back at fullll streennngth.'

Jack was studying her carefully, from afar. 'You're amazing,' he said. 'Are you really saying that you lay desiccated and in hibernation deep under the museum for years and years?'

'I believe sooo, Jaaack. I rememberrr sooo little . . .' Her face squinched up with concentration. 'Greeeat patches of my memory stilll seem to beeee coming to liiife. I rememberrr being in the seaaaa . . . after . . . yeesss, a shipwreck . . . I was float-innnng, floaaating for sooo long . . .'

Liza looked at her sharply, listening with keen interest. This was a detail of her story that Bessie hadn't brought out before. Quite probably it was just returning to her now. Her voice was quaking as she told them about the deep cold of the Atlantic.

'I believed I would sinnnk to the bottommm of the ocean, and that would beeee it for me. But . . . there was a hoook in my back. Someone took hoooold of meee and dragged me back to the surffface . . . They thought I waaaas a reeeal woman. They were

209

disappointed and horrified whennn they saaaw that I waaasss not. I was lucky that thossse sailors didn't simply throw meeee back intooo the freeezing waaaaves . . .' Bessie blinked her flaking eyelids hard. The images she was recalling suddenly faded, and she smiled at her audience benignly. 'Seee? A little mooore of my paasst returns every hooour, every daaay that I aaam awake.'

Jack was simply staring at her in amazement.

Shelley prompted him gently. 'So, Jack. You called in the middle of the night. Bessie said you sounded alarmed. What's been going on?'

He rubbed his face with both hands. 'Oh God. It's been horrible. I should have told you all earlier. I should have asked for help. I can't cope with this by myself.'

'All right,' said Shelley. 'Tell us.'

Liza scooted off to the kitchen again. 'I'll fetch those pastries you brought. And more coffee.'

'Tell us what's happened, Jack?' Shelley urged.

'Okay,' he said, gratefully.

He felt sure that if they could take the revivification of Bessie in their stride, then Liza and Shelley would have no problem in believing what had been happening round at his place lately.

When he had finished telling them, Liza wanted to go straight to Daniel's apartment.

'This old dame! We can't just leave her to them!' Liza looked stricken. 'My God, imagine running after your son like that and encountering . . .'

'But the vision I had,' said Jack. 'Was it true? Was I just dreaming, or am I going crazy or what?'

'I don't know,' said Liza. 'Did it seem real?'

'Very.'

'Have you had visions before?'

He shook his head.

Shelley had her head in her hands, sitting forward on the sofa. 'Oh God. I feel responsible for this.'

Her aunt tossed her head impatiently. 'You always feel responsible. I blame the way your mother treated you as a child. Why are you responsible?'

'I should have said something earlier,' she said. 'About Daniel. And what he's been like.'

'You mean he's been holding satanic orgies regularly for a while?' Liza snapped.

'No, that's all quite recent,' said Shelley.

'Yoouuu mustn't blammme yourseeelf,' said Bessie, patting her with twiggy fingers. 'The magic has got itsss hoookss into your mannn. I have seeen this before.'

'He wanted us to be King and Queen of New York City,' Shelley sobbed. 'He wanted me to be his vampire queen.'

Liza looked scandalised. 'I can see you've been leaving out a few details in the stories you've been telling me about recent events, young lady!'

'I'm sorry, Aunt Liza. I was just so embarrassed. I mean, I figured that he had to be crazy, right? And there was I, I'd moved in with him, thinking he was so great . . .'

'The vampire thing is real,' said Jack. 'Even before Ricardo, there were clues. There were stories downtown, and in the Village. It wasn't just some drag fad, some dressing-up thing. And then – we saw that boy, didn't we, Liza? In the subway. Covered in blood.

We both said the same thing then. Vamps. Real vamps. Here in the city.'

There was a prolonged silence between them as they stared at each other.

'Ohh deeaar,' said Bessie. 'It'sss a goood job you haaave meee heeere with yooouuu.' She flexed her noisy limbs and treated them to a ghoulish smile.

Jack didn't find her words at all reassuring.

Suddenly his phone bleeped. He took the call without thinking, and all at once Consuela's voice was filling his head – gabbling, panicking, spilling out of her near hysterically. Half of what she said was in Spanish; the other half made no sense at all.

'Calm down, please . . . Slow down, Consuela, and tell me . . .'

The others watched him nodding and squinching up his face in concentration. A few moments later he was finished. 'She's okay. She's at my place. The police took her home.'

'Thank God she's alive,' Shelley said. 'What are the police doing?'

'She says they're going to Daniel's. They're taking her complaint seriously.'

'Good!' said Liza. 'It all happened, then? Just as you saw in your vision?'

He gave a troubled nod. 'Seems like it.' He looked at his watch. 'It's almost eight.' Outside there was proper daylight now. The city's silhouette through Liza's tall windows looked like flats on a theatre set. That's what you got up here, uptown, Jack thought. Light and air and a sense of the scale. But he had to return downtown, to his tiny apartment. He had to console his boyfriend's mother and get her to seek medical attention. Why hadn't the police taken her to the emergency room? Wasn't she hurt physically at all? 'I'd better go,' he said. 'I've gotta be at work too today.'

Liza rode down in the elevator with him in order to fetch her mail. She was expecting some important stuff. 'Pay cheques. If I don't get 'em today, I'll be screwed all over Christmas.' She mugged, trying to make him laugh at her double entendre.

He appreciated her attempt at levity, but sighed deeply. 'What are we getting into, Liza? Both Shelley's boyfriend and mine are vampires, aren't they?'

'Sure looks like it,' she said, more breezily than she felt. 'I'm just glad neither of you have been bitten.'

Jack felt his neck and throat self-consciously as the elevator plummeted and picked up a few more passengers, stifling the frankness of their talk. He thought about hickeys and rough sex and unsafe exchange of bodily fluids. His stomach roiled at the thought of what he'd recently been up to with a creature of the night. But if he'd been nipped or sucked he would know about it by now, wouldn't he? He'd have felt the craving, the freezing in the blood . . .

In the lobby he kissed Liza goodbye and she hugged him hard, impulsively, telling him she was there if he needed any help in looking after the distraught Consuela. Suddenly Jack was very glad he had this sensible woman in his life. She felt like a rock, suddenly, with her resolute good sense and her salty language.

He hurried out and was gone before the whole busy lobby was treated to a prime example of that frankness.

*

'HOLY FUCK!'

Liza had received another letter from England. She had scanned the flimsy page quickly, expecting one more pleasant and mildly flirtatious missive from a fellow bibliophile, but what she read shocked her horribly and caused her to cry out.

My dear Ms Bathory,

I am afraid that we have done you a terrible disservice. I am so sorry that this has happened. In the short time we have had dealings with each other, you have become one of my favourite customers.

We had no right to take advantage of you.

I can only reiterate my apologies.

We should never have done it. We thought – I thought – it was just an old superstition. A silly piece of nonsense.

We sent you the grimoire because we thought you would appreciate it, as a book-lover of your discrimination surely should.

But now we are hearing alarming tales on the news wire and television services from across the ocean. Ah yes, we are old-fashioned and stuffy perhaps, here on Charing Cross Road, but we are not completely ignorant. We do manage to tune in to the news from around the world.

I was at home yesterday evening having my solitary repast and I heard the news from New York on the BBC's World Service.

I feel terribly responsible.

214

I should never have let the grimoire out of my sight. I was a fool to send it to you. I have no inkling of what I was thinking. What have you ever done to harm me?

I just wanted that evil book away from here.

That is the truth of it.

I was thinking about myself and my own peace of mind. *WHAT HAVE I UNLEASHED?*

I truly hope that I may prevail upon you to help, Ms Bathory. Elizabeth, if I may call you that. Will you return the book here to Charing Cross Road? Or better still, bring it back in person, and then we can make sure that its curse is lifted from your undeserving shoulders.

It may not be too late.

Yours in haste,
Mr K. N. Wright

Chapter Twenty-Two

Jack took the subway downtown, jolting along with the other commuters. He glanced surreptitiously at a few of the tired faces, wondering about them. Were they pale and drawn because of a poor night's sleep, or was it because of something worse?

Time was running away from him. He hadn't long to stop by home before he had to get to work. He was dreading hearing Consuela's tale. It wasn't even nine a.m and already he felt he'd been through enough to last him a week. He grabbed a coffee and a *New York Times* from the corner of his block and hurried up the alley where the entrance to his apartment was tucked away.

Consuela wasn't the gabbling basket case he had been expecting.

She was sitting on one of the chrome stools in his kitchen wearing an abstracted expression. She had dressed her wounds and scrapes efficiently, seemingly by herself.

'Are you sure you don't need medical help?' He brought her a large mug of steaming chai.

'I'm okay,' she snapped. 'What we need to decide is what we are going to do.'

'What do the police say?'

'They listened to me. They went round to the apartment where

216

Ricardo is. Belonging to this Daniel. But there was nothing there to make them suspicious.'

'Nothing?'

She shrugged. 'They had flown the nest in time. They knew they must, once I had escaped.'

'But the body parts and all the blood . . .'

She glanced at him sharply. 'They were gone. Cleaned away somewhere. I don't know. All I know is, when the police called, they just found a very untidy apartment and Daniel pretending that he had been asleep. He convinced them. He told them I was a mad woman, victimising him because I think he has perverted my son.'

'What?'

'The police even apologised to him, for waking him up.'

'That doesn't sound right.' Jack frowned. He wondered if Daniel could have nobbled the police somehow. He was intent on getting what he wanted. He claimed to want to take over the whole city. Perhaps getting some police protection was part of his plan . . .

'Ricardo is still there with him,' Consuela moaned. She put her face into her hands. 'But he is no longer my son. The creature who I chased and who laid his hands upon me, violently . . . that is no longer my Ricardo.'

'Don't say that,' said Jack, trying to soothe her.

'Why not? It's the truth. I have to face the truth here.'

He left her shortly after this bleak exchange, hurrying back to the West Village and arriving late at Fangtasm.

Lame Wendy looked annoyed at him only for a few moments.

She had been forced to open up the shop alone, but she had been working there longer than he had. She knew the routine. 'It's okay,' she grinned. 'Late night, huh, with your hunky Latino?' She winked at him and bustled away to tackle an elderly shoplifter. 'Hey, hey! Put that back!'

There was something breezy about Lame Wendy this morning. Ricardo thought about it idly as he propped himself up by the till. He watched her hurrying about stocktaking, dusting, and then opening up her secret file for the party they were organising for Mr Grenoble's seventieth birthday in January. There was no stopping Lame Wendy this morning.

'Is it just because I'm, like, nearly comatose this morning, or are you really full of beans?'

'Full of beans,' she laughed. 'I love that phrase. It's cute.'

Definitely something different about her. Not just her manner. Something about her hair, maybe. Were her clothes less dowdy?

'Have you had a makeover, Wendy?' he asked when she came back from the deli with sandwiches for lunch for the pair of them.

'Huh?' She shook her head. 'Nope, same old Wendy here. Why?'

'You just seem . . . kind of energised. Happy.'

'Ah!' She laughed at him, playfully taking the cellophane off a turkey salad. 'I got laid last night.' Her eyes widened. 'Hey, don't look so surprised, Jack. I could take offence at that expression you're wearin'!'

'No, no!' he protested. 'I'm not surprised! I'm just . . . surprised by the way you came out with it, that's all! Well, who was is it? Er . . . was it anyone I know?'

'Nuh-uh,' she said. 'You wouldn't know him. Just some guy.

Some random guy. My God, Jack. I've never done anything so reckless or stupid in my whole life! You've no idea what a good girl I've been. It's been nauseatin'. Seriously, last night – for whatever reason – I just decided that it was time I cut loose. I went out with some of my girlfriends. That same crowd who laugh when I'm first to go home, or when I'm telling them to be more careful . . . and something just clicked. I saw this guy, Christian. And something flipped. He's a total hottie. Jack, you will cream yourself when you see him.'

Jack stared at her. What had happened to Lame Wendy? She wasn't even talking like herself any more. 'That's great, honey,' he told her. 'Really. I'm pleased. You were . . . erm, safe and all, weren't you?'

'I made Sandra watch the end of the alley when I was behind the dumper with him, yeah,' she said, and then she was off again, surging into a full afternoon's busy work.

Jack watched her go, open-mouthed, still unable to adequately process what she had been saying. She'd done it with some guy behind a garbage dumper?

Just then Shelley phoned.

'Hey,' she said. 'How was Consuela?'

Jack brought her up to date. 'I don't know what to do about her now. When I left the apartment, it was like she had given up.'

'Hmm,' said Shelley. 'Well, Daniel's here at work, looking immaculate, and like butter wouldn't melt. He's still smarming round me. He's determined to get into my good books.'

'Huh.'

'He even lied to the board about the fate of the Scottish Bride effigy. He did all this paperwork and stuff claiming that the thing had collapsed and shattered. We should never have exposed it to public display. It was on its last legs, et cetera. There was nothing left but a heap of useless debris.'

'Wow,' said Jack. 'Well that gets you off the hook.' Even as he said this, images of the Scottish Bride flashed through his mind. Her strange, fluting, sonorous voice. Her twitchy, rustling fingers. Those hollow, ancient eyes. He shook his head to clear it. Something about Bessie disturbed him greatly, but it seemed impolite to mention that fact to anyone. 'Daniel's really after getting you back, isn't he?'

'Yeah,' said Shelley, and Jack could have sworn he heard her shudder down the phone. 'He's asked me out for a reconciliatory dinner. Up on the roof garden of Chez Harpo. Can you believe it?'

'How could he possibly imagine you'd go back to him?' Jack said. He was still watching Lame Wendy flitting energetically around the shop floor, lugging boxes back and forth. 'Still, Chez Harpo is meant to be fabulous. It'll be tough to turn him down.'

'Yeah, right,' she said. 'Listen, Ruthie's here. We're going for some lunch. See you later.'

Jack remembered Ruthie from the gift shop in the museum. He recalled the way she had shouted at Ricardo, and made him buy the slim-fit T-shirt with the picture of Bessie on the front. Suddenly he had a real pang of missing Ricardo. It seemed like they had hardly had any time to get to know each other, or to settle into the happy routine of being each other's boyfriend.

The door crashed open, startling him, and suddenly Liza was there.

'Hey, kiddo. Am I still barred?'

When did she start calling me kiddo? he wondered. Staring at her mismatched ensemble for the day – a kind of cross between sixties Chanel and seventies Bionic Woman – he decided he quite liked the endearment. 'Uh, I can't remember how long Mr Grenoble barred you for.'

'Never mind that,' Liza said, stomping in and shaking the snow off her shoes. 'We got a problem.'

Jack groaned. 'Another one?'

She produced the letter she had received this morning. 'Well, what I mean is, we've got a possible solution to all our problems. But getting to that solution is going to be pretty tricky.'

He wanted to yell at her for being so cryptic. Here she was in a mystery bookstore, and he was flailing after her like an amateur sleuth's stooge as she talked at gunfire speed. 'What do you mean?' he asked through gritted teeth.

'I mean . . . it's all down to that book. That's what brought all this bad luck. So we've gotta get it back, kiddo. Toot de fricking sweet.'

Chapter Twenty-Three

Because of Liza's letter and the realisation of what had to be done next, Shelley was left with no option but to go to dinner with Daniel. Chez Harpo's it was.

'Listen, honey,' her aunt told her as she beautified herself early that evening. 'Just go with the flow, huh? He may think you're getting the hots for him again, and you just gotta go along with that for a while. Long enough to get the book back, okay?'

Shelley stared at herself in Liza's dressing-table mirror, dabbing at her face with make-up, feeling coated with misgivings. 'Well I just hope he doesn't get rough like before. You never saw him, Aunt Liza, when he was round here . . .'

'You can tackle him, I'm sure,' said Liza. 'You've got your phone. Me and Bessie will be nearby. We'll tail you.'

This thought was hardly reassuring to Shelley. She imagined an awkward evening of bad acting on her part, her tactless aunt hiding round the corner with her strange best friend, watching her every move . . .

And on top of all that, there was Daniel.

She supposed she hated him now. That was the right way to feel, wasn't it? It wasn't like he had been taken over or possessed unwillingly by some malign being. His current doings were a result of choices he had made. Shelley just knew it. Daniel *welcomed* this surprising turn his life had taken.

She took a cab to the restaurant, feeling dreadful. What if Daniel started on the funny stuff again, and she was forced to cause a scene or punch him out in public? In a strange way, she was feeling bad about her own eagerness to settle the score with him. There was enough of her aunt in her to relish the idea of a fight, and enough of her mother to feel mortified before it had even happened.

The restaurant was at the top of a building sheathed in ebony glass. She had read the reviews, seen pictures in fancy mags. Chez Harpo was a heated tropical garden at the very top of the world. The kind of place she had fantasised about Daniel taking her one day.

She rode up in the elevator in her poshest frock, but still felt a little out of place beside the other diners. Did she look poorer, more nervous? Or was it just the unaccustomed feeling of wearing these spindly, fabulous shoes, this glamorous wrap belonging to her aunt? And the weirdness of carrying such a tiny bag. What was the point of this bag, big enough only for her keys and her credit card? Shelley was used to carrying something she could fit her whole life – and her aunt's dog – inside.

She took a final, hopeless look at herself in the polished metal of the elevator's interior as the bell pinged. The other diners shuffled eagerly out into the restaurant and she was borne along with them, feeling more excited than she thought she ought to.

Daniel was seated at a table at the extreme edge of the rooftop, where it was impossibly balmy for the time of year. Shelley imagined the wasted heat and the outrageous contempt for environmental issues that this place was flaunting. She felt guilty but contented herself with the fact that it wasn't her choice, and anyway – look at those stars. Amazing, having scallops under the bright constellations like this.

'Hey,' he said, jumping up to pull out her seat.

She lowered herself carefully, woozy with a sudden vertigo and a whiff of his lemon and verbena cologne. Oh God, Daniel. Can't we go back to how we were? Can't you just be a fruity English snob again? Can't you drop all the undead and neck-bitey cult business? She sighed and smiled at him, meaning it.

He looked perfect in a brown cashmere jacket she didn't recognise. But then, she thought, this frock of mine's new too. Maybe we've both splashed out on expensive things since our split. Maybe we've both consoled ourselves in that way.

'I've missed you,' he told her. They were hiding behind their oversized menus, aware of the waiter hovering at a discreet distance. Shelley was also aware of the two women who had entered the restaurant and were being shown to a table diametrically opposite. Oh God, she thought. Aunt Liza, no. That wasn't the arrangement at all.

'I've missed how things were,' she said. 'When we were happy.' She tried to crane her neck around, under the guise of fiddling with an earring, pretending it was caught up in her hair. She peered round and took a quick breath. Yep – it was Aunt Liza and her new best friend. Dolled up and painted and keeping a keen eye on the young lovers. Damn. They'd give her away, she knew it. They were bound to cause a ruckus, create a scene. Surely someone would notice something strange about Bessie?

'We were happy, weren't we?' Daniel smiled. He ordered for them both, curtly, quickly, and dismissed the waiter. He leaned forward and she saw he was wearing cufflinks she had bought him. He made sure he had her full attention. 'Before I started all this nonsense.'

She raised an eyebrow at him. Flim-flam, surely. He was buttering her up – rather more successfully than she was managing with her own warm roll. She fiddled with the curl of iced butter, distracting herself from that intent stare of his. 'You don't really think it's all nonsense. You want to be king of the city, don't you? You want your entourage. Your gang of vamps.'

'Ssh.' He frowned. 'I got mixed up in something ridiculous,' he said. 'For just a few days. I don't know, Shelley love. It was like something had got into me. Some spirit of devilment.' He sighed. 'All my life, I've been such a good boy. Well, mostly. Doing the right thing for the sake of my family and trying not to let them down. Being so respectable and nicely brought up. So perhaps . . . a little naughtiness . . . a little bit of being bad . . . maybe it was exciting for a while. Maybe I needed to get it out of my system.'

She knew she had the sob story coming now. She'd heard it before, and the first couple of times, it had made her breath catch and tears well up in her eyes as he melted before her. He'd tell her about his emotional diffidence and his inability to properly connect, the result of his being sent away to a harsh English private school when he was four. His lack of empathy stemmed from the competitiveness and ruthless drummed into him from that early age. His suspicion and paranoia were due to the fact that no one had ever taught him to trust or open out to another human being . . .

Yeah, yeah, Shelley wanted to say.

Tonight at Chez Harpo she got a mercifully curtailed version of his own self-analysis. She was sufficiently used to the highlights that she had time to cast a few glances at her aunt and Bessie as they ordered their dinner and stared back at her. Mortifyingly, her aunt even gave her a thumbs-up.

'I wish you had talked to me more about what you were getting into,' she told him.

'How could I?' he said. 'I didn't even know.' His voice cracked, and then the waiter was back with them, bringing the scallops she'd craved on the way up here, in some kind of vanilla sauce.

'You knew it was black magic.'

He sighed. 'It was the day your aunt received that book. That's when it all started. I had a kind of niggle in my brain. You know I love ancient secret books and suchlike. I love that sense that you're uncovering something forgotten and forbidden. When I look into those old artefacts, I feel like I'm teetering on the brink of rediscovering amazing knowledge that the rest of the world has passed over . . .'

Shelley could chime with that. She knew what he meant. She liked poking around in old neglected items too. 'But I don't think I can gain mystical powers from them. I don't think I can harness arcane forces and take over the world. Daniel, what were you playing at?'

He stared her dead in the eye. 'Something came out of that book. A force. A personality. An undead being. And he's here with us now. He's inside me, Shelley. I'm holding him in obeisance tonight . . . with all my will. I am trying to be myself . . . as much as I can . . . for you, my lovely Shelley. But he's taking me over. He's . . . taking possession of me.'

Daniel put down his golden cutlery and laid both hands upon hers.

Her stomach rumbled with anguish and a hunger she couldn't quite put a name to.

Their steaks came, and her eye kept being drawn to the blood pooling on his plate. His side salad was dripping with it, but he hardly seemed to notice. He devoured his dinner and exhorted Shelley to enjoy her own. The Daniel she knew would have started to get annoyed with her about wasting money. The vast expense of coming here, this swanky place at the top of the city. But this Daniel – this new, post-grimoire Daniel – was seemingly more relaxed. He relished his own meal and let her fiddle with her French fries.

She tried not to look at Aunt Liza and Bessie. In that restaurant of discreet murmurs, tinkling silverware and gentle, tasteful classical music, there was a persistent raucous laughter from Liza. And a guttural guffawing from Bessie that sawed through the air and disturbed other diners besides Shelley, she was sure. Why were the two women drawing attention to themselves?

Their dinner plates were taken away eventually, and she watched Daniel dabbing at his lips with his napkin.

'We did lots of things wrong,' he sighed at last. 'We weren't very kind to each other. I think we jumped into our relationship with both feet. Too quickly. It isn't your fault, Shelley. I blame myself. It was all down to me.'

'No, no,' she said feebly. Half of her was trying to remember what had been on the dessert menu. 'I was the one hurling myself at the relationship. I was so keen to have a proper boyfriend and a nice place for us both to live.'

He pawed at her hand again. 'We could still have that, maybe.'

'I think,' she said, a little stiffly, 'you'd have to give up the rough stuff with your cult. And all the black magic. And the drugs and the boys. What was it with that, anyway? You never said you were bisexual.'

His eyebrows went up. 'I-I'm not.'

'Oh, come on, Daniel. When I was round there, it was pretty obvious that you were messing about with the guys. Ricardo was wearing my dressing gown. I saw, remember. And you laughed at me for being so gauche. I should have listened to Ricardo himself, and Jack, when they tried to tell me you were gay . . .'

'Shelley, I'm *not*,' he said, looking flustered for the first time. 'I'm really not. But, like I told you, I've been under the influence of the entity that came out of that book.'

She eyed him sceptically. 'It's okay, you know. People can be gay or bisexual. You don't have to find some elaborate reason for it.'

For a moment he looked angry at her. 'You know there's real magic involved here. You know that impossible things have been going on. There are dark forces swirling about us.'

'I try to keep an open mind,' she said.

'The Scottish Bride is an impossible being,' he whispered. 'An animated cadaver. Hundreds of years old. Created by the hands of a madman. Filled with rage, despair and hatred. You are dicing with evil forces, letting her into your life.'

'Stop it, Daniel . . .'

'I can see her over there. With your crazy aunt. Trying to blend in with normal human beings. They've been keeping an eye on us all evening.'

'What?' Shelley tried to deny it, to feign surprise. 'Oh, look, can we just order dessert and—'

'No,' he said, suddenly gripping her forearm. He was on his feet and dragging her round the table. For one terrible moment Shelley thought he was going to yank her across the restaurant in order to confront her aunt.

But it was worse that that.

He pulled her roughly to the edge of the rooftop. She bumped into a couple of diners on the way, and there was a muttering of discontent. He made her stand at the edge and gaze down at the splendour of the city before them. They were midtown, and so high up it was as if the ground had ceased to exist. Up here she was aware of the vast sprawl of the city, and the mantle of clouds, heavy with snow, seemed cloying and thick. For a disorienting moment Shelley experienced both vertigo and claustrophobia, even as she took in the vast panorama.

'I could be king of the city,' Daniel said. 'And you could be my queen.'

He was misquoting David Bowie's 'Heroes' at her. She could have kicked herself for going a little weak at that. Him with his English accent, cigarette-roughened, vampish pale in the snow-light. Damn it, she thought. He's bruised my wrist to hell and I'm freezing away from the heating lamps . . . but he's doing something to me again. Something invisible and good . . .

Shelley refused to believe it was all to do with wicked magical powers.

Then he wrestled her to the very edge and threatened to step out into nothingness.

Screams went up in the rooftop restaurant as people saw what they were up to. There was the scraping of chairs, the whoosh of indrawn breath – and the deathly rattle of pearls being clutched.

Liza and Bessie had seen enough. Now that Shelley was in danger, they were persisting with the charade no longer. The two elderly ladies were on their feet and pushing through the tables . . . Too late.

Daniel snarled with laughter and propelled himself over the edge. He hugged Shelley to him with all of his considerable might. She felt his body twist and buck with immense force, and for an absurd second she thought of the strength and grace of a salmon, thrusting itself upriver. That was Daniel now, sending the two of them into the sharp, thrilling air all these storeys up.

And then the bastard flew.

She was looking for reasons to hate him for ever. She was only with him as a subterfuge tonight, to get the grimoire back for her aunt.

But then the bastard flew.

Holding her in his arms. Smoothing her hair down as it flapped wildly about her face and her elegant silver wrap fluttered around her like a superhero's cape. He whispered to her consolingly and stroked her suddenly frozen cheeks. He licked the hot tears away as the two of them tumbled and twirled and looped the loop. The lights of the city spiralled into a marvellous vortex all around them and they steadied and banked like a 747, skimming under the cloud cover. It started to snow, and it was as if they had unleashed that tide of soft flakes themselves, by coming so close to the canopy that smoothed over the city.

The bastard was flying her across the city's spires and murmuring to her.

She had the screams of the diners in her ears. She had her aunt's screams and Bessie's weird ululations rattling in her head. But then they were silenced by the scything noise of the wind all around them. The cold air didn't hurt as she rested in Daniel's arms.

He whispered, 'And the best thing is? We skipped out without paying our bill.'

She didn't know what to say to that.

'Come home with me, Shelley,' he said. 'Come back home right now.'

She nodded, feeling very small and very high up. 'All right,' she said.

Chapter Twenty-Four

For a few moments the staff and diners at Chez Harpo's rooftop garden simply held their breath and clutched with both hands whatever was nearest to them. Liza felt Bessie's sharp fingers digging into her shoulders until she shook her roughly off.

'My baby! My niece!' Liza squawked, but everyone was still paralysed by the sight of the couple from Table 1 soaring into the magenta clouds. They stayed quiet and still until the figures spiralled away and vanished into the mist and the new-falling snow. Then Liza swore loudly, and it was as if this was the signal for everyone to start talking at once.

'Did you see . . . ? Did I imagine . . . ? That guy flew . . . he took that girl. Did they fall . . . ? What the . . . ?'

Phone calls were being made to emergency services and the press. Some quick-thinking souls had snapped pictures on their cell phones, and already images of Liza's airborne niece and flaky boyfriend were being zoomed around cyberspace.

'Hot damn,' Liza said bitterly.

'Sssooo Daniel is nooow in posssesssion of all the deeemon's powersss,' Bessie mused, staring into the churning snow clouds. 'Thisss is baaad neeewsss.'

'Of course it's bad friggin' news!' Liza snapped. 'He's dangling my baby over Broadway! He's holding her to ransom! We should never have let her meet with him.'

'We musst act fasst,' Bessie said. 'With his queen, they will nooow perform the betrothaaal ceremony, and that will increase his powers tenfold . . .'

'You don't say,' said Liza. 'C'mon then, Bessie. Let's split.'

The two of them were drawing their own fair share of attention now, as the manager and security came stomping into the previously balmy rooftop garden. Everyone had heard Liza shouting about Shelley being her relation, and now they were coming to her for answers. She wasn't prepared to hang around any longer.

'Ma'am, ma'am,' someone was shouting, dogging their heels. 'You haven't paid you bill!' It was the maître d' coming after them as they headed for the lift, his elbows jerking and his forehead gleaming with sweat. Liza got Bessie to give him a quick shove into the shrubbery.

'Not so hard,' she added, as the man brought down a whole wall of trellis and honeysuckle. 'Jeez, lady, but you're strong.'

It proved a good distraction, though, allowing the two women to duck into the elevator and make good their escape.

In the gilded cage of the elevator, Liza tried to take stock and make sense of what had gone on this evening. Shelley whirled away into the sky by that madman. Bessie standing there before her in clothes that were slightly too small for her: an animated cadaver in Liza's 1920s party outfit. The Scotch Bride kitted out in a beaded dress and a cloche hat. How did we ever think the poor dear could fit in?

In the ground-floor lobby, the two of them set off at a run. But no one down there was taking any notice. News crews had arrived, trailing leads and wires, and people were shouting at each other about the flying diners from Chez Harpo.

As Liza and Bessie hurried through, they caught a few moments of CNN footage on a plasma screen behind the reception desk. It was jerky and fuzzy, but it definitely showed Daniel and Shelley doing a slalom across the Manhattan skyline. Liza shuddered and bundled her skinny friend into the street.

'Taaaxxiiiii!'

Even the cab driver had heard about the superhero and his girl. Word spread fast in this town.

'He ain't no superhero,' Liza said, and gave the driver her address.

'Sounds like the old *izzy a boid, izzy a plane* routine,' chuckled the driver.

'Huh,' growled Liza. 'Nope. He's an English queer with a black-magic fixation and he's probably biting my niece all over even as we waste time here yakkin' with you.'

'Whuzzat?' said the taxi driver. He hadn't followed her meaning at all. 'Jeez. I'd love to fly, with the traffic like it is. How 'bout that, ladies? How 'bout a flying yellow cab?'

'Jussst drive,' Bessie told him stertorously, tapping her twiggy fingers on the glass partition rather menacingly. The driver glanced round, and there was something in her dark stare that made him jump to attention and put his foot to the pedal.

Liza squeezed Bessie's hand. 'Weee'll sooon beee home.'

'And then what?' sighed Liza. 'What can we actually do to help Shelley? Two old dames like us?'

But when they arrived at Liza's building, they found they had company. More help, perhaps.

'Jack!' cried Liza, dashing up to him across the echoing lobby. As she hugged him, she realised that he had another woman with him. A tiny woman all dressed in black, as if she were in mourning.

He hugged her warmly in return. 'Liza, I had to bring her here. I didn't know what else to do. I figured, if anyone could be of any help, you could.'

Bessie had paid the cab driver and was coming in last, arriving in a flurry of snowflakes and looking rather wild from the swirling wind. She stood almost twice as tall as Consuela and was rather impressively terrifying in the bright lights of the lobby.

Consuela took one glance and gave a strangulated yell. 'Jesus Christ! It is another monster! Faaugghh!'

Jack took hold of her, trying to pacify her. 'Hey, hey, it's okay. It's just Liza's friend.'

'Uh, this is Bessie,' began Liza awkwardly.

'Goood eveninnng,' said Bessie scratchily, extending a hand for Consuela to shake. She was glad of an opportunity to try out some of the social skills Liza had been trying to coach her in.

'Get it away from me.' Consuela's eyes flashed and she rounded on Jack. 'I thought you said you were bringing me somewhere safe. You said you were bringing me to good people, people who can help a poor old woman in her hour of need.'

'It'll be all right, Consuela,' Jack said hurriedly. 'They *are* good people . . .'

'This is a devil witch!' spat Ricardo's superstitious mother. 'A voodoo creature!'

235

'Hey, ladies,' shouted Sammy from the front desk. 'Is everything okay over there? You seem kinda upset.'

Liza felt a wave of tiredness rush through her. 'Fine, Sammy. Sorry about all the noise. We're completely fine. We're all going up to my apartment now and givin' you some peace.' She gritted her teeth. '*Ain't* we, everyone? We can continue this ridiculous conversation upstairs.'

'I'm not going anywhere with you people,' Consuela sobbed. 'I came here for help. Jack said you would help me to get my son back from the forces of darkness.'

'We *will*!' said Liza, shoving her gently towards the elevator. 'Let's just not do it all in public, hey?' Liza was longing for the comfort and calm of her own rooms. After standing on that rooftop and screaming her lungs out tonight, she was feeling rather overexposed.

'Hey,' Sammy shouted after her, as the small party boarded the elevator. 'Did you ladies see Superman and his girlfriend tonight? They had great pictures on the TV. Didja ever believe a man could fly like that?'

The doors whooshed closed on him and Jack asked, 'What's he on about, Superman?'

'Daniel and Shelley,' Liza told him tersely. 'They took to the skies tonight and everyone saw. Did you miss the news?'

'I've been looking after Consuela. She's pretty distraught. What do you mean, took to the skies?'

Bessie answered him in her most ghoulish tones. 'Danniel can flyyy! He haaas come into the deeemon's powerrsss! Soooon nothing will be able to ssstop himmm!'

*

236

It felt like the most romantic thing in the world. Floating lightly, impossibly across the city rooftops, safely buoyed up in the arms of her man. For once Shelley felt she could relinquish all cares and anxiety and simply relax as he whirled her away through the snow. They danced through the endless cascades of silvery white.

She didn't know if she'd been bitten or nibbled or what. Had he taken control of her? Was she in his possession in more ways than one? There seemed no way of knowing yet. She was numb with bliss: that was how it was. When he kissed her, his breath was hot. His lips were scalding. Could the undead really be so warm? Maybe there was hope for Daniel yet.

They floated over the tree-lined streets of brownstones where Daniel had made his life – and until recently, so had she. A great longing rose in her as he prepared to descend to the snow-softened sidewalk. There was no one to see them or greet them. After so much fuss attending their take-off, and so many cameras and fingers pointing their way as they moved across the sky, their arrival here was wonderfully low-key.

'Here we are,' Daniel told her.

'All right,' she said uncertainly. For a moment it was as if he was giving her the choice, now that her feet were back on the ground. She could pull back and dash away from him. She could return to her sanctuary on her aunt's funky old settee in that overfull apartment with the dead woman in the closet. Or she could come with him.

Inside the building, they didn't bother with the stairs. She clung to him lightly and he took off again, floating serenely up the open column of the stairwell. Shelley laughed as they rose through the levels of fretted ironwork, thinking of how many times she had toiled up this staircase. Was that the thing: sell your soul and give your will up to the monsters and everything became so much easier? Was it all so much more fun?

The apartment was lit only by a few cosy lamps, but Shelley could see that Daniel had made a great effort. It was habitable once more, with no sign of the strange, rapacious, decadent guests who had for some days overrun it. Rugs had been cleaned, furniture mended, everything scrubbed and straightened.

He undressed her in the kitchen with tender accuracy. Piece after piece of her fancy outfit was plucked from her shivering body and flung away. For a strange moment her eyes fixed on the cooking utensils stacked neatly on the work surfaces, and she felt like a large joint of meat being prepared for the oven. He was tenderising her. She felt he was readying himself to taste her, and she didn't even care.

Then he led her into the bedroom – which was tidier than she had ever seen it – where he flung her down and shucked his own clothes with alacrity. They were both glad to be out of those garments. The fine ice crystals gathered on their night flight had melted in the heat. They shivered as they lay in bed together.

He gathered her in his arms and she had a moment to reflect on how they had never quite learned each other's bodies and rhythms when they had been girlfriend and boyfriend. One of them had always fumbled or got it wrong somehow during sex. But there was nothing fumbly or clumsy about what was happening tonight.

There was a new assuredness in his every move. She would never have believed it possible.

'Daniel,' she said. 'I . . .'

'Sssh,' he whispered, and bent to kiss her with a tenderness that made her want to cry. No one had ever been that careful with her, or that caring. Or spent that long in giving her just one single kiss. Should I want to cry? she thought. And then she thought, should I even be doing this? And the thought came back: no, I shouldn't. This is the last thing I should do.

Chapter Twenty-Five

Across the city, there was a kind of council of war going on at Liza's place.

Rufus was agitated, sniffing around everyone and barking fiercely at the intangible enemy he could sense in the air. He came to look at Bessie, who sat patiently on the bed settee, primly as usual, and cradling a hot mug of herbal tea. He frowned and sniffed several times at the Scottish Bride, but he didn't feel the antipathy he had experienced when she had first arrived at Liza's. He was used to Bessie now, and even came to rest at her feet quite happily, tail thumping on the Moroccan rug. Then he glared attentively at the newcomer – the tiny woman, Consuela – who was still making a fuss, wailing and occasionally shouting out.

'Brandy,' Liza said, giving the old woman a huge glass half filled with spirits. 'This will do you good.'

Consuela took it, and the first couple of sips stopped her shaking.

'We're having coffee, me and you,' Liza told Jack. 'We gotta keep clear heads so we can think about what we need to do next.'

Jack nodded, though he quite fancied the brandy, too.

'Who are you people?' Consuela asked at last. 'What is going on here?'

Liza sighed. Her nerves were frayed and her patience had almost gone. She tried to explain a little about what had been happening recently, in the hope that the woman would tell her own story and be less inclined to scream and thrust her crucifix into their faces.

Jack hurriedly told the tale of Ricardo, and how he had been enlisted into this army of young vampires that was taking over the city bit by bit.

'Poor you,' Liza told Consuela. 'It must be very hard to see your son involved in something terrible like that.'

'But is there any way back for him?' Jack asked. 'Can people be saved or cured?'

Liza frowned. 'I don't know. Whenever I've fought vamps before, in the past, they've been the normal sort, if that makes sense. The usual neck-biters and coffin-lovers. But this is different somehow. And it's all to do with that book and the spirit that inhabited it.' She realised that Jack was gawping at her. 'What is it?'

'Whenever you've fought vamps *before*?' he repeated. 'You make a *habit* of this?'

'Oh yes,' she said cheerfully. 'Though not for a while. I just don't like to mention it. It can get some very odd reactions from people, that kind of thing. Anyway, things have been relatively quiet on the supernatural front till this past month or so. I've lain fallow for years, thinking I was happy to be outta the spook-huntin' biz. Now all this. Tell you the truth though, kiddo, I think I even missed the excitement.'

Bessie gave a guttural laugh. 'Beee careful whaaat you wissshh foooor, Lizaaa.'

'Quite,' said Liza. 'So. New type of vamps. Or old type of vamps, they could be. Their guiding, presiding spirit has been exported from the Olde Worlde, remember. Daniel has been taken over by a malignant soul brought in from the heart of Olde London Town. He and it could be operating on rules that we aren't even aware of. He could have powers that we don't know the first thing about.' She was going paler and paler as she spoke. 'We should never have let Shelley anywhere near him. We've gotta get her back.'

Consuela was rummaging in her large handbag. She produced a handful of devilishly sharp knitting and crochet needles. 'Whatever kind of undead they are, surely they can still be staked through the heart? I brought all of these. We can stake them, no? And that will be an end to them?'

Liza frowned at her. 'Well, I've never known a vamp who couldn't be felled by a stake. But you'll need something better than knitting needles for the job.' She sighed. 'Jack, could you help me pull this bookcase aside? We need to break out some supplies.'

He gasped. 'You've got a hidden hoard of sharpened stakes?'

'Of course,' she said. 'And we need them right now if we're gonna do anything about poor old Shelley. Come on!'

Shelley lay awake in the dark, buzzing. Next to her Daniel had fallen into a deep and soundless sleep. Never had she felt more awake. Every iota of her body was humming and fizzing.

She'd never had a night like it. Somehow her recently estranged boyfriend had learned a whole new bag of tricks. He suddenly knew just what to do to her . . .

But that sounded crass. That was wrong. It was far more than anything simple and mechanical such as . . . technique. This was chemical. It was . . . spiritual, even. They had made some profound connection in a way they never had, ever before.

How could Daniel sleep? How could he not be sharing this? Shelley felt like all the lights of Times Square were pulsing through her. The noise and the restless energy of the city were flowing out of her. But there he was. Sleeping so deeply, breathing so deeply. He smelled delicious. He smelled like foreign spices and wood smoke and mulchy undergrowth in winter woods. And still that tantalising aroma of lemon cologne.

She knew she wouldn't sleep.

She slid out of their bed and wandered happily into the living room. She moved about easily in the snowlight from outside, flickering through the blinds in the tall windows.

I've never felt more awake. More alive. I've never felt better.

He had done something amazing to her.

The whole apartment looked so clean and tidy in the blue light before dawn. It was as if all that bad stuff, all that mess and those strange parties, had never happened here. Perhaps they could forget it all and start again. It had been a momentary madness. A strange fad of Daniel's. But now he had come back to her. Now he could fly and whiz her about the city. Now he could make love to her and make her come with the same celebratory glee as the chimes at midnight on New Year's Eve.

Shelley drifted through the living room of what had briefly

been her home. She was seriously considering simply moving back in with him.

And then she saw the thick black book lying so innocently on the coffee table. On top of a neatly stacked pile of art books and slick magazines, the grimoire seemed to radiate darkness and a faint whiff of spoiled meat. She sniffed and drew closer, and the movement broke the spell that had been upon her.

She sat down heavily on the sofa. This was the source of all their recent troubles. It was because of this book that everything had changed. It was only because of the eldritch powers somehow bound up in this volume that Daniel could fly.

He was still possessed. He was more possessed than ever.

And she had fallen for it. She'd flung herself into his arms and let him do anything he wanted with her.

She was his now. That was why he was sleeping so deeply and looking so pleased with himself. In the fug of his exhausted slumber, he knew that he had bested her and sealed her to his will.

For a second she gave herself up to despair and to feeling like a fool who'd been taken for a ride. A pretty amazing ride, but a ride all the same.

Now she had to take back control.

She got up and started hunting around for her clothes and shoes and her tiny chic handbag. She seized the ancient book. It felt almost hot to the touch of her fingers. It felt like warm human flesh. It felt like Daniel's skin as they lay there in bed and he moved away from her after making love. Her stomach revolted at the thought and she nearly threw up Chez Harpo's pricey scallops all over his coffee table art books.

She managed to wedge the tome into her silly little handbag, and then she was dressing in the dark, stumbling around in sudden panic, getting her bra twisted and snapping one of the straps of her brand-new dressy dress. She swore repeatedly under her breath, sure that she was going to wake Daniel at any moment.

She fiddled with those ridiculous shoes. Why couldn't she just have worn trainers? Something practical for running away in the night?

Running away. She had to do it now. She had to get away with the grimoire. And maybe if the book was away from Daniel and Aunt Liza could do something with it . . . destroy it or return it to where it had come from . . . then perhaps Daniel could revert to normal again. Clumsy and awkward in bed and unable to fly, but at least he wouldn't be possessed by demons any more.

Stop quibbling! she yelled inside her head. Just get out. Get out of here.

In a few moments she was out of the door and hurrying down the stairwell, with her legs shaking – out of fear and because they were still a bit trembly after the sexiest night ever. I'm running away from the most amazing night of my life, she thought – and then realised that it was the book getting to her. Trying to influence her thoughts and to send her back into his warm waiting arms . . .

Down on the street it was silent. The snow had stopped falling but the cold hit her like a wall of ice. She put her head down, took a deep breath and plunged into the night, clutching the bag to her chest. She marvelled at her ability to take her life into her own hands and escape.

Out here she felt raw and exposed. But less imperilled than she had suddenly started to feel in Daniel's apartment. At least out here and heading for sanctuary at Aunt Liza's, she was mistress of her own destiny again.

At the end of Daniel's block, she shrank into the shadows. She'd heard noise. Laughter. Raucous yells. Playing it safe, she withdrew into the darkness and almost immediately saw that she was right to do so.

Daniel's boys and girls were passing by on the other side of the street.

Loud and lewd, a ragtag gaggle of young vamps was racing through the night, back to Daniel's apartment. They didn't see her.

For a moment one of them – she recognised him: Ricardo! – paused and gave the air a curious sniff. She crouched down and thought her heart was going to burst. She knew he had scented her. But then he shook his head and hurried after the others.

Heading back to the nest.

Where she was supposed to be still. With Daniel – their prince. Her king.

Nothing had changed. She was a fool.

She watched them disappear, shouting and screeching, excited by whatever kills they had made in the city tonight.

At least they don't have their precious book, she thought.

Then, when it was safe, she emerged from the shadows behind the frozen bins and hurried on her way.

Chapter Twenty-Six

'We're horribly lost, aren't we?'

Jack, Liza, Bessie and Consuela had been traipsing the snowy streets west of the park for some time before eventually they had to concede defeat.

'I thought I could remember!' Jack cursed himself. 'From Thanksgiving and all, when we went over there . . .'

'My mind is in pieces,' said Consuela. 'I should be able to remember too, where this apartment is. But it is so late now . . .'

The poor old thing was dropping asleep on her feet, Jack realised.

'I wonder if there's some magical kind of thing going on,' Liza mused. 'Deliberately confusing us and putting us off the scent.'

Bessie was literally sniffing the frigid air at this point. Her thin breaths emerged as tiny plumes of smoke and she frowned deeply. 'I can smellll them. Death and corruption. The chiiildren of Daniel and his dark maaaster have been hunting toniiight. Not far from here. I can smell the blood congeeeealing . . . and the poison as it steeeeals into their soulsss . . .'

They all stared at her withered face and streaming hair and were disturbed by her words.

'Can't we just find Daniel's apartment?' Liza snapped. 'We need to get after Shelley . . . She's in great danger.'

Bessie shrugged, her old bones and sinews cracking in the cold. 'I have never been to that place. How could I knooow wheeere it lieesss?'

So, disheartened and exhausted, they had to give up. They lugged their makeshift stakes and Liza's emergency weapons back across twenty blocks, feeling utterly thwarted.

Home again, they found Shelley asleep on the bed settee. Snow crystals were still in her hair. She'd slung her belongings in the corner and dropped off in an instant, as if some magic spell were upon her.

They gathered round and gazed at her.

'Oh thank goodness,' Liza said. 'She's safe, she's safe.'

They all whispered and tiptoed around. Bessie grunted with satisfaction and sloped off to her closet in the hall to restore her energies. Consuela watched her go, eyes narrowed suspiciously. The old woman still didn't quite like what she had become involved in, but these people were her only allies.

While Consuela went to the bathroom and Jack was making them some early morning coffee, Liza checked her niece over a little more thoroughly.

Her breathing . . . was it too regular? A little too relaxed? Did her face look perhaps too placid and calm? And her complexion . . . how smooth and pure it appeared. In her sleep tonight, Shelley looked radiant, in a way that everyday cares and concerns had prevented in recent weeks. Liza felt nasty suspicions nudging at her.

She drew the comforter down slightly from where it was pulled right up to Shelley's chin. Nervously she peered at her niece's neck. The light was dim in this cosy nook, and she didn't like to put on the reading lamp. She peered closer.

There was something bloody there. A contusion, a blemish of mangled skin. Liza could smell the fresh blood. She caught her breath.

Shelley's eyes flashed open. 'You're back!' she gasped. 'I came home . . . I got away . . . but there was no one here!'

'We were out . . . looking for you,' Liza whispered. Her head was buzzing with confusion and fright. 'We got lost in the snow. It was ridiculous. We took weapons and all sorts and we went out searching the streets for you. Daniel took you away . . .'

'I know,' said Shelley. 'I'm so sorry for scaring you, Aunt Liza. I'm sorry . . .'

'Hush now, sweetheart.' Liza found herself pulling the quilt back up to her niece's chin, as if she could hide the damage and the blood from Shelley herself that way. 'Hey, remember when you used to come and stay with me as a little girl? And those times, a little later, when you ran away from home and came into the city, escaping your mom and stepdad? And you'd find sanctuary here?'

'I'm still doing it,' Shelley said. 'You've been so good to me.'

Liza bit her lip. 'You *flew*, Shelley. That slimeball took you in his arms and flew you into the sky! There was nothing I could do to save you or protect you . . . You were out of my hands.'

Shelley nodded dumbly. She was out of her aunt's hands. That was just how she felt. She was on her own and helpless and still squirming in Daniel's grip.

Then Jack came back with a tray of coffee things.

'She's awake,' Liza said.

'You're a celebrity,' Jack told her. 'They took some great footage of you, swooping about over Manhattan like Lois Lane.'

'Oh, please . . .' said Shelley.

Consuela came back from the bathroom. She had scrubbed at her thick mascara and made it worse. Now it was spidery all down her face. Her usually immaculate hair was out of its bun and hanging down her back.

'Are you okay, honey?' Liza asked her.

'We must destroy them all,' Consuela told them in a dead kind of voice. 'We must purge this city of the undead scum and not rest until we have succeeded.'

They were all alarmed by her quasi-religious fervour. Jack felt his heart sink in his chest, thinking he was going to be the one in charge of her. This rather determined old woman was his responsibility now, and she looked set on doing someone – lots of people – a mischief.

'Well,' said Liza brightly, handing round the coffee mugs, 'I certainly think we ought to get on with things and put an end to this shocking menace.'

Jack could have cheered for her bright commonsensical tone.

Then Shelley jerked and almost spilled her scalding beverage. 'Omigod! I almost forgot! Quick! Pass me my handbag.'

'This tiny thing?' Liza asked. 'Hardly a handbag at all. What have you got in here? Feels like a . . .'

Shelley had broken the bag's clasp, jamming her purloined

treasure inside. Now Aunt Liza yanked the bag open and there was a sharp noise of ripping silk.

'Whoops.'

And then they all saw that Shelley was holding the smooth and shiny *Little Book of Necromancy*.

'The grimoire!' Liza gasped. 'Oh, you wonderful girl! You stole it back off him!'

Shelley grinned. 'It took some getting.'

Aunt Liza whooped and hollered as if the answer to all their ghoul-hunting prayers had just landed in their lap. Consuela looked puzzled, Jack felt sceptical, but Shelley was content – for a bleary moment – to bask in the pleasure of her aunt's approval.

All the next day, Jack had a kind of mantra running through his head. It was in Liza's voice and it was the last thing she had said to them before their little party disbanded early that morning.

'We can't get complacent. Yeah, we got Shelley back and we got the book. But do you think that Daniel and whatever's controlling him will give up that easily? We gotta act. We gotta be decisive.'

He took Consuela home to his apartment with those words about being decisive going round and round.

'What do you mean, decisive? What do we do? Chase after every vamp in New York?'

Liza had looked grim. 'They'll be increasing their numbers exponentially, as vamp bites vamp. We gotta go to the source.' She had looked at him levelly, very seriously. 'You got a passport?'

He nodded, thinking about that disastrous trip to Florence and

Rome with his last boyfriend, Jed. But there was no time to dwell on past unhappiness or failures now. 'You're saying we have to go to London? Take the grimoire back in person?'

'We can't risk it falling into anyone else's hands.'

'Are you crazy?' Shelley had said, her voice going screechy. 'Just put it in the mail!'

'Christmas mail,' her aunt had said. 'I don't trust it. It's way too dangerous to send off by itself. We're going there. To Charing Cross Road.'

'I think we should cope with the crisis here at home,' said Shelley.

'Well,' said Liza, '*I* know best. Jack, take Consuela home. Wrap up loose ends. Tell your boss you're taking an early break. Be back here by six p.m.'

'We gotta be decisive' rattled through his head on his way downtown as he guided Consuela about. He was trying to calculate how much he had in his bank account and thinking he really didn't have enough to go on this hugely impractical jaunt. Well, maybe. But was it the right thing to do? And surely they couldn't get a flight at such short notice? His head was crowded with all the reasons ranged against them . . .

But wasn't a part of him excited? Hadn't a little bit of him thrilled at the easy efficiency of Liza's decision? We gotta go to haunted Olde England and take their filthy grimoire back to them. That's the only way of fixing this thing.

The morning actually went smoother than he was expecting. He dropped off the rather quiet, shellshocked Consuela at his apartment, made her tea and left her to recover her wits. He didn't have time to sit with her this morning and talk about Ricardo. It seemed cruel, but there was just too much to do.

He bolted out to the nearest branch of his bank and found out exactly how much money he had left in the world. With a bit of scraping, he could make it across the pond. Just! Though what he was going to live off when he got back – whenever that might be – he had no idea.

It's Christmas, he thought, hurrying through the snowy West Village. And I'm heading out of town. I'm heading into history, into antiquity. Into some kind of ghost story.

He bought a paper from the newsstand on his way to work and read about twenty-three deaths in the night. Thirty-four bitings. It was a rash, an epidemic – a serial killer's fad. The authorities were on full alert. But where were they? Jack thought about how his gang had traipsed the blizzardy streets last night with their crucifixes and stakes and had seen hardly anyone out in public. How eerie that had been, getting lost in the peaceful streets. You'd hardly have known the city was in crisis.

At the shop, he found that Lame Wendy hadn't turned up yet. Another assistant, Ralph, was doing the work of three. Mr Grenoble was tearing out what was left of his hair.

'What is this, when I can't rely on you young people any more? The world's going crazy. All these deaths and maimings going on. This bad stuff. And now Wendy letting me down and coming in late if she comes in at all. And getting sassy and giving me rough talk when she *is* here . . .'

Jack frowned. 'That doesn't sound like Wendy.'

Mr Grenoble shook his head sorrowfully. 'You've been so preoccupied, young Jack, that you haven't been noticing the queer changes in her these past few days. The revealing clothes, the nasty mouth . . .'

'I guess . . .' said Jack, but Mr Grenoble was wrong. Jack *had* known about it. Wendy herself had told him what she had been up to, and how it had changed her. She had very deliberately gone off the rails.

'And I find that she has been using my store computer while she has been here at work,' the boss went on worriedly. 'I have discovered that she has opened up my private files. Looked at details of my friends and family, all my personal stuff. And made notes on them all, as if she is planning something . . .'

Now Jack was torn. 'Ah, that's . . .' But could he really tell Mr Grenoble the truth? Could he willingly blow the surprise of the New Year seventieth birthday party? He could see at once that it was the right thing to do. His boss was stirred up, paranoid, writhing with upset in his green tweed suit. 'Mr Grenoble, that's just—'

But they were interrupted by a pushy customer, come to complain about the dirty words in a book she'd bought from them, and the moment passed.

How do I tell him I'm gonna need extra time off? How do I even start to explain what it's for?

As he mulled that point over, Jack realised that by now there was simply no question in his mind but that he was going to London with Liza. Wherever she wanted to go, whatever measures she wanted to take – he was with her. He had never been so unequivocal before in his life. Was it her easy, brassy authority? Or was it the excitement?

I think I'm just glad someone has an inkling what to do in the situation, he thought. Left to myself, I'd just be screaming and running away.

Jack headed out for a late lunch and left Mr Grenoble – still sore over Lame Wendy's no-show and suspected espionage – grumbling at the cash desk.

He slipped out with the intention of dashing home, packing a bag and finding his passport in whichever drawer he had flung it in after his ignominious return from Italy. He'd get everything ready now and be ready to flee in the early evening.

And he'd check on Consuela. See how the poor old dame was doing.

'Hello? Consuela?' He let himself in and was struck by the lack of TV noise. No soaps, no jangling commercials. Probably she was sleeping.

The first thing he saw was some upturned planters. Soil on the rug. Pale roots showing obscenely. Then he noticed a wooden stake, broken in two. He recognised it as one from Liza's arsenal.

Consuela had broken a stake and flung it on his carpet. What did that mean? Some kind of hot-tempered peevishness? A refusal to go any further in this charade? Or just plain old despair?

And then he saw the blood. Thick, gloopy and sprayed up the wall and blotted over the carpet tiles of the hallway.

He found her on her favourite bed settee, sprawled on the pink comforter with her detective novels splayed around her.

Oh please let it not be Ricardo . . . Don't let it have been Ricardo who did this . . .

But at one level it hardly mattered. It had happened. It was over.

Did it matter if Ricardo had returned and done this to his own mother? It was too late to worry about that now. Here she was. Her neck ripped open like a birthday card with money in. Her eyes full of horrible fright and rimmed with congealing blood.

Ricardo had done this. Jack knew it.

Chapter Twenty-Seven

'Listen, you just gotta get out of there. Right now. I mean it, Jack.'

That wasn't what Jack was expecting to hear. 'What? Liza, I can't just leave her lying here dead in my apartment.'

Liza was determined. Her voice had dropped to a machine-gun rattle. 'If you phone the cops and report this, what do you think's gonna happen? They're gonna seal the whole area and you're gonna be hauled in toot de fricking sweet, dearest heart. Now, you gotta get out of there and buy yourself some time.'

He stared at the receiver and then back at the ghastly form of Consuela. A thousand emotions were battling it out inside of him. Right now, he just wanted to run screaming out of that place that had been his refuge for so long.

He realised all at once that his home had been defiled and ruined for ever.

'I could report it anonymously maybe, and make my escape,' he said, thinking aloud and picturing himself packing a quick bag and bolting out of the place.

'You could do . . .'

'But then they'll come looking for me, won't they? It'll seem even more suspicious. They might stop me at JFK as I try to leave . . .' Already he felt like a hunted animal, and he hadn't gone anywhere yet.

When Liza spoke next, he heard the exasperation in her voice. 'Look, kiddo, we don't have enough time for this. We just gotta act. You went back there to get your passport and whatever you might need for a little trip. Just pretend you never saw the body.'

He marvelled at how cold and controlled the old woman could be. She had known Consuela, she had met her. She had seen her just last night.

'Think how many people are being attacked and killed all over New York right now,' Liza told him. 'Consuela is one among dozens. Our duty is to get to the root of this outbreak. Not have a nervous breakdown over one single fatality.'

'Y-yes,' he said. 'You're right. If you think we can do something about stopping them . . .'

'And I do,' she snapped. 'So getta move on. Come on. I gotta go now and get on to the airlines. I'll see you back at my apartment in an hour, tops. Okay, Jack?' She waited for his shaky agreement before slamming down the phone.

Next thing he knew, he had his overnight bag open on his messy bed and was slinging things into it out of his wardrobe, almost at random. He should be taking more than an overnight bag. He didn't know how long they would be away for. Surely a few days . . . maybe right through Christmas. But where in London were they going to stay? Had Liza even thought about that?

London . . . London . . . Then he remembered something

Ricardo had told him recently. His cousin in London. How he had disappeared. Paolo. He'd been checking out that shop of Liza's on Charing Cross Road. And something had happened to him.

Jack stood stock still for a moment, trying to figure out why that bit of information had reappeared in his head.

He went to the kitchen corner of his living room and easily found Consuela's capacious handbag. He dug through layers of tissues and knitting wool and found her ancient address book. Somewhere in there there'd be a contact in London. Her sister's son and wife. It would be a starting point, wouldn't it? That bloke had been and paid a visit to the bookshop that was waiting at the end of their quest. Was he still missing?

He fumbled through the pages of the book. Maybe he could phone them long distance and check what had happened.

So absorbed was he in his search that he was completely unaware that Consuela had left the settee.

Her eyes had opened suddenly, disturbed by the sound of Jack muttering to himself as he went through her bag and her address book.

She glided to her feet in one smooth motion. Her movements were much more fluid and elegant than they had ever been before. She floated silently across the room like a dancer. She grinned at this ease of movement. Her feet no longer ached. Her bones no longer troubled her. She chuckled low in her throat as she saw Jack there, riffling through her private things. He was going to get such a surprise . . .

He whipped around at the sound of her laughter and screamed.

She laughed louder. 'Please, please, don't fear me,' she said. 'And don't feel bad for me. I am feeling wonderful! I haven't felt like this since . . .' Her face was shining as she did a quick calculation. 'Since before the crisis with the Cuban missiles. That's a long time. Waaay before you were born.'

Jack stowed away her address book and fell with a clatter of pots and pans against the work surface. 'Who did this to you, Consuela?'

She advanced on him, smoothing her glossy hair back into its habitual bun. 'Why, my son. Ricardo was always good to his mother. Always did everything for me. We shared everything we could. And now he has given me this gift . . .'

Jack groaned. 'Where is he now? He isn't here, is he?'

She shook her head. 'He has returned to Daniel at the nest, where he is to be second in command. They are making plans. Big plans for this city. We are going to be rich, Jack. We are going to be calling the shots, for once, in this great big city.' Her eyes glittered. She looked thoughtful. 'I am very hungry. I am starved. Come here, Jack. Ricardo wants you. He needs you now, to be like us. Come to your new mamma . . .'

As Jack tried to get as far from the small woman as his kitchenette would allow, the phone rang again. 'Yes? Help!' he yelled.

Liza went rattling on. 'Look, have you got a really big case? Mine won't do. Bessie says she can fold up real small – we could even dismantle her, apparently, and put her in the hold – but we need one of those great big cases on wheels . . .'

Jack cut through her flow of words. 'She's here!' he cried out, as Consuela made a lunge at him.

'Who? Bessie? But Bessie's right here with me. What are you talking about?'

'Consuela! She's alive!' Without thinking, he flung open the cutlery drawer and picked up a meat skewer. He brandished it wildly and the woman hissed, then gurgled with laughter. What was he going to do? *Could* he stake her? Could he really bring himself to plunge it into her chest? What if he was wrong and she wasn't a vamp at all? What if she was just crazy and he went sticking utensils into her?

'Jack!' Liza shouted. 'What's going on down there?'

'I'll talk to you later!' he yelled and flung down the receiver. He lashed out with the skewer and caught his putative mother-in-law on the chunky top of her arm. Consuela howled. 'You keep away from me!' Jack warned.

'I know what you're doing,' Consuela said. 'I know what you're plotting. You and that Liza Bathory and Shelley and that hollow excuse for a fake woman. I know what you are planning to do.'

'No you don't,' snapped Jack. But maybe she did. She had been with them for hours. How much of their cobbled-together plans had she overheard?

'I know you have stolen back the grimoire,' she said. 'And Daniel wants it. He has been hideously betrayed by his love. He will do anything – absolutely anything – to get it back.'

'He won't get it back from where we're taking it,' said Jack, and instantly regretted it. He needed to stop talking to her and get out of here. He took one last wild, despairing look at his beautiful home.

'I will tell Daniel everything,' Consuela taunted him. 'You

came here for your passport. You have packed a bag. It is obvious what you are planning to do next.'

'Yeah?' he said, and lashed out again with the skewer, feeling terrible about it all the time. Consuela hissed and drew back. Jack took the advantage and lunged at the refrigerator, flinging open the heavy door. Taken by surprise, Consuela fell sideways. Jack picked up a huge bottle of rough white wine and just about brained her with it. Black blood flowed down her face as she sprang up, but her power seemed undimmed. Jack snatched the jar of Lazy Garlic and dashed its vinegary contents into her face. She sneezed loudly, but nothing more.

Jack pelted past her into the hallway. No time to get the big bag Liza wanted. He snatched his overnighter and checked he had his passport and wallet. With a great screech, Consuela came after him, reeking of garlic.

He was out on the fire escape and just about to thunder downstairs when he looked back and saw the most extraordinary thing.

Consuela turned herself into a bat and fluttered past him into the frosty air.

The creature gave a venomous hiss as she skittered and flapped away from him, and he flung his skewer after her like a spear. It clattered uselessly several storeys down, and by the time it hit the snowy alleyway, Consuela was gone.

Gone to report to Daniel and the others. Telling them where Liza and her gang were taking the book. He would know. Within the hour, Daniel would know.

Time to get moving.

There wasn't even time to think about the crazy stuff that had gone on. And there was no time to report back to the shop to explain.

He just had to go. Right now.

It was dark again by the time he arrived at Liza's apartment.

Chapter Twenty-Eight

He found Liza beetling about her apartment, flinging things into bags, dashing from room to room in a disorganised manner. She seemed feverishly nervous.

As she gabbled at him and explained that she had persuaded Mr Oblonsky upstairs to take Rufus in for a few days, and how painful her brief goodbye with her pooch had been, Jack realised what it was about her. She wasn't just scared. Liza was excited. Brimming with anticipation.

'And why not?' she croaked when he accused her. 'I've always wanted to go to England. Can you believe it? In all my years of reading about it, imagining it – I've never been! It's the wellspring of English literature . . . the home of the spooky ghost tale. This is my great opportunity!' She said 'litcheratoor' and 'opportoonity', and Jack reflected that she had never sounded more like a New Yorker than now when she was overexcited about going to London. 'C'mon,' she told him. 'You gotta help us. I think Shelley is kind of struggling . . .'

Jack followed her into the L-shaped main room and hesitated in the doorway, surveying a scene that several days ago might have filled him with horror and dread. After recent events – and

especially the surprising brutality of Consuela's attack this evening
– he was less fazed than he might have been.

Shelley was packing dismembered pieces of the Scottish Bride
into a vast suitcase on wheels.

'It's okay,' she said, looking up at him. 'Bessie told us to do it.
She needs to come with us in order to help. She says she's been in
bits like this hundreds of times before . . .' Shelley was holding up
one of the woman's skinny arms as if to reassure Jack that
everything was okay. The sight of those fingers twitching at
him from across the room did little to calm his nerves. 'Aunt Liza
told me about Consuela,' Shelley said. 'I'm so sorry.'

He sat down heavily on the sofa. 'Yeah, me too.'

'I know you liked the lady.'

'I did. She was eccentric, and hard work sometimes. But I
thought I really had a little family there, you know. With things
working out with Ricardo. And then his mother moving in –
which should have been disastrous. But it was okay, really. And
now . . .'

'I know,' Shelley said, incongruously patting the arm down
into a corner of the gigantic case, snug against Bessie's hollow
torso. 'This whole business has messed up everyone's lives.'

'And more lives will be ruined if we don't succeed,' said Liza,
who was calm and intent-sounding all of a sudden. In the middle
of checking the window locks she had paused dramatically and
was watching over the snowy rooftops and towers and the vast
pregnant sky of the city.

To Jack she looked like its guardian. The witch at the top of
the Eighth Avenue tower who had to make such a long journey
this very night . . . in order to confront the powers of unholy

darkness . . . in order to save the world. 'There is a great evil out there,' she said. 'And we have to rout it out.'

He saw that she was holding the grimoire. Strange that such a small, innocuous-looking thing could be at the heart of this. No, scratch that. The book didn't look at all innocuous. It seemed to radiate a dreadful kind of power, almost a vapour of wickedness that came streaming out of it. At some invisible point of the light spectrum, that thing was glowing a really shitty colour, Jack thought.

He watched Liza place the grimoire with great ceremony into her hand luggage. Then she turned to help Shelley stuff the rest of Bessie into the great big suitcase. 'Mr Oblonsky was so helpful. We must bring him back a present. Not only did he agree to look after Rufus along with his own three poodles over Christmas, but he lent me the biggest suitcase he had. Isn't it just the thing?'

Jack had to agree. He examined it and was shocked to find Bessie's face staring out at him from a tangle of her own limbs. '*Jesus Christ!* Can she hear us still?'

'I think so,' said Liza. 'But she said that while she's in pieces like this, she generally goes into a trance.'

'Will it be hard, putting her back together?'

'Nuh-huh.' Liza shrugged. 'She says not. She says clicking herself back together is a cinch.'

'But surely . . . customs and the security guys are going to wonder what it is you're carrying?'

Liza coughed modestly and Shelley spoke up. 'My aunt has cast a deflection spell. Just a small magic thing. It'll kind of deter anyone looking too hard at what's in the bag.'

Jack boggled at them. 'You've been casting spells? You can *do* that?'

'I told you I was a bit of a witch,' Liza said lightly. 'Not much of one, sure. But enough to know a few interesting and useful tricks. Like the deflection spell. But it costs me dearly to use even a tiny bit of magic. I'm worn to a friggin' frazzle here, y'know.'

Soon, all that remained for them to do was travel down in the elevator with their strange consignment of luggage. Before she turned out the lights of her apartment and triple-locked the door, Liza cast a last look round. Jack saw her glance at the sumptuous black and purple Christmas tree she had put up near her bookshelves, and at those shelves themselves, decked with ratty swags of tinsel. At first he thought she was sighing because she'd be missing the Yuletide season in her beloved home. But then he realised it was more. He was watching Liza look around at her place as if for the last time. She was preparing to meet her ultimate fate while away on this trip. Getting herself ready to face up to her own demise. He gulped, and she slammed the door shut and locked it firmly behind them.

Down they went in the elevator and across the lobby, where all their baggage garnered a bit of attention. Shelley was struggling with the massive bag on wheels. It was heavier than she was herself, and it kept trying to tip over. Luckily, no one stopped them wanting to chat. They didn't have to explain they were going away for Christmas. Liza doubted that at this point she could chat breezily about holiday plans.

When they flagged down a cab, the driver looked really pissed off about all their bags. He was bitching about the heaviest one so much that Liza shot around to his side of the trunk and said something to him that made his eyes bulge for a moment. 'Yes, ma'am,' he replied, and got on with the task in hand. Jack was keen to hear what Liza had said to him, or threatened him with, but once they were sitting three abreast in the taxi, he soon forgot to ask.

The car ducked and wove through the midtown traffic. There were a lot of people out on the street, shopping in the vast lit-up stores, even after all the warnings of danger. The city wasn't a safe place to be this season, and yet everyone seemed to be out and about, charging their cards to the max and waddling along with bulging shopping bags. Jack wound down his window and felt the wet snow whirling by, some of it landing in cold little dabs on his face. He heard snatches of overfamiliar Christmas tunes and suddenly he longed to be out there. Just being normal. Enjoying the evening like everyone else seemed to be.

Why did he have to be here with this lot? How come he got to be part of this crazy scheme involving evil books and women who weren't even real, women who were folded up inside cases and about to travel across the ocean to a city none of them even really knew?

Soon enough they had left the excitable, frightened, ghoulishly festive city behind.

They gripped each other's hands in the back of the cab, feeling as if they had escaped from something. The city receded brilliantly behind them in the darkness as they sped over the Brooklyn Bridge.

But they weren't escaping anything, were they? Jack thought.

They were leaving the city . . . but they were heading towards something even more deadly. Or that was how it felt.

Ahead of them they could sense the airport, with its planes running through the night, back and forth all over the world, efficient as clockwork. And one of those planes would take them to London this very night.

Jack felt underpacked, underprepared. Utterly overwhelmed.

Then Shelley cried out, 'Look! Oh look!'

She was craning round in her seat, looking out of the back window.

'Oh my God,' Liza said.

Jack looked. The traffic behind them had slackened somewhat. A great dark gap of bridge stretched out behind them.

It wasn't empty, though.

Something came running through the darkened slush after them.

A vast brindled wolf. Its tongue was lolling hungrily, and even at this distance they could see its eyes glowing like rubies.

It didn't try to catch them. It just wanted them to see. Somehow they knew the wolf wanted them to know that he was in pursuit. And that they would never get away from him. No matter how fast or how far they flew tonight, he and his kind would come after them.

Chapter Twenty-Nine

Their flight arrived at Heathrow in the early morning, wreathed in carnation-pink cloud. The whole city still bore the last vestiges of night, its dark corners sketched out in orange street lighting. Liza had been awake for several hours before their approach, avid for the first glimpse of the land she had dreamed about.

Jack had been shuffling in and out of sleep, his long legs cramped in the tiny space, his mind full of foreboding. But they had touched down without incident, and Shelley had slept through even that sudden, rapid jolt.

When the seat-belt lights went on, Liza bolted up and flung open the overhead compartment. She wanted to be first off the plane and collecting her luggage. 'It doesn't make any difference,' Jack grumbled. 'Everybody has to wait at the carousel just the same.'

'I know,' she said, looking pale and tired. 'I just keep thinking about Bessie down in the hold.'

Their anxious faces were incongruous on that plane filled with passengers arriving to spend Christmas in England. A good-natured – even jubilant – mood was upon all the strangers around them. Some were even wearing Santa hats and reindeer ears, and were hoisting expensive parcels they hadn't wanted to put in the frozen hold as the plane streaked over the dark Atlantic.

Shelley woke with a bad head. 'Do we even know where we want to go?' she said as they queued to leave the plane, nodding at the air crew's earnest grins.

'Well, the bookshop, of course,' snapped Liza tiredly. 'We gotta go straight there and get this book back to them.' The grimoire was heavy in her flight bag, still exuding its exotic and heady scent. Still, her winter coat smelled strongly of Rufus, and that masked a little of the reek of black magic.

'It's six in the morning London time,' Jack reminded them. 'We need somewhere to stay.'

'A hotel,' said Shelley, deciding she didn't care how much this was all going to cost them. She just wanted a hot shower and a place she could lie down for a few hours at full stretch without expecting someone to shove into her, tread on her toes or start biting her neck.

'I've got a better idea,' Jack said. 'I'll phone Paolo's wife and explain why we're here.'

'Who's Paolo?' Shelley asked, and he tried to explain as they followed the seeming miles of carpeted hallway and glass corridors leading to passport control.

Eventually they were in the vast hall where the luggage carousels shunted around emptily and a festive crowd was gathering. Jack sloped off to activate his cell phone and find the number in Consuela's address book.

They were in England. A whole ocean away from Consuela, Ricardo and all the terrible stuff that was happening over there in New York City. Standing in this white concrete bunker, with people waiting for mundane suitcases and shoving trolleys about, Jack could almost believe that the events of the past month were a kind of dream.

Someone picked up his call.

'Hello?'

'I'm sorry to have woken you . . .' he said.

'We've been up for ages,' said the woman's voice on the other end. 'Connie's overexcited about Father Christmas coming. Can you hear her?' It was true: in the background, Jack could hear a toddler whooping and screeching. He winced. 'Who is this?' asked the woman, sounding as chirpy and cockney as Jack had imagined.

'We are friends of Paolo,' he began.

'Paolo! You know where he is?' She sounded shocked – and then guarded and frightened, all within a few words.

'No, er, no . . . we don't, I'm afraid.' Jack paced around, wondering if he wasn't making a difficult situation even worse. He dodged a few bustling passengers with their clunky trolleys and peered across the hall to see that their carousel was moving round now, laden with bags. Well, Liza and Shelley would be sure to look out for his too, and be ready to grab it off the conveyor belt. He had to explain to this woman why they had come. 'I'm Jack Hoban, a friend of Ricardo and Consuela's. Paolo's cousin and aunt in New York. I've flown from New York in order to—'

'Ricardo and Consuela are here?' Her voice went up in alarm. 'They've come all this way?'

'No, I'm afraid not,' he said, feeling foolish. 'They can't come just now, but they were . . . we were . . . concerned to hear about Paolo disappearing. Is he . . . still . . . ?'

272

'He hasn't been home for over a week,' she said, her voice going cold and hard. 'No one will say or do anything. The police, no one. They just think he's run off with some fancy bird.'

'Fancy bird?' Jack repeated, before he got her meaning. 'Look, are you . . . ?'

'I'm his wife, Vicki. Sitting here like a lemon, waiting for him to get back before Christmas. He ain't ever done anything like this before. And Connie's a toddler, and this is the first Christmas she'll remember properly, you know what I mean? And her daddy's done a runner, kind of thing. What sort of Christmas is that gonna be? For either of us? I've literally got nothing in, no money, hardly any presents or food . . .'

'Er, yes,' said Jack, beginning to wish he hadn't started this. 'Look, we've come to help you.'

'With Christmas and stuff?'

'With finding Paolo,' he said. 'He went to the bookshop to investigate, didn't he? The one on Charing Cross Road.'

'I don't know where he goes. He used to like gambling. Horses and dogs it used to be, then he got into the casinos and he'd go up West alone sometimes . . . but yeah, you're right. This time he went off saying he was going to check out some kind of bookshop, which I thought was bloody funny at the time . . .' Behind her there came a crash – a clatter of cooking utensils, it sounded like – and then a child started howling. 'Shit! Connie! Look, mister, I've got to go and see to the kid, she's pulling the place to bits here . . .'

Jack said, 'Look, do you mind if we call in? We're new in London and we don't know anybody.'

'You think you know something about what might have happened to my Paolo?'

'Yes,' said Jack. 'I think we might. We're here to go to that same bookshop. Something's—'

'Well, if you know something, you'd better get round here. The police ain't doing nothing. No one's doing anything.' Her daughter's angry screams went up in pitch. 'Look, you got the address?'

'Yes, er . . . Rowley . . . ?'

'Rowley Way, that's it. You got it. See you here, Mr Hoban.'

The phone went dead, and Jack wondered whether he should have explained that he'd be arriving with an entourage in tow: two women and an undead effigy called Bessie, plus all their collected luggage.

He hurried back to the carousel, which had been picked clean of most of its baggage already. He was reminded of National Geographic films of ants carrying away the bulky carcasses of caterpillars. Shelley and Liza had a silver trolley apiece, with their bags loaded ready to go. He was glad to see his own modestly sized case included.

'Are we ready?' he asked.

Then he saw the pinched and anxious expression on Liza's face.

'What is it?'

'Bessie's case hasn't turned up yet,' she said. 'These last few bags have been round twice. There's no sign of her.'

Shelley swore under her breath, as if this was just what she had been expecting.

'She'll turn up,' Jack said. 'We've just got to wait here.'

'Nuh-huh,' Liza said. 'She's got lost in fricking transit, Jack. I just know it. Bessie's gone missing!'

Liza grumbled hysterically all the way to St John's Wood in the taxi.

'I'll never forgive myself if something dreadful has happened to her.'

Shelley was just as bad-tempered, snapping, 'Well she's my responsibility, isn't she? I was the one who found her in the first place.'

'You still think of her as a thing, an artefact,' said her aunt. 'To me, Bessie is a real, living person who's alone in the world. She deserves our respect and all the help we can give her. And what do we do? Lose her somewhere over the friggin' ocean.'

'They'll find her,' Jack said. 'Stuff goes missing like that all the time. They've got our details, they know where to find us.' In the rush of panic and bureaucratic stuff, registering their precious lost luggage, they'd had to resort to giving the authorities Vicki's address. It was the only one – besides the bookshop in Charing Cross Road – they even knew in London.

Now the taxi was pulsing through the streets, just as the morning rush was beginning, towards that address and the council flat home of this woman none of them had ever met before.

'She sounds very nice, anyway,' said Jack. 'And very concerned about her husband. I'm sure she'll put us up, especially since we're investigating where he's gone.'

'Are we?' said Shelley. 'I thought we were just returning the book to the shop and then getting out of here.'

'Jack's right,' Liza said. 'I think we gotta find out what's going on with this shop. Sending out dangerous parcels like that. Causing all this ruckus. It's down to us, guys.' Unconsciously she reached to knee level to pat Rufus's head, just as she normally would at this point. Too late she remembered that her mutt was spending the festive period with her uncouth upstairs neighbour, Mr Oblonsky. She sighed. She hoped the old man would feed him right. Oblonsky seemed to live off nothing but pickles and beer.

At last they came to a kind of concrete fortress. The council estate was organised in a series of terraces in a vast fake valley livened up with overflowing plant pots and some decorative graffiti. 'It's . . . charming,' said Jack, finding the exact address in the book.

However was he going to explain to these relatives of Consuela and Ricardo what had become of them? One step at a time, he reminded himself . . .

Vicki's landing was on the highest level. She opened the door to them with her daughter in her arms and looked politely mystified by their appearance. The apartment smelled delightfully of fresh ground coffee and the radio was jangling with some silly pop tune as the visitors shuffled into the messy kitchen.

'Sorry about all the stuff,' said Vicki. 'I wasn't expecting guests.' She turned the radio down and surveyed them all seriously. Jack was acutely conscious of the extra clutter that their bags made in the hall. He was also conscious that the young girl was staring up at Shelley, Liza and himself with the frankly interested stare that only kids could get away with.

'Are you American?' she asked.

'Connie, don't be rude. Come and finish your porridge.'

'It's okay,' chuckled Liza. 'Yeah, we are, honey. And we've come all the way from New York City.'

'My great-auntie lives there,' said the child. 'I've got the same name as her.'

Jack felt it hard to swallow his first sip of coffee. Once again he wondered how on earth he could tell these people what had become of their relatives.

'It's very good of you to let us drop in like this,' Liza told Vicki. 'We won't get under your feet. If we can just leave our things here . . .'

Shelley muttered something about how they should just have gone straight to a hotel. This was ridiculous, imposing on people . . .

'You're not imposing,' said Vicki. 'I gather you guys know something about my Paolo, right?'

'We may do,' said Jack.

'Then I'm happy you're here. Like I say, neither the police nor no one will look for him. He's a grown-up and he can look after himself. All this fobbing me off. And you can see how I'm fixed. I can't go hunting the streets. I went to the shop he said he was going to, on account of what his cousin had said, but I didn't go in. It looked a bit . . . I don't know.' In the bright winter sunshine of the kitchen, she shivered. 'It looked . . . skanky and forbidding, you know what I mean? I wanted to go in. I wanted to ask about Paolo. But somehow I just couldn't. I couldn't even get the pushchair up the step into the shop. Something in me just gave up and I came home. You'll think I'm such a coward.'

'No,' said Liza softly. 'There's magic in this.'

Vicki looked at her sharply. 'Magic?' She didn't laugh and she didn't overreact. She just stared back at Liza and waited for her to elaborate. It was as if she already knew Liza was right.

'I'm sorry,' said Liza. 'But we have come all this way to sort it out.'

'P-Paolo always said his aunt believed in superstitious stuff. Magic stuff. He said she was famous in the family for it. Curses and that.'

'It wasn't her fault, what's happened,' said Liza. 'I'm afraid that it's all kinda my fault.'

Vicki shook her head. 'Look, I can't afford to get mixed up in anything bad. Nothing nasty. I got my girl to look after . . .'

The child was looking at them all solemnly.

'You'll be okay,' said Liza.

Jack thought the old woman was a bit rash, to offer assurance so blithely.

As it turned out, he was right.

After their coffee, and then some discussion about Shelley looking dead on her feet, it was decided that the best thing would be to head straight into central London by Tube. The day was under way and the shop on Charing Cross Road was waiting for them.

'You can leave all your bags here. I've only got one spare room, and the sofa, of course,' Vicki told them. 'But you're welcome to stay.'

Her warmth embarrassed them. And Jack felt uncomfortable, leaving her and her daughter with all their stuff. Involving them in their troubles like this. He shivered as they set off once more in the frosty morning.

'She was very nice,' Shelley said.

'I just hope we haven't placed her in any danger,' Liza sighed. Then they hurried off in the direction of the Tube station, using the *A–Z* that Vicki had loaned them.

Chapter Thirty

Liza, you're such an old fool. Just get a grip on yourself, woman, and concentrate. You gotta sort this whole mess out. It's really down to you that these forces got unleashed in the first place, and there's only you who can deal with them.

Still, even as she gave herself this stern talking-to, there was a little part of herself that was disappointed.

This isn't a holiday, she intoned. This isn't the trip of a lifetime. It isn't everything you were hoping for.

Because, really, London wasn't living up to what she had expected of it. Not yet, and if she was honest, she didn't expect that it would *ever* live up to the mad expectations she had in her head. Somewhere between a lifetime marinading in English literature – with special emphasis on the Gothic – and the forceful energies of her own imagination, Liza had created an extremely vivid picture of what this first trip should be like.

So far it was a bit too much like the boring parts of home. Their hurried dash to the subway had afforded her glimpses of McDonald's, Starbucks, street markets and honking, congested traffic. It was more like being in the Bronx than anything else.

But don't be disappointed, Liza, she told herself. There are bigger things here than just the upset of some old woman. Some old woman who had spent her whole life imagining the sensation of setting foot on British soil, who had saved up every spare penny for the eventual trip . . . and who had just blown every damn dime in her savings accounts simply coming here.

But she was here at last. And they were on their way to the shop that had come to mean so much in these past few weeks.

She gripped Shelley's hand as they sat very close together in the Tube carriage. Jack was standing up, studying the poster map – and perhaps trying to look as if he wasn't with them. Maybe they looked rather bedraggled and mad and he was regretting ever getting mixed up in their cause. But it was his cause too, wasn't it? After his terrible ordeal with his boyfriend and Consuela. They were all in this together, and Liza was glad.

She fretted that Shelley was subdued and not quite herself. Was that jet lag – or was it something else, more sinister? She remembered the blood on her niece's neck just after the last time she had escaped from Daniel. Was it a scratch, a graze – or had it truly been a bite? An undeadly bite? Shelley was surely conscious of it, because she was choosing to cover it up with a turtleneck collar – like a teenager covering a hickey. I should ask to see it and examine it properly, Liza thought. But somehow she just couldn't bring herself to. There hadn't been a moment to broach the terrible subject. She simply had to hope that her niece was unscathed – and even as she had that thought, she was fidgeting guiltily, and with dread. Liza knew that she was making awful mistakes all over place and had done so throughout this whole debacle.

In her earlier years she wouldn't have made such mistakes. Not when she had fought against the monsters and horrors of the sixties and seventies. But she had retired from all of that. She was rusty. She had made some awful errors . . .

And maybe I've lost poor Bessie too, she thought, dwelling with shame on the image of poor dismembered Bessie stuffed into the suitcase they had borrowed from Mr Oblonsky. Bessie had survived hundreds of years of incredible tribulations. She had been cast to the bottom of the sea and she had voyaged alone from the Old to the New World and was wanted in neither place. She had been despised, rejected and not even recognised as human, but somehow the Scottish Bride had managed to survive, all in one piece.

Yeah, thought Liza bitterly. That was, until we pulled her apart and stowed her away among the luggage of a 747 one Christmas.

She was probably lost for ever. In a warehouse in Abu Dhabi. Or worse, some bright spark would X-ray the case and find a dismembered corpse, and the labels would lead them straight to Liza . . .

Enough. She was making herself ill with these ghoulish speculations. Her stomach roiled and threatened to heave up the black coffee she had taken at Vicki's apartment. And that was another thing – what was Jack doing, promising the girl that they'd investigate her husband's disappearance? Like they didn't have enough to do! Still, it was good to have somewhere to leave their cases. They didn't have to heave all their baggage into the city centre and . . .

Shelley was shaking her shoulder. 'Jack's trying to catch our attention.'

Liza blinked and realised that, quite suddenly, the shabby, brightly lit carriage had filled with passengers. It was jolting to a halt and Jack was by the sliding doors, trying to catch their eyes.

'I think we're here,' said Shelley.

He had brought them to the subway stop called Charing Cross. From a quick glance at the borrowed *A–Z*, Liza could see that, really, they would have been better disembarking at Tottenham Court Road, but she didn't want to argue or cause a fuss.

They emerged blinking into a honking, screeching street filled with tourists and pigeons. Everyone was shouting about something or other, and those that weren't kept their heads down and plodded along with determination. At least they got to see Trafalgar Square, coming this way, and Liza's heart lifted at that. Perhaps that was why Jack had chosen this stop to get off at – to give them a little glimpse of the kind of London they had imagined: lions and Nelson and stuff.

Negotiating the roads and the pushy taxis, they found their way to Charing Cross Road itself.

Liza took a deep breath. She pushed her hand into her bag, where the letters from Mr K. N. Wright crackled under her fingers. She checked them for the exact address – 66b – though of course she knew that by heart. Those few letters she had received from her friendly bookseller were with her as a kind of talisman more than for any practical reason. As she stowed them away again, and hurried to keep up with the young people, her fingers brushed the leathery binding of the grimoire.

It was warm, like lightly sweating skin. It was hot with anticipation. The grimoire was coming home again, its nasty work abroad swiftly accomplished.

It was returning to Charing Cross Road to roost.

'We're almost there,' Shelley said, counting doors.

They passed shop fronts, dark and streaked with dust. They passed ramshackle displays of books and barrows containing knocked-down bargains. Liza longed to stop and browse and to be just another book-buying tourist. That was all she wanted to do.

Bookshop after bookshop, all the way up Charing Cross Road. Some shabby, some rather grander. Antiquarians and floggers of cheap paperbacks. The road narrowed and bottlenecked, and it seemed to Liza that booksellers were peering at the newly arrived Americans, squinting over their counters and their pince-nez, aware of the horror that these interlopers were carrying with them . . .

But that was just her foolish imagination. No one really cared, did they, about these visitors and the small black book they were bringing back? No one either knew or cared.

She hoped.

At last Jack stopped outside a rather small, unassuming door painted black. A brass plaque told them that this was number 66b. There was no other sign and no shop window. Just this black door, its paint chipped and starting to flake away.

Liza gulped. Home to roost.

This was it. Here they were.

She raised her hand, shaking slightly, and rapped on the door.

Leaving Connie in front of morning kids' TV, Vicki applied herself to the task of manoeuvring her guests' bags into her tiny spare bedroom.

How had she suddenly acquired visitors and all this luggage?

She'd never clapped eyes on these people until about an hour ago. It was like her mum always said: she was too soft. She took the path of least resistance, every time. And that was how she'd wound up with a guy like Paolo. A loudmouth who could do what he wanted and she'd never complain. Vicki had brought this recent bad business on herself, her mother opined. Paolo had just wandered off on his merry way, hardly thinking he need tell his wife where he was.

What am I thinking about her for? Vicki wondered, wrestling with one of the cases. She read the label. An exotic address in New York. Second Avenue, indeed. She imagined going to New York one day. Paolo had promised her that when they'd saved enough, they could go and see his relatives in the Big Apple.

Well, as it turned out, half of New York had come to them instead. Vicki laughed at herself. It wasn't as bad as that. It wasn't all that inconvenient. And they seemed like quite nice people, anyway. Even if they had been talking pretty strangely about this bookshop of theirs. There was an odd urgency about them . . . an almost furtive urgency. It was as if they were wary of letting too much of their story out, in case they alarmed her. And then there was that talk of magic and superstition . . .

She was about half done with the bags when there came a heavy, authoritative knock at her front door. She turned to see a tall silhouette through the rippled glass. She peeked through the spyhole to see an impatient, handsome face looking sternly back at her. She left the chain on. 'Yes?'

'I'm afraid I need to speak to you, ma'am,' the man said, sounding quite posh and important, she thought.

'Who are you?'

'We're a special investigation squad, er . . . madam.'

Her heart leapt in her chest. 'Is this about Paolo?' Without thinking, her fingers were at work, unhooking the chain.

'Paolo?' asked the man, frowning. He looked at a little policeman's-type notebook. 'Er, yes. Yes, we are, madam.'

Vicki threw open the door. Later she would wonder at herself and her actions. She hadn't asked him to show his ID or anything. Pensioners had gotten their heads kicked in doing stuff like that, letting in strangers who seemed personable enough but were just thugs with a convincing manner. But there she was. Too trusting by half, as usual.

She let him in.

'Nice place you have, Mrs . . . ?'

'Delgado,' she said. 'I'm sorry for all the mess.'

'That's quite all right, Mrs Delgado. Now, I won't take up much of your time . . .'

She led him into the sitting room, which was bright with the sun pouring through the French windows at this time in the morning. Almost unbearably bright. The picture on the noisy telly was just about invisible, not that Connie cared. She stared at it anyway, singing along with the familiar tunes and ignoring the new visitor completely.

'Lovely kid,' he said. 'Got two of my own.'

Vicki motioned him to sit on the old G Plan settee she'd inherited from her mum. Did it look a bit shabby in the bright morning light? She tried to see it through the detective's eyes. Was that what he was? Special Investigations, he had said. Was that the police? He wore a very sharp suit, she noticed. 'What do you know about Paolo?' she asked him. 'It must be bad for them to send a guy round from Special Investigations, and not just an everyday copper. Do you want a cup of tea?'

'Er, no thanks,' he said.

'Have they found him?' she burst out. 'Don't tell me they've found his body. Don't say . . .' Her words petered out. She could feel great waves of panic beating at her.

'It's all right, madam,' the man said with concern. 'It's nothing like that. Honest. Rest assured that we haven't found a body. Don't upset yourself.'

'Oh, thank goodness.' She tried to calm herself, wiping her eyes on the sleeve of her top. She gulped and laughed nervously, seeing that Connie was watching them now, concerned. 'So what is it, then? What have you come to tell me?'

'You know, I think I will have that tea,' he said, smiling.

She smiled back and led him into the tiny galley kitchen.

He surprised her in the hallway by saying, 'You've got visitors?'

'Oh, yes. Strangers, really. People I'm helping out.'

'From New York?'

'Yes, apparently.'

He followed and watched her put the kettle on. 'Interesting,' he said.

'You know, I can't tell you how good it feels to think that you're out there looking for Paolo,' she said. 'I made a complaint, because the local police weren't bothered at all. No one seemed to care; they all thought it was fine and normal that he'd just gone wandering off.'

The man in the suit was staring at her. He said, 'Where are your New York guests now?'

Vicki shook her head in surprise. 'What?' She couldn't believe he hadn't been listening. 'I'm telling you about Paolo . . .'

'Yes,' he said, in that measured, cultivated voice. 'And I'm asking a question about these curious unwanted visitors of yours. I'm Special Investigations. I'm investigating. Now, answer the question, would you?'

She blinked at him, surprised by his curtness. 'They had to go out and do something. Something important. I dunno . . .'

'I think you can do better than that, dear,' he sighed.

Vicki frowned. 'Look, mister, I'm not liking your tone very much. Shouldn't you be listening to me?'

'Don't you think it's very strange?' he said smoothly. 'Your husband disappears. These strangers turn up.'

'They know him. At least, they know his family . . . his cousin and his aunt, over in New York.'

'Hmm,' said the detective. 'That sounds rather convenient to me.'

Vicki rummaged about with the tea-making, discomfited by his tone. 'They've gone to the bookshop he went to. They've promised to look into it . . . to find out what happened to him. I dunno . . . I trusted them. Just . . . instinctively, I guess. And they were promising to help. At the end of the day, you know, that's more than your lot, the police, ever did.'

'Oh dear,' the man said. 'I can see how upset you are. Let me help you with the tea things. And tell me . . . the bookshop? Which bookshop was this?'

Vicki grew impatient, setting out teacups with a clatter. 'I told them all this in the report I made! You've got it all on file!'

'I'd like to hear it in your own words,' he said. He spoke

purringly. He was standing too close. Vicki gasped. Whenever had he come to stand beside her like that? What was he playing at?

She stared him right in the eye. 'They've gone where Paolo went. Six six six Charing Cross Road.'

'Thank you,' he said. 'Thank you for helping with my investigations.'

And then, to her amazement, he kissed her.

She dropped the milk, but she didn't even care that it leaked two pints over the hardwood floor they'd only had since last spring.

She was kissing him back. Why was she doing that?

His arms went round her. She relinquished herself to his surprising strength.

And then he bit her, quite hard.

Chapter Thirty-One

Jack wondered how on earth a bookshop like this stayed in business.

They had to knock on the door three times before they attracted the attention of the skinny, round-faced man who eventually answered it. He let them in bad-temperedly. The narrow corridor inside reeked of damp and green mould.

The Americans glanced at each other before they followed the old gent down the whitewashed passageway, trying not to dislodge the stacks of papers mouldering against the walls. Old sheet music and unbound books, seemingly centuries old. Jack could tell Liza was longing to examine them.

A single unshaded bulb lit the passageway, making everything look sharp and eerie. It was bright morning light they had left outside, but in here it could have been four in the morning.

'Welcome to 66b,' said the tiny old man, and hacked out a wad of phlegm. He led them through a doorway and down some wooden cellar steps that felt a little too rickety. Jack was thinking about the bookshop's ad, which he had first seen in that glossy trade magazine. How they had no email, website, fax or even phone. That hardly surprised him now, seeing this place. It was like descending into a watery tomb. It was like the Thames itself was flowing through these lower rooms and tunnels, swishing fetid gunk, flotsam and jetsam through the dark corners of the shop.

He turned to see how Shelley was doing. She was moving along in a kind of trance. Her tiredness was threatening to overtake her and she was gripping on to consciousness with only the very tips of her fingers. Her touched her arm gently as they tried to keep up with the old man and the indefatigable Liza.

'I'm okay,' Shelley told him. 'It's just been a bit hectic recently. Jeez, this place really reeks, doesn't it?'

He pulled a face. He knew Liza was in her element here, amid all these crumbling, mould-spotted volumes arranged higgledy-piggledy on the shelves. There seemed to be no rhyme or reason to their ordering, though the old man led them very carefully, reverently, as if they were moving through some fabulous, opulent tomb of the gods. As if it was imperative that nothing was dislodged or spoiled.

'I am Mr Danby,' said the old man. 'I have worked all my life in this shop.'

'I'm Liza Bathory,' Liza began, but he cut her off.

'I know who you are. One of our most intriguing customers, if you'll forgive the impertinence.'

'Hardly impertinent at all,' said Liza. 'I'm glad you know me. And perhaps you know why I have come here in person?'

The old man turned, looking sly all of a sudden. 'Maybe you should talk to the owner about that, Ms Bathory. I'm sure he is better informed than I. These matters are his area, not mine, I'm afraid.'

'Okay,' said Liza. 'Where is he?'

Jack could hear the catch in her voice just then. He knew how keen she was to meet Mr Wright in person. The man who had typed those letters to her, and wrapped those parcels of books in brown paper. He hoped that she would remember that Mr Wright – charming as he was on the page – had been the one true cause of all their recent misfortunes.

Mr Danby led them through several more subterranean rooms. This was like progressing into the inner sanctum. Here the walls were drier and less stippled with fungoid life. The floors were even carpeted, in some richly embroidered Turkish affair. The shelves were better organised and the books more opulent, bound in fine leather and stamped with gold. Jack found his attention straying to their titles and authors, and he longed to examine them. Ahead of him, Liza looked as if she had been transported into heaven.

'This place must extend for miles underground,' said Shelley suddenly.

Jack had lost his bearings completely. 'It feels like we've walked several blocks down here.'

In one particular room they could hear a rumbling in the walls. It set flyblown pictures rattling on the walls, and a few stray teacups jingling in their stained saucers. It sounded like a herd of elephants rioting in tunnels quite nearby, and Jack suddenly realised that it must be the subway, somewhere behind the wall and underneath their feet.

Mr Danby took them down a further staircase, and then another. Eventually they could hear music playing. Something tinkly and baroque on a harpsichord. The rooms were lighter, suffused with a honeyed glow. And here, at last, was Mr K. N.

Wright, sitting at his vast desk and almost lost behind carefully stacked mountains of books.

'Mr Wright.' Liza sighed with pleasure. 'This is an antiquarian's paradise.'

He stood up and smiled at them over his glasses. 'Welcome, my dears,' he said.

Jack gasped. He heard the other two do the same, before they mastered their manners.

The first surprise was that the old man was wearing striped pyjamas and a fabulously embroidered scarlet dressing gown. Somehow the sight of him in night attire seemed shocking, even here in this timeless place.

The other surprising thing was that he was incredibly handsome. Old, but very finely chiselled and benign. His dark eyes glowed with humour and goodwill. But – and there were no two ways about this – his head was twice as large as it should be. His was the biggest face Jack or any of them had ever seen. Even Aunt Liza, who had met some very strange people in her time, looked surprised.

Mr Wright raised his bristly white eyebrows at them. 'Oh dear, I hope Mr Danby's rather gruff manner hasn't put you off? He hasn't spoiled your first visit to 66b, I hope? Go away, Danby. You may leave us now. Take your glowering little visage elsewhere, if you would. Why not try mopping out the map room, again, hm?'

They watched Mr Danby shuffle off. He groaned as he went, but Jack was sure that the old man was relieved to be out of their presence. Perhaps he was keen to get away from what it was they had brought with them. Jack had noticed him casting a glance, now and then, at the bag Liza carried with her. Danby had known what was inside. He had known why they had come here.

Mr Wright grinned at them. Far from being reassuring, though, the effect was ghastly. His whole face seemed to swallow the lamplit office. His bright teeth gathered all their attention.

'Now,' he said. 'I must say. What a delight it is to see you all here. You have come so, so far.'

'We have indeed,' said Liza. She couldn't take her eyes off his massive face. She seemed transfixed for a moment. 'I-I've brought the book back to you.'

The old man's tongue licked his dry lips, and the gesture seemed almost obscene. 'Oh dear,' he said. 'Oh dear oh dear oh dear. And what trouble has it brought in its wake, my dears? What trouble have you brought down about our ears?'

Liza opened the clasp of her bag and paused. Jack thought: she doesn't want to hand it over to him. She's gone like Gollum or something. She wants to hold on to its powers.

'Liza,' he prompted. 'Give him the book . . .'

'I should never have let it out of my sight,' said Mr Wright. 'I've been such a fool. An idiot. Please, please, give it back to me . . .'

Liza's hands hovered over her bag. She seemed to make a decision. 'No,' she said suddenly. 'First of all, I want – and I think I deserve – an explanation. We all do. We've been through a horrible ordeal, and I think you need to tell us why.'

The old man studied her through his glasses. The lenses were the size of dinner plates, reflecting the light from the oil lamps in an irritable flash. 'An explanation, hm?' he said, and laughed at them.

*

He was still kissing her when there was another loud knock at the front door.

It broke the spell.

Vicki took a step away from the stranger in the kitchen and stared at him. Her hand went to her neck. 'You bit me . . .'

'Answer the door,' he said.

She reeled away from him. Dark blotches were covering her vision. Threads of blood went scurrying past her eyes. She jolted and cried out as a weird pain lanced through her. Her veins were on fire. 'What have you done to me?'

There was another knock at the door.

He was implacable. 'You must answer it. It may be your new friends.'

Vicki pushed past him. She went to her daughter, who looked away from the telly and stared at her mother. 'It's all right, sweetheart. Mummy's just cut herself.'

Connie's eyes went huge. Vicki tried to stop the panic rising up into her throat. She could hear her own heartbeat pounding in her ears.

She hurried down the short hallway and threw open the door.

Bloke in a cap and a suit. Overweight, harassed.

'Y-yes?' Vicki asked.

'Delivery. You need to come down to the van to collect it. I'm not carrying it up all these stairs.'

She stared at him. 'What delivery?'

'Lost luggage. Heathrow. Big bloody suitcase. Big as a coffin. I'm not carrying anything that big on my own on account of my back, you see. I don't want them thinking I'm doing things for the compensation. So you need to come down to the van to help me with it.'

Her head swam with confusion. She vaguely remembered her new guests talking about the missing bag. 'Oh, all right,' she said woozily, swaying on the spot. She reached for the keys on the hall table. 'Connie? Come here, darling.'

The delivery man stared at her. 'Are you okay?'

'I'm fine. Really.' Somehow it seemed imperative that she didn't let another man into the flat. She covered up the still-bleeding wound in her neck.

'You don't look right,' the lost luggage man said.

'I'm okay,' she snapped, and went into the living room. 'Connie, fetch your coat, darling. You've got to come with Mummy to the . . .'

She stared at the scene in the living room. The telly was still playing mindlessly, but her daughter was sitting with the strange man.

Connie was grinning at her. She was sitting on the man's lap, and he was grinning too.

'Get away from her,' said Vicki. Her blood was cold now.

'She likes me,' said the man. 'She's quite happy, aren't you?' He smiled at Vicki. 'So who was at the door?'

'M-Mum?' said Connie. 'I don't feel well . . .'

And then Vicki saw the blood on her daughter's neck.

She bolted across the room to her, screeching. And then everything seemed to happen at once.

The delivery man was calling out, 'Hey, hey, what's happening in there?'

Vicki had hold of her daughter's arms, dragging her off the man on her settee. He was laughing, relinquishing the girl. He said, 'No worries. I've bitten you both. You've had it. You're both mine.' And then he started laughing like a drain.

'Who are you?' shrieked Vicki. 'What are you? Why are you doing this?'

'I'm Daniel,' the man said, as if that was the only explanation needed. Then his head jerked round quickly, as he noticed out of the corner of his eye that the delivery man had stepped into the room.

'Look, I, er, don't want to get involved in a domestic,' said the fat man, looking scared, 'But this don't sound right in here. This don't sound right at all . . .'

He took in at one glance the scene in the living room. The blood on the little girl's blouse. And then the dark man springing at him.

Vicki pushed at him. 'Nooo! Get out! Leave us!'

But it was too late. Daniel was upon the delivery man, who went down quickly, slumping to the carpet like a farm animal submissive at the slaughter.

Daniel laughed as he opened up a vein in the man's thick neck. 'This one's for feeding. Not like you two. This one's just to give me a bit of a drink. You two are different. Remember that. You're mine now.' And then he was on his knees, slurping and lapping at the man's neck. The delivery man's limbs were still thrashing and sparking with dead energy. His eyes were like two boiled eggs, staring up at the Artex.

Vicki pulled her daughter closer to her, burying her head in her stomach. But the child wanted to see.

'You'll both be hungry,' Daniel told them. 'The shock of my blood in yours. You need to drink now.'

Vicki shook her head soundlessly. To her horror, she felt her child break away from her. Connie went trustingly to Daniel.

'Good girl,' Daniel said. 'She knows what's good for her. Drink up, Connie.' He watched the child almost paternally as she stooped over the dying delivery man. And then his eyes flashed at Vicki. 'Where did he say this van of his was parked?'

Chapter Thirty-Two

'I'm afraid I can't tell you where the grimoire comes from,' sighed
Mr Wright. 'If I could, I would, I promise you. It has been in our
possession for some time, we believe. Mr Danby – whom you have
met – dug it out of one of our most obscure storerooms last year.
It gave us all quite a turn, in point of fact.'

'So you knew how powerful it was?' Liza snapped.

'Well, yes, we did really,' said Mr Wright. He looked hangdog
for a moment. His wattles and dewlaps were monstrous things,
and because of the size of his head, his expression came to
dominate the room. When he stood up, smiling brilliantly again,
it was as if someone had switched on an extra light. 'You see, it is
referred to in so many other volumes down the centuries. In
hushed whispers and reverent tones, you know. It's the great-
granddaddy of grimoires.'

'Then how come you wanted rid of it so bad?' Shelley burst
out. 'How come you palmed it off on my aunt?'

The old man smiled and shuffled round the room evasively. He
was scanning the top shelves of the bookcases surrounding him,
though whether he was looking for anything in particular, or just
avoiding their eyes, they weren't sure. 'It was a weak moment. A

tempting moment. I am very sorry. I can't tell you how sorry I am.'

'Not as sorry as I am,' Liza said. 'Do you realise what kind of a mess we've left behind in New York? And all because of this book. I'm expecting to go back and find the whole place heaving with freakin' zombies and vamps.'

Jack felt light-headed for a moment. It was all the doomy magic talk, but also the stifling atmosphere down here. Suddenly he wanted to be up on the surface again. There was a nasty, greasy feeling to the air here. It felt like breathing candle grease and mildew. 'Look, let's forget the recriminations and whys and wherefores,' he said. 'And just focus on what's to be done.'

Shelley glanced at him. 'We leave the book here with these guys and then we go home. That's all we need to do.'

'No,' said her aunt. 'We've got to see this through. And all the knowledge we need is here, somewhere in these books.' She glared at Mr Wright. Her disappointment in him came out like laser bolts, drilling from her shrewd eyes into his skinny body. 'Am I right?'

'Indeed,' he said, still glancing furtively around, as if for a means of escape. 'You are quite free to go through all the volumes we have here to help you. Anything you might need to combat the forces unleashed from the grimoire . . .'

Liza grunted at this and turned to the others, issuing instructions about what to look for. Shelley looked mightily pissed off, but Jack was too tired to do anything but what he was told. Basically, they were looking for the books that mentioned the grimoire that had fallen into their hands, plus anything that included useful advice about combating book demons, zombies or vamps.

'There'll be plenty here to help you,' Mr Wright said. 'And of course you may borrow them from the shop no charge.'

This earned him a savage glance from Shelley.

For almost an hour they scanned the musty shelves. They hocked out tomes whose titles spoke to them, and flicked hurriedly through rough-edged pages. Jack realised he was grabbing things almost at random. He glanced to where Liza was working. Her search seemed a whole lot more systematic.

Why couldn't Mr Wright just give them the answers? Why didn't he know?

'I gotta thank you, Mr Wright,' he heard Liza saying. 'Up until you sent me the Book of Unholy Evil and Disaster, it was a pretty good system we had going. I loved getting the anthologies and novels you were sending me.'

'All part of the service,' he said.

'Hmm.' Liza grimaced. 'I wish you hadn't spoiled it, though. Why me? Why pick on a poor, helpless, defenceless old lady in another country to send your evil book to? Were you so desperate for it to be out of your shop? What have I ever done to you?'

'But . . . but, my dear . . . you're *Elizabeth Bathory*,' the old man said, deliberately italicising the words. 'Did you think I wouldn't recognise your name? Did you assume I would just think it a coincidence? I know who you are and a little of what you have done in the past.'

'*What?*'

Jack was on the other side of the bookcase they were examining. They thought he had wandered further away. They had no idea he was eavesdropping on them. He heard the note of surprise in Liza's voice. No, more than surprise. Shock.

'Elizabeth Bathory,' the old man said. 'A name that any bookseller would recognise. Any specialist in books pertaining to the dark arts would know who you are, my dear. And so – clutching at straws fearfully, as I was – I knew that my only chance was to send the grimoire to you.'

'You did it on purpose?' she gasped.

'Knowing what success you have had in the past in neutralising supernatural threats and bringing various other-dimensional spirits to heel . . . I thought the book would be in safe hands. I thought you might achieve something rather spectacular,' he said sadly. 'And thus save all our necks.'

'Well nuts to that,' she said. 'I think I made it all worse. I let the book fall into the hands of a dangerous young man.'

'Yes, indeed. Very regrettable.' Mr Wright sighed. 'And so we must all work together to do what we can do. And rid the world of this menace. Again.'

There was a loaded pause. Jack drew closer to the bookcase, in case he missed anything.

Liza said, in a very quiet, controlled voice, 'You know more than you're saying about this.'

Another pause. Mr Wright said, 'Perhaps. But what I have is at your disposal, Ms Bathory. Seek and ye shall find!' And then he started laughing, so loudly that Jack drew back in shock, dislodging a pile of heavy volumes, which fell with a clatter all around his shoulders.

Shelley reappeared. 'I don't like this, Aunt Liza. And I don't like this crazy old guy. I say we just leave him with the book and get out of here.'

The old man's huge face regarded them solemnly. 'But she can't. You can't. You can't leave this battlefield now.'

'Battlefield?' said Shelley. 'Is that what it is?'

'Oh indeed,' said Mr Wright. 'Forces of good and evil and all that. Make no mistake. That's the devil you've conjured up out of that book. Beelzebub himself. Or rather, the devil's most dedicated disciple. He's born again and he'll create new vampires to do his wicked bidding. He'll raise the still-living dead to act as his zombie army. He'll lay waste to your city, our city, everything – until he is appeased.'

Liza said, 'We can't just walk out on this, Shelley.'

Shelley looked close to exhausted tears. 'I can't find what we're looking for in these books. They're all relevant and none of them are. They're all full of magic and junk. How do we even know where to start?'

'I know . . . I think . . .' said her aunt.

Then Mr Danby was back among them. His pale round face was sweating. His former composure was gone. He was wobbly on his skinny legs as he arrived in the room and told Mr Wright, 'There's somebody at the door upstairs. There's somebody . . . wanting to be in.'

'So?' snapped Mr Wright, impatient with the fussy little man.

'I think . . . I think it's *him*,' said Mr Danby.

Daniel didn't have any trouble locating the bookshop. Wrestling with the clunky steering wheel and controls of the delivery van was another matter, but he knew precisely how to get to his destination.

The radio on the dashboard crackled and hissed at him and voices came squawking out of it, wanting to know where he was and what he was doing. Was he on his way back to Heathrow yet? With a deft flick he switched it off and thought briefly about the dead man on the carpet in Vicki's flat. He wondered vaguely what she would do with him. Daniel had definitely killed him, rather than vamped him. But even as a corpse, the delivery man was a danger to them. The blood in him would be no good soon. Once the heart stopped, the clock started ticking and the blood would turn treacly and bad. It would make both Vicki and her daughter miserably sick if they carried on drinking from him.

There hadn't been time enough to tell them. This was all pretty new to Daniel, and he knew he'd made mistakes. In a way, he felt guilty because he hadn't taken the time to warn them about the dangers, and explain to them the intricacies of their new state. But then, he hardly knew those intricacies himself yet.

Vicki had stood in the sunlight of her terrace and said, 'Shouldn't the light destroy you? Shouldn't it be harmful to us?'

'Old wives' tale.' Daniel shrugged. 'Anti-vamp propaganda. We sometimes sleep in the day only because we prefer to go out at night. The sunlight won't harm you, or your lovely daughter, Vicki. You'll be okay.'

Vicki had lifted her daughter up then, as Daniel turned to go. He ruffled the child's hair and wiped a smear of blood off her teething-chapped chin.

'It's happened so fast,' said Vicki. 'You've changed literally everything for us.'

He nodded. 'I hope I've made your lives better. I really do.'

Then he was off to find the delivery van, and next thing, he was racketing through the London streets that he had once known so well.

Daniel had grown up here. This had been his first city. Knowledge of the place – its sights and smells, its devious twists and turns and eccentricities – was hardwired into his brain. He could feel his every fibre bristling with nostalgic joy.

The presence in his mind was pleased, too. He was home as well. And the man inside his mind knew Charing Cross Road very well indeed.

'I lived all over the world. I was a great traveller. I settled in many countries. But I know this street better than most. I spent a good deal of time haunting these bookshops for their secrets. Both in my natural life, my vampire life, and my disembodied life since. I sat waiting on shelves here, biding my time, for years. Slowly absorbing everything I could from the tomes around me . . . And now you bring me back, Daniel. To this city within a city. This necropolis of words.'

Daniel was used to that richly resonant voice in his head by now. These days it was no stranger than having the radio playing in his room as he worked. A British station, like those his father had listened to, with a fruity, self-satisfied voice rumbling on about classical music. The voice didn't chill him any more. He let it guide him, inform him. He let it tell him what to do.

Now the van was parked neatly in a no-parking zone, clogging the thickened artery of the street. He found the black door to 66b, obscured though it was by plastic bags of rubbish, and pounded on it firmly. With great authority.

Mr Danby quailed before him. Daniel shoved his way into the whitewashed passageway. He laughed as the moon-faced man backed away, stumbling over dictionaries and parcels of newsprint. 'You know who I am, don't you?' Daniel laughed. 'You know why I'm here. Go and run, little man, and tell your master.'

Danby ran, and Daniel took his time pursuing him into the papery labyrinth. He was content to pick his way gradually from room to room, because the vestiges of his former self left to him were very interested by everything they saw in those rooms. As he went down the steps and into a series of brick-walled chambers, he sniffed appreciatively, all the instincts of an expert coming alive. He glowed with pleasure in that cold place. His frosted skin began to seethe with joy at the sight of the strange and rare books before him. He breathed in the swampy scent of all those decaying volumes and tried to hold it in his tarry lungs.

'Intoxicating, isn't it?' said the voice of the man in his head.

Eventually he came to the warm room filled with peach-coloured light and lined with books bound in gold, oxblood and pale straw-coloured leather. He was in Mr Wright's office. Here was the man with the colossal face, looking stern and determined behind his antique desk. Beside him, Mr Danby had turned fish-belly white, wringing his hands as the young man stepped nimbly into the room.

Daniel felt like a dancer springing on to a stage. Cutting a stark, slim black figure in that windowless room. He turned to Liza, Jack and Shelley and smiled at them. He tried to make it a nice smile. He was genuinely pleased to see them.

'I don't believe this,' Jack said. 'Where the hell did you appear from?'

'D-Daniel?' Shelley said, taking a faltering, involuntary step towards him.

He snickered. He meant it to be an urbane chuckle. He'd have given anything for it to sound that way. But instead he gave a kind of smug giggle, and that annoyed him. 'Ah well. I can transform myself, you know? So travel's not such a big deal. You saw me as a wolf, I believe? And I've tried being a bat, but that's not so much fun. All that flapping about. Mist is good. Mist is quite easy. I quite like just . . . *issuing* about the place.'

'Mist?' Liza said. 'That's how you got on a flight? You came across the Atlantic as *mist*?'

'Bingo,' he said. 'On your plane, in fact. The whole time you were sitting up in the relative comfort of economy class, I was down in the chilly hold, just sort of hanging about. Being evanescent, as it were, and catching up on some sleep. And now here I am.' He shook his head and tutted. 'What a lot of bother you've put yourselves to. Coming all the way to London. Ruining Christmas for yourselves. And I must say, you've put me to some trouble as well. I've had to abandon my newly conquered kingdom, just as things were getting to be even more fun, and leave my second-in-command in charge. I just hope he's up to the job, frankly.' He shrugged and sighed.

'You monster,' spat Liza. 'Not you, Daniel. I'm talking to the beast inside you.'

Daniel chuckled and rocked on the heels of his handmade shoes. 'The beast inside me. Oh dear, Liza. You need some new material. And do stop trying to see the best in people. I'm quite complicit with this . . . possession business, you know. I know what I'm doing. He hasn't taken me against my will. No more than I have taken Shelley against hers.'

It took Jack a moment to realise what he had said. 'What?'

'Huh?' Liza gasped, and swivelled to look at her niece.

Shelley had moved another step towards Daniel. Her eyelids were flickering as if she was fighting against overpowering sleepiness.

'Shelley,' Liza warned. 'Keep away from him.'

But Shelley didn't waver. She walked over to join Daniel. She stood behind him, facing them, and they knew, all of a sudden, that she was lost.

Daniel grinned. 'Now, we won't take up any more of your time. You're bound to be frantically busy, this time of year.' He turned towards Mr Wright. 'Do you get much passing Christmas trade in the occult book business?'

'You fiend,' said Mr Wright. 'I'm asking you to leave my shop. Leave us in peace.'

Mr Danby had been fishing around in a desk drawer, and now he produced a battered crucifix, but Daniel just laughed at it. Then, in a flash, he was across the room, smacking the old men's heads together and seizing the book that Mr Wright had been holding under his palms. With the grimoire in his hand, he cried out in glee and turned to punch the bookshop owner in one of his hugely saggy eyes. The old man went down without a whimper. His head made a sickening noise as it hit the desk.

Liza and Jack threw themselves at Daniel, but he slipped through their grasp as if he had turned into mist once again. Then he was in the doorway, the book in one hand, his other keeping an unbreakable grip on Shelley's upper arm.

'Goodbye, my dears,' he told them. 'I think I've got everything now. Don't try to bother me again. Don't come after me. *Don't get in my way.*'

Liza pulled herself up roughly from the jumble of ancient texts she'd been pushed into. 'I'll come after you. And I'll keep pursuing you. I'm not gonna rest until I've staked you, cut your head off, stuffed it with garlic bulbs and stuck it up your ass.'

Daniel laughed joyfully at this. 'Saucy!' he cried, and then he was off, dragging Shelley with him. Liza gamely tried to follow, but stumbled immediately on fallen books. She sprawled, sobbing with fury, as Jack fussed round her.

When Liza had calmed down enough to make herself say actual words, she turned to Jack and said, 'He's taken her away from me. My little girl's gone for ever with that . . . monster!'

Chapter Thirty-Three

Their journey back to the Rowley Way estate was almost wordless. Liza was simmering with fury, sitting across the Tube carriage from Jack. Both of them were clutching jute bags crammed with books from Mr Wright's shop.

'This is the least you can frickin' do,' she had told the old man. 'Let us take anything we might need. Anything that might be of use to us. We gotta fight this thing and it's obvious we gotta do it ourselves. *You're* not gonna be of any help.'

Mr Wright had looked very miserable, holding a cold wet flannel over his inflamed eye. At first he thought Daniel had done him serious harm, but now he saw he was just going to have a huge shiner. He stared unhappily as Jack and Liza grabbed the books they might need and wished he could have been of more use.

'I'm so sorry,' he whispered.

Liza rounded on him, 'Just don't, wouldja? Don't start maundering and bellyaching at me. That guy's got my niece and God only knows what's gonna become of her and the rest of us. So just don't go yappin' at me. I've heard enough from you.'

Jack had wondered if maybe she wasn't being too harsh with

the old gent. It struck him that Mr Wright resembled a strange specimen of mushroom, nurtured underground in optimum conditions and grown to bizarre proportions. He looked fragile and helpless – of course he was of no use to them.

He knew Liza was being so hard on him because she was disappointed. She had built up her image of the old man as their saviour. She had expected so much more of him.

Now, in the subway, she sighed deeply and said, almost to herself, 'It's always down to me to sort it out.'

'What's that?'

'I said, that's the way it's always been. It's always me. I can never rely on anyone. Back in the day, I was left alone with kids to bring up and a career to keep going. And even when my kids were grown and gone away to their own lives and careers, *their* kids ran away from them and came to be with me instead. I'm always left with other people's problems.'

'And then there's all the supernatural mysteries,' Jack added. 'All the monsters and demons that you had to do battle with . . .'

She looked at him sharply, and saw that he was gently ribbing her. 'Yeah, that's true as well. But you don't know nothin' about that, remember? That's all a long time ago and el toppo secreto, okay?'

He laughed, because she was sounding like Jimmy Cagney or someone. This tiny, loud-mouthed old lady, wisecracking about her strange and arcane past. He shook his head. Just look at the stuff that had happened since the day he had started shooting the breeze with her in a Greenwich Village coffee shop. Would any of this have involved him if he hadn't talked with her and instantly become her friend?

Maybe, maybe not. But they *were* friends – and she had to see that she could rely on him. Even if there was no one else she thought trustworthy enough. But how brave was he really? He gulped. How much use was he going to be against the massing forces of darkness?

Ah, this was their stop. He called out to Liza, who was still in a glum trance.

Above ground again, they were glad of the stiff wintry breeze after the clamminess of the Underground. They hurried back to the concrete valley of the council estate, where they dodged past mothers with pushchairs and kids on skateboards who – as Liza pointed out – ought to have been in school.

They had to pause for a breather outside a row of shops. Liza nipped in for some cigarettes, some garlic bulbs and a bunch of ragged-looking freesias that would do as a gift for their hostess.

For a moment she looked haggard in the clear morning light. 'I can't believe we let that monster get away with the grimoire *and* Shelley,' she sighed. Then she stiffened her spine, grasped up all of her bags and marched them back to the flat they had visited early that morning.

Liza banged cheerfully at the glass door and called out, 'Yoo hoo!'

Jack shivered as they waited for Vicki to answer. He didn't know what it was. Something sickly in the air. A sweetish smell, like rotting garbage. Maybe the chute was overflowing, or some bins had been ripped open by rats. Or maybe it was sewage pipes leaking beneath the concrete walls. But just then he caught a whiff of horrible decay.

'Oh God, look, we're sorry,' began Liza cheerily, as soon as

Vicki opened her door. 'We've brought more stuff to clog up your flat. Just these books. But we brought you flowers, look!' And she held the tatty bunch up to the gap in the door. Vicki still had the chain on, and they both smiled reassuringly at the single deep brown eye gazing at them.

'It's you,' Vicki said. 'Come in.'

They exchanged a glance and stepped into the flat again. Jack took in at once the broken telephone table by the door, the wonky framed landscape. And again he picked up that weird scent, only it was stronger in here. It was as if Vicki had started cooking some meat that was on the turn, not realising it was rank until too late.

The windows were open, so that a cool breeze issued through the flat. The floor-length net curtains in the living room were billowing madly. Vicki hurried across to the French windows to shut them. 'Come in, Connie darling,' she called to her daughter on the terrace. 'It's freezing out there.'

The child did as she was told. She came in and stared levelly at the two guests. Her eyes were very large and clear and she was spotlessly dressed. That blemish of a rash on her chin had cleared up all of a sudden.

'Where's the other one?' Connie asked. 'The younger lady?'

Liza sighed. 'She's, erm, gone away,' she said.

'Is everything all right?' asked Vicki, the picture of concern.

'Not really, no,' said Jack.

Vicki got them to dump the books in the living room and ushered them into the kitchen. 'We'll have some tea and put some brandy in. You two look like you've had quite a time of it.'

Jack could have said the same thing about Vicki. She was paler, almost sallow-looking. He wondered if Liza was noticing anything odd about the woman's manner. He watched Liza lean against the refrigerator and close her eyes, suddenly looking about a hundred years old.

Vicki was staring at him. 'Did you get what you wanted at the bookshop?'

'Just a few leads.' He shrugged. 'But I think we made things worse than ever, to be honest.'

'Oh,' said Vicki. She spooned tea leaves into the warmed pot. 'And did you hear anything about Paolo?'

Guilt clutched at Jack's stomach. They'd completely forgotten about Paolo. He hadn't even mentioned Ricardo's cousin to the old man at 66b. Paolo had fallen straight off their radar. Jack stammered at Vicki.

'It's okay,' she said. 'I knew you wouldn't. I knew you weren't really all that bothered about him. There's something else going on here, isn't there? Something else you're mixed up in?'

'I . . .' Jack began. 'Er, well, that's to say . . . yes . . .' He turned to look at Liza for help. But Liza had wandered out of the kitchen and gone to lie on the sitting-room couch. 'She's exhausted,' he told Vicki.

'So tell me what's going on,' Vicki asked him urgently. 'Come on. I'm letting you stay here. I deserve to know a bit more about what you're mixed up in, don't I?'

'You're right,' he said. 'But it's kind of hard to explain it all . . .'

'Try me.'

He started to tell her the story from the beginning, as she carefully made them tea. He enjoyed watching her calm, precise movements as she moved around the narrow kitchen. This place was even smaller than his own apartment.

He had only got as far as telling her about Liza's grimoire and the queer effects it had had on Daniel and on the Scottish Bride when they heard Liza screeching in the lounge.

Vicki dropped the mugs she'd been laying out and whirled around with a shout. 'Connie . . . ?'

Jack hurried after her.

In the bright living room, they found Liza slumped like a bundle of old rags on the tiled floor. She was clutching her neck and sobbing.

Jack went to her, while Vicki stood paralysed in the centre of the room. 'Connie? Connie! Where is she? What have you done with her?'

Liza was breathing raggedly. 'Frigging kid . . . tried to bite me! Went for my goddamned neck!'

'Where is she?' said Vicki, turning a deathly glare on them.

'I fought her off. She went out on your balcony, I think . . .' Liza was dabbing at her neck with her fingers and examining them. But she couldn't find any blood. She calmed a little then. Jack assured her the skin hadn't been broken.

'You can't be serious,' he told her. 'The kid went to bite you? You fought her off?'

Liza's eyes blazed. 'I'm not shittin' you.'

Now Vicki was out on the concrete balcony.

There was no one out there.

'Connie!' she screamed.

'The kid's flown off,' said Liza.

*

Shelley stared at the contents of the minibar, and all the tidy miniatures stared back at her. She didn't feel thirsty or hungry; she didn't want alcohol. She didn't want anything, actually. She had never felt as empty as this before. It was a strange sensation. For someone usually so jittery and neurotic, she felt queerly empty of thought. No regrets, no rising panic.

She just felt empty.

She gazed around at the suite. It was all very tasteful and impeccable. There was a basket of fresh fruit on the coffee table. But all the fruit seemed to shrivel and suppurate as she stared at it.

The Savoy Hotel. It sounded like something out of a movie. Some fancy romance. Here she was, with her boyfriend, who had swooped in to reclaim her. And now they were back together.

Daniel came out of the bathroom. He looked perfect in his Armani. Not bad for someone who'd travelled through the night in the hold of a 747. 'Are we set?' he asked her.

'What do you mean?'

He grimaced with impatience. A touch of the old Daniel there. 'We've got to go and dump that van somewhere. You're coming with me.'

'Oh Daniel.' She felt hot tears springing into her eyes. 'I'm exhausted. Can't I just lie down here . . .'

'No,' he snapped. 'No, you can't. I'm not letting you out of my sight. As soon as I do, you start forgetting me and whose side you're on. That aunt of yours gets her claws back into you . . .'

Shelley groaned. 'It isn't like that. Aunt Liza only wants the best for me.'

Daniel rolled his eyes. 'Well she's getting in my way. Too much.'

'Don't hurt her . . .'

'Come on,' he said, hauling her off the vast bed. She had flopped down and fallen almost instantly asleep. He slapped her lightly and she blinked at him. 'We don't get tired. We're not the same as other people. You'll see. You'll perk up.'

'Leave me alone . . .'

'It's too late for that, love.'

He was just about carrying her to the door. He checked his man bag for key card, wallet, grimoire.

Shelley murmured, 'Where are we going?'

'We've got to dump that van,' he repeated.

It seemed to Shelley like a silly thing to prioritise, but what did she know? Daniel had his own reasons. He was very organised and he knew what he was doing. She tried to stand up straighter as they rode down to the lobby in the elevator. She felt rather ashamed of how dishevelled she must look, and thought longingly of her cases, stored at that woman's apartment. Daniel had promised her, though: she could have everything new. She would want for nothing now that she was unequivocally his.

The wound in her neck throbbed horribly. She knew what it signified. It was like having a second heart, pulsing there steadily, reminding her of what she had done.

The van was parked where Daniel had left it, a number of blocks away from the smart row of hotels. In a dirty alleyway off the Strand, there it stood, incongruous and bright red.

'Why not just abandon it here?' she asked.

'It's airport property. It'll be found. They'll check the rota.

317

They'll trace it, and the luggage, to you and your lot. I don't want it near me.'

That seemed fair enough. Daniel was logical, systematic. She'd always admired that about him. Shelley climbed up into the driver's cab beside him and off they went.

'Where are you going to dump it?'

'Stop asking me questions!' he shouted at her. 'What kind of vampire's bride are you anyway? You're supposed to be serene and ethereal.'

'I am?'

'*Yes!*'

Chapter Thirty-Four

Ssstrange.

It was a ssstraaange sennnsaaation.

But she was used to those. She had been manhandled and pushed and pulled all of her long life. She was used to being shunted and shoved and yanked about the place.

These past few hours and days had been like a return to the old days. When it was assumed that Bessie was just a thing. An effigy. A dummy without feelings or volition.

During the time she had spent dismembered in the case borrowed from Mr Oblonsky, she had let her mind float free of her body. It was the easiest way. Better to drift away from the tedium and discomfort. She had a touch of anxiety that scratched at her as she bided her time within the case, stacked amongst so many others. It reminded her of her years spent hidden away in that basement, before Shelley had found her. She imagined being lost again, for goodness knows how many more years, or even decades.

So Bessie let her thoughts float free, and went off into a kind of gentle reverie as the plane soared over the Atlantic and the Scottish Bride was returned, secretly, to the islands where she had originated.

But now . . . consciousness was returning to her dislocated limbs. Breath was stirring in her squashed chest. Her face twitched and her joints started to ache.

Where was she?

There was a sickening lurch. A sliding sensation. Horrible squealing noises of tyres. She felt the case she was in jolt and knock against walls. It felt unsafe. It felt like something awful was going to happen.

She was fully awake now. Blinking. Breathing. Heart racing.

It was time to take control of her own destiny again.

Shelley had absolutely no idea where this wasteground was, but Daniel obviously did. He had driven the van to some benighted landscape, heaped with trash and rusting girders. Somewhere in the undesirable outskirts, Shelley thought. Somewhere near ruined factories and gutted tower blocks. As they climbed out of the van, she felt a wave of depression flowing over her.

Daniel was businesslike. He hurried round the van and flung open the doors. 'Might as well check there's nothing valuable inside,' he said. 'Before we torch it.'

Shelley was shocked. 'You're going to torch it?'

'Oh grow up, love,' he told her. 'We leave a trail of death and destruction after us, don't we? Haven't you got that yet?'

'Oh,' she said. 'Right.'

The back of the van contained only a few items of luggage. It made her feel sad, that these bags had been on their way to their rightful owners. Those owners would have been so relieved to be reunited with their belongings. And now Daniel was going to burn them all.

Shelley had never felt so distant from her own belongings and her own life. This made her feel even more desolate.

'Not worth opening these,' Daniel said. 'Just a lot of crap, I expect.' He found a can of petrol in the back, and hefted it out. Already Shelley could imagine the thick, choking smoke of the fire he was planning. The whole van would explode and they would have to flee.

Maybe he would fly again. He would take her in his arms and fly her away from this wasteground, back to the city – across the shining rooftops of London Town. They'd be like Mary Poppins and Dick Van Dyke, and they'd go back to the Savoy and maybe she could have a sleep at last . . .

It was then that she noticed the large case belonging to Mr Oblonsky.

'Oh my God!' she gasped. 'That's ours!'

'This?' he said. He reached for the label. 'Yeah, that's your aunt's writing. What's in it?'

All of a sudden, Shelley couldn't speak.

'Well?' Daniel jeered at her. 'What's it full of? Don't tell me it's Aunt Liza's old bras and panties and stuff?'

'No,' said Shelley.

Daniel took hold of the case. He frowned as he touched it. 'That's weird . . .'

'What?'

'It . . . it made a noise.' He started fiddling with the locks. Shelley gasped as he took a miniature padlock in his fine strong teeth and wrenched it open.

'Not bad, eh?' he boasted. 'I've got all sorts of superpowers, you know, Shelley love. And you'll have them soon too, I promise.'

As he spoke, he was unzipping the case.

Shelley found herself backing away. She didn't know she was doing it. But her feet were taking her backwards steadily, across the cinder blocks of the wasteground.

Daniel frowned at her. 'What's wrong with you?' And he flipped open the heavy lid of the case.

Two hands shot out and seized him by the throat.

He didn't have a chance to make a noise before Bessie sat up and proceeded to throttle the undead life out of him.

Chapter Thirty-Five

Jack had serious qualms about this.

Things had turned nasty. This young woman had lost her baby. Somehow the child had disappeared from the balcony of her home. Vicki had become a gibbering wreck, unable to function or make herself understood.

Liza watched her almost dispassionately. She stuck to her story. 'The kid flew away. I'm sorry. What more can I say? I saw what I saw.'

Jack was trying to get Vicki to calm down. He glared at Liza. He believed her. He knew that she would never lie about something like that. But he just thought she could show a bit more compassion, perhaps. And be a bit more understanding about how . . . impossible it should seem.

'*You* caused this,' Vicki shouted at last. 'You came here and all this stuff started happening.'

'Look, Vicki . . .' Liza began.

'No, *you* look!' Vicki shot back. 'That's Connie! That's my baby! Where's she gone?'

Liza looked very solemn. 'She's gone to find her master, I think.'

'Her what?'

Jack put in, sensibly, 'I think we should phone the police.' He was over at the balcony, peering down once more, just making sure Connie hadn't fallen over the edge. There might be a more prosaic – if grisly – answer to this.

'She's a vampire, Vicki,' said Liza wearily. 'Or at least, her blood has been tainted by Daniel. She's well on her way to mutating fully. It happens very quickly in the extremely young. With adults it takes a little longer. With you, for example.'

Vicki drew back in alarm. 'With me?'

Liza said, implacably, 'Don't mess about and play games. You know what's been done to you. There's no time to fool about. I can do something to help both you and your daughter – if you do what I say.'

And this was what Jack had qualms about.

Liza was promising Vicki things she surely couldn't make good on. She was saying she could help her. But could she really? Vicki and her daughter had been bitten good. The kid could fly already. Vicki was clearly on her way to full-blown. Could Liza really reverse the process?

The old woman nodded. 'Yeah. Course I can. I just need to find out where Daniel is. Where he went with Shelley. Then we can set about putting this thing to rights.' She glared at Vicki. 'We need your help. As you progress through the transformation, your mind as well as your blood is connected to your vampire master.'

Vicki jeered. 'You're talking rubbish. I ain't never heard such—'

'Can it, lady,' Liza snapped. 'It's gone too far for trying to deny stuff. Now, do you wanna get your daughter back?'

There was no mistaking the horror and fear on the woman's face. To Jack it looked like she was at war with herself, and that turmoil became all too plain.

'You've gotta help us,' Liza said.

Vicki nodded dumbly, and Liza sat her down on the settee. She clicked her fingers and talked to her gently. Jack was astonished to see Liza reveal yet another hidden talent, as the young mother dropped suddenly into a trance.

Liza talked to her in a soft murmur for several minutes, and Vicki whispered back. At one point Liza instructed Jack to fill his backpack with some of her home-made stakes, and by the time he came back into the room, she was standing up, a triumphant look on her face, and Vicki was awake.

'I think we can find him,' she said.

They caught a cab out on the main road behind the estate. Vicki was shivery and pale. She looked much worse out in daylight. Or maybe the vampire virus was taking a stronger hold as the minutes went by.

The cabbie looked cross that they didn't know exactly where they were going. It didn't take long, however, for Liza to tune Vicki back in and start issuing directions.

'I can't believe it,' Jack whispered, hugging the bag of sharpened implements to his chest. 'You're using her as vampire sat nav.'

The taxi wove its way into town. Into the very centre. Eventually they found themselves outside the grand hotel where Daniel had made his base.

'Pay the man, Jack,' Liza said, helping Vicki out of the cab.

Jack pulled a face. He was already running out of money. Then he saw that Vicki was gliding along like someone in a dream, towards the main entrance. 'Daniel's living the high life,' he said.

In the foyer, they paused and waited as Vicki stood still and seemed to sniff the air. The place was festive with bunting and fabulously dressed Christmas trees. There were tourists and guests milling about, so that the newcomers were hardly noticeable. Don't we look conspicuous? Jack wondered.

'We're never going to be able to get into his hotel room,' he said. 'They won't let us just . . .'

But then Vicki was gliding towards the elevators, and Liza and Jack had to stumble after her across the plush carpeting. They almost lost her in the sudden rush for the doors as they slid effortlessly open.

They managed to stand beside Vicki, because the other people in the lift seemed to draw away from her instinctively. She was in sweatpants and an old shirt, but it wasn't the sloppy housewear that marked her out, Jack realised. There was a strange smell that she wore. Like a cologne that had gone stale.

'His room,' she said, 'is right at the top.'

'The fanciest suite,' said Liza. 'That figures.'

'Will my daughter be there?' said Vicki, suddenly anxious.

The others in the lift were trying to look as if they weren't listening to any of this. Jack was astonished by the way English people carried on. How hard they tried not to seem agog at this strangely stilted scene in their midst.

'I just don't know, honey,' said Liza. 'But you can bet that wherever Daniel is, she won't be far behind. He's the master, and he calls his creatures of the night to him when he wants them. Vampires, zombies. Anything that's hanging around, waitin' to be called into satanic service.' She noticed a frowsty-looking old dame staring at her. 'Can I help you?' she asked her sharply.

The other woman looked away, furious and ashamed.

By the time the lift was at the very top, they had it to themselves.

'Someone's bound to report us,' Jack sighed. 'We don't look like guests here.'

'So?' said Liza. 'Frig 'em. Who cares. We just want to get in and—'

The lift went ping, the doors swished open, and there was a short corridor to the suite at the very top of the hotel.

'Yeah, but how are we going to get in exactly?' Jack asked.

Liza rolled her eyes and reached with both hands into the silver bun she'd put her hair in for tidiness and ease. As well as hairpins, it was held together by her very favourite and most proficient lock-picks. 'Watch and learn, sweetheart,' she said. She rolled up her sleeves and turned determinedly to the door.

As she got to work, Jack's mobile trilled.

It was Shelley.

'Shelley, where are you? Where's he taken you?'

At that precise moment, the door to the suite gave a very definite click and swung inwards. Jack could have cheered.

'It's Shelley,' he told Liza. 'Are you in the suite?' he asked.

'What?' said Shelley. 'Back at the hotel?'

'She's not here,' Jack told Liza.

Liza was leading the way stealthily into the suite. 'Is she okay?' she hissed.

'Shelley, are you okay? And where are you?' Jack felt absurd, carrying out a phone call as they tiptoed into the lavish penthouse suite. 'Oh my God, there's a view of the river and everything.' He was aware of Vicki darting past him. She moved frantically from room to room, obviously searching for her daughter.

'She's not here,' Liza was saying. 'None of them are here.'

At the other end of the line, Shelley was puzzled. 'Look, where are you?'

'We're in Daniel's hotel,' Jack told her. 'We're at the top of the Savoy. We thought *you* might be here.'

'How did you . . . ? Oh, never mind. Look, we got trouble.'

'Ha!' laughed Jack bitterly. '*More* trouble! Where are you? Are you okay? When he led you away, I thought you were gone for good this time. You were completely under his . . .'

'Thrall,' called Liza from across the room, where she was conducting a rapid search in the drawers and the minibar. She produced some cashews and some dinky bottles of wine. 'Thrall is the word. That's what she's in – and so is poor Vicki here.'

'Okay, but where are you physically?' Jack asked Shelley urgently. 'Like, geographically?'

'I dunno,' she sighed. 'Some frickin' wasteland middle of nowhere. Daniel brought the van out here to burn it.'

'What van?'

'The van from the airport. It came to Vicki's flat with our lost luggage.'

'Lost luggage?' Jack frowned. 'You mean . . . ?' His eyes widened. 'Oh . . . *my!*'

'Anyway, he brought it here to torch it. We opened up the back and—'

'Wait a minute,' Liza said, marching over. 'What's she saying? What's that about luggage?'

'She's telling me,' said Jack. 'Daniel was going to burn the van with the lost luggage.' He looked at Vicki. 'Is that right? A van came to your flat with our missing bag?'

Vicki went even paler. 'The man from the airport. The fat man. Daniel . . . Daniel killed him. I had to get rid of the body . . . It's in my airing cupboard. There's blood on all the clean towels . . .'

Liza groaned at the woman's rising hysteria. 'Jesus wept.' To Jack she said, 'Where's Shelley now?'

'With the van. Daniel's going to burn it or something.'

Shelley spoke up suddenly. 'No, it's okay for now. Bessie scragged him. She burst out and knocked him flat out unconscious.'

'Whaaat? Bessie's there?'

'Of course!' said Shelley. 'She was in the bag at the back of the van. She's still in bits, but she was out of that bag like a . . . like a jack-in-the-box.'

Liza was staring at Jack, open-mouthed. 'Bessie is there? She's revived herself?'

'She's knocked Daniel out cold, apparently.' He asked Shelley, 'And how's Bessie?'

'She's coming back to full consciousness. She's rebuilding herself as quickly as she can.'

Jack shuddered at the very thought of that. Liza told him, 'Tell her to bring Bessie and the van and Daniel back to Rowley Way. Can she drive the van okay?'

'Yes, sure I can,' said Shelley, when she heard this.

'And you're okay?' Jack asked her.

'You mean am I under his power any more? I don't know! How would I know? I don't want to drink blood or anything. I don't feel very different to normal . . .'

'That's good,' said Jack. 'Okay, we'll see you back at Vicki's apartment.' As he said this, he hoped that Liza had money with her for a taxi. This spook-hunting business was getting expensive. He looked at Liza. 'Hey, why doesn't she just stake him right now? While he's unconscious?'

'She won't do it,' Liza snapped. 'Try her.' Her attention was caught by Vicki just then. The girl was wandering around the room, bending to examine one of the bedside tables.

'Shelley? You hear that? Your Aunt Liza says you won't stake him.'

'I won't *what?*'

'I said, just stake him. Right now, while he's out cold. You could end this right now . . .'

'I-I . . .' Shelley stammered.

'Well?' asked Liza.

'She won't do it,' said Jack. 'You're right.'

'I can't just shove a stake into his heart! I . . .'

'She's under his thrall, like I say.' Liza shrugged. 'Get Bessie to do it. Is she strong enough yet?'

'I don't know, but I'm sure Shelley won't let her,' said Jack. 'Look, Shelley. Just drive the van back to Vicki's. Okay? Put Bessie on guarding him.'

'Yeeeesss? Jaaaack?'

'Bessie? Is that you?'

'It isss.'

'Err, I'm glad you're okay, Bessie. And back to your normal self.'

'I will waaatch him, Jack. I'll make suuuure he doesn't get to hurt Shelley – or anyone elssse – again.'

Then Bessie was gone, and the phone clicked off. There was silence at the other end.

Jack whistled, shaking his head. He was at the top of the Savoy, and had had a mobile phone call to some weird hostage situation involving variously undead protagonists, one of whom was one of his best friends.

Liza cried out in triumph, 'She's found it!'

Vicki was drawing a familiar-looking book out of the drawer in the bedside table.

It wasn't the Gideon bible that should have been in there.

'The grimoire,' Liza grinned, 'is back in our hands! Oh well done, Vicki. Your supernaturally heightened senses led us straight to the grimoire, rather than Daniel! Your in-built vamp nav knew what it was doing after all! Come on, both of you. It's time we were off!'

Chapter Thirty-Six

Shelley knew she could handle the van. She had driven all sorts of vehicles for the museum in the past. What she was less sure about was her route. Coming out this way she had tried to keep a grip on her bearings, but London was unfamiliar to her. On top of that, she was just about fainting with fatigue.

Oh, come on, Shelley, she goaded herself. You gotta do this.

She swerved back off the blasted wasteground and headed for lights and life and busy traffic.

'Are you okay back there, Bessie?' she called.

Bessie shouted back, sounding gruff but cheery. She was keeping a wary eye on the unconscious form of Daniel, rolling on the greasy floor of the van as it rocked from side to side. As she guarded him, she was working busily at her own body parts. Shelley didn't like to think about that too much. The woman was literally pulling herself back together. Just before she had slammed the doors on her, Shelley had seen Bessie threading black twine through her left kneecap, securing her lower leg in position.

Where was Rowley Way? Could she even remember? She'd end up going round and round in endless traffic. Stuck in London for ever, and always on the move.

With monsters in the back of the van.

Her boyfriend had become a monster, and he was in the process of turning her into one too. Her eyes misted up at this and she shook the thought away. No point in getting upset now. Let all that come later. Right now she had a job to do. She had to be practical and gutsy like her Aunt Liza.

Now, where was St John's Wood? She flipped open the glove compartment. Bingo. Another *A–Z*. Well-thumbed. She tried to flip through the index as she drove. Heavy traffic now, protesting at her as she veered about. Christmas traffic, she realised, suddenly aware of the fairy lights strung through the streets and the glowing shopfronts.

With a shock she realised that it was Christmas Eve. Jesus Christ!

Come on, come on . . . She was caught at the lights. She took the opportunity to study the little book and make sense of the tiny street maps. Okay, she could do this. She was resourceful. She was a professional lady. Okay . . .

Daniel was unconscious and so her mind was clear. She didn't feel like anybody's slave. Nuh-huh.

'Ssshellleey?' came Bessie's voice from the little window into the back.

'Uh, yeah?' The lights were green suddenly and she accelerated with a lurch so that the van seemed to leap across the intersection.

'Heee iss waking up again!'

Once back at Vicki's flat, Liza's party set about securing the place and settling in for the night.

Jack suddenly felt sick as a thought struck him. 'You said there was a body in the airing cupboard?' he said to Vicki.

She went wordlessly to the hallway and flung open the doors. 'He's gone.' There were just a few blood-soaked towels and the lingering traces of that dreadful smell.

'Hmm,' said Liza. 'I think the delivery man walked out of the French windows too.' She was in the living room, where the windows were open and there was more dark blood on the carpet tiles. 'So he *was* infected after all. He was a Walker.'

Jack felt himself shuddering. He was trembling involuntarily, and it wasn't just the breeze coming in. 'It's happening here, too. So quickly. Daniel is spreading this . . . disease. He can't help himself. And he'll be drawing other vampires and creatures to him.'

'Making another army,' Liza agreed. She noticed that Vicki, having locked the French windows, had wandered out of the room, looking vague. 'Go after her,' she told Jack. 'Tell her we'll sort this out. We'll get her baby back. We'll make all of this better. You're good at that stuff. Make it sound convincing. We need her help. I'm no good at talking to people about mushy stuff.'

He stared at her. 'And *will* we? Will we make it all better in the end?'

Liza gave him a look as if to say *don't ask stupid questions*. He wasn't going to get any easy reassurances from her. She waved him away and was about to start sorting through the books they had brought with them when the doorbell rang.

'Shelley?'

But it wasn't Shelley. Liza stared in shock for a second at the man in the long dark coat and the oversized trilby.

'Mr Wright!' she gasped. He looked so out of place and

vulnerable, up above the ground. He was incongruous in so ordinary a setting. And his physical deformity was all too clear, here in the dim light of the fading day.

'I brought some more books,' he said. He looked uncertain of his welcome. He was wearing a large eyepatch and seemed very wary. 'I came to help.'

She ushered him in.

When Jack returned with tea and whisky and some cheese sandwiches, he was surprised to see Mr Wright sitting with Liza, amid piles of old books. Vicki looked disgusted by the old man's appearance.

'You're from the bookshop?'

He gazed at her steadily. 'For my sins.'

'What about Paolo?' she snapped. 'What about my husband?'

'I'm afraid I don't know . . . Your husband . . . ?' Mr Wright looked completely mystified. He turned to the others.

'Paolo went to your shop,' Jack explained. 'He's a relative of a . . . friend of ours. And he wanted to check out where the grimoire came from.'

'When was this?' Mr Wright asked. Vicki counted on her fingers and told him, repeating the well-worn story she had told the police so many times by now. Mr Wright looked at her with concern. 'You shouldn't be on your feet, young woman. You are infected. When night falls properly, you will experience some difficult hours.' He shook his huge head sadly. 'We must secure her and prevent her from leaving this flat. She will try to hunt. And we must protect ourselves, otherwise she will do us great harm.'

Vicki took a step backwards. 'S-secure me?'

'It is for your own good,' said Mr Wright. 'We will lock you in your room. Stuff garlic under the door and round the windows. Crucifixes. Anything we can think of. No superstition is too trivial or silly. We must keep you here.'

Vicki was glaring at him. 'Whatever. I don't care what you do to me. But I want my daughter back. It's . . . it's Christmas Eve, innit? And if you're the expert, you can get her back, right? In time for Christmas. And Paolo, yeah?'

'Paolo . . .' He shook his head, tutting. 'I don't know who comes into my shop. I am busy in the lower levels, always. Danby knows. He talks with the customers. He knows who comes and goes.'

'We'll find him, Vicki,' said Jack. 'And Connie. It'll be okay.'

Liza grunted. 'Look, get something to eat. And then we'll lock you in your room.'

'I'm not hungry,' said Vicki, turning away from them.

Mr Wright was already on to the next topic. He was withdrawing a slim, finely stitched book from his briefcase. 'This is what I have brought you. A monograph.'

Jack felt like giving a derisory cheer. Here comes the frickin' cavalry! A monograph! Just what we need!

But Liza took it carefully from the old man's pale hands. 'What is it?'

'It's the story of Mr M,' said Mr Wright. 'Or rather, fragments of his story that he dictated to one of his own disciples. Everything we know about him is in here.'

'Who the hell's Mr M?' asked Jack.

'Mr M is the man in the grimoire,' said Mr Wright heavily. 'The vampire who was trapped inside the book, and who now

336

resides inside Daniel. Mr M is our implacable and well-nigh-invulnerable enemy. And his secrets have lain hidden away in my possession these many years. Waiting on this moment.'

Liza brushed them all away. 'Okay, it's only a few thousand words. I'm gonna read it right now and see if I can get the skinny on this sucker. You two better lock and bolt Vicki in her bedroom. It's getting dark out there. And then you better get some sleep. You both look beat. I'll wake you in a few hours.'

Jack went gladly to his rest. As he drifted off, his last thoughts were about Mr Wright. How come it was only now that he was giving them the little book about this mysterious Mr M? How come he kept holding back on them? But at least he was here. And he seemed to be on their side, didn't he? Him and his huge head.

Chapter Thirty-Seven

The noise from the back of the van was horrendous now.

Shelley had no choice. She brought the vehicle screeching to a halt in a side street. She had absolutely no idea where she was. The A–Z had dropped to the floor some time ago, when the first sounds of struggle broke out behind her. Since then she had been flying blind, panicking in the driving seat and taking turnings at random.

It sounded like Daniel and Bessie were tearing each other apart back there.

He was awake! And it was as if all the lights and sprung on in the dark house of her conscious mind.

Daddy was home.

She hated herself for even thinking that.

She flung herself out of the cab and backed away from the van.

It was rocking and shaking by the kerb.

A few passers-by increased their pace and hurried on by. A black woman in a shiny blue jacket and a Santa hat gave Shelley a curious look as she bustled past, but Shelley didn't care. She was holding her breath and trying to fight the presence that was suddenly so strong inside her head.

But suddenly it was too late. It was all over.

The back doors of the van flew open. Daniel burst out of them – suitably enough – like a man possessed. In his hand he was clutching something damp, oily and black. Shelley recoiled from this trophy as he waved it around. She shuddered at the dark spatters and his madly grinning face as he rushed up to her.

'What is it?'

'Her heart,' he said, and looked at the sticky, discoloured organ with an expression of utmost disgust. Then he tossed it into the frozen gutter.

'Oh no, no . . .' Shelley moaned, shrinking from him as he wiped his hands on his jacket.

'Uh-huh,' he said. 'That's put her out of action at last. Come on.'

Shelley caught a glimpse of the collapsed form of the woman in the back of the van. She was sprawled in the shadows, lifeless as she had ever been. It was hard to tell, but Shelley thought she could see a great hole in her chest. Daniel had thrust his hands inside her desiccated body and ripped out her heart.

It was too horrible to think about too much.

He took hold of her roughly. 'We're going.'

She fought him. 'I won't go with you . . .'

He laughed. 'Too late, Shelley. It's all too late.' He threw back his head and his hair streamed out darkly. He sniffed the frosty night like an animal. 'My creatures are massing. They're coming together. Come with me now.'

'Are we going to fly again?'

'We could do.' He shrugged. 'Yes, why not?'

She found herself smiling, despite everything. 'All right,' she said.

*

Jack slept solidly for just under three hours. He woke thick-headed, unsure of where he was. The bedroom was very dark, apart from a line of light under the paper blind, and some luminescent stars stuck to the ceiling. As he lay there, he struggled to bring himself up to date. For a fleeting and wonderful moment he believed he was still home on Thompson Street. He thought Ricardo was in the narrow bed with him, and Consuela was in the living room, under heaped comforters.

Instead he was in London, in a toddler's bedroom, in a bed covered with stuffed toys.

Early hours. He rubbed his eyes. His sleeping pattern was shot all to hell, of course. He wasn't even sure what day it was. Was it Christmas Day yet? Was it already tomorrow? The approach to Christmas had seemed endless this year. It was as if he and his friends were stuck in the endless build-up. But how could they celebrate when it finally came? Knowing as they did about the foul poison seeping through this city and their own?

He lay back and tried to sleep again. He'd always been quite good at sleeping.

Was that a noise? Footsteps in the flat?

He thought of Mr Wright and Liza in the living room. They had probably been sitting up all night, scouring those old books. Liza would be gleaning what she could about the mysterious Mr M. They were indefatigable, those two, it seemed.

They've been doing this for years, Jack thought. For decades, those two, in their separate ways, have been at war with the forces of darkness. In a quiet and surreptitious way, nipping these wicked things in the bud. Mr Wright had been quite outspoken about

340

being aware of the work that Liza had done, back in her prime. Though she had demurred and played it down, she was famous for it, within their own, shared, arcane world.

What have I strayed into? Jack wondered, not for the first time.

More footsteps. Someone banged a door. There was knocking on a wall. He sat up abruptly.

Ah. It would be Vicki, wouldn't it? In the darkest part of the night, she'd be widest awake. The surging infection in her blood would be keeping her up. She'd be wild-eyed and keen to get out into the streets.

They had bolted her bedroom door. But if she was at full power, surely that couldn't hold her? Jack didn't know. He realised that the little he did know all came from novels on the subject, most of which contradicted each other. This was real life, he reminded himself. Things worked differently here . . .

The sounds quietened down and he was massively relieved. He tried to subside gently into sleep. He wanted to forget what was going on. He wanted to dream about Christmases. Family Christmases at home . . .

And then came the tapping at the window.

Jack continued to lie still. Willing the noise to go away.

But he knew he had to get up and see what it was. Maybe just a tree branch outside the window. Did it sound like twigs against the glass? Or did it sound like small knuckles? He realised he had no idea whether there even was a tree out there. Before sleep he had collapsed into bed and barely peeped outside at the view.

There it was again. A little rhythm picked out on the glass. That wasn't random. It was someone knocking.

He got up heavily, lumbering across the room in his

undershorts. Stepping on squeaky toys and littered plushies. He stared at the paper blind and it was like a blank screen. Something was moving and shifting out there. Just inches away from him.

Was he crazy? He could hear a high little voice singing: '*Away in a manger . . . no crib for a bed . . .*'

He lifted the cord for the blind and yanked it hard. Too hard. The cheap blind ripped away from its fixings and clattered down. For a moment he was tangled up in strings and dusty-smelling canvas, and he cried out in shock. Then he realised what he'd done, and swore loudly.

He pushed the broken blind away from himself and looked up to see that it was snowing.

'*. . . The little Lord Jesus lays down his sweet head . . .*'

And the toddler whose room he was borrowing was on the other side of the window.

Her small palms were pressed against the glass, very white. Her wispy hair was streaming in the night breezes. She was smiling at him as she hovered there, several storeys above ground. She laughed at his so-serious expression on seeing her, then thumped hard against the glass, wanting to be in. Her flesh looked pale and squashy as uncooked dough.

Jack stepped backwards, stumbling on the toys.

'*. . . The stars in the bright sky looked down where he lay . . .*'

She would freeze out there. He had to let her in.

She's already frozen, the rational part of his mind told him. She's too far gone. If you let her in now, *you're* dead.

He shouted at her to go away. He flung up his arms and tried not to look. But the child – Connie – just giggled at him and

342

mimicked his movements, as if they were playing a game. She knocked on the window again.

Jack watched in horror as another figure came floating out of the night. A dumpy, motherly form. She emerged from the obscurity of the silently falling snow and swam gently towards the window. She too was grinning at Jack. Beckoning to him with warm familiarity.

Consuela.

How on earth was she here? What was she doing floating about in north London, when they'd left her in New York?

Consuela took hold of the baby and cradled her softly against her vast bosom. The child laughed and kicked and pointed at Jack. Yes, yes, we both want to come in. Let us in, Jack.

Consuela was Connie's great-aunt. Her namesake. Had she come over with Daniel on the plane? Had she turned herself into mist as well, and stowed away with him in the hold? Jack remembered seeing her turn into a bat. Could she have flown all this way on her own silky dark wings?

Either way, she was here, smiling and floating in the freezing air. She was united with her great-niece, and they looked so happy to be together.

Jack shook his head violently. Don't even think like that. They're nothing now. They're dead. Undead. They're not even real people any more.

Are they?

He stood there, transfixed.

Who would be next? Ricardo?

Was he dead and gone as well? Was he no longer a real person?

'Go away,' he moaned, in a small voice. 'Please go away. I don't know what to do.'

Somehow the two figures in the falling snow understood what he was saying, or the gist of it. They looked at his stricken expression and laughed fondly at him. To them it was easy. Just open the window. Invite us in. Nothing could be easier. Just do it, Jack.

Would that be easier? he wondered. To give in now. No more fighting it. And then . . . then he'd belong to something, wouldn't he? To *someone*.

He was more than half tempted.

The bedroom door flew open. Light streamed in from the hall.

Liza stood there on the threshold. Defiant. Furious.

'Get away from the window, Jack,' she told him. 'Don't look at them.'

'But they're . . .' he began. He stared at her. Her hair was straggly and long, witchlike and free of its bun. She was brandishing one of her home-made stakes. She looked terrifyingly calm.

'I know who they are,' she said. 'And what they want.'

'They want all of us,' he said. 'They want to take us all over.'

'That's right,' she said. 'Till the whole frickin' place is turned into vampire world. Well they're not getting it.' She shouted at the floating matron and the toddler outside. 'You hear me? You're ain't getting us.'

There was a loud crash from the bedroom next door. 'Vicki,' said Jack.

In an instant, he saw that the two figures at the window had melted away.

'They're after *her* now.'

Liza's words were interrupted by an even louder crash from the next bedroom. The terrible sound of splintering glass.

'She mustn't let them in . . .' Liza gasped.

But by the time they'd raced down the hallway and grappled with all the locks and barricades, they were already too late.

They found Vicki's bedroom empty and abandoned and littered with broken glass. The snow was pelting in. Consuela and Connie were gone – and so was the young mother. All three had flown into the night.

Chapter Thirty-Eight

Something was missing.

When Bessie woke up, sometime after dawn, she knew that something significant had gone. She sat up cautiously, taking stock of the usual dull aches she was prey to.

The back of the van was freezing and half packed with drifting snow. It had been abandoned, with its doors hanging open. The snow was still falling. The morning light seemed clean and freshly laundered, even in this stinking alleyway.

She lumbered heavily to the open doors, and that was when she felt it. The sickening lack of noise in her chest. The gaping wound left by Daniel. There was no ticking inside her. She was hollow.

It was as if time itself had been stolen from her, since she had nothing to measure it with.

Bessie remembered those last few moments of their fight. They had tussled and rolled about, close and hot as lovers. His fingers had gripped and wormed their way through her soft, tender flesh. They had taken hold of her heart and drawn it out of her body.

She couldn't even scream, she had been so shocked. The surprise of it had blotted out the rare moment of pain she had experienced. Real pain! *Her!* It was amazing. Almost like a gift.

Raw, savage, gut-wrenching pain – bestowed upon her. She who had felt hardly anything that extreme in years. Nothing more than the constant aches and shivers and the occasional buzz of pleasure.

Now she was feeling. Now she knew what it was to feel real human pain and anguish again.

She found her heart in the gutter, under the snow that had been falling all night. It was frozen to the stone. Brittle and glistening with a beard of frost. Like something stuffed way back in a butcher's cold storage.

She took her heart and stowed it away again in her hollow chest. It rattled and rolled around in the dry chambers, looking for its place. She didn't know if it would melt again and warm through.

Maybe a cold heart was what this situation merited.

Lately she had been feeling too soft and tender. These new friends of hers. The human connections she had made again. Perhaps they had made her too soft and pliant. Vulnerable to other monsters. But now her heart was frozen again. It had been disconnected.

She listened hard. People were approaching.

Bessie concentrated. She saw the city in her mind. She could sense it all, spreading out for miles around her. All that hot, jumbled-up life. Slippery, promiscuous, selfish. And where was Liza and her other friends? Could she find them? And Shelley? Ah, but Bessie suspected that it was too late for Shelley now. Her trail had turned icy. She had fled into the skies with Daniel. She had flown again, and now nothing could bring her back.

But the others . . .

Iiii haave tooo finnd the otherrsss . . .

Now there were little men around her. They wore blue uniforms and they had parked their car by the stolen van. They were looking at her strangely. Like she was something out of the ordinary.

I am, I aaaam, thought Bessie. They don't knooow hooww out of the oooordinary I aaam . . .

The police were looking at her in horror. At the great black hole in her chest.

She smiled at them as warmly as she could manage. She knew that the police were meant to be helpful. 'Haaave yoou seeen my friendsss?' she asked.

It was anarchy.

All that night, a stream of odd-looking people arrived at the hotel. The desk staff were overwhelmed. Alarm bells were rung, phone calls made.

Ted the doorman had seen nothing like it since the late sixties and the days of the Rolling Stones.

Such a mix of people, though! Bag ladies, bus conductors, glamour models and a duke. One by one they came through the golden revolving doors. They were in their night things, many of them, walking with a shambling gait. Some of them even had their eyes closed, pushing roughly past the hotel staff.

They knew where they wanted to be. It was as if they were responding to some silent, urgent summons or subconscious need. Ted had heard all about sleeper agents and the strange things the secret services got up to. He'd been pally once with a few of the more loose-lipped gentlemen who'd stayed at the Savoy, up to murky business with foreign agents. He could well believe this was all their doing, the way these folk were carrying on.

By dawn he had stood by helplessly as more than forty of these waifs and strays had lumbered past him. Some of them milled about in the foyer, others wandered to the stairs. Some wove their way through the hotel's lavish, endless corridors. They were going to the suite at the very top.

The manager was at reception now, ringing the suite but getting no answer. He looked flustered and disturbed.

These weren't spies or agents, or any of that malarkey, thought Ted, smoking outside. Agents and that – they were all subtle, weren't they? You never knew they were there. That was the point of them. This was different.

Damned if he was going to stand in their way.

There was a strange smell coming off the ones arriving now. It was dawn, and the smart lane leading to the hotel's grand entrance was steeped in blue gloom. Here came older ones who reeked of grave mould. They walked jerkily and their clothes were tattered and decayed. They wore periwigs and buckled shoes, some of them. Others sported high-necked shirts with cravats. Ladies limped by in ballgowns streaked with mould and gore.

No way Ted was standing in the way of this lot.

They hissed at him, some of them, as they lumbered by, revealing their flashing fangs as if to ward him off. Ted didn't need telling twice. He drew back and raised his hands in supplication. No problems here, mate. You just go where you want. Have it all. Have the Savoy. I've no problem with that. I'm not daft.

The newcomers – the Walkers – made their way stiffly towards the top of the building.

A few of the other guests emerged from their rooms, coming face to face with the visiting dead. Shrieks rang out. Long-disused limbs stretched and flexed, grabbing warm flesh, breaking necks, caressing warmth where they could find it.

The visitors met no obstacles.

Their master, Daniel, awaited them. He cried, 'Welcome, welcome!' as each new wave of half-asleep vampires and zombies made it to his suite.

Beside him, Shelley wondered vaguely if there would be enough room for them all. For a moment, she felt absurdly like a hostess, fretting that everything was just so for their guests. Then she stirred out of her trance for a moment, and became horribly aware of the rank odour of decay, the dusty clothes hanging on rotting flesh, and the savage eagerness of those newly made vamps, who had come to join the deadly throng.

But her moments of doubt and dismay were few and far between. Most of her personality was thoroughly submerged. She was Daniel's concubine, and she delighted in his moment of triumph. He had put the call out, to the dead and undead alike, as they had flown across the night skies of London. She had felt like they were Peter Pan and Wendy, streaking through the velvety clouds, calling out indiscriminately to all the Lost Boys and Girls of the ancient metropolis.

She and Daniel watched them – barrow boys, dolly birds, soldiers and chars – come to pay court to their new monarch.

Now Daniel opened the drawer in the bedside cabinet closest to him.

'Erm, Shelley . . .' he said. 'Where is it?'

Chapter Thirty-Nine

Liza woke to hear banging at the front door.

She came alert instantly, curled up on the sofa in Vicki's living room. She glanced at where Mr Wright was sitting upright in an armchair. His one visible eye was closed and he was perched like a gigantic owl, with a hefty book upon his lap. He was quite still, unmoved by all the clatter at the door.

Liza struggled through the heaps of books, swaying on her feet with tiredness, and saw a uniformed figure standing on the other side of the pebbled glass.

'Yeah?' she shouted through the letterbox. Her voice quavered slightly, and her heart was playing merry hell. The last thing she needed was the police getting into all of this.

'Madam, would you open up, please?' said a polite and young-sounding voice. 'We've picked up a lady here. She was on the streets last night and in obvious distress. She wouldn't be taken to hospital and she gave us directions to come here. She says she's a friend of yours.'

'What?' Liza fumbled with the locks and chains. Could it be Vicki? Maybe she hadn't flown off to Daniel last night after all. Perhaps she'd been able to resist him.

But it wasn't Vicki on the doorstep. Liza stood in the wide-open door and stared amazed at the figure behind the cowed young policeman. 'Are you the friend she's looking for, madam?' he asked.

It was Bessie standing there, looking large as life and twice as ghastly.

'Liiizzaaaa!' she said, in a loud and jubilant voice. 'I haaave fooounnd yooouu!'

'Where's what?' asked Shelley nervously. Less nervously, perhaps, than she would have done had she not been as possessed as she was. But she felt nervous nonetheless. Daniel had a very funny look about him. Glowering. Black scorn and menace were dripping from his face. She could see the emotions pouring off him in great waves and she wondered vaguely if that was some new power she had – the ability to see people's feelings so acutely. Or it might just be that Daniel was incredibly and hugely pissed off with her.

'What do you mean, *what*? What do you think, Shelley? What's this whole thing been about, you dozy bint?'

She felt like she had been slapped. 'Don't talk to me like that!'

'Shut up. You're in my power, remember?'

But she wasn't. Not totally. His mind was off her as he tugged the drawers out of both bedside cabinets and tossed them about. Next he was ripping the pillows out of their cases and flinging the bedclothes around. His mind was straying off his other subservient visitors, and they were murmuring and moaning at his strange behaviour. Shelley glanced at them – this weird hotchpotch of deathly looking creatures from all times and places; this potpourri of sleek vampires and unkempt zombies in varying states of undeath. She had been avoiding looking at them too closely. Some of them had the bloated, glassy-eyed look of corpses dredged up from the bottom of the river. They were moaning more loudly, seemingly in sympathy with Daniel's rage.

'Daniel, you're disturbing them . . .'

'I don't care!' he barked, grinding his perfect teeth together. Fangs! She could actually see his fangs now. They were fully mature. Terrific. Just what you would expect to see. Her Daniel. Fully fledged. Fully vamped up.

Shelley took a backwards step. 'The grimoire. It's not there,' she said.

'That's right,' he said. 'Someone's been in and nicked the flaming thing. Any ideas?' Suddenly he was right in front of her and had her by the shoulders. He was shaking her.

'Daniel, stop . . .'

'You know, don't you? You know something?'

'My aunt, she was here,' Shelley said, and it felt like he was shaking the words out of her. Like she was a piggy bank and he was shaking her till he got what he needed.

'She took the book?' He swore savagely.

'She phoned me, or Jack did, while they were in here,' Shelley said. 'Yeah, she's got it.'

Daniel roared and tore at his hair with both hands. Then he reeled away from Shelley, scattering zombie guests as he went. 'That woman! That frigging woman! Everywhere I go! Everything I try to do – she's there!'

Shelley felt she had to defend her aunt. 'Listen, without Aunt Liza, you'd never have been transformed in the first place.

Remember? It was she who had the book first. She passed it on to you . . .'

He rounded on Shelley. 'Yes! It's all her fault! But the least she could do is let me get on with it now! Let me take control of my own destiny!'

'She wants to stop you,' Shelley said. 'She wants to . . . stop us.' She hung her head miserably. Now she knew which side she was on. She felt that she could never break out of Daniel's control. She had about as much volition as these skanky vamps clogging up the luxury suite. She was no better off than those lost souls.

Aunt Liza would never trust her now. Never again.

'We need the book back,' Daniel said. 'Without it . . .' He looked stricken for a moment.

'Without it what?'

'Mr M's control is slipping. Because I don't have the grimoire. To fully manifest, he needs the book in my hand. His very essence is still partly in that book . . . he wants to come out of it and fully into my form . . .' As Daniel said these words, it was as if they were only just occurring to him. As if the words were speaking him, rather than the more customary way round.

'If he does that . . .' Shelley said. 'What will happen to *you*, Daniel? Where will you be?'

Daniel looked confused for a moment. Then he looked shiftily at the nasty disciples around him. More were coming in the door every minute, and soon the suite would be full. He dragged Shelley into the immaculate and vast bathroom. He sat her down.

'I think Mr M wants to take me over completely,' he said.

'And what about you?' she repeated, gazing at him. Beseechingly, she thought. I'm looking at him beseechingly. At the old Daniel. The Daniel's that still in there. He was arrogant and snappish and not altogether nice – but at least he was mine. And not evil or dead.

'I'll be . . . I'll be gone, I think,' he said.

They stared at each other.

'I think I'm almost gone as it is,' he added.

'Don't say that,' she told him. 'You're still *you*. It's not too late.'

'I think it is.'

'Who is this Mr M, anyway?' she said.

'A sorcerer. A vampire. From a long time ago. He talks to me . . . a little. I have learned a bit about him. But only so much. Only as much as he wants me to know . . .'

'It seems a rubbish deal,' Shelley said. 'What do you get out of it? He gets to live again in your body. He gets to become you. And after everything you've done for him!'

'I've had no choice,' said Daniel. 'Right from the start, Mr M has been in command.'

'You can fight it, Daniel . . .'

'No,' he said. He realised he had been holding both her hands. Squeezing them. He dropped them suddenly and turned away. 'This is me now. This is my destiny. We need to get that book. And I know where it'll be. It's obvious where that old cow will be taking it. She'll be getting back-up and help. She'll be there right now.' He swung round and glared at Shelley. She gasped, seeing that Daniel was mostly gone again. His eyes were blazing crimson and that malign intelligence had returned to them. 'You will go there first, Shelley. You will talk to them.'

'Will I?' she said.

'If you ever loved Daniel, yes, you will. I can make him suffer terribly, you know, while we're in this form together.'

Shelley gasped at this. 'Get out of him. Leave him alone!'

Daniel chuckled. 'You think you can defy me, Shelley?'

'Yes. And I will.'

'Not for long. You'll do as I say. And you *will* go to them.'

'Where?'

'Where do you think?' He smiled horribly. 'They'll be trying once again to take the book back to its home. To 666 Charing Cross Road.'

Chapter Forty

'She'll be all right now,' Jack told the policeman. Was it bad that he thought the young cop was hot? Happy Christmas morning. What a gift on the doorstep. An ancient effigy with a hot police escort. I'm delirious, Jack thought. With everything going on, I'm reverting to my basest instincts. He shook his head and shut the door on the cop's stammering protest. 'She'll be fine with us,' Jack reassured him, shouting through the letterbox. 'She's our friend.'

What must the young cop think of them, though? Having a friend that looked like Bessie did now. He was amazed she hadn't been dragged off to the emergency room or the drunk tank. She looked like someone who'd been living rough for months.

He turned towards the living room, from where he could hear Aunt Liza's muttered imprecations. 'Now are you sure, dear? You look dead on your feet . . .'

Bessie chuckled ominously at that.

When Jack came into the room, he saw that Mr Wright was sitting bolt upright in his armchair, staring at the new arrival. His whole body was filled with electricity and his single visible eye was wide open with shock.

'Ah, yeah,' Liza said awkwardly. 'This is a strange meeting. Mr

357

Wright, this is our friend Bessie. Bessie, meet the owner and proprietor of—'

'I am the guardian,' said Mr Wright in a chalky voice. 'That's my main role. Guardian of the bookshop at 66b Charing Cross Road.'

They all watched Bessie's weather-beaten face twist and gurn at him. She studied the timid man carefully from a distance and then took a lumbering step towards him. 'Amongg the thiiiingss you were guaaarding wass a certain booook . . .'

'Indeed.' He nodded, looking shamefaced. 'And, having quite by chance learned of the whereabouts of a certain lady, I sent it to her in order to be rid of the responsibility.' He hung his massive head and his shoulders shook. 'I was a selfish idiot. Everything that has happened is my fault.'

'Noooo,' Bessie said. 'I wassn't going tooo blame yoou, Mr Wriiight. I was goooing to thannnk yoou.'

He looked up sharply. 'You mean because the grimoire brought you life?'

She nodded creakily. 'It maaade the diviiine spaaark retuuurn to my old bonesss and sineeewsss.'

'She was on display in a museum,' Liza put in. 'And I was in there with the book in my handbag. Somehow, the grimoire being close managed to . . . work magic on her. But no one knows really where she's from. Or who she is.'

Bessie seemed to be struggling with all kinds of emotions as she said, 'My memoories arre damaaaged and I juust don't knooow much . . . I know I hail from these iisles originalllly . . .'

Mr Wright sat up stiffly to attention. 'You don't remember who you are?'

She shook her head, her dry hair rustling like straw.

'I . . . I think I might know,' he said.

They all stared at the old man. Liza was dumbfounded. 'What do you mean? How would you . . . how could you know anything?'

He was on his feet, galvanised and beaming with excitement. 'Think, Liza Bathory! *Think!* Of the legends and myths. The rumours and tales! Think about Bessie and who she might be. Reach back into arcane lore . . .'

'Do we have time for this?' Jack asked. 'Haven't we got enough on our plates?'

Liza said, 'Jack's kinda right. No disrespect, Bessie. We'll sort out your mystery soon enough, but in the meantime, we got vampires swirling about in the skies above London, and Daniel coming to the height of his powers.'

'Daniel has been possessed by Mr M, Liza,' said Mr Wright. 'Mr M who was trapped inside the book. But whatever has animated Bessie's inert form was also inside the book. The sorcery trapped therein brought her to life. I'd be very surprised if that isn't inextricably linked to Daniel's shenanigans.'

Liza nodded. 'I'm sure you're right. But we haven't got time to go over it all now, have we? Let's just be glad Bessie is here with us, in order to help in our hour of need. She's pretty good in a fist fight, aren't you, honey?'

But Bessie's attention was riveted on Mr Wright. 'Yooou said yooou sussspect you knooow whooo I aaam.'

'Er, yes,' he said shiftily. He gingerly lifted his eyepatch so as to boggle at her with both eyes as she came closer to him. He gagged a little at the whiff of necromancy that still followed her around.

Behind them, Liza was shouting out orders, 'Jack, better call a taxi. I'm not messing about on that subway today. But get a big one, mind, we got Mr Wright's head and Bessie's long legs to think about . . .'

'Sure thing,' said Jack, hurrying into the hall.

Bessie stared into the antiquarian's huge eyes. They swam with wonder and twin reflections of her own amazing self.

'Telll meee whooo yooou think I aammm,' Bessie intoned, in a voice that brooked no dissent.

'You are the fabled Scottish Bride,' said Mr Wright. 'That's what I think. I've read about you in books from the nineteenth century. You were thrown into the sea by the folk of a small fishing port on one of the islands.'

'I waass in the seeaa for a long whiiile,' agreed Bessie. 'I rememmmber the cooold briiine of the seeaaa, and the sailors fisssshinng me oout. I wore a ruuinned wedding dress. It had barnacles and eeeels among the seeeed pearls and laaace.'

Liza asked, 'But why did they throw her in the sea?'

'Because she was an abomination,' sighed Mr Wright. 'Or so they thought. In their infinite wisdom. After they murdered her, they commemorated the fact, each year afterwards, by repeating the sacrifice with an effigy, rather like a Guy Fawkes dummy. Their descendants do it to this very day, I believe. To appease the restless spirit of the Scottish Bride, who was put to sea so long ago.'

'Yeeesss!' cried Bessie harshly. 'Thaat iss it. I dooo have a restless spirit ssstill.'

'The taxi's on its way,' said Jack. 'But I don't understand, why did they throw Bessie in the sea in the first place? Why was she an abomination?'

Bessie twitched her head around to look at him. 'Can't yoou seee, Jaaack? I aaam indeed an abommminaation. I was not of woooman booorn. I am unnaturaaal.'

'Oh, honey,' Liza sighed. 'We all got our back stories, you know.'

'Hm,' said Mr Wright. 'Except Bessie's is a real humdinger. You see, those Scots villagers found her in a castle turret on their island. One recently vacated by a certain mad European scientist. A surgeon and practitioner of the darker arts.'

'Huh?' said Jack, sounding dumb, but suddenly realising what the old man meant.

Ditto Liza. 'You mean . . . ?'

'He *made* her,' said Mr Wright. 'He created her. Amongst other . . . experiments he was conducting, that scientist was messing about with the body parts of the dead. That was his great discovery. How to bring life back to the dead. He'd stitch pieces together and make humans of his own design. The villagers knew what was happening. He robbed their graveyard and mortuary. They suspected him of even worse. They watched him make a man. And a woman. They watched him try and fail and try again. And they watched him fight to the death with his creations when they rebelled. They were relieved when he went, at last, and left their bloody shores.

'But when they went to his makeshift laboratory, they found that some of the fruits of his labours lay abandoned there.'

Bessie squawked in shock. 'I waaass there. Meee! That wasss mee! But . . . how dooo youuu knoow thisss?'

'I read a lot,' said Mr Wright grimly. 'And the story has been passed down. I thought it was merely a legend, in a book of quaint Scots tales of the macabre.'

'I neeed to seeee this booook.'

'It's in the first Book of Manifestations. That compendious study of the hidden and forgotten. It's back at the shop. In the deepest depository.'

'Myyy storry,' said Bessie, breathing raggedly. 'I haave a sstorrry. My ooown!'

'You weren't alone,' said Mr Wright. 'There was another there, when they found you. Another woman, created by the same man. You . . . you have a sister, Bessie. You're not alone on this earth.'

Just at that moment, the phone trilled.

'Taxi's here already,' muttered Jack, amazed.

Chapter Forty-One

Shelley would have to go to the bookshop by herself. Daniel explained that if he went with her, all the vamps, zombies and Walkers that were gathering at the Savoy would follow him mindlessly. It was flattering, but not that helpful. Getting the grimoire back was going to be a delicate job.

'And only you can do that, my wonderful girl,' he told her. She wasn't sure if it was him talking, or the Mr M inside his head. She wasn't even sure if that even mattered. She sighed and squeezed past the raggle-taggle throng now filling up the suite. She wasn't scared of them any more, even though they were hissing thirstily like a nest of mad snakes and were icy to the touch. She was their monarch's concubine, and she suddenly realised that in this position, she had nothing to fear from anyone.

I've spent half of my life fearful, she thought. That was the thing about having massively competent and brave relatives like Aunt Liza. Knowing she could never measure up. Knowing she'd always be left far behind or in the shade.

'I will watch through your eyes,' Daniel told her. 'I will direct your feet.'

Yes, yes, I'm surrendering everything to him. It feels like such a relief in away, doesn't it?

She rode down in the elevator, finding the lavish foyer in a state of horrible chaos. The vamps weren't attacking anyone any more, or attempting anything else unpleasant. In fact, they were being pretty well behaved by now. They were lounging about and milling almost excitedly, as if at the start of a convention. They had come here to be with their master. They were here for the beginning of the end of the world. The Savoy was to be their new headquarters.

Many shrewd and hungry eyes flicked and glanced as Shelley hurried by. They knew who she was. She put her head down and scurried on her way. Thrilled, if she was honest with herself.

The sight of Consuela on one of the squashy sofas, holding the toddler, Connie, in her arms, brought her up short. Vicki was sitting close by, and they were all drinking coffee and nibbling fancy biscuits.

'Oh!' Shelley said. 'You're here.'

'We're here to be with Daniel,' said Vicki. 'He made us. We all belong with him.'

Shelley nodded. It was hard to know what to say. She could see herself having to be rather accommodating and tolerant when it came to Daniel's affections. What was he after? A harem?

As she thought that, she felt him laughing, somewhere towards the back of her mind.

She stepped outside and breathed in the morning air.

Yet even out here there was that musty smell. As if many graves had been turned over that night. The stench was still lurking in the brightness.

Daniel directed her feet across roads and through side streets. She hardly had to think at all.

'I'm here, I'm here . . .' he told her.

At last she came to Charing Cross Road. Here she caught the eye of a few stumbling cadavers, clearly on their way to the Savoy. They smiled at her, tipping their hats and winking and smirking. They looked so pale in the daylight. What was that nonsense about not going out in the day? All the vamps she had met seemed to be up at all hours. They never seemed to take any rest at all.

Like me, thought Shelley. I should be dead on my feet, all these days without sleep.

Her heart thumped harder. Dead on my feet. Is that what I am now?

She saw the large taxi cab at the kerbside on Charing Cross Road. It was just pulling away, revealing the blistered paint of the half-hidden black doorway: 66b. She was here again.

She banged loudly on the door.

'They're here, my love,' she told the Daniel in her head. 'They have arrived here with the book. I know it. I need you, Daniel. I don't think I can face them alone . . . Aunt Liza will shame me. She will convince me that you are in the wrong . . .'

The Daniel in her head was quiet. She panicked. 'Where are you? Where have you gone? Daniel!'

The bookshop's door swung open and the blandly smiling face of Mr Danby was there before her. He looked scared when he saw who it was.

*

'We can't destroy it,' said Liza.

They were in the heart of the bookshop. Liza, Jack, Bessie and Mr Wright. Back in that pink and golden glow of ancient books, deep under Charing Cross Road. Here time had stood still for decades. Until recently it had seemed as if nothing bad could enter. Nothing could puncture the calm equilibrium of this inner sanctum.

But they all knew that was a false hope. Daniel had already been here once. He could get in any time he wanted.

Mr Wright was flipping cautiously through the thick, warped pages of the grimoire. They all stared at the crabbed writing and strange drawings in many colours. Distorted, faded, discoloured by time and other weird substances, the book's very contents were radiating sheer malignity in the gentle glow from his desk lamp. He paid special attention to the bloodstained and blackened pages. He sniffed them and studied them.

'The book has changed since I sent it to America,' he noted. 'There are extra pages. Graffiti and notes have been added. More suspicious stains have appeared or been made. This book is constantly evolving. It grows in power and malice.' He sighed deeply. 'And that is why we must destroy it. We must attempt the ritual as described in the fifth Book of Manifestations.'

'You and those Books of Manifestations,' said Aunt Liza. 'You act as if they contain the answer to everything.'

He looked surprised. 'They do.'

Bessie was standing transfixed by the grimoire. She reached out to touch its pages reverently with the twiggy fingers of one hand. 'Thiss brought mee life again . . .'

Jack was startled to hear her speech becoming less slurry as she touched the book. It was very strange. 'Are you saying that in order to put a stop to the . . . erm, entity possessing Daniel, we gotta destroy the book. And that if we do that, Bessie bites the dust as well?'

They all looked at him. 'To put it bluntly,' said Liza, 'yes, Jack. That's exactly right.'

'We can't do that!' said Jack.

'But we must,' said the old man. 'It should have been done years ago. I should have done it myself. But I could never stomach the idea of deliberately destroying an old and valuable book. Even an evil one.'

'What does the ritual involve?' Liza asked.

'Liza, we can't! We can't let Bessie be destroyed!' Jack burst out.

'That's the other thing,' said Mr Wright. 'The ritual for destroying the book also needs lots of blood. Contaminated vampire blood. It's got to blot out every page. Only then can the book be burned, apparently.'

Bessie stirred on the spot. She took her hand away from the grimoire. 'Sooo . . . ifff I help you do the ritual and destroy the boook, then I alsssoooo sacrifice myssself . . . and diiieee yet again, and then aaall will be saaaved? The vampires will sink baaack intooo the earth and the wooorld will be saaafe for Chrisssstmassss?'

Mr Wright coughed, rather embarrassed. 'Er, yes, my dear. That's right.'

Bessie seemed to be chewing this over. Her whole form trembled with suppressed emotion. Her face was contorted and her eyes were livid. Her next words ripped out of her with a force that made them all jump.

'Wellll ffffuuuckk that for a game of ssssoooldiersss!'

With that she snatched up the book and hugged it to herself. Before they could stop her, she had hurried off into the labyrinth of corridors. Deeper and deeper into the dark city of books.

The others were struck dumb and still for some moments.

'Get after her!' somebody shouted.

And they realised it was Shelley, standing there with them all once again. She was clearly possessed, and mad as hell.

Chapter Forty-Two

Bessie ran without thinking where she was going or where she might end up. She knew she was deep underground. She could hear the trains and rats and underground rivers running all about her, hidden away behind the stacks of books. The tunnels and runnels twisted and knotted like sinews and veins. She felt as if she was inside some vast body, running for her life.

The book nudged against her wounded chest. She held it there as she lolloped and staggered, dislodging other old volumes as she went. The ground here was soggy, even puddled in places, and she felt the rank water soaking into her.

She could imagine being lost down here for ever.

The book spoke to her. Just as it had that first day in Shelley's museum, when it had brought her back to life. Bessie hadn't mentioned that fact to anyone, but the whispery, sepulchral tones of Mr M had spoken to her as well as to Daniel.

Now the old vampire was telling her to give herself up, to go back. To find the others. To surrender to Daniel and his growing army.

'They're coming into the bookshop right now, Bessie,' he said. 'They're swarming down Charing Cross Road and ducking in through that black door. Mr Wright's shop has never been so busy. There's no escape for you or your friends. Not now.'

'Frrienndss?' Bessie shouted aloud, inside the tight confines of the corridor. The space was growing more constricted, harder to negotiate. She was exhausted, she realised. 'Aaare they reeeally my friendsss? Theeeey were willlling to sssacrifice me.'

'Oh, the ritual,' laughed Mr M. 'Well, perhaps. They thought they could be rid of us both, Bessie dear. The vampire king and the hotchpotch monster. We're both embarrassments to them, I think. But they would never have done it. They care too much for you, the fools.'

'Caaare?' sighed Bessie. 'They caaaare?'

'Oh, I think so. They've grown sentimentally fond of you. They're coming after you now. Down these tunnels. Calling your name. Can't you hear them, Bessie dear? They want to remonstrate and beg your forgiveness. Of course they weren't prepared to do away with you. They weren't willing to sacrifice you to save everyone else. You, apparently, mean too much to them.'

Bessie's eyes grew wide at his words. She trembled. 'I . . . do not belieeeve you, Mr M.'

'But it's true, my dear. Can't you hear them calling, pursuing you down these infernal tunnels? They've lit pen torches. They've brought Mr Wright and Mr Danby with them, the men who know where these passageways lead. They are hunting you, Bessie.'

'A ruuuse,' said Bessie. 'When they fiiind meee, they will saaacrifiice me.'

'They love you, Bessie,' said Mr M.

'Looove?' Bessie asked. Then she laughed, barkingly, and started walking again, stumping tiredly down the corridor. As she went, she pulled deliberately at bookcases, letting the contents tumble down. The books splattered and heaped on the wet dirt track she left behind her. If she could have sealed the passage, she would have.

But Mr M was still in her head. So long as she carried the grimoire with her, so close to her chest, she could hear him murmuring on.

'Daniel and my subjects are inside the labyrinth, my dear,' he said. 'Only a matter of minutes away from catching up with your friends. They will take them. They will bite and infect them. You've abandoned them to this fate. You have done this, Bessie. Why not turn back and save them? Why not . . .'

She shook her head to clear it of his voice, and kept on running, stumbling into the dark.

Shelley stopped shouting at her aunt and stiffened. She sniffed the air.

'Daniel is here. In the shop.' She looked both alarmed and delighted at the same time. 'He's coming after us.'

Liza cursed and pushed her niece ahead of her. 'Well he ain't getting you. I've had enough of his interference. Thinking he can just take anyone he wants.'

'But you must let me go to him,' Shelley said. 'I—'

'I nothing,' Liza said. 'When you're away from him, your mind reasserts itself a bit more. You're not a lost cause yet.'

'You haven't seen the army he's amassed this past day or so,' Shelley told her aunt. 'They came to us. Out of graves and out of the river . . .'

Mr Wright and Mr Danby looked fascinated and appalled,

respectively, at her words. 'It begins in earnest,' Mr Wright said, plying his torch beam into the dark gallery ahead. 'This is just how the books said it would be.'

'Don't tell me,' said Jack. 'The Books of Manifestations, right?'

'Indeed, young man,' said Mr Wright. 'All of this was foretold. More or less. Well, most of it. I didn't see these legends interconnecting quite so much. Bessie is a bit of a red herring, actually. It's strange that she's been revivified as well . . .'

'We've got to find her,' Liza grunted, shoving the reluctant Shelley ahead of her. 'You keep movin', lady, and don't give me none of your sass.'

'You won't stop him,' Shelley said. 'Daniel's too strong.'

Mr Danby asked his superior, 'Are we going to use the girl's blood to destroy the grimoire, then?'

They all stared at him, shocked. The moon-faced man looked perplexed. 'Well,' he said, 'I just thought. After what it says in the . . . and the legends and so on . . . the tainted blood you need and everything . . . I thought it was obvious.'

Liza's voice was steely. 'What is obvious?'

'Well, slit her throat.' Danby nodded at Shelley. 'Take her blood and Bob's yer uncle. You can be rid of her, the book, the vamps and that ghastly patchwork woman all in one fell swoop.'

'We're not doing that!' Jack yelled. 'That's not what we're doing!'

Shelley was quiet, staring at her aunt. 'No, we're not going to do that.'

Mr Wright turned to them, his torch uplighting his huge and doleful face. 'You must admit, it would sort everything out . . .'

'No!' Liza screeched, pushing past him, and dragging Shelley with her. 'That's not what we're doing! We're escaping, right? We're taking Shelley to safety, and we're gonna find Bessie and get out of here.' She coughed and spat. 'And if I never see another dirty old ancient book again, I don't care.'

'Very well,' said Mr Wright, his voice and oversized visage full of misgivings.

'These tunnels emerge where, did you say?' Jack asked him.

'Various locations, all over London,' Mr Wright said. 'The actual details and maps are lost. But I know that my ancestors in the book trade had a number of exits and bolt-holes available to them. They were rather lawless, I'm afraid.'

'You don't say,' snapped Liza.

Mr Wright stiffened. 'Look, my dear, I'm doing my best. Danby's last suggestion was simply that – a logical suggestion that would save all our necks, and maybe the whole world as well. But I respect and abide by your descision not to murder your own niece. I can understand that.'

'Bully for you,' Aunt Liza said, mollified only slightly.

'Do I get a say in any of this?' asked Shelley.

'Not really,' said Liza. 'You've caused enough trouble. Getting yourself bitten in the first place, you foolish girl.' She tutted. 'So, Mr Wright. Where are we heading?'

'If we can only find our way to the tunnel that branches off east . . . yes, here. Butterflies. Spiders. Molluscs . . . Yes . . . look. This tunnel. Keep left and left and left again. You'll come up somewhere near High Holborn.'

'What?' Jack couldn't believe it. 'Isn't that miles away?'

'We've already walked for miles, it feels like,' Shelley pointed out. She was gritting her teeth, so Jack knew that Daniel was calling out to her. Raging at her to stay still, to bring them all back to him. 'Oh, this is such a mess. We've lost the book. Everything.'

There came a crash, then, from the tunnel behind them. It was as if someone had wrenched a bookcase away from the wall and smashed it to the ground.

'Bessie?' Jack asked, thinking of the woman's uncoordinated, jerking movements.

'Wrong direction,' Liza said.

'It's Daniel,' said Shelley. 'And the others he's bringing in his wake. They're not far behind now.'

'Oh God,' said Jack. 'We're going to die down here.'

Mr Wright elected to send his minion back down the passageway. 'Danby, fend them off for as long as you can. Take my crucifix.'

'I will,' said the little man.

'Be brave, Danby,' his boss told him.

Danby nodded smartly and hurried off, back the way they had come. There was more loud, threatening noise coming from that direction now.

'He's prepared to die for you?' Liza asked.

'Oh, indeed,' said Mr Wright. 'And much more. You simply can't get staff like him these days. If we survive today, I shall tell you his story. Poor Danby.' Mr Wright watched after the little man for a second or two, then swept back into action. 'But first we must make sure that we live to fight another day. Come along! Follow me!'

He was amazingly energetic and strong for a man of his age. When they encountered obstacles and fallen furniture, he thrust them out of the way without much effort.

'Bessie's been and gone this way,' Liza said. 'This damage is recent. She's come through here ahead of us.'

Mr Wright nodded. 'I can smell the grimoire. We can follow its scent from here.'

As they turned to hurry on, they blocked their ears to the noise pursuing them through the book-lined maze.

Chapter Forty-Three

Daniel rather regretted the fact that his newly resurrected and assembled horde insisted on accompanying him to 66b. They were trashing the place. The vamps surged through the book-filled rooms, ripping and shredding everything they came across. The zombies stamped on precious volumes and ripped into tender bindings with their teeth. What did they have against literature? Daniel wondered.

His former self would have been appalled. But the person he was now knew he had no choice in the matter. These cadavers were bonded to him; they must follow him and destroy everything that stood between them and their quarry. That was how it had to be.

Fires were breaking out. Some of these creatures had strange powers indeed. When they touched the older, more arcane books of magic, the volumes went up in showers of sparks and flame. Perhaps it was some kind of magical defence system. The books were protected against the touch of evil.

The beautiful subterranean rooms grew chaotic and hot, and smoke started to billow and churn.

Daniel saw there was no going back. The way behind was

blocked by lumbering undead bodies and flame and falling books. They're creating a death trap, these creatures of mine. But what did they know about health and safety or self-preservation? Most of them were still cool from their tombs.

Shelley . . . He could sense her, hundreds of metres ahead. They had quite a start. Was she thinking for herself again? No, she couldn't escape him. She never would. She was after the grimoire and using her aunt to fetch it.

'The abomination has the book in her grasp,' Mr M told him.

'B-but didn't I rip out her heart, somewhere near Stoke Newington?' Daniel cried.

'It wasn't enough,' rumbled the presence. 'Her kind always rise again.'

A short, well-dressed figure came staggering out of the tunnel ahead.

'I bring a message,' said Mr Danby, breathing hard. He sniffed the smoke suddenly and looked frightened. 'Oh my! You're setting light to the catacombs! It'll all be gone in a flash!'

Daniel grimaced. He was pretty annoyed about that himself, as it happened. 'What's your message?'

'Leave us alone,' said Danby. 'Spare us. You can have the others. The witch, the boy and your harlot. You can even take the Scottish Bride.'

'The abomination,' Daniel corrected him.

'But leave us our shop and our stock intact,' quavered Danby. 'Don't destroy it.'

Daniel laughed bitterly. All around him his children were tearing books apart and pulping their precious pages. 'It's a little late for that, sir. I think we can say 666 Charing Cross Road is having its final closing-down sale.'

'P-please!' Danby cried out. 'This is our life! Our very souls! This is the collection we are supposed to guard for ever!'

'You've made a poor job of that.'

'I can't believe your master would condone the destruction of our books.'

'This was his prison for all that time,' Daniel snapped. 'He hates this place as much as my children do. Now, what about the grimoire? Fetch me that, and I'll consider helping you.'

'The grimoire?' said Danby slyly. 'Why, that's . . . that's perfectly possible. I can get that for you, sir. I'm sure I can show you where the abomination is . . .'

Daniel was pretty sure he could trace the book and the bride himself, but the little man might have knowledge he could still use. He wouldn't kill him.

'I'll spare you,' he said. 'Show us where they are.'

'My name is Danby, sir, at your service.' He bowed.

Daniel looked round at his ravenous subjects. 'Somebody bite him, would you? I'd rather not.'

With the noise of pursuit and wanton destruction came the horrible smell of burning.

Mr Wright stopped and took a long sniff. 'Oh dear.'

'This place is a tinderbox, even with all the damp,' said Jack. 'Or will the damp put it out?'

Liza shook her head. 'It'll all go up. All of it. It'll be an inferno.'

'The Books of Manifestations . . .' whispered the bookseller.

'Hundreds of years' worth of vital knowledge and necromantic lore and—'

'Yeah, yeah,' said Liza, unsentimental as ever. 'C'mon. There'll be time for all that later.'

But the old man sat down heavily on a nearby stack of out-of-date dictionaries and bestiaries. 'I'm afraid I'll be staying here, my dear. To go down – as the captains of old once did – with my sinking ship.'

'It's a burning shop, not a sinking ship!'

'Nevertheless, the world outside holds no charm or future for me. But you, my dears, must flee at once. I will try to hold back our enemies for as long as I can. Just around the next corner there is a kind of chimney, going straight up through the earth to the surface. There should be iron rungs still, if they haven't rotted away by now. It must be a hundred years since this escape was last attempted. The chimney should emerge into safety.'

'We're almost there?' Liza said. 'And you're giving up?'

'I'm too old to keep on running,' said Mr Wright. 'And without my shop and my books . . .' He shrugged and smiled sadly.

The air was thickening and misting up. Soon the whole place would be filled with poisonous smoke.

'Come *on*,' Jack urged.

'Daniel's back there,' Shelley said.

They stared at her.

'You think we should run back and rescue him?' Jack asked. Suddenly his eyes were streaming with tears from the smoke.

'I-I don't know,' Shelley agonised.

'I think he can look after himself,' said Liza. She turned to the old man once more. 'Are you sure?' she asked Mr Wright.

He waved them away. 'Go! Now hurry!' His huge eyes blinked sadly at them and they looked like twin headlights in London fog. Such wisdom there. Such a lifetime of knowledge garnered here underground, still glimmering at them brilliantly as they turned to go.

They left him.

'What about Bessie?' Jack asked. 'And the book?'

Liza had found the chimney flue in the next corridor. She looked up and saw, impossibly far above, a disc of blue sky. 'I think maybe she's already been this way. Look. She's made her escape. And she's shown us the way out.'

Jack and Shelley stared up the chimney at that inviting blue.

The explosive noise of destruction was catching up with them. They could hear Mr Wright somewhere in that chaos, and he was yelling at someone. His voice went up in pitch, sharply. He shrieked and then was quiet.

'Daniel!' Shelley cried, recognising another voice, and made as if to go back to him. Her aunt kept a firm grip on her.

'Oh no you don't . . . Now, climb! Both of you!'

She just about pushed her niece and her friend up the chimney.

As she prepared to haul herself up after them, Daniel stepped out into the corridor. For once he was looking rather dishevelled, and dirty with grease and smoke.

'Where is Shelley?'

'You can't have her,' Liza told him.

'I've killed Wright and Danby, you know,' he said.

'That was quick work.'

'And I've set about the destruction of these books. Everything down here at 666.'

'Absolute wickedness,' Liza blazed at him.

'I know.' He shrugged.

'Well,' said Liza. She wouldn't give him the satisfaction of listening to him gloat. 'I believe I'll be off. Cheerio, Daniel. You've been such a disappointment. I thought Shelley could have done better for herself.'

He nodded, as if he quite understood. 'You're going to seal that chimney once you're at the top, aren't you?' he said politely. 'I guess that will trap us down here. Me and my horde. We can't go back the way we came. We've sort of set light to everything.'

Liza clambered on to the first rung. She peered upwards to see that the youngsters were making good progress. 'Yes, that's right. I'm going to shut you all in down here. If it's the last thing I do.'

'Hm,' said Daniel. 'I feel a little outmanouevred by that, actually. I could, of course, just rush over there and kill you and then simply fly up the chimney to safety . . .'

'Yes,' Liza conceded. 'I suppose you could.'

'Or I could seize control of Shelley again and get her to scupper your escape.'

Liza nodded. 'That's quite true, too. There are loads of ways you could kill us now and make good your escape. But that ain't gonna fill me with despair. And it ain't gonna stop me tryin' my best to get away and leave you down here. You can't panic me. You ain't got me beat.'

He grinned. 'No, I don't suppose I have.' His tone was almost as mild as hers. For a moment they were both reminded briefly of the people they might have been – the fond aunt and the niece's boyfriend. They should be trying to get along, for the sake of the girl they both loved. But instead here they were . . . in some infernal tunnel, locked in a death match.

Liza took one more cautious step up the rusted ladder. Daniel was wondering how she managed to keep her cool. She'd have tricks galore up her old-lady sleeves. He'd heard enough about her to know that Liza Bathory was far more than she seemed. She was used to fending off monsters such as him.

And that's what I am now, he thought. This is how monsters end up. Fighting for their lives.

Liza could see that Daniel was bracing himself, ready to trip lightly across the dark tunnel as it filled up with smoke, to take her by the throat. He faltered. She could see he was thinking, why doesn't the foolish old hag look more frightened? What stunt is she about to pull? He stared into her eyes. She was tricky. A worthy enemy. She'd have something ready for him. Some kind of trap . . .

And then he knew.

It was as if he could see the reflection in her bright, determined eyes. The twin reflections of shadows emerging from around him in the fetid smoke.

Liza had been watching the tall, vengeful figure rising up from the darkness behind him.

A figure too tall, really, to make a fully convincing woman.

A figure with a grimoire where her heart should be.

And she was standing right behind him.

Liza nodded quickly at Bessie, then closed her eyes briefly, wincing at the horror of it, as Bessie plunged a stake with deadly, hefty accuracy into Daniel's back, so that the tip emerged from his chest.

A terrible expression of surprise burst on to the young man's face as he crumpled to the ground. The two women watched him slump into a heap. His whole form crazed and crizzled in an instant, crumbling into a tidy heap of ashes.

'We'd better hurry,' Liza said. 'Otherwise we'll be reduced to the exact same state by the flames.' She grinned at Bessie. 'Hello, dear. Well done! Where the devil did you get a stake?'

Bessie lurched across the room and heaved herself on to the ladder. 'Aaahh. Whenn he ripped myyy heart ooout he snaaapped off one of my riiiibs. I've been waiiiiting to get himmm baaaack for that.' She retrieved the deadly bone and waved it about triumphantly.

Then, as acrid smoke and flames engulfed the tunnels, the precious books and Daniel's undead army, the two women hurriedly set about climbing to safety.

It took some doing, but they made it. The ladder was growing hotter against their hands and feet. It scorched and hissed and pulled at the skin on Liza's hands, raising blisters on her palms and shins and melting her tights. The inferno raged behind them, underneath them, and hideous screams pursued them from below. A leaping golden torrent of flame ran under them, bringing an updraught that just about smothered the life out of them both. It was as if hell itself was reaching out urgently to claim them. Black embers and rags of ash came rushing past them, billowing at their backs.

They climbed and climbed and climbed.

Somewhere near the very top, Liza lost her grip and cried out in stark terror as first one hand, then the other slipped free. She windmilled madly with both arms and knew she was about to fall backwards down into the pit.

She felt Bessie ahead of her lurch into action. Regardless of her own fears, the Scottish Bride executed a strange, almost gymnastic manoeuvre, and Liza felt her own arms being gripped and clasped together in one massively strong hand. The fingers squeezed hard about her wrists, hoisting her upwards again, guiding her back to the rungs of the ladder.

Liza sobbed with pain and relief. She tried to shout her thanks up to her friend, but Bessie growled something about their needing to hurry up. Liza blinked tears out of her smarting eyes and saw that Bessie had reached the very lip of the chimney. She was suddenly out in the clear, fresh blue air, and – putting on a miraculous burst of speed – Liza wasn't far behind.

For some moments they lay on the ground in the open air, panting and heaving for breath, their ruined clothes smouldering slightly.

Jack and Shelley were waiting for them. Everyone looked at each other in relief, dismay and horror as they each struggled with the thought of what they had escaped from. After some time they regained enough breath to speak. Jack started laughing with relief – sounding insane to himself. Bessie joined in, 'Hurrrr, hurrrr, hurrr . . .' and it was the first time that her laughter had sounded anything like human to him.

They appeared to be in a yard at the back of an old pub. 'Somewhere near High Holborn, the old man told us,' said Jack. 'Wherever that is.'

'We made it,' Liza panted, on her hands and knees, watching as Bessie rolled the iron manhole cover back into place. 'We made it out!'

'And Daniel?' Shelley asked, her face filthy and unreadable. She hurried over to them. 'What about Daniel? Where is he? You left him down there?' She was clutching her head suddenly. 'I-I can't hear him inside my mind any more . . .'

Down below, it was just a river of incandescent flame. There was no chance that anyone could have survived. Liza looked at her niece as if she was crazy, and saw a dozen different emotions flash across the girl's face.

She's gonna need help, Liza thought. She was still in thrall and in love with that asshole. She went to give Shelley a motherly hug.

'He's gone,' she said. 'I'm sorry.'

Liza was glad that Shelley gave in to her embrace. If she had drawn back and started hurling accusations, Liza wouldn't have known what to do. Yeah, we killed him. We left him down there, where his minions foolishly set light to the whole of the labyrinth.

There was nothing that could have been done to save Daniel. Even Shelley could see that.

Maybe I'll not tell her that Bessie aced him with her spare rib. That particular detail might prove too much for the poor girl to take . . .

'Is that an end to it?' asked Jack. 'What about Mr M?'

Liza bit her lip, glancing at Bessie. 'I don't know. Yet. We'll have to see.'

'I haaave the grimmoire tucked awaaay,' said Bessie. 'As looong as it exisssts, then I exissst, and so doesss the vampire maaaster.'

'I see,' said Jack.

'It's okay,' said Liza. 'This time we'll make sure he stays inside the book.'

And that was what they did.

For a while, at least.

Epilogue

It was New Year's Day and they were back in New York.

'Of course, it was quite tricky, getting both Bessie and the grimoire back through security at the airport,' Jack told his work colleague, Lame Wendy, at the party she'd organised for Mr Grenoble. The whole of Fangtasm was packed with well-wishers.

'I'm not surprised!' Wendy – in a sexy new outfit that had surprised a few of those people she hadn't seen for a while – was agog at Jack's tales of what he'd been up to in England. He was quite frank with her about the outlandish details. In the day or two since their return, there hadn't been many people he'd been able to confide in. Lame Wendy always listened – that was the thing about her. 'So, I guess they just went back in the hold with the other luggage?'

'Actually, no,' said Jack. 'Bessie's a bit more human recently. Something to do with the grimoire. She didn't stand out so much on the journey back. And Liza managed some kind of . . . erm, spell, kind of thing, to get her a passport and everything she needed. So the Scottish Bride could fly back in style with the rest of us to her newly adopted city of New York. Looking just like a natural-born woman, in a brand-new outfit. She and Liza went shopping the afternoon before we left.' Jack shook his head and took a deep swig of eggnog, still not quite able to credit everything they'd been through. 'Hey, here's Shelley.'

Looking much like her old and capable self, Shelley came nudging through the crowd of writers and readers bearing a paper plateful of nibbles. Lame Wendy studied her. 'You're looking well for all your recent ordeals.'

Shelley boggled at Jack. 'What are you telling people? We just went on a shopping trip, right?'

'Oh sure, right,' said Wendy, grinning. She slurped her Bloody Mary and Shelley gave her a funny look. A searching look. She knew Lame Wendy had been vamped. Just one more victim of Daniel's army. There were dozens, even hundreds of them, in both New York and London. They would take some watching out for. And, in some cases, mopping up.

And somewhere in New York was Daniel's second-in-command. Ricardo.

Jack hadn't even let himself think about that yet. Not much. His feral and satanic most recent ex-boyfriend was a problem for the New Year. He thought they all deserved a little rest before facing that one . . .

Shelley agreed with him. She was just glad that she still felt like herself. She didn't think she had been fully transformed. Not quite. She hoped.

'Everything okay?' Jack asked her. 'Is your aunt on her way?'

'Yeah.' Shelley nodded. 'She texted to say she was delayed. She'd been on the phone for ages with Vicki.'

'Vicki! Oh, good.'

'Yeah, they're doing all right. Vicki, Connie and Consuela. All back at Rowley Way. Connie attacked the postman yesterday and drew blood, apparently, but they managed to laugh it off and get him to promise not to report it.'

'Jeez.'

'But they're okay. Consuela's staying with them in London, for a bit at least. Oh, and guess what? Paolo turned up. Turned out he was just in some place called Eastbourne. Drunk and gambling and shacked up with a woman. Soon as he heard about what was happening at home, he was straight back there, all concerned. So – it's happy families for them back in Olde England.'

Jack smiled and they clinked glasses. Sure, he thought. Happy families all right. Happy family of neck-biters. He shook his head woefully.

He looked up as the record changed (why were they still playing Christmas tunes?) and there were Liza and Bessie entering the shop, bringing a somewhat giddy Rufus the beagle on his leash. They were dolled up to the nines in their new English outfits, and he had to admit, they looked the height of sophistication. Bessie had on a glittering purple frock with frou-frou layers of lace and beads. Liza was sporting a kind of turban and a velvet wrap over her vintage dress. The party crowd drew back to admire them. Mr Grenoble hurried over, beaming, to welcome his most treasured customer.

'That's not what you called me when you were banning me,' Liza laughed, kissing his rubicund cheek.

'Oh tush,' laughed Mr Grenoble. 'My staff have given me a wonderful party, and all is forgiven, my dear! I don't even mind you bringing your mutt into the shop!' He raised his glass and urged everyone to join him in a toast. 'Dear, dear friends and supporters of Fangtasm books,' he announced. 'I am sure you have all heard about the terrible things that happened in England right before Christmas. The legendary Charing Cross Road – famed for its string of bookshops – was hit by a terrible conflagration, damaging stock and several shops, and completely gutting one particular store. Miles of tunnels and storerooms underneath the shops were entirely destroyed. We must commiserate with our cousins across the ocean, and thank our lucky stars that we are all right and still here.'

Everyone at the party muttered and agreed. Yes, terrible news from the famous Charing Cross Road. All those old treasures! All those wonderful books! Gone in a puff of smoke! And all those bodies they found there afterwards. Terrible, terrible.

'We think we have problems here in New York with our monsters and vampires,' Mr Grenoble muttered to Liza. 'But who knows what really went on under Charing Cross Road on Christmas Day, eh? It must have been terrible.'

'Oh, awful,' agreed Liza, and completed his toast for him. 'To bookshops and book-lovers everywhere!'

As the party guests returned to their drinks and their conversations, Liza realised that the wily old shopkeeper was looking at her appraisingly. 'You were over there in London, your friend Jack was telling me. You were all there for a few days, weren't you? About the time of this . . . tragedy?'

'Oh, we were just shopping and visiting.' Liza grinned at him, and patted his arm. Then she pointed to a space that had briefly opened up on the plush carpet, where some of the guests had started dancing. 'Do you fancy a twirl, Mr Grenoble?'

He did, and as they waltzed with the others under the shop's moody lighting, they were joined by Jack, Shelley, Rufus and even Bessie, who had discovered, during her first New York Christmas, that dancing was something she adored.